The
Lucy
Effect

DEREK MELLOR

AuthorHouse™ UK
1663 Liberty Drive
Bloomington, IN 47403 USA
www.authorhouse.co.uk
Phone: 0800.197.4150

© 2015 Derek Mellor. All rights reserved.

No part of this book may be reproduced, stored in a retrieval system, or transmitted by any means without the written permission of the author.

Published by AuthorHouse 01/21/2015

ISBN: 978-1-4969-9914-6 (sc)
ISBN: 978-1-4969-9913-9 (e)

This novel is a work of fiction. All characters and descriptions of events are the products of the author's imagination and any resemblance to actual persons, living or dead, is entirely coincidental.

Any people depicted in stock imagery provided by Thinkstock are models, and such images are being used for illustrative purposes only. Certain stock imagery © Thinkstock.

This book is printed on acid-free paper.

Because of the dynamic nature of the Internet, any web addresses or links contained in this book may have changed since publication and may no longer be valid. The views expressed in this work are solely those of the author and do not necessarily reflect the views of the publisher, and the publisher hereby disclaims any responsibility for them.

Thanks to Linda my wife, Maria Shevkina for her invaluable artistic support, staff at the Manx Museum, Vera Lalyko regarding help with research and German, the Chainbridge Hotel Team and Miraz and staff at 'FM Caffe', who each provided a perfect setting for writing.

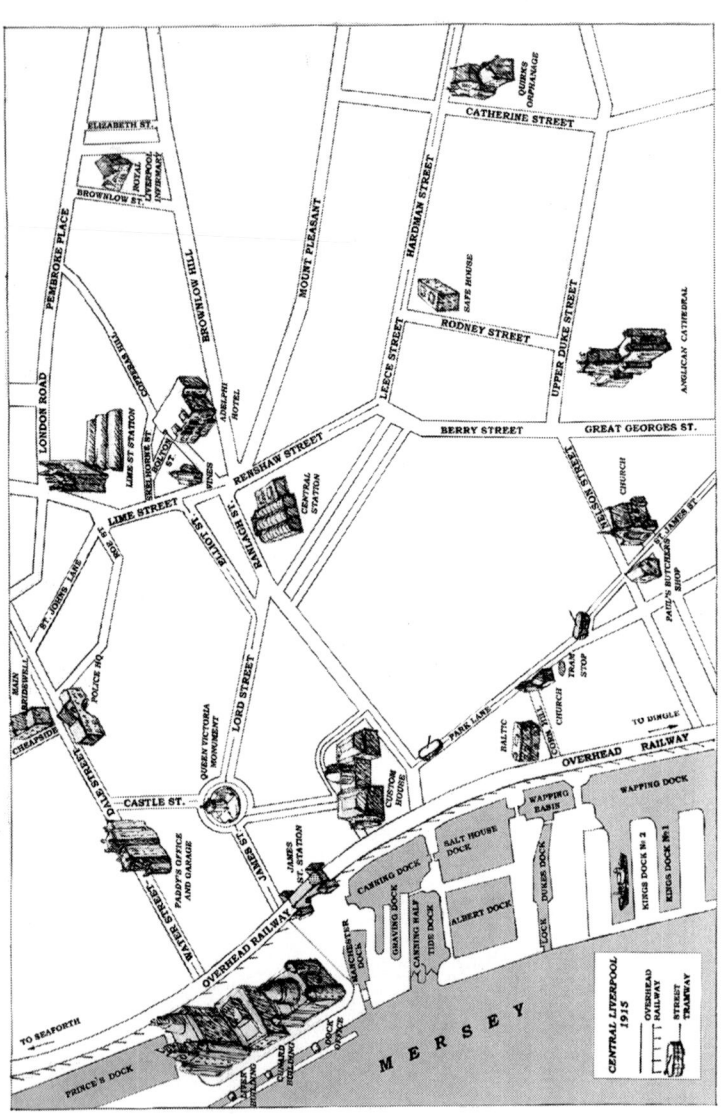

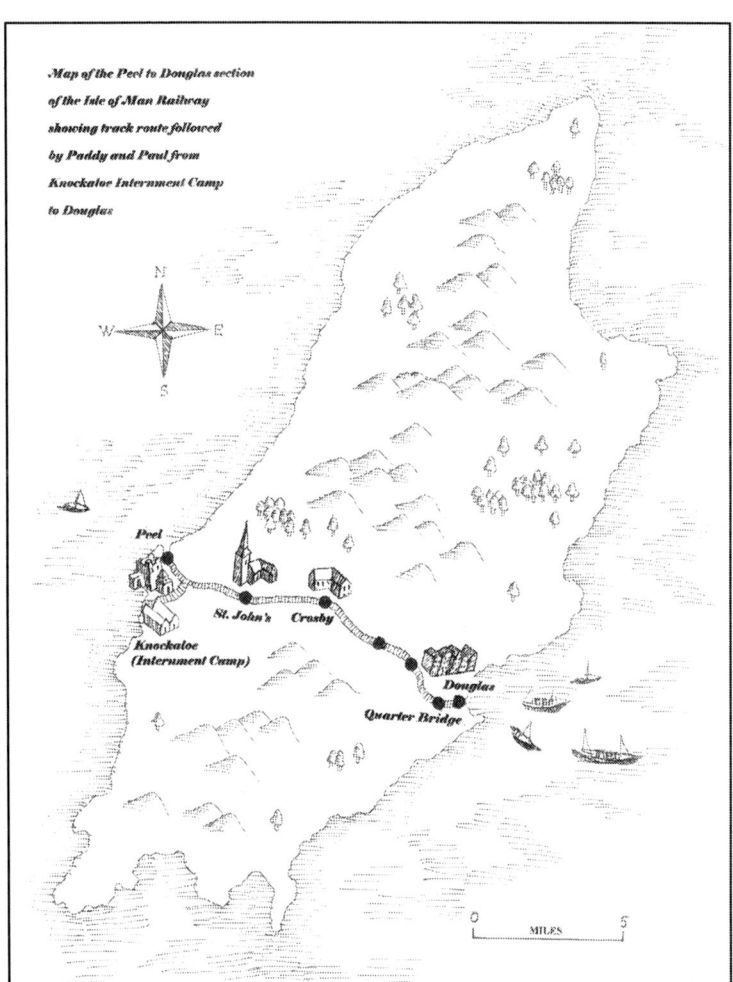

On May 7 1915 the Cunard Liner RMS Lusitania, sailing from New York to Liverpool England, was sunk by the German U boat 'U20' off the coast of Southern Ireland. 1198 passengers lost their lives, many of them were American citizens. The British losses included passengers and also many seaman from Liverpool. The event led to attacks on Germans and their property, firstly in Liverpool spreading to other cities and towns in Britain.

Part I
Separation: 10th May 1915

Chapter 1

Two rickety and well-worn straight-back chairs stood too close to the fire. Over them were draped damp underwear and starched shirts. The room was full of steam. The tiny window was misted over so that the backyard it looked onto had vanished. The front page of the *Liverpool Courier*, 10 May 1915, with a black-framed banner headline, covered the fireplace surround acting as the fire's lungs. It suddenly exploded into flames and blasted up the chimney. Black confetti was ejected at speed from the pot on the roof only to float down gently to the ground. A cat surprised by raining flies sprang again and again after its wafer thin prey only to be disappointed. From another room Paul Roth heard the commotion. He ran into the room, grabbed the chairs, felt pain, and dropped them immediately. The scorching hot chairs fell to the floor. It was then he saw her. Flames burst from a log in the centre of the fire. He saw Emily's face. The face he'd looked on as she lay in the coffin. Her lips opened and moved. His whole body recoiled. In that split second he heard a faint cry. Emily must be warning him. The voice became louder and more agitated. Then it dawned on him. It wasn't Emily's voice; it was his son's.

His heart pounded. He ran through the shop, slipping on the sawdust-covered floor exposing traces of animal blood. When he reached the road, he couldn't believe his eyes. It was bedlam. Jorgen was running, chased by an angry mob. Some brandished long sticks. Others clutched at household objects and clothes. As they ran, people threw objects mindlessly onto the cobblestones from doors and windows. Furniture hurled from open or shattered bedroom windows crashed onto the pavement. Further down the road he noticed small fires consuming wooden chairs and tables.

'There's his pa, Mary!' yelled a woman dressed in a shabby, torn dress and a woollen shawl that covered her head. 'There's the butcher's shop at end of row!' Flaming-red-haired Mary, who appeared to be the mob's self-elected Boudicca, pointed her chair leg in that direction, and the mob obeyed without question.

When Jorgen was a few yards away, his father started to run back to the shop bawling at his son in German, *'Komm, schnell, schnell, schnell!* This, of course, wound up the crowd even more.

Mary shouted with all the venom she could muster, 'Get the Huns! They butchered our innocent lads! Fer sake of all us greavin' widders!'

As they entered the shop, Paul pointed to the ice room, the only secure room in the place. Its door was unlocked, and he plucked the large brass key out of the keyhole as they went in. In panic they collided with hanging carcasses. Jorgen was attacked by a rebounding one that sent him flying onto the icy floor. Paul struggled to lock the door. He thrust the key into the lock and applied as much pressure as he could with his large muscular hands, which were used to cutting and tearing the toughest of carcasses. At the back of his mind he was conscious that the key might snap. He could hear the mob smash the front door in, although it had been unlocked. The shop window went next. He kept as motionless as he could. The door to the ice room remained unlocked. There was little he could do if it was charged. The mob flowed past the ice room door. He could hear furniture being smashed. Paul's guts turned over when he realized they'd surely pick up the knives and saws in the shop. Mary must have other plans though; he heard her shout at the top of her voice,

'There'll be time enough for wrecking and theivin'! Grab us Huns first. Some out round back others up th'stairs. We'll weasel the cowards out yet!'

Those who'd gone upstairs shouted down that all was clear and went about smashing up furniture and lobbing it through the bedroom windows onto the street.

Paul carefully withdrew the key from the lock and put it back in slowly, making sure it was fully engaged. Luckily, to his amazement, it worked.

Unlucky for Paul, however, hearing was one of Mary's finest tools of the trade. She'd been a petty thief over the years.

'Here they are fer sure, lads! Batter door down! That's where they'll be, mark me words.' Mary, who was of Amazonian proportions, rammed her shoulder against the solid wooden door without any affect. Scowling, she beckoned two male acquaintances to assist. They tried to crash through it several times without success.

'You'll not get through that, Mary. It's one of those new fangled things,' one of them said nervously. 'With iron inside.'

The other disagreed.

'It's a' ordinary wooden one, maybe a bit thicker. Not as thick as you though.'

'Stop blarting,' Mary said. 'Talk about wooden – ye're both as thick as two short planks!'

Then an odd thing happened. The two men looked on in disbelief as Mary fell to her knees and started sobbing. That powerful lady, cock of the St James area, and the scourge of many a man, had been reduced to blubbering jelly. She beat the floor with her fists, and through her sobs she gasped,

'Me son went down in *Lucy*, and these Huns are gonna go down too!' The men tried to help her up, but she shoved them away, ashamed at what she'd just done. And as quickly as she'd been reduced to her jellyfish state, her sting was back. Once again she was commanding and in control. She moved to the shop door, put her finger to her mouth indicating they ought to be silent, and waved the two men over. 'Look, they'll hav' to be comin' out soon, as they'll be frozed, so we'll wait here till job's done. But be quiet about it.'

Before they could say anything, she pushed one of the men back into the shop. He'd been ordered to bolt the back door and stay near the ice room door. The rest of the mob had moved on to where there were more pickings. The sweet taste of booty was a stronger draw than any allegiance to Boudicca and her ranting. It was only the two she knew well, who were in her debt, quite literally up to their necks, who stayed true.

In the ice room, Paul managed to light a candle, which he placed on a shelf near to where ice was stacked. The soft light revealed an army of carcases hanging on hooks that were secured to the ceiling. On one of the walls, the carcass shadows, encouraged by the candle's flickering light, played out a menacing war dance as if they yearned for revenge. Paul and Jorgen had no room to sit down, and they stood huddled together close to the frost-covered door attempting to quell all movement for fear of being heard. As time went on, this became more difficult as their bodies were affected by waves of shivering fits. Paul became concerned about Jorgen, whose face was pale as his breathing quickened.

'Jorgen, we'll have to make a run for it now. We can't stay in here any longer. The cold will get to us. It's gone quiet out there. Listen,' he whispered moving close to Jorgen. 'They'll be after me, not you, so you leg it when you get the chance.'

Paul reached up and grasped a leather bag that sat high up on a shelf next to the door that was stacked with ice. The bag was easy enough to open, but handling its contents was another matter. The gold sovereigns were frozen into a solid mass. Paul tried to use the heat of the candle to melt the ice, but the candle kept going out. He put the sovereigns back in the bag and desperately threw the bag on the floor. The resulting clatter was much louder than he'd anticipated, and he placed his ear on the door for as long as he could. They were in luck; he couldn't hear a sound. The sovereigns were still frozen together, but had separated into smaller blocks of three or four pieces.

'Stick these in your pockets and get a train to St Helens from Lime Street,' Paul told Jorgen. 'Your great aunt lives there, Frau Stocker in Windle. Tell her to take you in for a few days.'

There were tears in Jorgen's eyes.

'But I want to stay with you.'

'You can't. It's too dangerous. I don't want you to be hurt. It's not going to be safe for any German here now that *Lusitania* has been sunk. They've taken some to the camps already. If this happens to me, they'll shove you in the workhouse. Do you want that?'

Paul, himself, did not want any of this but there was no choice. The worst scenario – his death at the hands of the mob outside – was unthinkable. But if it happened, Jorgen needed to be with relatives. Though his great aunt was not an ideal choice, and he wasn't sure whether she'd agree, it was the only chance he had.

'Right, son, when I've unlocked this door we'll make for the back. When we get to the end of the entry in Nelson Street, you run to the left and I'll go the other way. Do you understand?'

'But, Papa...'

'There'll be no buts, d'you hear me? It's for your own good.'

Paul forced back the tears, and in order not to weaken his resolve, he grabbed Jorgen's arm as he turned the key in the door as quietly as he could. As he did this, some of the sovereigns fell to the floor. With no time to retrieve them, he flung the door open. The door rammed into the man on guard outside. He was flung backwards by the momentum and collided with Mary and her other henchman. Paul and Jorgen rushed to the back door, and Paul wildly pulled the bolts across cutting his thumb badly. Turning round, he noticed a photograph of himself and his wife in a picture frame. He grabbed it as he and Jorgen both rushed out into the backyard.

Mary and her comrades had landed in a heap on the floor; they were coated in sawdust. She pulled herself up swearing, but stopped abruptly. Her blood lust had been quenched, albeit briefly, as in disbelief she noticed the bright lumps of gold on the floor of the ice room. The two men were breathing down her neck as she scooped up the frozen lumps and hid them in a pocket designed for holding less valuable contraband. She thought she'd got away with it.

'We want some of that!' one of the men shouted, breaking Mary's spell.

'No one's gettin' any of this till we've caught Huns!' Her words, spoken in a deliberately slow manner, were full of anger. She was kicking herself that they knew. 'Come on, yous, they'll be away!' Mary darted past them and ran into the entry. She saw the trail of blood on the ground and followed it.

Jorgen disobeyed his papa's order to run in the opposite direction at the end of the entry. He tailed his father, who'd reached Nelson Street. They heard the angry cries of Mary closing in. Blood was gushing from Paul's thumb, and he felt faint. He misjudged his footing on the kerb, went tumbling over, and fell awkwardly, injuring his ankle. Jorgen caught up with him and knelt down to help.

'*Geh, geh, geh...*' his father shouted repeatedly. 'Get the train...' he sobbed. Jorgen had never seen him so angry and agitated. Paul thrust the picture frame into his hand. Jorgen started to run as fast as he could with words *geh, geh* crashing about in his brain. The words stayed with him all day and for many days to come. They were like the bangs of a chopper blade rapidly cutting into raw steak, the once-perfect steak being mutilated.

Chapter 2

Edward Aughton stood in a queue that snaked out of the enquiry office into a narrow passageway along a corridor into a vast hall, walled and floored in ceramic tiles that echoed with the cold click of footsteps and whispering voices. The queue extended out of the Cunard building and snaked its way a short distance down Water Street and around the corner into Rumford Street. He was now at the front of the queue at the snake's head where venom flowed and devoured families as if they were playing a game of Russian roulette. An attendant allowed ten people at a time to check the lists of survivors of the *Lusitania* that had been placed on the wall adjacent to the main office of the shipping company. The people were herded along roped barriers, a soulless lane of control. People bawled at the staff who couldn't provide the information they desperately needed to hear. Others, unable to hold back the tears, broke through their Victorian corseted facades and wept uncontrollably. Those of the fortunate minority subdued a joy beaten into pulp by the wild unstoppable grief of their neighbours.

Edward stared at the lists in front of him. His son's name was absent. The single black cloud that appeared on the horizon when he'd first heard of the sinking became a raging storm. His body started to shake. He had no control. Unlike others, desperate to hold on to their silver-lining endings, disbelief was far away from him. Edward knew instinctively his son was gone, just as he had known about the others in his family. He ran out of the building, his sixty-five-year-old stout body soon exhausted. He found himself overlooking water, clutching a rail. There were steps nearby leading down to boats tethered at a dock. He thought about joining his son in the water. He put one foot on the lower railing and was about to haul himself over the top when a constable, who'd been observing him, ran up and asked if he was all right.

Edward found himself walking past rows and rows of terraced houses. At the end of one street he would go round the backs of properties and start on the next row. A soothing numbness came over him. He lost all sense of time and whereabouts until he heard children's voices. They begged for money. He didn't respond, and the voices became louder. He turned round and shouted obscenities at the top of his voice. The children screamed and scuttled away in all directions. Mothers came out of doors with young infants in their arms or clinging to their legs. One of them picked up a stone and threw it. The stone knocked his top hat off his head, and it blew away in the breeze until it was snatched up and whipped up the road by an urchin who was gone in a blink.

This assault brought him back to his world of unbearable grief. Its close ally, guilt, was on its tail. He raved at the lack of interest he'd shown when his son announced he was to start work with Cunard on the transatlantic runs. Edward saw this decision as an obvious knee-jerk reaction to the death of his son's wife and boy in a railway accident six months before. His son desperately wanted to get away from all the memories that plagued him. Edward thought he should have tried to talk some sense into him. But pride – his own – had stood in the way. He'd been upset. His son hadn't thought about the impact his leaving would have on him. But his son wasn't to blame, for Edward had withheld his true feelings about how the deaths had affected him and how much he had pined for his grandson and daughter-in-law. He never told his son the coldness he knew he'd feel being totally on his own. These raw painful thoughts, each like a grotesque animal impaled on a merry-go-round turning round and round in his mind to continually incense him, were only broken as he came to the end of a terraced block. For in the distance, as if miraculously, he caught a glimpse of the new cathedral that was under construction. Without hesitation, he started to make his way towards what he desperately hoped would offer some comfort and relief. There was nothing else he could do. Nowhere he could go.

It was late in the afternoon. Edward had been on his knees for some time. The sunset gently bathed the delicate gilt filigree of the alter triptych in gold, each screen topped with crowns of thorn and embossed with New Testament images. Edward observed the changing light streaming through the massive leaded windows. It projected a dazzling display of colours onto the screens, and his eyes were awash in tears as he contemplated the animated figures. To his left at the foot of the altar was Giovani's *Madonna*, her face showing joy and compassion. None of this eased his pain; quite the reverse. How could a God be delighted in his creation at such a time?

He cried out hopelessly,

'Why me? Why me?' He repeated this like a mantra, but the mantra increased in volume until he was bellowing at the top of his voice. Nearby a candle's flame was extinguished with the force of his breath, and a wisp of smoke rose until it died below one of the low-strung hanging lanterns. The few people who had been kneeling around him in silent prayer gradually moved away.

Eventually a curate appeared and assumed a posture of prayer. He said softly,

'Oh, Lord, please help your servant in his hour of need and bestow upon him your peace.'

This touched a raw nerve in Edward. He pushed past the priest, almost knocking him over, and began to run along the aisle towards the wood-panelled foyer at the rear. Not looking back and stammering he shouted,

'How… how dare you? What do you know, wrapped up in all this cotton wool? The… the… the cheek of it… the… the very cheek of it!'

Edward ran in the direction of Upper Duke Street. The sound and physical experience of rhythmically placing one foot down after the other allowed him to keep at bay the feeling of dread that seemed to be snapping at the pit of his stomach, a dread he thought would overwhelm him. He imagined his mind slowly splintering away in all directions, scattered about, until there was nothing – absolutely nothing – left of him, the person inside.

Part II
Paul's Story: 10th May to 19th July 1915

Chapter 3

'Nein, nein!' he spluttered. Blood oozed from his mouth, but the blows didn't cease.

'Take that for Harry an' that fer Smith twins!' Mary repeatedly beat him with a chair leg. Paul passed out, and Mary threw the cudgel down on the ground.

'Think you've done 'im in Mary!' said her companion.

Before she could respond, they heard the sound of whistles.

'Rozers! Leg it!' someone cried out, and in no time the street was clear of rioters.

Two constables, batons drawn, checked to see if Paul was all right.

'The buggar's come off bad. Looks like a Hun, or if he isn't he's unlucky. Let's get him over to quack's in Duke Street. See what he thinks.'

As they lifted him up Paul moaned,

'*Mein sohn...*'

'He's a Kraut... chuck him into black wagon and off to shop.'

Paul was barely conscious as he was roughly assisted by the two constables through the big fortified door of the main Bridewell in Dale Street. They crossed the cobbled courtyard into the main hall. Through the windows in the corridor he could see into the charge room. Apart from the usual drunk customers on a Monday night, the place was heaving with women, young children, and men mainly shouting and cursing. 'Ye're as bad as em Huns, you are. Should be ashamed of yourselves, dragging us in here. You should be helpin' to get every man jack of 'em, yer traitors!' yelled a woman wearing a tattered coat tied with string. Her pockets bulged with the night's takings. She observed Paul through the window.

'There's one of em! Isn't he that "Rotter" fella from St James's Street?' But before she could muster any support, the officers bundled Paul into another room and bolted the door.

'You've had a rough time and suffered several fractures. Who did this to you?' a very young-looking police surgeon asked in an absent-minded way as he awkwardly stitched a wound on Paul's forehead. Paul could smell port on his breath; it seemed to be taking its toll.

'I don't know,' Paul said. But speaking was extremely painful, and he wanted to get away with the fewest words possible. He did remember the name Mary, and he could see her face, twisted in anger. He wasn't going to say. He couldn't. His body moved instinctively as if another blow was on its way, and he cried out.

'There, there,' the surgeon said softly but automatically. We'll get you sorted out, but it's hospital for you I'm afraid.'

Paul gathered all his strength to speak.

'I have a son. We were separated.' But all was in vain. The surgeon had disappeared, obviously thinking of the evening ahead. But even if the surgeon had remained, Paul's effort would have been to no avail as, utterly exhausted and affected by the morphine, he had fallen into a deep sleep.

Chapter 4

The smell of carbolic woke him up. As his eyes focussed, they fell on a pretty girl with green eyes and dark-red hair that was tucked into a white linen cap. She wore a starched white apron. Then he realized exactly where he was, although he'd never been on a hospital ward. The nurse was talking to someone nearby. He noticed a police officer on a small wooden bench leaning against a panelled wall. The experiences of the previous day all came flooding back to him – the pain and the deep sadness.

'Mein sohn! wo ist er?' He thought his voice sounded strange; it wasn't his.

As the nurse leaned over the bed, he got a whiff of her perfume. It was like one his wife used to wear.

'Pardon?' she said, seeming to be a little taken aback.

'Where is my son?' he repeated in English. Her perfume had acted like smelling salts, focussing his mind. The police sergeant stood up and said that he would deal with the situation, and the nurse moved away obediently but with irritation showing in her eyes.

'Now look here, you, 'said the policeman, clutching the side of the bed and bending over so his face was close to Paul's. 'Just you watch it. You're not in any position to make demands. Remember, you're an enemy alien and don't have any rights.' He straightened his back, brushed the sleeves of his uniform as if removing some imaginary dirt, and went back to his seat and started reading a newspaper.

'Wo bin Ich?' Paul shouted.

The sergeant looked up from the newspaper, 'Will you knock off with that foul language unless you want me to wash your mouth out!'

'Where am I?' The question was aimed at Bridie. She glanced briefly at the sergeant, He was reading. She went over to Paul's bed, tucked him in and whispered,

'You're in the Liverpool Royal Infirmary'.

Several hours passed. Paul drifted in and out of sleep. Occasionally he would be awakened by the routine activities of the nurses or the cries of men newly admitted who were being placed into freshly made beds. In the centre of the ward was a table that was used as the nurses' station. It was situated next to a stove and a ventilation tube that ran from the floor to the ceiling. The sister was discussing duties with staff who had just come on duty for the second shift of the day. Ward M1 was an acute male medical ward. Patients who were moved there were seriously ill, and their chances of survival were slim. Each nurse had four patients to deal with personally. Nurse Bridie O'Sullivan had left Paul as her last patient to attend to on her shift.

Noticing that he was awake, she went over to his bed and leaned over carefully so she wouldn't surprise him.

'Hello, Mr Roth. How are you feeling?' He nodded his head slowly and smiled. She checked his notes and started to look at his wounds. She did this in as gentle a manner as she could, carefully taking the linen bandages first off his arms. She applied new dressings. Then she repeated the process with the wounds on his face and legs.

'You have a deep gash on your head, Mr Roth,' she said. 'Last time I examined it I thought there might be signs it was turning septic, but, mercifully, now that's not the case.' She quickly redressed the wound. Having checked his other bodily functions, she began to make him more comfortable while she waited for the doctor to administer morphine.

Paul, half drugged yet still in pain said, 'Thank you. Thank you.'

On Bridie's face there was the most fleeting of blushes. She fiddled with the sheets and said,

'Oh, that's a pleasure, Mr Roth.'

'Please call me Paul,' he said, and in the next laboured breath he managed to get out, 'And what's your name?'

Bridie knew that it was hospital policy that communication with patients had to remain reasonably formal. Certainly the use of first names was out of order. She knew it went on, though, and in fact had increased with the reports of nurses dealings with the dying wounded on the front in France. Paul could die. But that wasn't the only reason. She looked around to check the whereabouts of sister.

'I'm Bridie.' She blushed again, only it was more noticeable. She turned around in embarrassment only to find the bully of a sergeant staring at her, and as she averted her gaze, he suddenly stood up and checked his pocket watch. His current shift and duty were not his normal ones. He'd been posted to the Royal Infirmary with a prisoner owing to the shortage of men. The riots were taking their toll. His relief was late, and as he walked out of the door to stretch his legs, he collided with a constable dashing at some speed. The momentum pushed the two men into the ward. For a second they had to hold on tightly to each other, and they almost danced a jig in order to keep their balance.

Witnessing this, Bridie couldn't stop laughing, even though she tried to desperately. Like other patients on the ward, woken by the commotion, Paul joined in, although his voice was barely audible. It was like a scene from a Chaplin film and acted as a natural release of tension. In the end, Bridie had to turn her back on Paul. The sergeant who was leaving gave her a dark look but suddenly pointed at Paul. The bandage on his head was weeping blood.

Chapter 5

Nine days later Paul was back at Dale Street Bridewell. He took his time getting out of the police van, which had pulled into the courtyard of the prison. His fellow prisoners jumped off the vehicle with ease, unlike Paul who was careful not to increase the pain he was still experiencing. They'd discharged him from hospital early, on the instructions of the police. It was a miracle he'd survived, having picked up infections in a couple of his wounds. If it hadn't been for Bridie's care, he knew he wouldn't have made it. Her tenderness had shone through all her professionalism and captivated him. They were attracted to each other. She was so like Emily in her manner and looks he couldn't believe it. There was a possibility the lingering grief he felt coloured such a view, but he was totally unaware of this. On his departure from the ward, Bridie promised that she would visit him, and she secretly gave him some aspirins to take for the pain. An observant officer in the police escort witnessed the transaction and confiscated them. They said his having them was too risky, as he might want to take the lot and end it all. This alarmed Bridie and made her more determined to visit Paul as soon as she'd finished her duty.

Inside the Bridewell, Paul was taken to the sergeant's desk to be booked in. They both recognized each other immediately. Sergeant Frank Roberts had ginger hair with a complimentary ginger moustache and receding chin. In addition he was of considerable bulk. With gusto he said,

The Lucy Effect

'I know you, lad, don't I?' Paul shuffled his feet and looked up at the ceiling and quietly mumbled.

'Don't deny it. You're that bloody insolent Hun at the Royal, aren't you? Listen...' The policeman got hold of Paul's jacket lapels and, lifting him up, he pulled him close, so close that their noses touched. Paul inhaled stale breath as the sergeant continued. 'I've got my evil eye on you, son. Better watch out. Any little incident in here, and I'll have you up before the beak in the twinkle of an eye, and you'll be off to do some very bloody hard labour!' The sergeant put Paul down with a jolt that nearly caused his legs to collapse beneath him, but he suppressed any sound of discomfort, unwilling to give the sergeant a morsel of pleasure.

Twelve hours later, Paul awoke in one of the underground cells at the police station. He'd been disturbed by footsteps outside. It was pitch black. On realizing there was an absence of light, he suddenly panicked. Since an experience in early childhood, Paul had always feared total blackness. He imagined he'd lost his sight. Was it the head wound? Had it been diagnosed wrongly? If only Bridie were there with him. Then there was relief. His pulse rate fell; his breathing became calmer. Over by the door he saw light, and the door swung open. There silhouetted by the lamplight in the corridor stood a large form.

'Attention, lad. Up when an officer is in your vicinity. Up, up, up!' he shouted, pulling at the prisoner roughly and deliberately pressing his bandaged arm. 'Just thought I'd drop in to tell you, 'cos I thought you'd like to know. That hospital tart of yours came to see if she could visit.' Paul heard laughter in the corridor. 'You'll be delighted to hear that I gave her a right rollicking and sent her on her way. No visitors for you, me laddie.' He pushed Paul back onto his bed and banged the cell door hard as he went out. Paul began to cry uncontrollably. Pain didn't exist in the moments that followed. It was as if a great, black imaginary wall had descended that had no footholds. He desperately needed to climb it. He couldn't. He wasn't in control. The sergeant looked through the grill in the door and smiled. There was scant illumination in the cell, but he'd sensed Paul's fear.

Paul was in near total darkness, but he'd picked out a faint source of light that comforted him. Time stood still. He didn't know whether it was night or day. Perspiration tickled his ears and trickled down his cheeks. Anger was welling up inside. It had kicked out and demolished the hopelessness. The normally prudent Paul became a raging animal. He gripped the iron sides of his bed in frustration, and his fingers touched the chamber pot lying underneath. It was half full. He had an idea. An idea that brought a smile to his face as he floated images through his mind of scenes that might follow. But what of the consequences? *Beggar the consequences*, he thought. There was now only one path he could go down. These thoughts were being driven by an anger that was overwhelming. Nothing could stand in its way. He had a target.

It all happened quickly. He saw the chink of light under the door as it opened. The silhouetted figure was standing a few feet away. Paul caught a whiff of his smell. It was him. He grasped the handle of the chamber pot. His feet were on the floor. Raising himself up slowly to avert suspicion, he suddenly lifted the pot up from behind his back and deposited its contents over Sergeant Robert's head.

Chapter 6

'Your name and address,' the clerk of the court said curtly.

'Paul Roth, 64 Great James's Street, Liverpool.'

The clerk hardly gave him a chance to finish. 'You are charged with assault to a member of His Majesty's constabulary. How do you plead?'

'Guilty,' Paul mumbled.

One chief magistrate asked him to speak up, so he shouted 'Guilty!' as hard as he could. The sound filled the chamber and seemed to echo softly along nearby corridors. The magistrates looked on with disgust written all over their faces.

'Mr Lambert, please proceed.'

The prosecution lawyer stood up and slowly looked at the three magistrates in turn. 'The facts of the matter are that, on Friday May the twenty-first of this year of our Lord, nineteen fifteen, in the cell in which the offender was residing at in the Dale Street Bridewell of this city, the offender did wilfully throw the contents of his chamber pot at a Sergeant Frank Roberts.' There was a titter from the public gallery. The magistrates ignored this, as they were deep in discussion. One of their number wanted clarification on a point. The lawyer stopped speaking, scratched his head, shuffled his papers, and started drumming his fingers on the table as if he'd witnessed these scenes many times before.

The chief magistrate, red in the face and casting his eye on the offending magistrate, said,

'Mr Lambert, my colleague wishes to clarify what the contents of the pot were.'

The court broke into uproar; there were whoops of laughter from the gallery. The clerk, carefully placing his hand over his mouth, sniggered. The only persons who didn't seem amused were the magistrates and Paul.

'Order, order!' the chief magistrate shouted. 'Or we'll clear the court. Please proceed, Mr Lambert.'

'Both kinds', he said quickly with half a smile. The offending magistrate nodded in satisfaction. More laughter from the gallery followed. The lawyer continued with his statement outlining the sergeant's momentary blindness, and the fact that he'd slipped and suffered a head injury that was serious enough to keep him from appearing as a witness. What was so outrageous was that the defendant had not shown any remorse for the injuries he'd caused. The magistrate recommended that the court deal with the accused as severely as they could.

The defence lawyer outlined the mitigating circumstances: the beating that Paul Roth had received from the mob. The separation from his son. And the vendetta that he had suffered at the hands of Sergeant Roberts. The lawyer summed up by saying that, although Mr Roth was an enemy alien and that the offence was inexcusable, circumstances had harangued him and brought him to the sorry state where his only release from his unbearable pain and anger was to pour the contents of the chamber pot over the sergeant. 'Might I stress that my client did not push the officer,' he finished. There was another titter from the public gallery, but it was more subdued this time.

The chief magistrate did not have to confer with his colleagues. He said, 'Paul Roth, you have been found guilty of this heinous offence by your own admission. Listening to the facts of the case, I have no alternative but to sentence you to six months hard labour.'

The Lucy Effect

Before the magistrate could finish, the clerk jumped up and had a word with him. The chief magistrate continued,

'I have been informed that, owing to the defendant's injuries, he will not initially be sent to prison to carry out the sentence of this court. He will be sent forthwith to an alien internment camp, and when he has recovered from his injuries, he will be duly sent to serve out his term of hard labour. I would further recommend that the internment camp that he is sent to ought to be the severest one available, but with adequate medical services.'

Paul had sat motionless throughout the proceedings. He was perspiring, and his head banged. His eyes were fixed on the royal heraldic plaque fixed to the wall behind the magistrates – the lion and magical unicorn rampant, a crown between them. He imagined the lion was laughing, and the unicorn was nodding its head ferociously. The crown in the centre became the smiling face of the sergeant. It gradually became larger and larger, and the smile changed to an evil grimace. Finally, the plaque had gone; it was just the face. Then all went black.

In the gallery a woman stood up. She shouted, 'Paul, I'm here! I love you!' There were angry shouts of 'Hun lover', and obscene names were bandied about. People, particularly women, competed to outdo each other in their name-calling. A man grabbed the woman's arm, and he was about to strike her, but two constables quickly appeared on the scene and restored order. As all this was going on, with the chief magistrate shouting for order and then clearing the court, Paul was being carried out on a stretcher.

****

Early the following morning, Bridie stood in an office doorway opposite the Bridewell. After the court session, she'd used her womanly guile, which oozed sincerity, on a sympathetic constable and managed to worm out of him Paul's fate. She was surprised. He knew the schedule but said he had been sworn to secrecy, as if all had been decided even before the court case began. In a lowered voice he told her to be outside the main gate of the Bridewell at six sharp the next morning. That's all he could say.

Dawn had broken, and the day matched her mood. The sky's back screen was completely grey. Black clouds scuttled at a furious pace and acted out scenes of chaos as they clashed together in an unending drama that desperately needed a curtain to be drawn on it. The wild wind and rain had chilled her to the bone. She stamped her feet, an unconscious response as her thoughts were only of Paul. How would he survive? There were new cuts and bruises on his pale, worried face. Had he given up? He'd said little in court. Had her efforts been in vain? What was she going to do when the van emerged carrying her beloved Paul?

It was nearly seven. She'd been there for two hours. Perhaps the officer had been wrong, or he'd deliberately misinformed her. Dockers in flat caps looked her up and down. Trams rattled past together with carts loaded high with sacks, new from the docks, pulled by straining old horses, their drivers whipping freely. Suddenly the doors of the Bridewell opened disgorging a black van pulled by two fresh horses waiting to gallop, the driver holding back until the rig was on the straight. It turned her way. She crossed into the middle of the road between the tram tracks and waited. Trams bells rang out warnings. Just a glimpse, just a glimpse of him… but there were no windows. Following close behind was a cab. She raised her hand nervously. This was new territory for Bridie. She didn't know whether it would stop, or as important, if she had money. It halted, and Bridie climbed in, politely requesting the driver, who looked quite puzzled, to follow the van.

To Bridie's relief, the van joined a queue of traffic that she knew was headed for the Irish Steam Packet terminal at the pier.

They were moving slowly. She'd found a silver three-penny piece in her pocket and asked the cabby to stop. The van was three carts away, and she ran to the back of it, making sure the driver didn't cotton on. A barred window. She was in luck. Perhaps he'd see her. She pulled herself up onto the high step at the rear of the van. The window was grimed over. She couldn't get her hand under the bars to wipe it off, so she began to bang the door with her foot. Would this be seen as damaging police property? Then she saw it – the underside of a fisted hand rubbing away at the glass, and then a ghostly smiling face. She mouthed, 'I love you.' He responded by what seemed a shake of the head. It was hard to tell. Then he was gone. The van pulled up. She heard shouts. She jumped down and ran for her life. She was smiling though. It could have been anyone's face, but in her desperate need she converted anyone's face into Paul's.

Chapter 7

Paul was sitting with his legs bent and his back against the cold steel wall of the ship's hold. As an enemy alien, he was considered a danger to the state and not permitted to roam the decks of the steamer, whose course was set for Peel on the Isle of Man. So Paul, along with 400 other German alien internees, was below decks in one of the holds. There were no portholes. Light was provided by oil lamps that were attached to the walls. The air was warm and stale. Smells of recent animal cargo were rampant. The temperamental Irish Sea was as rough as it could be and was overdoing the showing off. There was no seating. Some of the younger men stood erect, almost at attention as if they were about to salute as they held onto whatever object was near at hand, not wanting to show any signs of weakness. Others, usually older and wiser like Paul, sat on the deck of the hold with their backs against the wall. Hands firmly placed on the deck, they kept pushing themselves backwards with their heels to ensure they didn't topple over when the ship pitched.

'Wow that shiner… you look the worse fer wear,' said the man sitting next to him in a cheerful Irish accent. 'Who did that to you? Hope he come worse off.'

Paul didn't feel like talking. His head was banging, and it seemed there wasn't any part of his body that didn't ache.

'Me name's Paddy,' said his companion. 'Can I get you somethin', mate? You look done in.'

Paul didn't respond right away. Paddy seemed to be losing interest, as he shifted his attention to someone more receptive when Paul said quietly,

'Have you any aspirin?'

'Come again, mate?' He seemed surprised at Paul's words, but his expression reflected the pain written deeply in Paul's eyes.

Paddy sprang up immediately, stepped over bodies of men who were vomiting, slipped in the wretched stuff, and collided with one of the stern men who stood erect fiercely holding his position. Eventually an older man, who glanced at Paul and smiled, handed over a small bottle. Just before Paddy returned to Paul, the ship was struck by one of the Irish Sea's best googlies, totally unexpected from the flow of play as the vessel was punched in the opposite direction than was anticipated. Paddy was thrown backwards and eventually landed on top of Paul's benefactor. With a twinkle in his eye he said, 'I'm back, sir. Wasn't sure if I'd said t'anks, mate.' The winded man twisted his face into a reluctant smile.

Paul gratefully took the aspirins, but couldn't open the bottle. Paddy took the bottle from him, removed the top, and handed the bottle back. A look of amazement crossed Paddy's face when he watched Paul shove two lots of three tablets into his mouth. As Paul fell into a deep sleep, Paddy climbed the ladders to the hold's bolted hatch and banged and shouted at the top of his voice. The sea and the wind had joined forces with gusto and carried the sounds aloft into the dark stormy night, ensuring no human or other beast could interfere with their sport.

Paul and Paddy were woken by loud cheers. Paddy had survived, but he looked deathly white. The door to the hold had been opened, and sunlight poured in. The steamer had docked, and the sea was calm. There were the cries of gulls and another cheer from the men. The trials of the long, tortuous night were, for a brief moment, forgotten. They'd been met by a less-fearsome adversary – the military who guarded them with fixed bayonets. The internees were lined up on the upper deck in rows of four, and a count took place. Some men joked about how anyone could have escaped that night. They looked around in disbelief at the green rolling hills, the curve of the bay, and Peel Castle, which towered above them. The Isle of Man seemed like a magical place for many who'd lived all their lives in the cities. Perhaps things weren't going to be so bad.

Chapter 8

The internees were given breakfast on the quayside. All had to stand whilst they ate. Paul was excused; he sat with his legs stretched out in front of him. Some men complained and accused the guards of favouritism. Paddy helped Paul with his breakfast and stood beside him. He'd attached himself to Paul and was looking out for him. Men would approach Paddy occasionally, and he would take them to one side. Paul tried to hear these conversations, but Paddy kept his voice down, so they were a complete mystery to him.

Four abreast they set off through the town heading for Knockaloe Internment Camp, which was about two miles away from Peel. As they marched almost in step, the noise of their boots echoed around the port's stone buildings. They encountered seagulls that would scatter and squawk, displeased about their disturbed early-morning hunting forays. The men were surrounded by armed guards. Most of the locals ignored them; they had seen so many pass through their streets. There were occasional cries of 'dirty Hun' and 'baby killers', mainly from old women. The men were used to this, and anyway the sun shone, and as they left the town, distant hills and green pastures burst into view. To their right occasionally, as the vegetation thinned, they'd glimpse the land rising, blotting out views of the emerald sea to the west. The winding hilly road with its gentle up-and-down gradients took them past wooded thickets. They were dazzled by sunlight suddenly searing through trees as they turned bends. There were streams running through glens. But it was the May blossoms that blew their minds. They were glorious in their abundance as well as their myriad of colours and tones. Paul saw little of this, for he was being carried by Paddy and the man who'd given him the aspirins. He had his arms round their necks. His feet hardly touched the ground, and the sergeant in charge of the party finally showed his concern. He shouted, 'Company halt!' Some of the internees were unused to this command and collided with the men in front of them. Pointing to Paul, the sergeant ordered four of his men to carry him to the army van that was following in the rear.

The company marched past cottages and stone walls. They sang marching songs. One was about men leaving their sweethearts to fight on the front for the Fatherland. Fortunately none of the guards spoke German, so they innocently sang along with them. The sergeant was easy going; he could understand some German, but wasn't bothered. Some prisoners didn't sing. They found it too much of a paradox. They were marching to a prisoner of war camp, and some held no enmity to the British, considering themselves as much English as they were German.

The van slowed down as it approached the main entrance to the camp. To Paul's surprise, as it turned onto the main drive, he heard shouts: 'Baby-killer Huns! So they've got you at last!' This was chanted rhythmically in the style of fans at a football match. There was laughter, and he realized it was the inmates themselves. Paul smiled along with some of the guards. The marching prisoners veered off to Camp Number Two on the left, and the van rattled along a road, if it could be called that, constructed of railway sleepers. It pulled up at a small compound some distance away from the other camps. As with all the compounds, of which there were usually five per camp, it was surrounded by a twelve-foot barbed-wire fence. Paul was so tired he paid little attention to his immediate surroundings. His tired gaze was fixed on the light that was coming from the open hut door. He remembered nothing else.

The following day, Paul woke up in a bed. He'd had the best night's sleep he'd had since his nightmare had begun. His bed, along with twenty others, was in a long hut, ten along each wall. There were toilets at one end of the building. The hut resembled the hospital ward he'd been in without the decorated walls, chairs, tables, flowers, equipment, and the smiling faces of the nurses. There was nothing else in the hut except for the wooden beams and rafters of the roof. Most of the men were out of bed, either standing around talking or sitting on beds. They were looking anxiously towards the end of the ward near the toilets where there was a bed that was partially enclosed by screens. The man in it was gasping for breath. A doctor was in attendance, and some men in white jackets were assisting him. Paul later found out that they were orderlies. All were German prisoners who'd had some experience providing care in previous occupations, or they were doing it for the perks involved.

A silence came over the ward as the body was taken out of the hut. The men voluntarily stood at attention as the body passed. Outside, men stubbed out their cigarettes and bowed their heads. The hushed tone remained for five or ten minutes. The man in the bed opposite Paul's kept looking over at him. He seemed to be waiting for a response. Paul ignored him. Impatiently the man got up and shuffled over to Paul, but Paul had closed his eyes. Clutching onto Paul's bed with one hand and balancing himself on his stick with the other, the man bent over him. 'You know,' he said, his voice lowered, 'that lot killed him. He came in here with a simple complaint, got better in days, but they wouldn't let him go, and he caught something else from one of the others. Wasn't the doctor, you know, it was *them*, the orderlies. They're on a good number here. They're after all the perks they can grab.' The man looked round when he heard a noise. Someone had come in, but left. 'You see,' he continued in hushed tones, 'if you have money, they want to keep you here for as long as possible. As soon as doctor comes, which ain't very often, they huddle round him like wasps around dished-up jam and tell him – that one's bad, he's doing this or that. They know the words to say, the words that'll keep 'em in. Mind you, they look after you. Stands to reason, done it? They don't want to lose money!'

One or two men filed in, and Paul's visitor crept back to his bed. He was nodding to himself as if wishing to affirm all he'd related to Paul.

****

Several days later, Paul was sitting on his bed. He was feeling much better. His wounds and fractures were healing. An orderly came over to him. He clutched a brown paper envelope in his hand.

'This is yours,' he told Paul. 'You should have had it when you first came in. If you want anything from the canteen, and you'd be surprised what they've got, just give us a shout.' He handed the envelope over to Paul, winking at the same time.

Conrad, the man in the opposite bed, had got up when the orderly entered the hut. He was eavesdropping. Once the orderly had gone, he stared at Paul, obviously unsure whether to approach him. Paul made eye contact with Conrad. The old man gingerly hobbled over leaving his stick on his bed. He seemed eager to talk, especially as his pace quickened as Paul gave him a welcoming smile.

'You've got money coming in I see,' Conrad said, anticipation written on his face. The anticipation turned to confusion, however, when Paul said with sincerity that he didn't know what the man was talking about.

'The envelope. It's money in the envelope. It'll be ten shillings from the camp bank. You've got money coming in!' He paused and waited for a response. Paul just smiled and asked Conrad if his bed was comfortable.

'Now you've got money, you can buy bedding from the canteen. They'll buy it for you, and they'll expect a treat. Don't you see what I'm getting at?' Paul half nodded and got back into bed and pretended to go to sleep. He was now feeling the bedsprings through the thin sheet. When Conrad had disappeared outside for a smoke, Paul opened the envelope and removed the ten-shilling note. But there was something else inside crumpled up at the bottom. He was astounded when he read the flimsy chit, which appeared to be a statement. He had £75 in the Knockaloe Camp bank. His life savings in sovereigns, or the major part of it, had followed him to the camp.

The man in the next bed stopped reading his newspaper and said,

'Don't take any notice of Conrad. He gets a bit confused, and he can't cope with not knowing what's going to happen. He's not the only one, of course. The place gets you down. I've been five months in Camp Three and then come here.' He paused in order to cough. 'In the compounds, everyone's in each other's way. You're sleeping, eating, washing, shaving, and peeing together day in, day out. They've not sorted the latrines out yet, so you do it outside with a bucket with everyone watching.'

'You sit on a bucket, with everyone watching?' Paul commented with a huge smile on his face, and they both burst out laughing.

'It's worse here in the Isolation Camp. Don't mean the toileting of course. He half smiled. Paul didn't pick up on it. 'There's nothing to do. At least in the other camps the men are starting clubs.'

'Like what?' Paul asked.

'Sports clubs, pottery, art classes. And they're starting a theatre group in the camp I'm in, would you believe?' The man stopped and began a coughing bout that lasted a minute or so.

'Who pays for all this?'

'The Quakers and the YMCA, but the men put their bit in too.'

Paul asked about the canteen and whether it was true that you could buy almost anything.

'Well, of course, within reason. There's extra food and cigarettes, and some of them buy materials they use in making things.'

'What if you don't have money?'

'You have to work for it. Prisoners who can afford it pay for jobs they want to do. Some posh prisoners even employ their own private stewards. There's lots of barbers and shoe shiners. Others make things to sell to people at the camp or to the Quakers who sell them on.' Another coughing bout occurred, and Paul was anxious that the man might be overtaxing himself. But he went on.

'Conrad's wrong. The orderlies can't keep men here for longer than they need to be. Doesn't make...' He couldn't finish; he started coughing again, only this time he was coughing up blood.

As Paul was shouting for the orderly, a thought beat a path into his mind. If Conrad was right about the delays in discharging wealthy patients, he ought to think about using the fact to his advantage. As soon as he was fit enough, they'd send him to prison on the mainland for the hard labour stint. He had to find some way to escape from the camp and locate Jorgen. In this he was like an infant – invincible. Any action was possible. It had to be. Adult responses were blocked by the drawbridge in his mind that barred anything that placed obstacles in the way of this desire. All obstacles bar one – the thought that it could take time. As the orderly approached, Paul gave him a smile. It was the same orderly who'd delivered the envelope. The orderly shouted to someone to get the doctor quickly. In the next breath he said,

'I know, you want something from the canteen. What is it?'

****

Later Paul had a walk around the perimeter of the hospital camp close to the barbed-wire fence for the first time. The doctor who'd carried out an examination was pleased with his progress and said getting some air would aid his recovery. Paul had formed an impression of the Knockaloe Camp and its surroundings from glimpses through the dirt-covered windows of the hut. But stepping outside and taking in the view; its beauty captivated him. As the hospital compound was in an elevated position, he could see for miles. On the horizon were views of rolling hills painted in shades of greens, browns, and yellows. Some hills were covered with lush dark green areas of trees; others were more barren. Nearer the camp, vistas changed to agricultural land with pocket-handkerchief patterns of hedged fields broken by thickets. This view was repeated on all sides, except the west. Here the hills closed in, and he could smell the salt of the sea. He watched sea birds on the hilltops. One moment they were in full view, and then suddenly they disappeared. It brought troubled thoughts. How long would he be around?

These views were in stark contrast to Knockaloe Camp itself. It was made up of the sort of structures that might fit superbly on the outskirts of a city, but it had been thrown down literally by the Home Office and hurriedly built in the midst of meadows and moorland with soft hills as a backdrop. It consisted of four camps plus a hospital. Within each of the four camps there were five or six compounds a hundred yards square. Each contained five long huts that slept two hundred prisoners, and each compound was served by a kitchen, recreation room, bathroom and latrines although these were added later. Between the compounds in each of the four camps ran passageways. Constructed with railway sleepers with towering barbed wire on each side, these passageways were like steel tunnels without roofs. Outside the compounds were recreational areas, again surrounded with barbed wire. Paul saw hundreds of men dotted all over the fields singly and in groups. Most were walking; others played football. They were like animals in a zoo, trapped in a huge enclosure without an audience, only the guards with fixed bayonets marching slowly along, occasionally looking at their antics as a keeper would, but with faces that reflected benign indifference in place of interest.

With his back against the hut, Paul slid down to the ground. He was shaken by a bolt of utter disbelief. It had come from nowhere. Instinctively he closed his eyes and was back in Liverpool. He could hear the habitually comforting sounds of horns from the river. He was in his parlour kneeling before the fire he'd just lit. The fire was casting its warm, red glow on the heavily polished and prized furniture. Outside he could hear the happy banter of Jorgen and his friends. But the image in his head was disturbed by a slight pressure on his arm. He opened his eyes slowly. His heart sank. They were still there – the cruel roads of barbed wire; the lines of black-roofed brown army huts that seemed to go on forever; the distant figures of toy soldiers in khaki so alien; and, worse, he himself as part of the unfolding scene. Turning his head left, to his great surprise, he saw Paddy.

'What are you doing here?' Paul half shouted.

'I'm ill like you, aren't I?' They both laughed. 'Didn't recognize you, though, at first. When they gotcha in the van yer wos half dead. I'd have bet me shirt on yer goin'to Jesus and Mary.' He crossed himself.

'What's up with you then?' Paul couldn't see any visible sign of an injury.

'It's the smokin'. The doc says not doing me lungs any good. Doin' a lot of coughin' lately. Some people in the hut had been getting on to the Tommies about it. Didn't want to catch anything.

So Doc sent me here to get me away from the others.' He cleared his throat and spat its contents on the ground. 'Told me to give up smokin'.' At this moment he took out a cigarette, lit it, and took a long draw. 'That'd be like me givin' up breathin!' After a moment he said,

'Whats goin' on in here anyhows?'

'Well, men come in sick and then go out well. That's the theory. If you've got money, you can't get out, and if you can't get out, it's likely you'll die with all these germs floating about in here.' He deliberately moved away from Paddy, who smiled.

'Ah it's smokin wid me. Nottin else. Are you worried about not gettin' out? Didn't take you as a moneyed one though.' He took another long draw on his cigarette, which was now the length of the width of two fingers. 'Are you?' he asked.

'Yes and no. I've some. Not a lot – my savings.' Paul wasn't comfortable talking about his money, so he quickly changed the subject. 'How come you're in here? You're Irish, aren't you?'

'As the shamrock, born and bred. It's the name.'

'What, Paddy?' They both smiled.

'Lieber. T'was me father's. A German. He's the culprit. T'was on the ferry goin' back to Dublin just after the *Lucy* went down, and they spied me name on the list when we docked. Before I knew, I was in a police station and banged up in a cell. They sent me back on the same ferry to Liverpool, and I landed up at a camp near Chester. Was in there a few weeks, and then I met you on that bloomin' cruise coming here. What about you?' he said lighting up another cigarette.

Paul wondered how much he could trust Paddy. He seemed a handy person to have as a friend. It was obvious he had the knack of making others work for him, sometimes even without their knowledge – a rare gift indeed. Paddy liked helping people, and they were taken in by his rich Irish charm and gift of the gab. Paul wasn't a person to make quick decisions; he was always careful. He liked to weigh matters up slowly, take his time. But could he afford to act like this? Perhaps he should bide his time and see what happened. But he didn't have time. The doctor had mentioned that morning that he was getting better by the day, and soon he could be moved out of the hospital. A police escort could be on its way from the mainland at that very moment. They wouldn't waste time, and God knew where he'd be taken. He had to act, and perhaps Paddy was the person to help.

'Paddy.'

'Paul.' Paddy imitated Paul.

Paul hesitated for a moment.

'Paddy, can I trust you?' He looked Paddy straight in the eyes.

'Like a cow's hind half trusts its front half to get along.'

'I mean seriously...'

'Yes, as God is me judge. But I can't give you any references.'

Paul realized he wasn't going to get Paddy to be any more serious, so he told him his story, particularly about his separation from his son, Jorgen, and his desire to escape from Knockaloe Internment Camp as quickly as possible because of the court sentence. When he'd finished, Paddy was speechless. It was a new experience for both of them.

Chapter 9

Living in the hospital camp gave Paul and Paddy greater time and opportunity to talk than they would have had as part of the general population. Free from the normal pattern of life in the compounds, where the men existed in cramped conditions without privacy, they spent hours walking around the perimeter of the fence together. Nobody bothered them. The authorities weren't interested; they literally treated the internees as numbers – prisoner numbers, which had been issued to them when they entered the camp. Paddy became friendly with some of the older guards who enjoyed his chirpy company as they paced slowly around the camp on the outside of the fence. Paddy had said that it would be a good idea to develop these contacts, as they might come in useful in the future. But Paul noticed that Paddy was genuinely interested in whomever he spoke to.

It was during the first week of these talks that they made plans for Paul's escape. At first there were heated arguments. Should Paul go ahead with this plan? Nobody, so far, had succeeded. The longest period of time anyone had been at liberty was two days. Why should Paul's attempt fare any better? And Paul's attempt at escape would prove to the authorities that he was as 'fit as a flea' as Paddy put it, and he'd definitely be sent to do his hard labour immediately, miles away from Liverpool. Paddy thought going to the authorities would be more sensible. Paul could explain the situation to them and leave it in their hands. They could approach the Red Cross and get them involved in tracing Jorgen. But Paul was sure the camp commandant wouldn't have any dealings with a convicted person who'd assaulted an officer of the Crown. No, escape was his only choice. He needed to protect Jorgen and anyone else who had been helping him. He had to do it on his own.

Arguments continued even after Paddy reluctantly accepted Paul's point of view.

'Look, it won't be any good when I escape if I hang around in a run-down building about four hundred yards away from where we're standing waiting for things to quieten down.' Paul and Paddy were looking at the very building as Paul spoke. It was situated in between the Hospital Camp and the beginning of the wooded area at the bottom of Corrin's Hill.

'Everyone else who's escaped has run off or hung around without any plan and handed themselves in,' observed Paddy. 'What I'm sayin' is that we first of all stock that buildin' up with food and other stuff yer'll need to last yer a week or so. Then yer can go and head east. They'll be t'inking the quickest way to the coast is over them hills west, and that's where they'll bound to be lookin' – not on their own doorstep.'

They covered this argument several times, and on the last occasion Paddy had a wide grin on his face. Paul stepped ever so slightly towards Paddy. At that moment Paul knew his friend had realized that he was coming round to his way of thinking.

'All right, you know it all,' said Paul. 'How do I get from that ramshackle hut to the east coast of this island and find that darn boat that's going to get me across to England?'

'Ah, don't be worryin' yer little head with such things, will yer?' Paddy said with a wink. And a guard suddenly approached from their rear on the other side of the wire.

'Ah, Fred, well, the top of the morning to yer. How's it goin'?'

'Yer bet, Paddy. I need sixpence off you for Saturday's race.' Fred looked around to see if any of the other guards were looking. 'And thanks for that tip last week. I won a packet on it.' Paddy handed over his sixpence to Fred, and the guard ran off in the direction he had come from. Paul was amazed that Fred and Paddy were on such familiar terms. Paddy usually preferred to speak to Fred on his own. Sometimes Paul could hear them laughing from the hut as they exchanged jokes. Fraternisation was frowned upon between the guards and the internees, but somehow Paddy got away with it.

'What we need to do is to get a needle and thread and do some sewin',' said Paddy. 'What did you say you was in your past life?'

Paul was still vexed with Paddy by the way he'd got round him about staying near the camp on his escape. What made it worse was that he was probably right.

'Butcher,' he said in an irritated tone.

Paddy ignored him. 'It'll be me, then, with the needle. You'll be havin' clumsy hands only fit for the chopper.' Paddy gave his special beaming smile, threw his arm round Paul, and started to pretend box. Paul took up the challenge, and in the end, they were both laughing.

'Look, what we need to do is make some bags to carry over yer shoulder.'

'What for?' enquired Paul.

'You'll need food and stuff to take with you unless you want to have the strength of a mouse without a tail, yer idiot.'

'Where can we get needle and thread?'

'The same place we'll get the cloth from – the canteen.'

So plans were made for Paddy to buy the items they needed, including food. He said he'd get a special rate. And Paul was to buy food as well, as it was essential they had plenty. Paddy had said they'd need ladders, and Paul had questioned this. He thought a blanket would be adequate to cover the barbed wire. But Paddy assured him it wouldn't. Paul was to become an artist, too, as a cover to the devious activities in hand.

So the other internees in the Hospital Camp would become used to Paddy busily sewing and Paul outside sketching landscapes and sometimes sitting on a chair on a cold evening drawing the heavenly constellations. The orderlies were pleased with their newly found interests and the food that the two were consuming. It meant that their coffers were increasing at a steady rate. The orderlies, of course, never disclosed any of this to the overworked doctor. They would report setbacks that Paul and Paddy had experienced and would project that their recoveries were going to be long and drawn out.

Owing to the state of the often water-clogged clay earth, the huts were raised off the ground. Beneath each one was a base of stones and pebbles that provided drainage. It was underneath the huts on the blanket of pebbles pushed out of sight that Paul and Paddy stored the food and other items they needed. They'd worried about mice having a nibble, but the hospital cat, always on duty at night, took care of this. Paddy had completed a few shoulder bags. At night he and Paul would place items in them, careful not to wake the other prisoners. In the morning Paul would place his sketchpads on top of the items in one of the bags and would take the bag with him when he went outside. He'd sit against the hut and store the jars of food and utensils one by one under the hut whenever he got the chance. At one point Paul complained to Paddy that they were overdoing it. They had enough food. But Paddy wouldn't have it.

'We'll be havin' to get the search lights out on the back fence,' Paddy said casually on one of their walks.

'How the heck are we going to do that?' exclaimed Paul. 'Have the heavenly forces arrange a lightening strike? Even you, Paddy, might find that a mite difficult.'

'You gotta imagine it happenin'! Faith they call it. Just imagine it happening, and it will.' If anybody else had said this to Paul, he would have dismissed it out of hand. But this was Paddy the magician who had the knack of making the impossible happen.

'Just t'ink friends in strange quarters,' Paddy said mysteriously and left it at that.

It was later that Paul saw Paddy at the fence with Fred. It seemed no different from other times they talked and joked and laughed. Then Fred walked away swiftly.

'That's done then,' Paddy said with a sparkle in his eye when he returned to Paul.

'What is?'

'Friends in strange quarters.'

There was one last thing they had to do. Again, it would be Paddy who'd be doing it. Paul had given up raising any objections. Paddy had all the ideas and made all the decisions. It was as if he was the one who was going to escape. Paddy said he was going to call in a favour from a friend. He showed Paul what he'd written:

> Dear Kirwen,
>
> Just to let you know, if you don't know already, for my great sins I've become a prisoner on that beautiful Island of Man. Is there any chance you can visit me here? The address is The Alien Prisoners Camp Knockaloe near Peel, Isle of Man.
>
> Patrick
>
> *Feach ar aghaidh le comhra mor.*
> *Patrick.*

'What's that last bit?'

Paddy hesitated and said,

'Patrick... no, it's a bit of the ol' Irish. It's special. Just means looking forward to a good *craic*.'

'What's a *craic*?'

'It's somethin' we do a lot of.' It took Paul several seconds before he cottoned on.

Chapter 10

Paddy waited two weeks for the response from the authorities. It had been delayed as neither the military censor nor the civilian staff in the administration hut had any idea what 'Feach ar aghaidh le comhra mor' meant. The officer who delivered the message to the ward was the doctor. It was only the second time he'd seen Paddy in the month that had elapsed since his admission. Kirwen was to visit the following Wednesday at 1300.

'That means you'll be out of here maybe a week later,' Paddy said to Paul. He got hold of a calendar and checked the dates. 'It'll be better to go at the weekend. Less military about and maybe on the Sunday even quieter. That's the twenty-seventh of June,' Paddy said.

'Do I get any say in the matter?' Paul said.

'No... oh... er... you could choose the butties to take.' And he waltzed off. His hackles raised, Paul was about to have it out with Paddy, but he saw that his friend was chatting with one of the orderlies, and by the time the conversation had finished, Paul had calmed down. Actually, he'd come to the conclusion there wasn't any point. Everything worked out for Paddy – luck of the Irish or what? More importantly, Paul had been impressed by Paddy's knowledge of the island. But whenever Paul had questioned him about it, he'd never received a straightforward answer. Paddy would answer in nonsensical riddles, which subtly changed to humour, and Paul would hear himself laughing. Paddy would walk away, and Paul would be left scratching his head.

Paddy turned to Paul,

'Look, mate, there's a reason I'm working this out for you and not lettin' you into things. I know it's winding yer up at times, but it's fer yer own good and the good of others. If yer get caught and yer know the ins and outs, yer could squeal to the authorities. Then, them others involved would be for the high jump, and they wouldn't take to kindly to yer now would they?' Paul was speechless, and Paddy added, 'Anyways, yer talents lie in other directions. I mean you make crackin' sarnies!'

Paddy was marched over to the administration block under an armed escort. They were not the usual older men who patrolled the health camp; they were from a Lancashire regiment. He'd tried to make a few jokes, and he'd seen some mouths move and eyes sparkle, but overall the mouths kept shut tight.

In one of the rooms, Paddy was ordered to sit down at an empty table. The hut looked like any other hut in the camp, but without the knick-knacks of the internees. There were about forty tables, and already people were sitting down chatting. Whenever voices were hushed, a sergeant would come round and rattle the table with his baton. Around the room stood riflemen with fixed bayonets. There were twenty in all. They stood at attention. It seemed to Paddy that all the tables in the room were within earshot of at least one or two soldiers. All the visitors were females of mixed ages and a few children. As he was looking round, a man was escorted to his table. Paddy's immediate reaction was to stand up and take Kirwen by the hand and give him a hearty welcome, but the sergeant wasn't having any of it.

'All present must abide by the rules,' he said. 'To wit, there must be no standing up by prisoners unless they are ordered to do so!'

'T'wit t'woo,' sang Paddy softly. 'That's the song of the wise bird,' he whispered. 'Not much wisdom or wit around here though.'

Kirwen smiled and shook hands vigorously with Paddy.

'Same old Paddy. How are you? Long time no see. You was supposed to come up and see us in May and you preferred this place did you?' He looked round. 'Well, takes all sorts as they say. That Gaelic greetin'—'

Paddy stopped his friend in his tracks, putting his index finger to his lips, but withdrawing it in a flash. He said several sentences in Gaelic. One sounded rather like an address if one imagined it spoken in English.

At that moment the sergeant rushed over and banged the table.

'There'll be no talking in that heathen tongue, d'you hear me?'

'Sorry, sur, I didn't know, sur, 'twas in the rules.' Then Paddy started coughing.

'I'll have none of this impertinence,' shouted the sergeant. 'The visit's ended! Up! Get up! Guards! Take this tinker back to his camp immediately.' Paddy's coughing attack continued. He stood up and then collapsed into the arms of Kirwen, who looked bemused. Paddy could see that his friend realized he was feigning the attack.

'Come on, Paddy,' said Kirwen, 'the joke's over.' But Paddy remained limp in his arms.

****

'You're all right,' said the doctor encouragingly. 'I think you might have been overawed by that visitor of yours. It was just a common faint.'

Paddy sprung up from his bed as if he was proving a point.

'Ah, fer sure faintin's fer womin, not a growd man like me. T'ink I'd had enough of that visiting lark, or the fags were not right.'

'Well you just take it easy,' the doctor said as he left.

Paul sauntered into the room. 'Hello, Tricia,' he said with a becoming smile.

'Oh, don't you start. I'll never live this down.'

'Come on, now, you can't kid me. You were faking it.'

Paddy quickly changed track.

'Twas the only way out. That sergeant smelt somethin' funny going on. He'd have been on to us if I'd given him the time. Only hope Kirwen got the message.' Paddy's voice displayed anxiety an emotion that Paul had rarely witnessed in him.

Chapter 11

It was the morning of 27 June. The sun was blazing in a cloudless sky. Knockaloe Moar was showing off its irresistible charms. Paul and Paddy had finished their breakfasts, and they were on a walk along the perimeter of the camp close to the wire. They were arguing. Paul's face had a sullen look about it. Paddy had recently been smiling, buoyed up by nature's dazzling close presence and its promises. But his mood had changed. No longer was he concentrating on the sounds of Knockaloe Camp on a summer's day with nature and man's soft calls intertwined – voices of dissonant choirs of gulls, the chants of grasshoppers, the calming nature of familiar farm sounds, and men's dulled joyful shouts in a football game coming from the huge sloping field that was one of the camp's recreation grounds. On the contrary, he was listening to the grating steely voice of an angry Paul – a voice that Paddy imagined encouraged birds of prey to be insanely excited by the chance of tasty pickings.

'But you don't know if Kirwen got what you were saying. How can I chance my neck on something that can't be confirmed? It's completely reckless,' Paul said.

'Yer've got to trust me, Paul,' Paddy said, turning and looking straight into Paul's eyes – eyes that blared out stifling anxiety. 'Look, didn't I get that letter back from him? And wusn't there that mark at the bottom?'

'That mark at the bottom… that mark at the bottom!' Paul's voice rose. 'That was a censor's mark, nothing else. All that was in the letter was "how are you?" and "bye for now" and his name. Where's the confirmation in that?' He flung his arms out wide.

'Twas the bit after his name. It was the ol' Irish—'

'It was the damn censor's mark, that's all!' interrupted Paul. 'And even if it was what you said – that greeting – "let's have an important chat" – it's not saying everything is ready for the escape. The house in Douglas, the fishing boat—'

'Hold yer horses!' Paddy smiled. 'That ol' Irish is magica!' His whole face grinned at this as he thought about what he was going to say. 'The meanin' of them words can change as quickly as the fiddler's bow goes up and down. You take the meaning as you understand it.'

'What do you mean by that? And I believe in the little people as well,' said Paul.

'He'd savvy that the letter would be censored, and he'd also know I needed an answer. The answer was the ol' Irish under the name not on top of it. If it weren't there then the answer would be "nottin doing." You see the magic in it? Now don't yer be botherin' yourself.'

Paul was still angry, but the beginning of a calmness was setting in as usual. It was that fathomless innocent smile of his friend. And that Paddy was always right. If he said it was going to happen, it would. But Paul still had to move away from him smartly. In frustration he wanted to let Paddy know that he wasn't the best pleased with him.

****

Everything was ready for the escape. Lights out at ten o'clock, and there was another hour to go. They both lay down fully dressed under their pyjamas and pretended to sleep. Paul was in a state of panic. One part of him shouted out he must go. Time was slipping by. The sentence hung over him. But more important was the burning image of Jorgen moving further and further away. In his mind, Jorgen was still running as he'd done mindlessly on that fateful Monday night in Liverpool.

The other part of him was raging about what could go wrong. There was a strong chance he could be shot while trying to escape. Jorgen would be an orphan. Even if he managed to get away from the hospital, surely the guards would be crawling all over the area, and one of the first places they'd look would be that run-down hovel where he was supposed to spend the week twiddling his thumbs. Then, as far as the rest of the plan was concerned, he knew not a dot. He hated not having any control. He was perspiring heavily. His left eye started to twitch uncontrollably. He turned this way and that. He heard Paddy snoring. How could he be asleep at a time like this? But this involuntary and so normal an activity eventually took the edge off the panic. It was Paddy to the rescue again, and the man from Ireland wasn't even aware of it.

Paul checked his pocket watch. It was eleven o'clock. The light had faded outside. He could hear the wind blowing. The calmness of the earlier part of the day had gone. It had turned colder. All the other men in the hut were asleep, and much to Paul's annoyance, this still included Paddy.

Paul crept out of his bed. 'Wake up. It's time.' He gently nudged Paddy to no avail. The Irishman slept on. So, as quietly as he could, Paul got hold of both his friend's arms and shook them. This did the trick. It was some moments before Paddy came round.

'I'm sorry. I wus dreamin' we wus in Liverpool having a pint of Guinness together in that posh Adelphi—' Paul told him to shush. They both stuffed their pillows in their beds to give the impression they were still sleeping. Both moved to the toilets at the end of the hut as silently as they could. The hut doors were firmly bolted. They had to get out through the toilet windows, which they unfastened, as quietly as they could, with tools they'd earlier bought from the canteen.

They were soon outside. It was blowing a gale. The sky was hung with black clouds. To Paul it was a bad omen.

'This weather isn't going to help,' he whispered gloomily.

'The darkness is good. We won't be seen as easily – if anyone's able to see.' It was six minutes past eleven, and the searchlights on the fence they were to clamber over flickered out. 'Well, what did I just say?'

Paul could not see in the darkness, but he imagined Paddy's face beaming. They hurriedly removed the items they'd stored underneath the hut. Their first job was to put on gloves made from strong suit material. Then they carefully tied footholds made of cloth and reinforced with leather onto the fence. Paddy had found this the most difficult task in all the sewing he'd done. They'd kept testing the strength of the footholds, trying different combinations of cloth and leather until they were certain they'd work without too many problems. The darkness and the wind were making the task more complicated. Eventually they fixed all the footholds on securely and placed a layered piece of cloth over the barbed wire at the top of the fence.

'How did you conjure up the darkness dead on time like it was ordained?' Paul said. His torn trench coat flapped in the wind as they walked back to the hut for the rest of the gear.

''Twas a favour, pure and simple. A favour from that lovely man, Fred.'

'But won't you get him into trouble?'

'No, would I do that? The cable was nibbled by rats, or maybe mice with tails,' he added in a teasing manner, 'to make it look like it weren't deliberate.'

'How though?'

'Perhaps he had a pet ferret. Just trust me. Now come on, Paul, don't be asking all these questions. We've got work to do!'

With tears in his eyes, Paul went over to Paddy, taking him by surprise, and began to hug him. 'This is goodbye. How can I thank you enough for all you've done?'

But to Paul's amazement, Paddy gently pushed him away. 'Now we can't be doing with all that soppy talk. Don't you know it's not goodbye, yer idiot? Yer don't t'ink I could trust yer out there on yer own. It'd be like throwin' that spaniel into the lions' den, and 'Im not surviving as you wouldn't!'

'*Daniel*, you idiot,' Paul said wiping the tears away. 'But why should you risk your life for me? It doesn't make sense.'

'Gettin' you and that son of yours together makes purfect sense,' answered Paddy, his voice almost drowned by the wind. 'And anyhows, I've tings to clear up out there. Comin' here stopped me from doing that. So there's no arguing. There's no time. Come on. Let's go, cos they won't let us if they sets an eye on us, and that's fer sure.' He shoved Paul ahead of him.

In Paul's mind, events over the past weeks were fitting into place. The one thing that he had repeatedly questioned Paddy about – the quantity of food they'd bought – now made sense. He felt guilty, yet relieved. He couldn't form the words that he wished to say. And the strength of the wind discouraged chatting anyway.

The two were aware of a guards' hut on their left, which was positioned in between Camp Three and the Hospital Camp, so they worked as silently as they could. Paddy was now on the other side of the fence; Paul was on top of the fence. Most of the food and drink was in bottles and glass jars. They'd tried to pack these in the bags as well as they could, protected with paper and cloth. When Paul dropped the bags from the top of the fence, sometimes Paddy was unable to catch them. Along with Paddy's curses, which were always followed by a couple of Hail Marys, there would be the noise of splintering glass. But the wind was their ally; it killed all sounds.

Once they had delivered all the food and the small items of equipment to the other side of the fence, Paul jumped from the top. But he landed awkwardly and winced in pain. He knew instinctively that he hadn't broken anything. They had to make three trips in all to transport their goods to the dilapidated farm building. On the last lap, Paul was limping badly. As soon as they were in the building, he sat down on a large stone to take the weight off his leg.

'Look at the mess in here,' Paul said. Pieces of dressed stone that once had been part of a wall lay scattered on the floor. 'It's much worse than I thought it would be.'

'Ah, it's a wonderful hovel,' philosophised Paddy. 'Can't you just feel the freshness of freedom? It makes yer nose twitch like a bunny's when it furst comes out of its burra!'

'But see up there? Gaping holes in the roof. I can feel the moisture on my face!'

'Twill be yer very own perspiration,' Paddy quickly retorted. But for once Paul was right. It had started to rain heavily. Water now seemed to be entering every orifice of the structure. As the wind swirled, its best friend, the rain, joined in the fun displaying as much versatility as its partner. As the two men tried to settle down, the holes they'd never imagined would be there suddenly caught them off guard. So they moved round, climbing over stones, squelching in the mud, and when they considered themselves in a dry spot, they'd settle down only to be showered on again as the wind sang in triumph.

The wind and rain died down at about three o'clock. The men were sodden, so they changed into dry clothes and managed to sleep for a few hours. At five in the morning, they were awakened by the warm rays of the sun shining through the very same holes that earlier had given them the dampest of receptions. The severe storm, though, had made their escape a much easier affair than they'd anticipated. Any noise they'd made had been swallowed up in its wildness. The downpour had eradicated their footprints and meant that attempts to use sniffer dogs in their capture would prove useless.

Then it happened. Sirens wailed, whistles blew, sergeant majors blasted orders, boots pounded the ground. All in all, an exotic cacophony rang around Knockaloe Moar. They had been found out. Paul shot up in a panic, his ankle slowing his pace down as he moved across the hovel to a find somewhere he could view the camp from.

'Paul, relax. Don't move. It's better we don't. T'ink that yer a stone in here lyin' in the sun, not a care in the world. Let them all be runnin' about blowin' their whistles. There'll be plenty of runnin' fer us in a couple of days.'

As the commotion in the camp died down, they relaxed. There was no sign of troop movement between themselves and the Hospital Camp. They had their breakfast – a jar each of herrings. They took the saltiness away by swilling down their ginger beer.

'This doesn't come anywhere near beatin' the kipper, but it'll do fer now,' said Paddy. 'Agh, one day we'll be swillin' down champers and oysters at the Ritz, trust me!' Paddy oozed confidence. Paul wasn't so sure. The Ritz sounded a million miles away from his life, as did the champagne and oysters. He couldn't imagine Paddy – the thin, tall figure with curly red hair and a rough and thick Irish accent – ever getting anywhere near even the back door of the place. But then he'd never have thought that Paddy would have the knowledge and contacts that he possessed. No, he was going to keep a rain check on the Ritz.

Chapter 12

That first day set the itinerary for the rest of the week. They took it in turns keeping watch on movements around the camp from dusk until dawn. At the same time they looked at ways of hiding themselves in nearby thickets if the troops decided to check the hovel. In the end they gave up, as they quickly realized that, if the guards did come their way, the only option would be to stay put and give themselves up. On one of Paddy's shifts, he'd noticed with horror a machine gun post well hidden in the extensive gardens to the extreme right as he viewed the camp. They'd not counted on the machine gun being there in their planning. It was positioned a few hundred yards from camp three and four times the distance away from their hovel. There was nothing they could do now, and he wasn't going to mention it to Paul. There was no point; he'd only worry himself sick.

It was Paul who finished the night shift on the Tuesday. He said to Paddy that he was amazed that they'd been left completely alone. Paddy winked, and smile lines covered his face. 'Others who's had a go at escaping tried to get as far away from the camp as they could. Stands to reason the authorities won't be lookin' our way.'

'If I was the commandant, I'd check everywhere nearby and then fan out.'

'But d'you not see they don't have that many lads to do that?' Paddy's smile changed to a playful grin and he added, 'Bet yer five guinnies they won't come. I'll even add me granny's slip as well!' Before Paul could respond, Paddy started to laugh, and they both stumbled round the stones laughing hysterically until Paddy said,'Shusht will yer? Or I'll be given yer that slip.' The laughing continued but stopped abruptly when they heard the sound of a siren and whistles coming from the camp. They crouched down in silence, both looking towards the camp. They kept this silence up for five minutes. Finally Paddy said,'Agh, it's a practice or somethin' like that. But I'll not be talkin' about me granny's slip again too soon!'

'Could be someone else has escaped,' Paul suggested.

'Aye, lad, yer could be right. An' that's gonna count in our favour if he's out fer long.'

Wednesday passed without incident, but the waiting and idleness meant that they kept eating for the sake of having something to do. They were quickly using up their supplies. Thursday was different. It was their last day, and they ate normally in between the tasks they'd set themselves. The sun was blazing, and the sky was cloudless. Paddy thought that, as the weather was set, they could expect a full moon that night. It would make them more visible, but it would also allow them to get their bearings when it was necessary.

'Now look, Paul, we've got to agree right here and now that, if we get run down by the Tommies, we won't put up a fight. But if one of us has a chance of slipping away, then he does, and we don't bother about the other. D'you agree, Paul?'

Paul paused. He seemed to be thinking long and hard.

'D'you agree, Paul?' Paddy repeated.

'Yes,' he said slowly, but there was reluctance in his voice.

But Paddy ignored this, thinking that, if all went according to plan, they'd get away with it, and anyway, going on past experience, he thought he could manage Paul. Paddy continued,

'Look, in case we get separated, I've got an address here for you to head to when you get to Douglas. Take it now. I've also written this letter to a friend of mine in Liverpool. I'll let you have it when we reach Douglas. You read it and let me know what you t'ink. Paul read:

> Dear Seamus,
>
> The person before you is Paul Roth. The one I mentioned when you visited the camp. He's a good, honest man, and the reason he's escaped is that he's searching for his son who he's not seen since he was arrested for being a German even though he'd been in Liverpool as a shopkeeper for 15 years. His son has got no one else to care for him, and Paul is desperate to find him.
>
> I've told him that he can stay with you, and you'd fix him up with food and clothes and anything else he will need to help him find his son.
>
> I know it will be putting yourself in the way of a little danger, but I also know that, like me, you think this war is a mess and it should never have happened. And I believe you are a man of integrity.
>
> I will reimburse you when we meet again after I've got out of this damn place.
>
> Your friend,
> Paddy
>
> Mr Seamus Kirwen, 31 Rodney Street, Liverpool

Paul was amazed. Not only because of the serious nature of the letter's contents, but that there was no light-hearted banter threaded into it in pure Paddy style. Also, the last few words puzzled him. He thought that Paddy had planned the escape with both of them in mind.

'Thanks so much, Paddy.' Tears were welling up in Paul's eyes, but he managed to control himself. 'I really appreciate what you're doing for me, but what I don't understand is that, according to the letter, I'm supposed to be on my own.'

'Just coverin' my tracks. Agh, well how could I ever let you do it on yer own? From what you was sayin', you'd fallen at the furst fence like a novice headstrong jockey and horse. Don't be frettin'. I'm enjoyin' the ride, but don't be goin' round tellin' everybody wills yer? And remember, if you get to Seamus's without me, remember to destroy that letter after it's been read.' Paddy could see that Paul was getting more upset.

'Don't be blubbering lad. We've got serious work to be getting' on with. Furst, the route to Douglas. Just run through what you remember we agreed about in the camp.'

Paul obliged: 'We leave here at about nine. Head north towards Peel keeping to the woods on Corrin's Hill. Have to keep walking until we clear the camp and woods. Then we take a bearing from Corrin's Tower in Peel. Then cross the fields heading east until we meet up with the railway line. Walk along the line until we reach Douglas – about fifteen miles'.

'Correct. Only yer make it sound a doddle,' said Paddy. 'I t'ink the furst bit will be dodgy as it'll still be light. But we need the light to see when we have to cross the moor. There'll be about half a dozen stations on the line to pass through, and we'll have to avoid these like the plague, and of course we don't know when the last train will be comin' along. It'll be a case of keeping yer eyes and ears open and prayin' at the same time.'

They'd agreed that it would be sensible to cover their tracks. In the unlikely event of the authorities checking the area, a lack of tracks would give the two a head start. So they cleared away the jars and bottles they'd used and stashed them in the four shoulder bags. They crept silently out of the hovel and walked for five minutes or so through the bracken and trees that covered the bottom of Corrin's Hill. This would be the start of their journey later on, and it was useful to get a feel for the terrain that they would encounter. They buried the items as best they could and covered the burial sites with branches and other loose foliage.

On their way back, they heard noises – faint at first but gradually became louder as they progressed. Individuals were raising their voices shouting to each other. Some were blowing whistles sharply. It was the unmistakeable sound of a football match that was being played in a nearby field, and hundreds of internees had gathered to watch the game. Guards were patrolling around the perimeter of the recreation enclosure. Paul and Paddy had a clear view of the Hospital Camp, the moor, and their hovel. It was impossible for them to get from behind the bushes and trees and make a beeline to the hovel without being seen. Even Paddy admitted it was too risky. Paul realized how anxious Paddy was. Paddy started to hurry his sentences and speak his thoughts out loud:

'These games can go on for hours – even late into the night. There's no knowing when they'll finish. There's more clearing up to do, and we can't run behind schedule, as we can't be arriving at Douglas in the light. We shouldn't have left the clearing up until we was on our way out of this place. Bloody hell!' Momentarily their relationship had flipped 360 degrees. Paul was consoling, and Paddy was just muttering on, recounting the events of the week and how well the plan had gone until this moment. Sometimes there was no coherence to his words. It was almost as if Paddy had keenly felt the loss of his magic.

'C'mon, Paddy, there's nothing more we can do. Only sit tight and wait.' Paul kept repeating these words until Paddy had calmed down and became his old self.

****

It was just after six that the internees were finally marched out of the recreation field, and the number of guards on sentry duty was reduced. Crouching, Paul and Paddy ran to the hovel. All the time Paddy was mindful of the machine gun position. He hadn't been as bothered earlier on, as it hadn't appeared to be manned. The fact that the gun and its attendants faced Camp Three was of little consolation. He knew that those guns could rip a man to pieces; he'd heard all the reports coming from the Somme. Additionally, the guns could be turned quickly. Paddy and Paul safely returned to their makeshift home, and Paddy was pleased that Paul's ankle seemed all right. It would have to be for the midnight hike that faced them in a few hours.

At seven, much later than they'd originally planned, they ate their last meal. This time it was tins of corned beef – they had no other food left – and bottles of ginger beer. They filled their bags with drinks and the leftover tins and bottles and packed the oilskins they'd bought at the canteen. Paddy had drawn a map that showed their planned journey. It was a rough approximation of the layout of the land from what he remembered from trips he'd made on the train from Peel to Douglas. He had marked out the stations on the route. Some of the major stations could be manned, so they would have to go around them if necessary. He thought the route would be clear of ordinary passenger trains after ten at night, but he didn't know whether the military made use of them through the night. They would have to be on their guard at all times.

'There could be trains at night run by the army,' Paddy explained. 'We don't know, fer I've never taken a stroll after midnight that way, would you believe! It's twelve miles roughly between Peel and Douglas, so it should take us no more than five hours without any breaks apart from latrine stops. This ginger beer is fearsome fer that sort of t'ing.'

Paddy announced their final task:

'Now, lad, yer moight of been wonderin' what that bag of flour and paint brushes that's sittin' there on the ground would be for.' Paul looked over to the area where they'd kept the food and looked at the bag of white flour and brushes. 'It's our war paint, lad.'

Paul looked at Paddy in utter bewilderment.

'War paint? What d'you mean?'

'We'll be needin' to disguise ourselves if we don't get to Douglas before the sun rises. We can put the flour in our hair, and we can stick moustaches on our faces. They won't recognize us then at all... nobody would.'

'But how would they recognize us?' Paul said, smiling. 'They haven't got any images of us.'

'Oh, yes they have – of me at any rate. A photographic image. The police take images of everyone taken into the Bridewells in Dublin. T'ink they're afraid of the Finnians.'

'Well, you can count me out,' declared Paul. 'I'm not covering myself with flour and making myself look like an idiot. No one's ever taken an image of me.'

'But some in the hospital camp might remember how you looked, and they'd make a drawing of your face.'

Paul's face was suddenly covered in a grin.

'What if it rains? You'll be looking like one of your banshees, and then someone will notice you for sure!'

Paddy had to laugh, but he was determined to go ahead with his plan. Paul wondered whether Paddy was doing all this to take their minds off the planned events of the night. It would be something right up Paddy's street, making fun to lighten the load.

Paddy turned away from Paul when he applied the flour. Then he began to pull the bristles out of the paintbrushes. He made a paste with some flour and ginger beer and attempted to stick the strips of bristles onto his upper lip, but he abandoned this after several unsuccessful attempts. He couldn't get them to stay on. He slowly turned round to show Paul the finished product.

Paul couldn't stop laughing. Paddy just gazed at him, keeping a straight poker face, which made him laugh all the more.

'What's wrong?' Paddy said with a glint of a smile. He wondered if his red hair was showing through the white of the flour.

When he'd calmed down, Paul said,

'Strawberries and cream comes to mind, but what about the moustache?

'Oh, no, lad, twasn't up to much. They felt too tickly fer me nostrils. I'd be sneezing all the while. Was like having a tin of snuff tied to me nose.'

Chapter 13

A large, brilliant, white moon cast its silvery fingers over Knockaloe Moar. It was reflected on the barrel of the machine gun, creating a sinister cameo. Paddy was relieved. There were no Tommies in sight. He was not so pleased, though, with the brightness he saw all around him and the stillness that seemed to go hand in hand with it. He was overjoyed they were finally leaving, but the first task of reaching the cover of the nearby trees made him feel uneasy. They would be exposed the whole time. But then he reproached himself. There would be other dangers he wasn't aware of. So there was no point in worrying. He blurted out,

'Enough's enough!'

'What did you say?' Paul asked. He was standing next to Paddy ready to go, bags slung over his shoulders. "Have you seen something?'

'I said, "Have we got all the stuff?" Are yer ready to go?' They shook hands and hugged each other. 'Come on. Yer'll be blabbering soon. Let's be on our way.' Paddy crossed himself.

They reached the woods without incident, and they discarded the remainder of the rubbish before getting on their way. The course of the route followed the lower contour of Corrin's Hill, which was to their left in a northerly direction. On the march to the camp in May, Paddy had noticed a tall tower on the hill. This was in line with a road bridge that ran over the River Neb south of Peel. They would have to use the road bridge to access the track that was on the other side of the river. The walk to put them in line with the tower lasted about fifteen minutes. This time would have been halved if they hadn't needed to deviate around a quarry that lay in their path. But they were keeping to their schedule. It was just after ten. Looking east they could just about make out the thickly wooded area that screened the road bridge. In between the bridge and where they stood on Corrin's Hill was the problem. They would have to travel through open fields until they reached the Glenfaba estate. They decided to follow the lines of hedges, keeping close to the ones that would obscure them from the view of the camp.

It was a further fifteen minutes before they reached the woods of Glenfaba House. All had gone well apart from them both being stung by the swarms of midges they encountered as they neared the woods of the estate.

'It'll be the bloody water,' cursed Paddy as quietly as he could, and there'll be more of them as we go on.' As they were both laden with shoulder bags, they found it difficult to swat the insects. Soon they saw the lights of the hall through the trees. It quickly took their minds off the pests.

'There's got to be a drive from that hall that goes near to the bridge,' said Paddy. 'So when we hit the drive, it's just a matter of following it to the road.' They heard the sound of cracking twigs, and they crouched down. It was a gamekeeper with a lamp. Paddy thought the man couldn't be out because of them, as they'd only just arrived. The man must be on his rounds. Paddy flapped his arms as a signal to Paul to sit for a while until the danger passed. Half an hour elapsed before they could venture on. They noticed that the gamekeeper had been tending to some traps he'd set. When he'd returned to the hall they continued, at a slower pace, and followed the sweeping drive, walking as if treading on eggs. Before the road and bridge came into sight, they were surprised to hear the sounds of motor engines, and not just one, but several. As they peered through the vegetation near the roadside, they were in for a shock. A column of twelve military vans had stopped. Their engines were still running. Paul panicked and almost shouted,

'They're on to us! Let's get out of here quick.' He grabbed Paddy's arm, but Paddy placed his hand gently on Paul's.

'Calm down, Paul. Can't yer see what I see? One of them van's broken down, and there's a fella with a crankin' handle trying to get it goin.' He pointed towards the bridge were a soldier was starting to crank the engine of a van. 'They know nothin' of us,' he continued. 'We'll just have to stay put till it's started again.'

But five minutes had passed, and still there was no sign of life in the engine. The soldier had given up trying to crank it, and was under the bonnet tinkering around. By this time, the two vans in front had set off for the Knockaloe Camp. The other vans behind were trapped. The bridge was narrow. There was no possibility of getting past the other vehicle.

'I'd get that bloody thing cranked up properly if they'd give me quarter of a chance,' whispered Paddy. 'But that lot would probably look a gift horse in the mouth an' not be havin' anythin' of it!' Paddy had emphasized the word *look*, and was lost in his grey matter for a few seconds before he shook his head slowly. 'No. We'll give them a few minutes. But then we'll have to do somethin'. Can't wait around here all night doing nothin' like wood lice under attack, as we'll be scuppered.' They waited for ten minutes. During that time, the Tommies had tried to push-start the van without success. So they began to push the vehicle along the road looking for a place to park it out of the way. The weight of the van and space restriction caused by the stone-and-brick walls on either side of the road hampered the task.

'Any ideas about what we should do?' asked Paddy. 'Those vans behind are movin' at a slow pace. At this rate, all the hall will be out wantin' to investigate.' Paul thought it strange that Paddy was asking him what they should do. He said,

'Well, there's no way we can cross by the bridge, either over or under it. Best bet is to ford the river further downstream.'

Paddy looked away from Paul. Several seconds passed, and then, in a weak voice, he said,

'I can't swim though'. Now Paul realized why Paddy had asked him.

'Don't worry,' Paul assured Paddy. 'It can't be that deep, and I'll look out for you.' There was no time for further discussion. They tracked north towards Peel through the thick vegetation of the estate until the river narrowed.

'This'll do, Paddy,' said Paul.

Paddy made his way onto the riverbank.

'Still wide. Looks about twenty yards or so.'

Paul was having none of it. He was behind Paddy, and with his arms on Paddy's shoulders, he propelled him into the murky water.

'It's icy cold!' Paddy yelled.

'I'm right behind you. Just keep walking.' Paul, too, thought it was cold – much colder than he'd anticipated. As they reached midstream, the strength of the current increased. Just then Paddy sank several feet all at once. His shoulder bag had floated away. The water had reached his shoulders. He stopped. Paul paddled around him anticipating the gulley that had caused his friend to sink. Paul could see that Paddy was so petrified he couldn't move. Paul jettisoned his bag and faced Paddy. He took hold of his arms,

'You're safe, Paddy. Look into my eyes. Grasp my hands.' Paul started walking backwards, holding Paddy's hands firmly.

'I can't!' Paddy shouted.

'Just look into my eyes,' Paul said. 'We're doing fine. The water level will go down as we reach the other bank.' Paddy took several steps. As the water level lessened, Paddy's panic started to recede. Once they dragged themselves up onto the riverbank, they took stock of the situation.

'You look like a very wet ghoul,' Paul said. Several tufts of Paddy's hair had congealed with the flour and stuck up on his head. There were streaks of white down his cheeks.

'At least I'm a live ghost, thanks to yer good self!' They'd lost their bags, which had contained the oilskins, pullovers, the ginger beer, and Paddy's rough plan of the route. Thankfully, he told Paul he remembered the address they were heading for and had a rough idea of the direction to go once they reached Douglas. 'Sure I'll have to get some hauntin' done this night and frighten away anythin' else that's lurkin' out there intent on stoppin' us.'

Chapter 14

Once they reached the narrow-gauge track of the Isle of Man railway, they headed east. To warm themselves up, they began trotting along placing their feet on the sleepers in unison. Paddy would up the tempo from time to time causing Paul to stumble and curse. Clouds had come in from the east and would occasionally take away the silvery light that helped them pick their way over the track, slowing them down. But they made good progress and reached the first station out of Peel, St Johns, at around one in the morning. They thought they heard sounds coming from the carriage sheds when they were working their way over sidings to avoid the platform area, but nothing came of it. It was later, after they'd skirted round Crosby Station and rejoined the track beyond the road bridge, that a noise did have substance. It was the sound of someone singing. Paul thought he saw a man walking along the track some distance away. A passing cloud obscured their view for a minute or so. When the light returned, the sighting was confirmed. A man carrying a dark object in his hand was making his way towards them. Paul and Paddy jumped into the undergrowth at the side of the track. The man was singing an Irish jig and was as drunk as a person in need of track to keep him moving, going somewhere. As he sang, he swayed from side to side and sometimes would stop and take a few steps back in keeping with his idea of the rhythm.

'It's one of yours, Paddy,' whispered Paul.

'Aye, a man after me own heart. Perhaps we could do a duet.' Paddy joined in with the song. But the man, who'd by this time nearly drawn level with them, seemed unaware of their presence and Paddy's harmonizing. He took a few steps backwards, but this time he lost his balance and fell onto his back, cracking his head on one of the rails. The bottle he was holding smashed on the sleepers. Paddy immediately ran over to him. He took his pullover, shirt, and vest off and tore his vest into strips, which he wrapped around the drunk's head wound and lacerated arm to halt the bleeding.

'We can't leave him here,' Paddy said. 'He mightn't be found for hours. The poor man will bleed to death. We'll have to get him back to the station and leave him there.'

The two picked the man up and retraced their steps back to the station. They passed the rear of the station building and crossed the road by the level crossing and walked past cattle pens. They noticed a house with a light on about a quarter of a mile away down the road.

'I t'ink we should head for that house,' said Paddy. 'We can leave him, knock them up, and then scarper. There won't be anybody around at the station till at least seven, an' he's still bleedin'.

They'd nearly reached the house when the drunk opened his eyes, turned, and had a good look at Paddy through bleary eyes. Paddy's white-and-red hair stuck up in tufts, and his face was pasty grey.

'It's one of them spirits of the little people,' the man bawled. 'Go away! Go back to them fiends!' He tried to push Paddy and Paul away, but they held on tightly and pulled him along a pebbled path to the front door of the house. The orange hue of gas lamps shone through the downstairs windows of the farmhouse. They propped the man up against the door. The door opened. They ran, just managing to catch a glimpse of the drunk as he fell into the arms of a man who was holding a shotgun. The gun discharged.

It was only when Paul and Paddy were back on the railway track beyond the bridge at Crosby that any conversation took place, and it didn't occur for several minutes. They were too exhausted, but more to the point, going over what had happened was to make it real. It was Paul who reluctantly broke the silence.

'D'you think he's a goner? If he is, we'll be up for hanging.'

'Now stop saying such codswallop, will yer? We don't know whether he wus shot. The farmer was holding the gun upright as I remember—'

Paul interrupted, 'But the fella saw us, I'm sure.'

'We can't be sure of anythin',' Paddy declared. 'We wus up that path as fast as them expresses run. Our injured fella fell into the arms of the farmer. The farmer couldn't see, and especially with the gun goin' off as it did. There'd have been too much goin' on. He'd have had to help our friend down.' Although Paddy couldn't be certain about anything he'd said, he didn't want Paul to be worrying. They'd know one way or the other in a couple of days' time, as their adventure would be all over the papers. There was nothing they could do.

They passed through the next two stations without incident. It was at Quaterbridge, a mile away on the outskirts of Douglas, that they had to divert from their journey along the track. Their target was Alexander Drive in the northern part of Douglas. They had both thought at the beginning that this part of the plan would be the most dangerous. But compared to the hair-raising events they'd managed to steal through, they were prepared for anything. As they neared Quarterbridge, Paul placed his hand on Paddy's arm and turned round to face him.

'Have you seen your mug?' he said with a smile. 'It's a face that could be a murderer's!'

'Agh, we'll have enough of that.' Paddy stopped short. He could see the grin on Paul's face, and then he understood. The

The Lucy Effect

humour melted the iced tension of the last few miles as tiredness set in. 'Is it that bad?',

'Worse. That fella was right to call you a ghoul. You'll have to wash it off.' Paul pointed to the stream on the other side of the embankment. As they approached the stream, they noticed the day was gradually beginning to dawn.

'If I remember right,' Paddy said as he finished sluicing himself with water, 'when we get off the track at the next station, we go over a bridge and follow the road, staying off it of course. Then it's the furst road on the right. Number thirty-eight Alexander Drive. As easy as pie it'll be.'

'If you say so,' added Paul as they set off for Quarterbridge Station, quickening their pace as they raced the approaching dawn.

And so, as Paddy had predicted, it was as easy as pie. Exhausted and having the thirst of spaniels after a two-mile, non-stop crashing dash through hedgerows, they reached number thirty-eight Alexander Drive. They entered the building through an open downstairs window. Desperately seeking water, they checked the three ground-floor rooms of the large, three-storey Victorian terraced house. Eventually they found bottles of ale sitting on a table. They found Woodbines and matches in the scullery. Underneath one of the bottles was a note:

> Don't make a sound. Neighbours think we're away which we are of course! More ale and other stuff in the pantry. On Sunday, get to the junction of Quarterbridge Road and Alexander Drive by midnight. A horse and cart will pick you up and take you to the coast where a trawler will be waiting to take you across to the mainland. Please destroy this note. Good luck. You owe me a massive one.
>
> Brian

'So that's it!' Paddy said. 'Some rest for the wicked at last.' He wiped his mouth on his sleeve. He'd downed the bottle in one go – the first beer he'd guzzled since his captivity. It tasted just like that; it didn't matter who'd brewed it. 'We've wun a few days when we don't have to t'ink. Others'll be doin' that fer us. Come on, me lad, let's raise our bottles to that luverly t'ought. Let's be gettin' in that pantry and at the grub. Don't know 'bout you, but I'm starvin' after all that fish paste.'

But Paul, who'd carried his bottle to the nearest settee in the house, was fast asleep. The bottle was half full and sat on a small card table next to him. Paddy sorted out a blanket and laid it over his friend. The exhilaration of his arrival at the safe house was keeping the approach of fatigue at bay. After demolishing several rough sandwiches of ham and pork he'd made without buttering the bread – he'd been too famished for such ceremony – he explored the rest of the house. He decided to sleep in a large bedroom on the first floor, and brought four bottles of ale up, placed them on a chest of drawers next to the bed, and lay down. He stared at the four bottles for several minutes. The bottles began to move and sometimes merge into each other, and then they would become four bottles again. Not a particularly religious man, Paddy began to pray. He prayed for their deliverance. He kept looking at the bottles, and then they were gone.

Chapter 15

They both woke up in the afternoon and were soon tucking into the cold meats that had been left for them. There were noises of shutting doors from one of the adjoining houses. Then they heard cheery voices of children outside along with footsteps. Paul went over to the window to look. He was just about to move the curtains slightly so that he could peek outside when Paddy, in a hushed voice said,

'Keep away from them curtains! We can't risk doing anythin' that'll make people curious, and there's not supposed to be anybody here. Come and sit down. Let's have a good crack. There's nothin' much else to do. It's the first time we can do it comfortably sittin' on proper chairs without mindin' who's behind or in front of us!'

Paul sat at the table and resumed eating. Neither of them said anything for a minute or two. Paddy was deep in thought. It was the four bottles on the chest of drawers in the bedroom, and how they had changed their form before his eyes. The bottles hadn't really changed; neither had he. It was his mind that had done it. It'd moved to another way of thinking, just as two people could view what was before their eyes in radically different ways. Paddy looked up at Paul and said, 'What happened to your wife and other son? You've told me a little about it already, but you've missed parts out. I've willingly put me neck on the line for us. I must be family be now. Isn't that so, lad?' Paul poured himself a mug of tea.

'Aye, you're family – the best all right.' He paused. 'I'm not a man for talking. I keep them to myself; they're my own.' He looked down at the tea.

'I understand that, lad, but sometimes it helps to get it off yer chest. I know – I'll start off by telling yer a few of the t'ings I've held back on, and then it'll be your go. But yer keep the t'ings that yer really don't want to talk about to yourself. Agreed?'

Still looking at his tea, Paul agreed, but his voice was full of reluctance. A floating tealeaf struggled to keep being drawn down in the swirl of hot liquid. It lost.

Paddy talked about his early life in Dublin. His German father died suddenly when he was four, so he hardly knew him. His ma was left money. She was all right and fortunately had a good family, so he didn't miss out too much on family happenings. He didn't like most subjects at school, but arithmetic was the jewel for him, and he outshone the others by a mile. He left school at fourteen even though the arithmetic teacher visited his home and tried to persuade his mother to let him stay on. But they needed the money, and he got a job with a shipping company in Dublin, as tea boy at first and then later as a clerk. But he couldn't stand being hemmed in by the walls of the place, so he rented a stall at the main Dublin Market and concentrated on selling clothes. He enjoyed every bit of it, especially his lively dealings with the public. But Paddy realized that he got most of his kicks from the buying escapades. He had a knack for getting the best deals. After saving some money, he started a small import-export business using the knowledge and contacts he gained in the shipping company. He had many contacts all over the world, but most were in Great Britain.

When he'd finished Paul was nodding his head.

'So that's how you know about the Isle of Man.'

'Well spotted,' Paddy said with a gentle smile. 'So, it's your turn.'

'What d'you deal in on the Isle of Man then?'

'Normally cats with no tails and the kippers they eat,' he said quickly, the words racing into each other so it sounded like one long word. He winked and continued,

'Now come on, fair and square, it's your turn.'

Paul had missed out his early life in Frankfurt. Paddy thought there was some ill feeling there. Paul talked about his wife being an orphan. He said they'd met working on the transatlantic boats. He hurried through his story, but then paused as if he wanted to get it out but was having second thoughts. But then, like an express train encased in darkness in a long tunnel suddenly blasting out into the lightening brightness with the deafening clamour of pent up steam, wheels on rails, and sweep of thundering slippage of air, for the first time in his life he found himself talking about the day the course of his life was changed forever, and the very black times that hit him in waves from that day on. But like an express, the quiet was deafening. It was here one moment and gone the next. Paul had moved on with the story.

Paddy interrupted holding his hand up.

'Tell me what happened on the day of the accident again.'

Paul, perspiring, obviously in some discomfort, was silent. Paddy gave him a look, a mixture of caring shining through his deep blue eyes tempered with assurance that the time was right. Paddy nodded, and Paul began falteringly.

'That night I was with Jorgen. He hadn't gone to bed. We were waiting for Emily. She'd gone to Manchester on the train with Nigel. She didn't come. There was a banging on the door at one in the morning. Jorgen was asleep on the sofa. When I opened the door I got the fright of my life. It wasn't that I hadn't expected it. I had this urge to shut the door in his face. To shoo him away. I didn't want to know what he had to say. He started speaking. I remember it was raining. The constable wore a full black cape, the bobby's helmet, and shiny silver buttons. But what I noticed more was the rain running off both ends of his long moustache. The drops were almost in strict rhythm. I heard the words and didn't hear the words. I closed the door, and he was gone. Then I remembered those words. The words "you must not". He hadn't said "I wouldn't advise you", but "you must not". I went over to Jorgen. He was still in a deep sleep. I lifted him off the sofa and carried him upstairs. I kept kissing him, but my tears weren't there. I remember that I wondered at that.'

'But what did the bobby say exactly?'

There was silence and then Paul continued, '"You must not see her body. It's so crushed. And your son's the same,"' Paul banged the table with his fists. 'It was the way he said it. Such a harsh voice. Is it because I'm German?' He started wailing.

Paddy put his arm round him.

'There, there you get it out. It's better out.' The wailing and banging of fists went on and on until Paul was exhausted. He rested his head on his arms on the table.

Paddy felt tears, a long-lost visitor, flowing gently. They remained in silence, heads bowed, for several minutes.

Chapter 16

It was half past eleven. In half an hour they were to be collected by a cart on Quarterbridge Road. They'd had a bath and a change of clothes. They'd picked up the fake Liverpool identity cards that had been left for them. Paddy gave Paul the letter for the man he was to make contact with in Liverpool in case they were separated. They had bid farewell to the house at ten to midnight. It was important to leave this late, as they didn't want to be waiting around for too long in case they were spotted. It took them three minutes to reach their destination. The cart was already there. The driver beckoned them over and turned up the tarpaulin cover so that they could get under it. No words were exchanged, and the pony pulled away at a trot.

The cart made a few stops along the way, but they got to the docks smartly. The wind had started to pick up. The driver pulled back the tarpaulin and pointed in the direction of one of the quays. Someone was waving a lantern. He didn't speak a word. Paul and Paddy made their way to the source of the light. When they arrived, they found it was held by a man wearing a dirty oilskin and sou'wester. The man pointed to some rusty ladders on the quayside that took them down onto the deck of the trawler. Paul noticed the name on its bow: *Star of Peace*. The trawler had a tall stack, and black smoke was pouring out. Paddy, who was following Paul onto the vessel, said with what seemed like forced enthusiasm,

'Let's hope it's a peaceful voyage. My sea legs have never been legs, but knees, if yer know what I mean.'

Paul didn't answer, but wondered about Paddy. He'd been all right on the crossing to Peel.

'You can call me Rod.' The sailor on the quay had jumped from the ladders halfway down with the thick casting-off rope in his hand as the trawler started and edged away from the quay. He stood next to Paddy and continued, 'Don't think it's the weather you should be worrying yerselves about. No, it's them darn whoo boats. Like sharks they are, around here. It's a good job it's gettin' a bit rough. They're wary of that. But this black smoke is nay so good. They'll spot us from miles away.'

'Can't yer do anythin' about the black smoke?' Paddy asked.

'No, it's the coal, you know. Can't get any better these days, what with the war on.'

Paul and Paddy were shown to the crews' quarters, which were behind the tall stack. The area was small and squalid, and the stench of stale fish and smoke brought Paul very close to wanting to heave. Two small portholes revealed the white-foamed waves that were increasing in size as the trawler passed out of the safety of the harbour into the open sea. They were surprised that the crew consisted of only four men including the skipper, whom they'd spied in the wheelhouse. Puffing his pipe with a dour look on his face, he didn't pay them any attention. They were cargo like the fish, but a shave more valuable.

Rod came into their cabin as the trawler lifted up forty-five degrees at the bow. They heard the wave crash onto the deck. Paddy, who was standing at the time, was thrown backwards. He hit the cabin wall and then jolted the other way as the boat righted itself.

'Skipper says were in for it tonight. It's nay gettin' any better.' Rod seemed to savour the words especially the 'nay gettin', which he strung out. Paul helped Paddy up.

'That's good of him to tell us 'bout that,' Paddy said. 'In case we didn't notice.'

closed, feet apart, clinging for dear life to the deck railing. Paul knew he had to help him. He bided his time waiting for the right moment, then he sprang out of the hatch in the direction of Paddy. At that precise moment, a huge wave pounded into him from the starboard side. It carried Paul over the port side railings. Paddy watched in horror as Paul disappeared over the side.

Rod, who was below preparing a place for them to hide, heard the crashing sound of the huge wave and the cries of Paddy that followed. As he reached the hatch opening he was amazed to see Paul squeezing through the railings. He told them both to stay put. He danced over to Paddy just after a wave from starboard drenched Paddy once again. He told Paddy to grab his left arm with both hands. He shouted 'Go!' as the port side went down below the horizon, and they both slithered in that direction. Rod bundled Paddy down the open hatch. Paddy misplaced his footing on the steps and fell, crashing onto netting in the hold. Rod then called over to Paul, 'Hold on! I'm coming!'

'I'm all right,' Paul managed to say. Rod knew that Paul would be much heavier with all the water that had soaked through his protective clothing. He knew the extra weight would be a problem. Before Paul had a chance to move, Rod was next to him. Within minutes they were both down in the hold, and Rod was showing them the large chest they would have to hide in, one on top of the other.

'It's only if they come on board, and that's not looking at all certain now with the storm and all that.'

Rod was gone before they had a chance to thank him or ask any questions.

'I'm surprised he helped us like he did,' Paul said. 'He wasn't showing any fondness for us – none of them was.'

'Agh, 'tis the unwritten law of the sea. They'd even rescue a murderer,' said Paddy. He paused. That reminds me, one of the crew might have a newspaper. It'll tell us if we're a couple of 'em.'

'Cap'ain didn't ask fer you to be told. But I thought it only right that you was, as you could prepare yourselves like. No, he wouldn't be out here tonight if it weren't for the cash. Too risky sailing the tack we'll be takin'. The whoo boats yer know.' Suddenly there was a ringing of a bell, which coincided with another huge wave crashing on the bow. Rod shot out of the cabin. Paul thought that Paddy's face was looking green. Just as he was about to speak, the door burst open and Rod appeared again.

'Both of you down into the fish hold. There's a British warship on our starboard. We're not supposed to be here. Chance is they'll board us, so we're not takin' any chances. Just be careful on the deck. Hold onto the rope.'

'Thought you said it was whoo boats we should be bothered about, not our own bloody lot!' Paddy couldn't help throwing this into the net. Unusually for him, he'd taken an instant dislike to Rod, and he wanted the sailor to know it. But it was more to do with his own emotional state. Sometimes he hated the sea, and this was definitely one of those times that his hatred engulfed him. There was no response from Rod. He issued them with oilskins and led them out onto the lurching deck that was awash with sea water. They desperately held onto the railings while Rod exhibited his artistry in manoeuvring across the slippery surface of the deck. He yanked open the hatch of the fish hold, and he went down into the black chamber.

Paul waited for the deck to be at an angle that would enable him to stagger down the hatch. He let go of the railing. But the deck's downward slope was more acute than he'd anticipated, and his balance was affected. He was in danger of being snatched by the waves and swept over to the port side of the boat. He dived, his arms stretched out, and made a grab for the handle of the open hatch door. Holding on, he waited for the vessel to pitch again in the opposite direction, and then managed to place his feet onto the hold's ladder. From there he shouted as hard as he could for Paddy to follow him. Paddy was frozen to the spot where he stood, eyes

'What d'you mean?'

'Murderers, of course,' he said with a wink. They heard steps approaching and voices.

'C'mon,' Paddy said. 'Get that light out, and get into the casket t'ing. You furst.'

'No, you first.'

'Listen, we haven't time to argue. They're comin' to search this place. You get in quick, and we can toss a coin fer it after.' Before Paul had a chance to respond, Paddy pushed him into the chest and threw himself on top of him. It was smaller than Paddy had thought, and when the lid came down, neither could move. What made it even worse was the state of the interior of the chest. The walls were greasy and smelt of decaying fish.

'Good practise fer our coffins,' Paddy observed. 'But I don't fancy sharing with you, no offence like.' He stopped abruptly. They both heard the door of the hatch open and footsteps coming down the ladder. Paddy could see the light of a lantern shining through one of the knotholes in the side of the chest. It grew brighter. His heart was pounding.

'Come on!' The voice was hoarse. 'Stop messing about. Show yourselves. I can't stand about here all night.' It was quiet. The man was apparently waiting for an answer. Paddy and Paul remained silent.

'Okay, suit yourselves!' They heard footsteps walking up the ladder. Then they heard the hatch door opening. The light went out, and the hatch door banged down. After a couple of minutes Paddy spoke,

'That was a queer do.' He didn't wait for Paul to speak as he knew he was indisposed, and he also knew he was still alive, as the warm fishy air continued to be expelled from his nostrils at two second intervals. 'Have they snitched on us, and are those navy fellas holding us down here as it's as good as anywhere? Funny, though, you'd t'ink they'd want to see us jest to make sure. 'ang on, if that's the case, we don't need to stay here whichever way yer t'ink on it. Idiots we is, don't yer t'ink, Paul?'

Paul's response was to knee him. Paddy got the message. He shot out of the chest. After a moment, Paul stood beside him in the darkness and took out a coin from his trouser pocket.

'As you promised. Here's a coin. Toss it. I want heads!' Paddy caught the angry glint in Paul's eye and realized he meant business.

'Okay, me friend,' he replied almost cheerfully, 'here goes.' He flipped the coin into the air, but it went high, out of sight.

'You did that deliberately!' said Paul. Suddenly the vessel's bow rose several feet into the air, and they were both thrown to the other side of the hold where they became tangled in old netting. No sooner had they freed themselves than they were pitched to the opposite end of the hold as the stern rose. The noise of the propeller changed in pitch as it beat air rather than water. At that moment, they heard footsteps on the deck above. The hatch was opened, and a lantern was lowered.

'Ahh,' a voice said. 'I see that you've stopped playing, silly beggars!'

Paul and Paddy were provided with clean, dry clothes and fresh oilskins and sou'westers. Most importantly, they were given money and fresh, up-to-date identity cards.

'Ye must know fellas in high places and ha' buckets o' money,' Rod said, obviously hoping to be let in the know about the goings on.

'Lady luck has her winning ways, and don't yer t'ink that money is the root of all evil? And don't the monkeys say, "see no evil, speak no evil, hear no evil"?' Paddy said in the rapid way he could shove words out of his mouth. Rod looked vexed, and he became silent.

The storm had subsided, although the sea was still on the rough side. It was three in the morning and pitch black. They were told that they were in sight of Liverpool Bay and the dropping off point, Blundellsands. The lifeboat in the stern was to be lowered, and Rod would pilot them to the spot that they'd been ordered to take them to.

'Ahh I've passed through Blundellsands on me way to Southport many a time. Posh place, full of the monied,' Paddy said, winking at Paul. 'Big estates an' lots o' gamekeepers.'

Paul was surprised that Paddy didn't know the details. He'd always been so meticulous in his planning.

The lifeboat was riding up and down on the waves. Rod and another crewman were on the oars battling the sea. Paddy's seasickness had returned with a vengeance. He threw up several times, and on one occasion hit an oar blade, narrowly missing Rod's face. Rod shot him angry glances, but Paddy was too far gone. He was in a world of prayers and mantras. As they got closer to the shore, the waves lessened in ferocity. They saw the lights of Blundellsands and the layout of the place more clearly as the boat settled onto a more even keel.

As they beached the craft, Rod shouted above the wind, 'You can't go yet. Give us a hand at turning this thing round and launching her.'

Paul and Paddy looked seaward at the figure of Rod and his mate thrashing the sea with their oars. Further in the distance they saw the trawler rising up and down with its red and green flickering lights shining on the wheelhouse. They'd thanked Rod, but he'd remained silent.

'Is that fella glad or not that we're out of it?' Paddy murmured, and they turned round, sloshing through the shallow water aiming for the beach. On the horizon they noticed the light coming, and they quickened their pace.

Chapter 17

Silas was on his bike, just about. He was hanging onto it as the wind battered into him. His rifle, slung on his back, was not helping. It was affecting his balance as he tried to keep riding in a straight line. He was a private with the Kings Own Volunteer Corps and was on night patrol along the coast from Crosby to Southport. An order had gone out since the sinking of the *Lusitania* that this part of the coast had to be patrolled owing to the U-boat threat. There were two soldiers on patrol during shifts riding in opposite directions. He was to be relieved when he reached Southport. That was supposed to be in another three hours. But the going had been tough because of the weather.

Personally, Silas considered that it was a pretty useless task – two soldiers patrolling miles of beach. The assignment had been a knee-jerk response on the part of the military. They had to do something. He pulled off the sandy coastal track into Victoria Road West. He wanted to get behind a high wall that protected a massive place called Beechwood Tower House to relieve himself and have a cigarette. He got out his packet of Woodbines, and on the first intake of nicotine, he started to relax. As he turned to look towards the sea, this feeling of peace was hammered out of existence. The cigarette fell out of his hand. Two figures were approaching from the sea. In the distance he caught sight of a vessel. He assumed it was a U-boat. It couldn't be anything else. All shipping in the area had been restricted. He was in a state of exhilaration bordering on panic. Now he could have a go at the Huns. His family would be proud of him. He let his bike fall and took his .303 rifle off his shoulders. It was loaded with five rounds. He ran towards the two figures and then crouched down behind a sand dune and took aim. Subconsciously he rapidly worked out distance, wind speed, and direction. He wasn't going to miss. Oh no, he wanted to bag the two of them. According to His Majesty's rules of combat, in such a situation, it was obligatory that personnel concerned should shout out to the suspects to halt and be identified. If they refused, one was granted permission to open fire. Silas was having none of this. He grunted a few words and then opened fire. His first shot missed. But he bagged one of them with his second shot as the two made for cover. He moved towards them. Suddenly, one of them was running at some pace in his direction, shouting in what he thought was German. He quickly took aim and fired a shot. It hit the target, but the man kept running. He was now about a hundred yards away, and for the third time Silas took aim and fired, but nothing happened. The rifle had jammed. The man was closing in on him. Silas started to run. He flung the rifle away, only to hear a shot go off. In confusion, he thought he was being fired at. He turned round, and the man was upon him. He was wild, shouting like a madman, and he was definitely German.

Paul kept hitting the soldier with his fist, pounding his head and body. He was boiling with anger, and the hitting was like a steam safety valve just blowing and blowing. Silas was no match. He fell in a heap on the side of a sand hill, unconscious. Paul was about to have another go when he remembered the words of Paddy just before they left the Hospital Camp – or was it the hovel? Paul ran back to Paddy, who was bleeding from a wound to his stomach. Paul ripped a piece off his shirt, held it against Paddy's wound, and told Paddy to press hard.

'Go, will yer, Paul? Yer've got a chance on yer own. T'ink of yer son. T'ink, man. That's what it's all about. That's what it's been about for me as well. You'll be lettin' me down as well. The Tommies will be here soon. They'll have heard the shots.'

Paul was in turmoil. How could he leave his friend there? Just then he caught sight of the lifeboat, which had turned and was heading for them.

'Here's the boat. We can both get picked up,' he shouted.

'No, Paul, you'll be banged up fer ages, an' you might never see that son of yers again. Just t'ink an' have some sense, will yer?'

Reluctantly, and with tear-blurred vision, Paul left Paddy on the beach and ran back to the spot where the soldier lay. Silas was moving, so Paul tied his legs together with his belt. His body shook intermittently, and his eyes illuminated stark fear. He tried to speak. The first word, *please*, was just about audible, but it quickly turned into incomprehensible blubber. Paul left him lying in the sand. It was then he felt pain in his arm and remembered he'd been hit.

As Paul reached what turned out to be a golf link, he heard the sound of police whistles in the distance. He was thankful in one way that the soldier – and perhaps Paddy – would receive medical attention, but it meant his chances of escape were slimmer. The man would be able to give a good description of him. He was now on the run, a hunted man. There was no chance of handing himself in now. They wouldn't give him an ounce of clemency, not a man on a likely murder charge and two offences of assault on His Majesty's forces. Although he didn't have any idea where he was going, his plan was to make for Liverpool and pay Paddy's friend a visit. Paddy, Paul's thoughts lingered on his friend who'd done so much for him. He could be dead, and it was all his fault. There'd been plenty opportunities to turn down his friend's offer of help. Why on earth had he gone along with all of Paddy's plans? He should have stayed at Knockaloe. The Red Cross might have been able to help. But Paul couldn't stand the idea of Jorgen being out there alone. The boy had lost so much – a mother and brother taken away in an instant. Paul started to sprint. He ran and ran.

Paul had been told that the landing would take place at Blundellsands. Where he happened to be was of little consequence. He knew he was quite close to Liverpool, and there was a station in the area on the main line to the city. He was nearing what he estimated to be the centre of the golf course and slowed down to a walking pace. The perimeter of the course was edged with huge mansions, self-contained in their own estates. Paul started to feel edgy. Morning was breaking in earnest, and he felt the rays of the rising sun on his face. They were like a searchlight picking him out, a huge, dark, maimed game bird. He felt sure that someone out there in one of the waking mansions was ready to have a pot at him. His heart was banging away, and he leapt into the nearest bunker.

Several minutes later, Paul was climbing over a large fence into an estate. He'd noticed outbuildings in a small cultivated pocket of vegetation. The door opened easily. Suddenly he was overcome by fatigue. He'd had little sleep since leaving Douglas, and he flopped down on a bench and fell asleep.

Torrential rain battered the windows, and he woke with a jolt. Although it was light, he had no idea of the time. He was warm – very warm – and he wondered if he had a fever. As he raised a hand to check his forehead, he realized that he still had his oilskin on. He took the coat off and noticed the holes at the top of the right sleeve. The coat had slowed the bullet down, and although it had grazed his upper arm, it had passed through the coat cleanly. He'd been lucky the wound was superficial and it had already begun to heal.

The building he was in was made of stone. It was clearly a storeroom of some sort, and large cutting tools hung on the walls. Boxes of nails and screws and small hand tools were placed neatly on a long shelf that ran along the bottom of the dimpled-glass window. Paul got up and ran his hand over the tools thinking of the knifes and choppers that he used to use regularly six days a week and more and his butchers shop in Liverpool. But his thoughts then were of waving sticks and his son running towards him, and his fear. He looked out of the misted window through one of its small frames, and his eyes fixed on a sight he just couldn't believe. It was impossible. It didn't make sense. Surely his eyes were failing him. Then there was an adrenalin rush. He dashed to the door and flung it open. It was real.

Chapter 18

About fifteen feet away there was what appeared to be a hastily dug mound of earth. A spade was sticking out of it. But that wasn't all. On the edge of the mound nearest the building, clearly visible, poking out, were a wrist and hand. What's more, it was ghoulishly pointing towards him, almost beckoning him. He ran back into the building and grabbed his oilskin. He worked out that the torrential rain had partially washed away the soil and uncovered parts of the body. As he approached the grave, he saw that it was a man who looked to be in his fifties. The person who'd been digging had found it hard going; it was heavy clay soil. The digger had made a pig's ear of the job. Maybe it was temporary, and as the thought skimmed through his mind, he sensed somebody near to him and turned round sharply.

Facing him was an attractive woman in her early thirties. She was pointing a shotgun at him menacingly. Her charm dissolved rapidly as she opened her mouth and he saw rain dripping off her nose and chin.

'What on earth are you doing on this property?' she asked him. 'You're not that escaped alien Hun that every one's going on about, are you?' Her voice was cultured but curt. It was oozing power and authority. 'No need to answer,' she said slowly. 'Your face gives you away. D'you know you're going to be a godsend for me? A bloody godsend!' She raised the gun level with his head.

It was now or never. Paul crouched down, and in the same movement sprang at her. He heard the bang as the bullet whizzed over the hood of his oilskin just as his head began to tilt upwards.

He knocked her off her feet. She still had the shotgun, but he quickly disarmed her. He pushed her into the out building. Anybody in the mansion hall would have heard the gunshot. So he waited half an hour for any signs of life. She'd started yelling out all kinds of abuse in between cries for help. He'd had no alternative but to man handle her. He'd tied her hands behind her back, strapped her to the bench, and gagged her. They stared at each other. In Paul's mind it had become a competition to see who would be the first to look away. He noticed faded bruising on her face and neck and other marks on her hands and wrists. She'd obviously had a few batterings recently. Paul thought of the corpse and wondered if this was the reason the man was resting stiffly on a bed of clay, his beating arms now stiff.

They'd reached the hall without incident, although he'd had to drag her along for most of the way, and his shins stung from the kicks she'd given him, especially when he'd freed her from the bench. The place was deserted. He'd taken her round the back, and they'd entered the kitchen. It was a massive room; the only furniture being several tables. The larger one stood in the centre of the room; the smaller against a wall. But the strange thing was that the tables were completely bare. There were two Aga ranges. They looked as if they hadn't been used in weeks. Unused too were the tens of brass pans of various sizes that hung on the walls. After ensuring his prisoner couldn't move or speak, Paul hunted for food. He hadn't eaten or drunk anything for at least twenty-four hours. He checked all the cupboards, but the kitchen had nothing to offer – no food or drink. Even the water taps were dry. There was a large storeroom nearby. At first Paul thought the room was completely empty. There was nothing on the shelves or in the large plywood boxes, but on the floor were half a dozen large fermenting jars covered in dust and cobwebs. They contained an amber-coloured liquid. He noticed several ginger roots in the bottom of the vessels. He lugged one of the jars out of the room into the kitchen and poured some of the liquid into a tankard. In no time, he'd drunk two pints of ginger beer. He went back to the storeroom. On shelves near the demijohns he discovered several jars of jam. And so Paul consumed one of the strangest of meals in his life – strawberry jam and ginger beer – while an unwitting companion looked on with eyes that were raw with anger and disgust.

Paul looked all over the empty massive house. The furniture in most of the rooms was covered with white dustsheets. In one of the bedrooms, to his amazement, he discovered a pistol and some ammunition. At first he was reluctant to pocket them, and he put them back into the drawer. He wasn't a criminal, was he? He'd never use it, and he remembered Paddy's words about not fighting back. But then there was the lady of the unlived-in house downstairs desperately waiting for an opportunity to get away. He needed to be able to coerce her in some way. Then it hit him. He could use her to travel to Liverpool. They wouldn't be looking for a couple. She'd need to be persuaded. If only Paddy were here, she'd be putty in his hands by now. But he wasn't, and so Paul slowly pulled open the drawer again and took out the weapon. He tilted his head upwards and in his mind apologized clumsily to Paddy. But then thanked fate and the owner of the gun for giving him an opportunity he desperately needed.

On his way back to the kitchen, he noticed something he hadn't spotted before – a set of keys lying on a small table in the hallway outside the kitchen. On the key ring was a tag that listed the address of the hall and a Liverpool estate agent's name. The jigsaw of the empty house, its lady, and the dead body had started to fit together, and the plan of moments before had just become firmly rooted in his head.

Paul returned to the kitchen. The woman had been dozing and woke up with a start. He was holding the gun uneasily and hoped she wouldn't notice his lack of experience with the weapon.

'We're going to Liverpool shortly,' he announced to her. 'It's definitely in your interest to do exactly as I say. There's no need to deny it. I know what's happened here, and you obviously know who I am. But don't believe...' Paul stopped. He had noticed that she was nodding her head in agreement. What was she playing at? He untied the gag on her mouth, and she held up her bound hands. He untied them.

'Look!' she said. She took her coat off and then her shirtwaist. This revealed a flimsy petticoat with a plunging neckline. He saw the bruises of varying colours. They covered her shoulders, her arms, and her upper chest. There was also a fresh looking bandage at the top of her right arm that blood had seeped through. The gun in his hand felt heavier. He thought of its probable owner. Then she raised her skirt over her knee and adjusted her petticoat. Paul reckoned that half the flesh she uncovered was bruised.

'And he did this to you?' She nodded. Paul expected tears, but there were none. Only deep, seething anger in her eyes.

'Can I trust you?' he asked. She nodded again. He was about tell her about Jorgen, but stopped himself. He had a nagging doubt that this might not be in his interest. As he began to untie her legs, remaining alert to the possibility that she might try to escape, he said as forcibly as he could,

'This is what's going to happen. We're going to walk to the railway station and get a train to Liverpool. We'll be acting as man and wife. We'll link our arms together, and my hand will be in my pocket holding this gun. If you attempt to communicate to anyone about your plight, I won't hesitate to use it. Do you understand?' She nodded defiantly.

It was still raining as they neared the station. The rain had partly worked in his favour, as he held her umbrella in his free hand. This disguised the fact that he was not wearing a bowler. An essential accessory for the smart navy blue suit he wore. It would have seemed out of place and attracted unwanted attention. He'd picked the suit up on the trawler; the bowler wouldn't fit. But the weather had also meant there were fewer people around, and those who'd ventured out were in carriages or cars. The rain was easing off, and he spotted the station. He noticed that his woman – she had refused to give her name – was looking around anxiously. He gripped her arm more tightly. As they entered the hall of the station, he noticed the clock. It was ten past eleven. He knew the journey would last about half an hour, so he reckoned he'd be in the city centre by twelve. More importantly, he was aware that he was a day late, and of course without Paddy. He wondered whether this would make a difference.

There were few people on the platform, and Paul kept as far away from them as he could. As the train halted at the platform, he dragged his woman along looking for an empty third-class carriage. He wished he'd gone for second class. Most of the thirds were full. Eventually he found some seats just as the guard, flag and whistle in hand, was bearing down on him. There were only two free seats in the compartment, and they were not together.

'My wife is of a nervous disposition,' Paul announced to the travellers, 'and she needs to be sitting next to me. Could anyone move please?' As he was saying this, he dug the barrel of the gun that he was holding in his pocket into her body. Reluctantly a man got up and offered them his seat, which would allow the couple to sit together.

The suburban coach was old. As the train started up, it jolted, and Paul and the woman were thrown into the empty seats. The woman, once she'd sorted herself out, started to give the eye to two middle-age ladies sitting opposite. One was knitting; the other was looking out of the window. He pressed the gun into her body, but it didn't have any effect. It was going to be an uphill task with her, and he still had a journey of fifteen minutes to get through before they reached their destination. Fortunately, both of the ladies, who were together, started gathering their belongings as the train approached the next station. Everyone in the coach alighted at the stop, and to his relief, no one got into their compartment.

'Look, I don't know what you were playing at a few minutes ago,' said Paul. 'But I warn you, one more move like that and you'll be for it. I'm a dead man and have got nothing to lose, and I'll bring you down with me whichever way you want. He felt that his words lacked conviction and was about to say more but stopped. He'd already said enough. His words implied that he felt guilt, and he knew she would use everything in her armoury to get at him. These thoughts were halted when he realized they were pulling into another station. Luckily their compartment remained empty, and it wasn't long before they reached Central Station. At last Paul had arrived in his city. Paddy should have been next to him, not his present companion who, from head to toe, showed signs of wanting to burst out of his grip and nail him good and proper. His problem now was to separate himself from her and to get away to the safe house in Rodney Street. The other issue worried him: he was a day late. Would the occupant still be around?

Paul directed the woman to the middle of the crowd that was making its way to the ticket barrier. He held her close, making sure she could feel the pressure of the gun through her clothing. There was a hold up at the gate. A family in front of them were looking for their tickets. The ticket collector became suspicious, and he hailed the police constable who was patrolling the station parade. As the officer approached, Paul's unwitting companion yelled, 'This man has a gun. I've been abducted!'

Paul quickly, but reluctantly, yanked the gun out of his pocket waved it at the crowd, and tried to grab her with his other hand but failed miserably. She ran into the arms of the constable. At the same time, Paul bolted onto the parade, crashing into people and into Ranelagh Street. His stomach turned when he heard a

The Lucy Effect

multitude of police whistles. He felt like a hunted animal. Luckily this fox knew the city centre like the back of his hand and was soon away from the area. But he also thought his best chance was following Paddy's advice of staying put where the hunter would least expect him to be. Having discarded his jacket in a back street in an attempt to disguise his appearance, he walked at a pace back to a side entrance of the station. His stomach was knotted. He was invoking Paddy to assist him, but he could hardly walk as he got onto the station parade and indeed halted. His legs wouldn't move. What was happening to him? For one weird moment he thought it was Paddy's doing. There was no sign of the woman or the constable, or for that matter any uniformed officials. Then he found himself automatically walking into the gents. He found an empty cubicle, put the toilet lid down, locked the door, sat down, and placed his face in his hands. He was sure he could hear the laughing voice of Paddy.

Chapter 19

About half an hour later there was a banging on the door. In terror Paul sprang up onto the toilet seat ready to pounce.

'Is there anyone in there?' a thin weak voice called.

'Yes,' he replied abruptly.

'Oh, okay. Are you all right?'

'Yes, thanks,' Paul said in the most cultured English he could manage. The toilet attendant walked away talking to himself and then started whistling. Paul knew he'd be back before long, and he'd get suspicious. He wondered what he should do to stall the possibility. It was the hunger pangs that jolted the grey matter into action.

'Excuse me, janitor.' He knew it was respectful to address him with his title. 'Is there anybody around? I need some privacy to talk to you about a delicate matter.'

'No, sir, indeed there's not.'

'I have this dreadful toilet problem. Had it since I was a nipper. When I get hungry and don't eat, I have the most awful trouble. Well, this morning I got up so darned late…' He paused, having noticed that his twang was becoming ever so slightly Teutonic sounding. Correcting the voice, he went on, 'Didn't have breakfast. Thought I'd make it to my office – Cunard's, you know – but got caught as soon as I alighted from the Southport train. Then there was all that commotion with the police here at the station, which delayed me further. So what I need now is some nosh to stop this pesky disease. You know what I mean?' The

The Lucy Effect

janitor on the other side of the door said the only thing he could say, 'Well, yes...'

Just the words Paul was waiting to here. He had him.

'You couldn't get me a bite to eat could you, man? It'll stop then, and I'll be out of your way. I'd be ever so grateful.' Paul figured that this was probably the first time the old gentleman had ever had such a request, but he was probably a simple-minded soul who wanted only to please.

'Do you want a sandwich? I can get one from the cafe. But I need money.'

'That's not a problem. But before you go, will you promise not to mention anything about this affair to anyone? It's my reputation as a gentleman, you know. I wouldn't like my colleagues at Cunard to hear such a tale. I'd be the laughing stock of the place.'

'Yes, of course, sir.'

'Well here's sixpence. Keep the change for your trouble.' He handed a sixpence under the door, and the man was off.

A few hours later, still in the toilet cubicle, having eaten his beef sandwich and dozed on and off for an hour or so, Paul was preparing to leave. He waited until he thought there was no one in the building and walked over to the janitor's small office. The attendant awkwardly propelled himself upwards out of a rickety chair. He couldn't take his eyes off the gent. Paul figured it must be his clothing – only a shirt, waistcoat, tweed trousers, and definitely no bowler. Paul quickly picked up on this and said,

'Oh, had to get rid of my jacket. Messed it all up you know.' At that moment some people entered the toilet, and so he continued in a hushed voice, 'Thank you so much for all your assistance. I'll be off now. By the way, what's your name?'

'James, sir, but people call me Jimmy.'

'Right, Jimmy. Here's sixpence. Please keep my afflictions of this day to yourself. Mum's the word, hey?' And with a wave, he strode off as confidently as he could out of the toilets. Jimmy just stood there, mouth wide open. *What a day*, he thought. What with the excitement of the criminal earlier on at the barrier and the kind gent and his toilet problems, he'd never known such a day. He couldn't wait to get home and go over everything in detail with his adoring family. But he'd swear them to secrecy. Oh, yes, the odd stranger was such a gent, he deserved nothing less.

Chapter 20

Paul made tracks to an outfitter in Ranelagh Street to amend the way he was dressed. All the assistants were busy and didn't notice his entrance. He hadn't wanted to arouse any suspicion by coming into the shop improperly dressed. So he grabbed the first lounge jacket he laid his eyes on that he thought would fit and put it on and went to the counter. He bought the jacket, a pair of trousers, a coat, and a silver-embellished walking stick to go with it. Although some tailoring was needed with the trousers, he declined the offer to have the work carried out. To this outfit he added a top hat. He had become the well-dressed, upper-class businessman that it was necessary for him to be.

With his confidence boosted, and sticking to the rule of lingering near the crime scene, he made for a nearby Lyons tea shop and ate a hearty meal. Occasionally when talking to the waitresses, he noticed his English voice taking on continental tones, so raising its pitch, he deliberately manufactured a sing-song Italian sort of accent. His former neighbour was Italian, and he'd had a fair amount of practise mimicking him. Still elated, he bid everyone *buonanotte* in his best Italian. He hurried along the few streets that led to Rodney Street. It was six o'clock on a beautiful summer's evening. His anxiety about being recognized had evaporated. Even a police constable had bid this gent a good evening, and Paul had even returned the greeting. The torrential rain and the darkness that had followed him for the last few days had gone. He was overjoyed to be walking in familiar territory at last, and he welcomed the expectation of a pleasurable end in sight after the sheer exertion and worry of the past week. This mood changed as he approached the large terraced house in Rodney Street. To check the address, he read once again the piece of paper that Paddy had given him. It was number thirty one.

Before him was a huge, imposing Georgian terraced house consisting of three storeys and a cellar. Steps led to a canopied double front door with Grecian-style columns on either side. On the second floor were railings surrounding verandas that overlooked the street. They were festooned with tubs of flowers. In the warm air of that July evening he was hit by a wall of subtle aromas. He couldn't resist standing there to take it all in until someone passed by on the other side of the street and struck a sideways glanced at him. He knocked in a conservative manner and turned round. A couple were walking by; he raised his top hat, bidding them a good evening. He thought he was getting too much into the role of gent. It could be overdone. Nobody came to the door. Placing his ear to the open letter box, he realized there was a silence in the house, apart from the ticking of a wall clock. Panic hit him. He gave the doorknocker a brisk, hard three bangs. Perhaps not arriving the previous day had made this Seamus think they'd been caught, so he'd gone off on business. Paddy had mentioned they'd be spending the first few days on their own. Just as he was about to leave, wondering what on earth he was going to do, someone came bustling out of the house next door. It was a middle-aged woman who smiled brightly at him.

'I'm Joan,' she said. 'Sorry I took my time. I couldn't find the key!' She spoke rapidly, not pausing for breath. 'Mr Kirwen told me you were coming, although he mentioned two of you and that you would be arriving yesterday. He asked me to keep an eye out for you, and he gave me his key. He should be back this Thursday. Here's the key. Oh, help yourself to anything you fancy, and if there's anything you're not sure about, give us a shout.' Then she shot back up her steps and closed the door. Paul thought she was rather like a figure

The Lucy Effect

in a cuckoo clock that pops out to strike the time and then quickly returns to its little house rather smartly. He walked into the large, airy, square hall. Off the hall were the various entertaining rooms. Some of the doors were half open. He was stunned by the sumptuous nature of the interior fittings and the tasteful blend of colours in the different materials and furnishings within each room. It took him a minute or so to work out where the kitchen was. When he found it, he helped himself to some cold meat and poured himself a scotch from a decanter conveniently placed in the centre of the kitchen table. He wondered whether Seamus had servants. From outside he'd seen sash windows at ground level indicating the cellar area might be used for servants' quarters. But there was no one around, and Joan hadn't mentioned them.

    Paul didn't bother looking around the other rooms in the house. He made straight for the bathroom and had the best soak he'd ever had in his life. He was in a strange, vast space of the palest of blue porcelain tiles. They covered walls, which were punctuated by ornate mirrors. Normally at home he'd taken baths in a tin bath in his small kitchen with water boiled on the stove. This occurred once a week on Sunday nights. The last one he'd had in his home was on the night before all the present hell had broken out. At the camp they'd used makeshift showers. The water was always cold and they were made to hurry. Here the water was luxuriously hot at the turn of a tap, and he found bathing quite a new and pleasurable experience, something to be enjoyed rather than a chore that had to be accomplished quickly. He dried himself with the largest cotton towel he'd ever encountered. His body seemed to dry immediately as the towel touched his skin. He used another towel to wrap around his torso, and he entered the first room he came across and sank into a huge bed. It was like being on his back supported by a calm sea. He had the distinct sensation of floating. In this relaxed state, the demons of the past two months retreated slightly. It was the warmth permeating his body between the silk sheets that subdued all, and he fell into a deep sleep.

Paul enjoyed the soundest sleep he'd experienced for some time. There were none of the nightmares featuring that Amazonian of a woman and her cronies, and Jorgen running. These were the dreams he'd experienced just after his beating and more recently when his anxiety levels had been high. As he sat up in bed, he became aware of familiar city sounds. He walked over to the double window that opened onto a balcony, and as he stepped out his towel fell off and he stood there fully naked for a split second. He was spotted by a young woman being escorted by a gentleman. She blushed and smiled at the same time. The man followed her glance, but saw only an empty balcony. Paul assumed that his wife hadn't said anything to him, as in normal circumstances the man would have been knocking on the door and probably alerting a constable. Paul sat on the floor clutching his knees, laughing and crying at the same time. This went on for a minute or so. He thought he must be more careful in future – much more careful.

Paul discovered that the bedroom that had been prepared for him was next door to the one he'd slept in. The room was larger and much more luxurious than the other. There was a wardrobe full of clothes that, amazingly, were his size. He suspected they belonged to Seamus, although most of them seemed unworn. He tried on different shirts and suits. In the end he decided on a navy blue morning suit with a frock shirt and cravat. Although Paul hadn't thought about going out, preferring to wait for the return of Seamus, he changed his mind when he made an amazing discovery in a bedside table drawer. He found false moustaches, beards, and an assortment of other disguises. They'd been professionally made – probably theatre stock. Paddy's friends had obviously been thorough in their preparations for his arrival. There was no way Paul's identity could be discovered if he were to wear what he saw before him in this theatrical treasure chest.

He was now impatient to visit his shop and the neighbourhood and search for Jorgen. His expectations weren't high, but he knew he had to act, had to do something no matter how insignificant. The theatrical props would help. It meant he could directly approach his neighbours without placing them in any jeopardy if something went wrong. Aiding and abetting the country's most hunted man would carry heavy costs.

Chapter 21

A woman was standing on the steps of Joan's house next door when Paul walked out into Rodney Street complete with top hat and stick. She was a maid, and she was carrying a parcel in her hand. Paul noticed she'd turned round quickly to have a better look at him. He wondered whether he'd gone too far in his disguise. In the long mirror in the bedroom he thought he'd glimpsed a slimmer version of Edward VII. Joan would wonder what was going on if she cast eyes on him. So he hurried off and followed the route to Central Station he'd taken the previous day intent on buying a newspaper, intent on testing out his disguise on the helpful toilet attendant. He approached the station from Lawton Street and found a newspaper vendor's stall outside one of the entrances. He froze as he read the bold headlines on a placard: 'Hun Murderer on the Run'. So he'd been correct. The woman had nailed her husband's murder on him. His first thought was to hurry back to the safety of Rodney Street. At that moment a red-faced constable drew near to him. He was feeling the heat of the day in his thick serge uniform and was wiping his brow with a white-gloved hand. As he passed Paul, the gloved hand shot to the side of his forehead, fingers stiff, and stayed there several seconds. It was a sign to Paul that he must persevere with his plan. Once again, a constable had seen before him a fine, upstanding gentleman of the highest order who could do no wrong.

Paul entered the station, forgot about the toilet attendant, and bought a newspaper at Smith's kiosk. He was in a hurry and took a cab to the Catholic Church opposite his shop in St James Street. The shop was boarded up. The mob had tried to burn it down, but it hadn't been badly affected. He crossed the road in a world of his own and was brought to his senses as a tram had to break severely in order to avoid him. The driver shouted, and a few of the passengers who'd been thrown about openly banged the windows. All this he could have done without. His apparel was bad enough for attracting attention, so he cursed himself over the episode.

He walked past the property and down Norfolk Street. He had a strong desire to go round to the back of the shop along the entry, but realized it would be too much of a risk. A gentleman would never be seen at a back entry in the area. The events of that afternoon, which seemed such a long time ago, were played back in his mind. He retraced his steps to the end of Nelson Street and the gutter where he'd been half beaten to death. This is where he'd last seen Jorgen running away sobbing his heart out. Paul was overcome with the same feelings of powerlessness and frustration he'd had on that afternoon. The road he was glancing at was the one Jorgen should have taken to Lime Street Station. But it could be that Jorgen hadn't left Liverpool; in fact, he could be somewhere close by in an institution.

Paul returned to the shop and walked across the road to the church and into the graveyard after discovering his Italian friend was not at home. There was a low perimeter wall around the church grounds, so he could see people a distance away who were passing the shop. There were children around as it was the beginning of the school holidays. His intention was to approach a friend of Jorgen and to ask general questions about the shop. As he was reading the wording on one of the gravestones, he observed a group of children walking on the pavement on the same side as the shop. He recognized one of the boys, so he rushed across the road and pretended to be peering through one of the holes in the boarding. Then he turned round as the children passed the shop and said in as friendly way as he could, 'Hello, lads, can you tell me what happened to this butchers shop?'

A boy whom he'd never set eyes on before answered,

'It belonged to a Hun. They smashed it up and then after tried to burn it to ground.'

'But what happened to the people in the shop?'

'Don't know,' he said in a matter of fact way, and he started walking on. The others followed.

Paul caught the eye of a boy he recognized, but he couldn't remember his name. He looked straight at the boy and said,

'But doesn't anyone else know what happened to them?' The boy looked at the lad who'd spoken who was obviously the leader of the group for permission to speak. The leader looked away placing the other boy in a quandary as to what he should do.

Paul continued staring at the boy. Realizing he might miss the opportunity of finding out crucial information, he said with an air of authority, 'You know something about this matter. Out with it, my boy.'

The leader had started walking away by this time, and the boy was about to follow, but Paul blocked his way. 'All I know, mister, is that the butcher was arrested and sent away somewhere, and that's it.'

'But what about others in the family?'

'There was a lad.'

'And?' Paul raised his voice.

'Just that he ran off and no one heard 'bout him anymore.' The boy darted away and was round the corner with the others in no time. Paul thought he heard some obscene language directed at him. Some passers-by were looking his way, and he realized that it was time for him to leave. At least he knew from his contact with the boys – and they'd surely know – that Jorgen was not in the city.

Chapter 22

The following day Paul waited in for the arrival of Seamus, but it was not until late in the afternoon that he heard keys in the front door. It was a stroke of luck he'd stayed in, as he was able to intercept the newspaper boy who might have pushed the newspaper into a locked box attached to one of the walls in the porch. He'd taken the paper off the boy just as he was about to shove it in. There was a chance that Seamus might have read the newspapers, but they would be London ones and wouldn't cover local news of the week until at least the weekend. So if he'd picked a paper up at a station there might be nothing in it about events in Liverpool. The headline on the paper he'd rescued from the paperboy was more muted but just as damning as the previous day's. It was a statement by Lady Winnington that read 'Shot with my husband's gun.' And there was a head-and-shoulders drawing of him in the middle of the front page; its likeness was uncanny. His situation had become even more hopeless, for the nation now believed that he, the Hun, had shot a lord of the realm. It also disturbed Paul that he might be in possession of the murder weapon. Part of him felt he ought to get rid of it right away, but holding the cold steel gave him a feeling of security – invincibility even. So he thought he'd leave that decision till later even though Paddy popped up in his mind wagging his finger muttering the phrase, 'Do it now. No violence.'

When Seamus arrived, he was holding a London newspaper, and he greeted Paul like a long-lost friend, so Paul relaxed. As Seamus hung his overcoat up there was a knock at the door. Paul, without thinking, grasped the gun in his inside pocket ready to pull it out if necessary. But it was only the neighbour with a tray of steaming food, and she was followed by a younger woman whom Paul thought was Joan's maid, but it turned out that she was her daughter. They both hurried with the dishes into the dining room and were out again in no time.

'You've timed that to a *T*, Joan. Thank you so much,' said Seamus. 'I take it you've met Mr Roth.' Joan shot Paul a cursory glance, which got him worried. Perhaps she knew something. She would have seen the newspapers.

'Yes, I have Mr Kirwen.' The fact that she didn't say anything else worried him further, but maybe that was her way. Joan turned on her heel and beckoned to her daughter. There had been no introductions. Paul felt his stomach knotting, and perspiration appeared at his temples. She was out of the door in a flash.

'Strange,' said Seamus, 'it's unlike her not to be going twenty to the dozen and not leaving anyone a chance to get a word in.' He spoke with a soft cultured Irish accident.' He abruptly changed the subject.

'Is Paddy around? I've not cast eyes on the scoundrel in months.'

'You've not heard then…,' Paul said as Seamus pointed towards the first sitting room. They sat down in sumptuous leather armchairs placed facing one another, and Paul went on, 'He was shot as we landed at Blundellsands.'

'Is he all right?' Seamus cut in. He clutched the arms of the chair; the smile on his face vanished, replaced by a look of disbelief.

'I don't know…' Paul's voice trailed off. He cleared his throat nervously. 'They managed to get him back on the trawler.'

Seamus was clearly shocked; his reddish complexion had lightened.

The Lucy Effect

'I must put feelers out to get to know his condition.' He paused. 'This is dreadful news. I'm sorry to say, Paul, that I was against Paddy going through with this escapade, but there was no way I could get my views across to him, what with the censorship of the letters and that useless meeting with him at Knockaloe. But having said that, I don't think I could have changed his mind. You must know how he is.' He hesitated. 'Once he'd got something in his head, you had the devil of a job to persuade him to change his mind.' Then there was a silence. Seamus seemed to be mulling through what had just been revealed to him, and Paul was anxious not to go into any more detail for fear of making matters worse. He waited for Seamus to continue.

'I'll get a telegram off to our friends in Douglas.' Seamus stood up, deep in thought, and then touched Paul's arm, obviously aware that he was not being as hospitable as he ought. 'Oh, please come through to the dining room for something to eat and a glass or two of wine or champagne. We must at least celebrate your freedom if nothing else.

After dinner they retired to a pleasant room on the first floor at the back of the house. They sat on the balcony overlooking the rear garden. There was no grass to be seen, only concrete. But that was the garden's trump card. The patio was full of tubs containing different varieties of tulips. The tubs were raised off the ground and positioned so that, from their viewpoint on the balcony, they took the form, in Paul's eyes, of a giant Catherine wheel firework. The curving lines of pots radiating from a central hub blazed with vivid flame-like colours. Seamus read Paul's thoughts.

'Yes, it is all rather beautiful, a creation of Paddy's, of course, with a little help from his fiancée. She'll be devastated to hear the news. She was so looking forward to seeing him again.' There was another silence, and Seamus continued,

'Look, I must send that telegram off now. I'll catch up on your news shortly. Just help yourself to drinks, and there's some cold food in the kitchen if you're still feeling hungry.'

On his way to the kitchen, Paul noticed that a letter had been bundled under the door. Someone was in a hurry to get a message to Seamus. He realized right way that it was probably from Joan, although he was desperately hoping it wasn't. The top of the envelope was marked 'URGENT' in capital letters. Paul didn't like what he did next, but he had no option. He tore the envelope apart, and there was Joan's signature at the bottom. His stomach knotted, and seconds later he found himself sitting on a straight-backed green velvet chair in the hall clutching the letter. He had read just a few words – *murderer* and *newspaper*. They had been enough. A newspaper cutting had fallen out of the envelope onto the floor. It was the front page of the paper he'd bought the previous day. It was his mug shot that must have convinced her. The letter finished off, 'For your sake, I'll leave it to you to contact the appropriate authorities.'

The frustration and anger he felt at the collapse of his plans welled up inside him, and he tore the letter and the newspaper cutting up and rolled them into a ball and jammed them into an inside pocket of his jacket. He decided against visiting the kitchen and went back upstairs, returning to the wicker chair on the balcony.

Paul and Seamus talked, drank, and smoked until the early hours of the morning. Paul, of course, didn't mention the Lord and Lady Winnington affair, or Seamus' neighbour's request to take urgent action. He couldn't cope with trying to explain the ins and outs of it all. He seriously wondered whether he'd be believed. In his mind he kept seeing his mug shot and the headlines. The drink helped him to ram it to the back of his mind. Paul wanted to impress upon Seamus that his immediate concern was finding Jorgen and escaping with him from England as quickly as

The Lucy Effect

possible. Seamus seemed sympathetic, but sometimes he'd stare right through Paul deep in thought as if he had doubts. The drink flowed, and Paul moved onto descriptions of their mutual friend's comical escapades in the last two months. To this Seamus added his three pennies' worth of Paddy tales. Paul worked out that they had known each other for over ten years, and Seamus was Paddy's second in command. He could imagine him trying to reign in Paddy from what he thought were his more extreme ideas, but he could equally imagine Paddy going his own way. As they parted to retire to bed, Seamus, slurring his words said,

We can talk about plans to start looking for Jorgen after a little trip I've planned for us tomorrow – a view from the air of the business Paddy and I are involved in. Oh, you'll need to disguise yourself just in case the police have an image of you. There are some items in the bedroom – beards and what not. They're in the bedside table drawer. You'll have to be up early. I shall see you for breakfast at seven then, all right?'

'That's fine. I've seen the disguises. Where'd you get the stuff from? It looks real.' Paul didn't mention his venture out that morning in monarchical character. He wasn't sure about the trip in the air either, whatever that meant. He just wanted to get on with the job of searching for Jorgen.

'Hasn't Paddy mentioned the theatrical side of his family? Contacts, you know, always contacts.' Seamus half waved his hand and left.

Chapter 23

Paul woke up at five the next morning with a hangover and just one thought in his head. He had to get away from Seamus and the house as soon as he could. Joan could be around at any time, or she could even telephone Seamus. Maybe the local newspaper was delivered in the mornings on Fridays. The temporary euphoria of the previous evening had deserted him. He'd persuaded himself, just before going to sleep, that he would tell Seamus everything that had happened since the landing at Blundellsands. They'd got on well together, and he couldn't imagine Seamus not believing him. He would tell the truth. But the bright, hopeful thoughts of the previous night, as often happens in the cold light of day, had changed to a more anxious reality. Now he firmly believed that, once Seamus found out what had been going on, he'd follow the line everyone in the country was taking – that Paul was guilty of the murder of Lady Winnington's husband. Paul figured it would be better for Seamus if he left without saying a word. Seamus would react more naturally to events as they gradually unfolded, and his story to the police would sound more plausible.

What Paul had to do now was to find anything in the house that might be of benefit to him on the run. He dressed quickly. The fact that he was taking action made him feel calmer. His bedroom was at the opposite end of the landing to Seamus's. He was in his stocking feet and managed to move noiselessly down the stairs and into the room that looked like a study. He searched the bureau. At first he thought he wouldn't come up with anything, and he nearly didn't. But as he was closing the rolling lid top, he noticed a tell-tale looped piece of braid in the writing surface of the desk and noticed the outline of a cut-out section in the felt material. In the secret chamber he discovered a ticket for an Atlantic crossing for an adult and child from a shipping line he wasn't familiar with, and a bag containing sovereigns and five-pound notes. He couldn't believe what he was seeing. He said a prayer and hastily stashed these items away in a pocket. The ticket and money were obviously meant for him. From this evidence, Seamus seemed to have much more knowledge than he'd supposed. It could be Seamus hadn't wanted to incriminate his friend, and the less knowledge about plans that Paul possessed the better. Paddy had mentioned this to him in Knockaloe. But how on earth had Paddy got the information to Seamus? The strict censorship at the camp meant internees could talk only about how many seagulls flew over the camp on Sunday at midday, and certainly not about the price of fish in the canteen. They probably would have blacked the seagull line out too. He smiled to himself; it could be a code.

Paul heard the doorbell ring. The person ringing was impatient and rang several times. It could only be the police. He went to open the door of the study, and he heard movement. Seamus was rushing down the stairs to answer the front door. Paul dashed back to his bedroom in panic and threw his shoes on. Then he ran to another room at the rear of the house where he'd noticed a fire escape. By this time, Seamus was careering up the stairs, shouting at the top of his voice, 'It's a telegram! Paddy's alive! He's safe!' Paul was just flinging the fire escape door open, and he halted. He thought he must go now. The adrenaline was pushing him onwards. But the news glued him to the spot. He swayed with indecision.

'Where are you, Paul?' Seamus had gone into Paul's bedroom, and then he flew down the stairs shouting excitedly that Paddy was all right. Paul shut the fire escape door firmly, but almost instantaneously wondered whether it was the right thing to do. In the end, he sprinted to the bathroom and quietly locked the door. He was over the moon to hear about Paddy. It could change the whole situation. If Paddy were here, now he'd be believed. But Paddy wasn't here. Paul heard the clocks chiming six and waited a few minutes. What was Seamus up to? Paul started to panic again. Perhaps Joan had alerted the police. He heard footsteps on the landing, and he began to unlock the door. As he was doing this, the door was pushed open. Seamus waved the telegram and, no longer the controlled gentleman, placed his other arm around Paul and hugged him.

They were sitting at a breakfast table that was laid as elegantly as one would see at any posh country house. The silver cutlery glistened in the sunlight that poured through the large dining room windows. The crockery looked Japanese and expensive. A lanky young girl rigged out in a smart black uniform with lacing and a petite cap was waiting on at the table. She had a raw Scouse accent, which seemed out of place in the surroundings. But Paul was fond of the accent and found himself gently teasing her. Seamus looked at Paul, who was having a joke with the girl about the way she said *condiments*; it sounded like 'con-*dee*-ments.'

'Ah, I see you're feeling more settled this morning,' said Seamus. 'You were stressed and tight last night until the drink softened you up. It was a damn good night. Did you sleep well?'

'Like a log,' Paul responded and turned his attention to the telegram lying on the table in front of him:

> Has your guest arrived (stop) Is he well (stop) I am slowly getting better (stop) Doc says will make full recovery (stop) please give your guest all he needs (stop) I mean all he needs (stop) He deserves it (stop) Hope to be in Liverpool in near future (stop) I drink a toast

to you both (stop) May God be with you (stop)
Pads.

He read the message through several times and let the words sink in. Initially it made him feel he ought to reveal all to Seamus. The message was so supportive. But something held him back. Would Paddy ever recover? He was trying to read between the lines interpreting what he thought Paddy really meant.

'Perhaps Paddy will be with us in a few weeks, hey?' Seamus said, pushing his plate to one side with vigour.

'Doubt it,' said Paul. 'He took quite a hit in the stomach. It's going to be a few weeks before he's up and about.' He excused himself from the table. The maid was clearing up the dishes in the dining room, and Seamus had spread out some business documents and was signing them. Paul entered the kitchen and frantically started opening cabinet doors until he found what he wanted. At that moment the maid came into the kitchen with a pile of plates. He spun round quickly. She couldn't hide her surprise and stuttered,

'Oh, I – I'll go out!'

He wondered why she'd responded to him in such a subservient way. Paul blushed violently. The guilt was steaming from him, but he managed to recover.

'No, no don't go. It's all right I was just looking for a remedy, something for my stomach. Heavy night.' She'd come closer, and he noticed she was staring at the jar in his hand.

'Gravee brownin'?' she said incredulously.

'Yes, one of my mother's remedies. He went over to the sink, emptied some of the brown liquid into a cup and swallowed it down as quickly as possible, not letting her see his screwed-up face,

'Well... ', she said half laughing,

'I've seen everythin' now!'

Chapter 24

Paul was clutching a bag. It contained the gear he reckoned he would need in the foreseeable future. Paul and Seamus got on a tram heading for the Pier Head. It was full of dockers. He was surprised that Seamus hadn't used a more fitting form of transport. But not as surprised as their fellow passengers who shot questions:

Are you comin' to do a proper days grafting, then, for the first time ever? Why aren't you in khaki? Have you bought yourselves out? Think we'll be needing to send the feathers? Most jibes carried a thin veneer of good nature, but underneath there was anger mixed with envy. Paul and Seamus didn't respond, but occasionally smiled. Paul was thinking that, if their companions had the slightest iota of who he was, then white feathers would certainly fly. Seamus thought only of his aim to give Paul the whole picture of what Paddy and he represented, to emphasize what they were both risking for him.

The conductor was concerned. He didn't want any trouble on his shift. Who'd ever heard of gents riding on the trams? It wasn't done. They were more out of place than a women conductor would be. Completely wrong. Their scheduled stop couldn't come too soon for anyone.

At the James Street Station, a fair number of the other passengers got off as well. They were mostly dockers, but there were some clerks. The covered footbridge that led to the overhead railway station was a mass of workers barging up two steps at a time in order to make sure they didn't miss the train they heard clanging over the tracks above them. This seemed to strike terror amongst some of the passengers coming the other way who didn't know any better. When Paul and Seamus reached the Northern Line platform, a train crawled into the station going the other way. With brakes squealing, it noisily stopped at the opposite platform. It was heading south for the Dingle terminus. Paul had one of those insightful moments. Here he was, dressed as a toff complete with moustache, beard, and cane. Shouldn't he either be one of the milling, joke-a-minute dockers or miles away from the place searching for Jorgen? A strong impulse to bolt hit him again, but he held back. He was curious to know what Paddy and Seamus's business empire might be. It could be of use to him. Seamus would know about shipping lines and their destinations and where they berthed.

After they'd established themselves on the platform with enough elbowroom at the back of the crowd, Seamus asked, 'You've been on this bone rattler before Paul?' As Paul was about to answer, the train travelling north rolled in. It disgorged its passengers, a pushing, rushing throng encountering fierce competition from adversaries with the single intention of getting onto the contraption whatever the cost. Seamus and Paul observed the melee, and as the crowd thinned, Seamus took hold of Paul's arm and guided him to one of the two first-class carriages. The doors were closed. There was no one inside the coach save for a guard. He opened the door for them at the same time he gave them a half salute.

They sat down, and once the guard was out of earshot, Seamus began his tale.

Seamus had met Paddy in Dublin. Seamus's family had been landowners for centuries in Ireland and were well off. He'd gone to public school in England and then finished his formal education reading law at Trinity College. He then joined a shipping group and was employed in its legal department. He was on the first rungs of a career ladder that would have led directly to the higher echelons of the Dublin business community. That was the plan. But then Paddy came along – Paddy, who had been born in Dublin and was a self-made man of exceptional gifts. He'd never had any formal higher education even though his German father, Gustav Lieber, a Jewish émigré, had been a professor of philosophy at the University of Cologne. Paddy's father had died when Paddy was four. He'd been a publican in the dock area of Dublin. There had been few other occupations open to him. He had been master of the Clipper, a hostiliery that was smartly run in contrast to the squalor and unsanitary conditions of the nearby housing. It was a popular meeting place, not only for the locals, but also the foreign seamen who appreciated what it had to offer. He'd been known as the 'Great Prof' because of his knowledge and the way he actively used it to help people sort out their problems. They all thought he was a foreign seaman who'd fallen in love with Dublin and its people, for that was the way it seemed.

Paddy's mother gave him his wonder for life, his joy, and his charm. She'd trod the boards of the music halls in her younger days, and her eldest daughter followed in her footsteps, achieving a certain level of popularity in London. Gustav had left his wife sufficient funds for them to live comfortably in a nice area of Dublin. Most of this Paul knew from his conversations with Paddy, but it was the detail and the personal nature of the information that Seamus related that convinced Paul that Seamus and Paddy's was a close relationship.

Seamus and Paddy had met as opponents sitting on opposite sides of a large, highly polished table in one of the chambers of the Dublin Steam Packet Company at Wood Quay. Paddy's outfit was in dispute with Seamus's company over their shipping rates. Paddy had discovered a discrepancy in the company's charging policy and had been able to prove that the company was discriminating against certain merchants, particularly the smaller ones. There was some skulduggery going on involving one merchant who had a great deal of influence on the company's board and who was attempting to lessen the competition in the city. Although Paddy's firm hadn't been affected, he'd realized that this could change. So there he was, representing himself with three other merchants' lawyers. Paddy, who quickly took up the leadership of the group with his charm and ability to get to the core of the argument, stitched the meeting up and won the day. Seamus had been frustrated and annoyed that this smooth-talking man with a broad Dublin accent and no formal legal training had outclassed him. But secretly he'd been impressed, and the fact that he'd not been happy with his own company's policies softened the blow. The next day he'd received a long phone call from Paddy and, in a daze, had put the phone down realizing that, in ten minutes, he'd just given up his career of ten months.

Paul had not interrupted Seamus from the time he'd started talking at James Street till they reached the end of the northern line at Seaforth and Litherland Station. Paul was about to get out of the carriage, but Seamus indicated that they were to stay on for the return journey.

'Now I want you to see part of our business empire from the air,' Seamus said, smiling. Paul was about to mention to him that they were near to the spot where he and Paddy had been dropped off on the shore, but Seamus didn't give him a chance.

'We'll do the stretch of the line now to the other terminus at Dingle. I'll explain how certain docks are at the heart of our little empire – that's if you don't mind.'

Paul left him to it. He'd listen now and again, especially when shipping lines were mentioned, but other times he was deep in thought about the next few hours and where he'd go. It was when Seamus mentioned the business killings he and Paddy had made when they'd opened up trade in Hong Kong that Paul really took notice. Seamus and Paddy had become very rich, nearly but not quite joint millionaires. Paul thought the term *joint millionaires* was interesting, but what really shook him was how much wealth Paddy had accrued. It set him off thinking. Why hadn't Paddy been able to rapidly extricate himself from his internment? Didn't money speak above politics? What had driven him to become a desperate prisoner on the run and expose himself to so much danger? Surely he must have known that in time he would have been released or at the very least sent to one of the posh internment camps at Wakefield where internees lived the high life. Paul wanted to interrupt Seamus here, but just couldn't get a word in.

As they came out of the tunnel returning on the northern line from Dingle, Seamus mentioned that he was going to conduct Paul to their offices in Water Street. Paul half listened. Glancing out the carriage window, he'd noticed the word *Hun* in a newspaper headline at one of the train stops, but hadn't been able to catch the rest of the headline. Raw panic set in. He imagined a hangman's noose floating towards him. He was stuck in the coach for another three stops before they reached the James Street Station. It was the panic of being trapped. The need to run just anywhere as fast as he could was boring into him. Should he open the carriage door as it slowed down and jump? He took some deep breaths – oriental style, as Paddy might have done – and calmed down. He decided to stay put. At least it would give him that little bit of extra time to get away. Bolting out of the carriage door could make Seamus suspicious and feed his doubts about him. Paul could lose himself in the crowd as they descended the covered footbridge, and Seamus would think they'd lost each other accidently. Paul wondered why he felt so strongly about keeping in Seamus's good books. Why did it matter how he parted from him? The man would soon know about the pack of lies plastered all over the city.

Chapter 25

Paul walked into the spacious reception hall of the Adelphi Hotel. He'd given Seamus the slip, but it had been a clumsy operation. Seamus had seen him running off and called after him. But it was done, and he was on his own again. He tipped his hat to the receptionist. He saw his face in the mirror behind the reception desk. It was shiny red in appearance, and trickles of perspiration were running down his cheeks into the ends of his moustache. He noticed she was staring at him. Had she noticed he was the Hun?

'The best room,' he said, trying to make his voice as posh as possible as he caught his breath.

'That'll be four fourteen, fourth floor. D'you want help with your?' She stopped after gazing at the floor.

'No, as you see I'm travelling light.' He paused and muttered as an afterthought, 'It'll be coming later on.' He moved towards the stairs, which were framed with square marble columns that sparkled in the light of the chandeliers.

'Sir, d'you not want to use the lift? Before he could respond, the receptionist went on,

'The porter will show you to your room, sir.' He felt completely out of place. He'd have to be sharper and imitate what others were doing. After climbing four flights of stairs and walking partway down a long hall, the porter stopped suddenly at room 414, and Paul nearly collided with him. The porter, who wasn't exactly calming Paul's nerves, had been talking about the escaped 'Hun' at thirteen to the dozen. Paul was shown into a sumptuous room furnished in a style that wouldn't have looked out of place in a country house. There was marble everywhere. Finally alone, he sat on the edge of a bed that was swathed in curtains and ribbons. It looked as if he'd been given the bridal suite. Every nook and cranny hid some love token, and the room was flowing with flowers. He wondered why he'd been given this room, but suddenly found the answer when he looked out of the window. There was scaffolding. It looked as if repairs were under way. He stole down the corridor at the back of the building checking on bedroom doors. They were mostly locked. Finally he came across one that was open. There were cigars still smouldering in overflowing ashtrays. He opened the window and was in luck. About thirty yards away, he observed a fire escape. Returning to the corridor, he found a door that led directly onto the escape. He was down it in seconds, ripping off his false beard and moustache and making sure he had the gravy browning and the other gear. He was gone in a jiffy and heading towards the centre of the town, his heart pounding.

****

Signor Alfonso sank into the deep green leather seat and realized the driver had been telling the truth about the state, as he'd described it, of his exceptional cab. It had been completely refurbished. He sat back and tried to relax as much as he could. This wasn't helped by the driver who was shouting obscenities at a group of people hindering their progress as they pulled into the short, crescent-shaped driveway in front of the Adelphi Hotel. The driver jumped down from his seat and held the throat of someone who'd just kicked the shining paintwork on his cab. Signor Alfonso had wanted to slip into the Adelphi unnoticed. This wasn't going to happen. As fists started to fly, he deliberately stepped out of the door on the opposite side to where the commotion was occurring.

The Lucy Effect

He ran up the steps of the hotel through the revolving door and went straight to the reception desk.

'Havva you a granda rooma for me for two days or so? *Grazie.*' The receptionist couldn't take her eyes off the face from which had emanated the smooth foreign voice. With any ordinary guest she'd be checking the books before he'd finished the first word. He had the most marvellous tan and the blackest of black moustaches, thin and long with drooping ends. The black suit he wore was the latest in Italian couture.

'Excusa, signora,' he began.

'Miss'. She smiled as she corrected him.

'Oh… ahhma sorry, signorina.'

'That's all right,' she said leaning over. 'How can I help you?'

He tucked his chin in so she wouldn't notice his pale neck.

'Canna I havva a room, pleasa? Last time I wassa here I wassa in room four sixteen. Is possible fora me to havva thisa rooma again? Pleasa?'

For the first time since he'd walked through the doorway she tore her eyes away from him and quickly checked the book.

'Oh, yes it's free, but there is a problem.' Paul felt perspiration running down his cheeks and wondered whether it would affect his face. 'Oh, but we can get round this if you don't mind scaffolding obscuring the view from the window.'

'Scaffdina? Whatta isa this? A cafe righta nexta door to the Aldephi? Buta ita wasn't there lasta time I was here.' He thought he'd overdone it at this point, sounding like an idiot. But he heard police whistles as the dispute he'd left and forgotten outside had suddenly flared into a minor riot with passers-by getting involved. He knew he must hurry, 'I'll take that then please', he said hastily. Fortunately the receptionist hadn't noticed the slip from one accent to another. Pointing to the door he said, 'Canna you not involve me ina all thata?' He left some money on the desk to cover the cab fare. He didn't know whether she might view the money as a tip.

As he walked away towards the lift she shouted after him,
'Do you have other bags, sir? Would you like a porter?'

He refused and got into the lift. As the door was closing, he saw the cab driver, escorted by a constable, enter the reception hall. He pressed the button, and the animated scene disappeared. He made straight for room 414 and rescued the bits and pieces he'd left there, and then went next door to room 416.

Chapter 26

Early the next morning the receptionist picked up the bundled newspapers that had just been delivered. She was sorting them out and checking the list of rooms and the newspapers that had been ordered when her eyes were drawn to the front page of the *Courier*. The headline read, 'Have You Seen this Man?' It was the eyes that gave it away. Room 414. The man who'd arrived without any luggage. She'd not seen him on the previous morning's shift after he'd gone to his room. She spoke to the manager, who told her to ask the staff on duty whether they'd seen or heard anything about the man. He told her to report back to him. He picked up the phone and rang the police.

Fifteen minutes later, constables, some carrying rifles, surrounded the hotel. A high-ranking officer entered the reception area with about twenty armed officers and plain-clothes men carrying pistols. 'Everybody stand just where you are!' he announced. 'Don't move.' There were no guests in the reception hall; it was too early. Only a few staff members were about, and they did as they were told.

'Who's in charge here?' the officer growled.

'I am.' The manager gingerly lifted his arm. The officer beckoned him over and asked which room the Hun was in. After he got the information he needed, the officer told the manager that no one was to leave the hotel. For their own safety, staff members were told to go to their rooms and remain there. Several constables were ordered up the stairs to the fourth floor, and the officers and plain-clothes men took the lift. Hearing the commotion, some guests had run out onto the corridors in their nightshirts and were swiftly ushered back into their rooms and ordered to stay put in no uncertain terms.

The police banged heavily on the door of room 414. 'Open up!' shouted the officer in charge. 'This is the police! We're carrying arms. We know you're in there!'

Paul, in the adjoining room, shot up bolt like from the deepest of sleeps. His heart was pounding, and his mouth was so dry that he could hardly move his lips. He hadn't thought the police would have been so quick off the mark. At least now he knew they were looking for a man with a beard and moustache who came from northern climes. This thought was of little comfort. His body was shaking uncontrollably. The noise of splintering wood and the accompanying heavy thud as the door to room 414 gave way brought Paul to his senses. He leapt out of bed and hurriedly dressed. He took a long draught of water, applied more gravy browning to his face and hands, and prepared himself.

It wasn't long before there was a heavy-handed knock on the door, accompanied by a gruff order to open up. When Paul opened the door, he thought he recognized the face and the voice, but the notion was shoved out of his mind as he was barraged with questions about the man next door. Paul kept repeating – in pigeon English – that he'd never seen the man they were after. Then there was some shouting outside in the corridor, and Paul thought he heard the words *'We've found him'*. He was about to follow the sergeant out of the room, but the door was flung in his face. He pushed it ajar and noticed a man bearing a close resemblance to what he'd looked like a few hours ago being frog marched along. He was dressed in a striped nightshirt that came down to his ankles, and he was shouting at the top of his voice that he was completely innocent. The police were having none of it. They kept thumping and foul mouthing him; each sentence always ended with the word *Hun*. From a lift emerged a uniformed inspector. Suddenly the abuse stopped. The inspector yelled,

'You've found him have you? Well, prove it. Pull his beard!'

The sergeant hesitated then he replied meekly,

'Beg your pardon, sir?'

'Pull his bloody beard!'

'Sir.' The sergeant took hold of the beard and yanked at it as hard as he could. The still-bearded, night shirted man shrieked. At the sight of this, Paul broke out into a chuckle. The sergeant spun round, and that's when Paul noticed the scar on his forehead. He shut the door quickly.

It was pelting down with rain and windy at the same time as Paul alighted from a cab in Elizabeth Street behind the infirmary a day later. This sort of weather would have kept him indoors just a few days ago, as graving-browning make-up wouldn't have stood a chance. But he'd managed to buy some theatrical greased-based colouring with an assurance that the weather wouldn't touch it unless he happened to be in the tropics. He had the cabbie drop him off a little distance away from the hospital entrance in Brownlow Street. He wanted to ensure that he attracted as little attention as possible. As he crossed the cobbled streets, the events of May slipped into his mind. The sight of the hospital inspired painful flashbacks – the gutter; the kicks; the blood; his harsh words; the separation from Jorgen, the boy's red, swollen, pitiful eyes as he ran sobbing.

Paul calmed down as he approached the hospital entrance and stopped next to a family who were distressed. They had tears in their eyes and were hugging each other. Nearby a flower seller was smiling and shouting at passers-by, cracking jokes, sometimes crude. The two groups contrasted vividly. At first, Paul identified more with the family. But thoughts of Bridie checked these feelings, and the groups' proximity to each other didn't seem so out of place. He walked over to the flower seller and bought a bunch of red tulips. The benefits were twofold. They allowed him to blend into the background, and they would be a pleasant surprise for the person he desperately sought. But it was all a waste of time. He was still there as the evening visitors wended their way home. He beckoned a cab and pitched the tulips into a bin.

It was the next day when he saw her. He'd been spending some time at a tea room across the road to avoid suspicion and was paying his bill when he nearly missed her. She was with a friend. They were laughing and playfully pushing each other as they walked along. She looked younger than he remembered. But perhaps it was because she was so happy at that moment. He had second thoughts about approaching her. Her happiness – would it last? If she'd been on her own it might have been different. At least he knew the time she went off duty, and maybe she would be alone the following day. But he just couldn't let her go. It was too much of a gamble. How much time did he have? So he decided to find out where she lived and take it from there. They'd walked for about five minutes, and suddenly Bridie turned round.

It was as if she knew that someone was following. At first she was unsure who the man was. He looked foreign. Maybe it was a former patient. The facial hair and dark complexion put her off the scent. But it was his eyes that gave him away, and then she knew immediately. Her friend, obviously realizing that she had to make herself scarce, quickly left the two on their own. Paul and Bridie spent time walking around and talking.

There were many silences. Neither of them could get around the embarrassment that stilted meaningful conversation. Paul had thought it would be easier. Surely they'd continue where they had left off. But where was that? Then, there had been no holding her, or kissing. There had just been looks and smiles and their eyes connecting. In the end they parted, but agreed to meet the following day. Both felt dissatisfied and frustrated.

Part III
Jorgen's Story: 10th May to 12th August 1915

Chapter 27

Edward Aughton had reached Berry Street and was forced to slow down to a walking pace. Conscious of pain building up in his arms and legs, he turned in the direction of the Adelphi Hotel where he was staying. Across the road running out of Nelson Street he saw someone he recognized. He was amazed. He thought it was impossible, but looked again and realized it was true. The uncontrollable fear that a second ago had been about to devour his identity – his very being – vanished. Yet more, it was replaced by an exhilarating spark of energy that spread throughout every cell of his body. It was inexplicable. His body was cleansed as if he'd taken a hundred baths one after the other. With renewed vitality he started to cross the road junction. His face beamed. He fixed his eyes on the boy and experienced a body free of pain – a new, yet still the old, Edward.

'Nathan!' he shouted as he began to run. He was nearly caught in the wheel of a trap that was moving along at a quick pace. But Edward didn't pay attention. Edward continued to run towards his Nathan.

Jorgen, who'd reached Duke Street, could hardly see because of the tears and was unaware of Edward Aughton's looming presence until it was too late. Edward grabbed his arms.

'What are you doing, mister?' Jorgen shouted, trying to push him away.

'Shush, shush, boy. Don't you know your grandpapa? I've not seen you for some time. How you've changed in your face!

And you've shot up a foot or so, but I'd recognize you anywhere!' There was no stammer.

'But I haven't a grandpapa,' Jorgen protested between sobs.

'Come, come, now, Nathan, don't upset yourself. You must be as surprised as I am about this whole affair. Let's make our way to the Adelphi and then catch the train to St Helens.'

The stranger said this as if it would be completely understood and not open for question, and Jorgen didn't question him when he heard St Helens mentioned. He became quiet. In a state of shock and confusion, he let himself be led away. He didn't listen to the string of benign and meaningless words that Edward spoke, or the sounds of the trams clanging, or the distant sounds of ships on the Mersey, or the cry of the evening newspaper sellers. It was the words *geh, geh* that rang in his head and reminded him about what his papa had said about his great aunt.

Jorgen had hardly spoken. Edward had picked up the boy's belongings, and taken him to a hotel room at the Adelphi. Jorgen sat down at the table, but he hadn't touched the sandwiches Edward had ordered for him. He just stared into space. Edward talked at him non-stop and rapidly. It was as if he was replacing the mortar in between bricks that had disintegrated over time. On the train to St Helens from Lime Street, Edward had given up attempting conversation with the boy. He'd fallen asleep, and when he'd awakened, for a moment, he wondered who the boy was sitting next to him. Arriving in St Helens Edward was different again making conversation although none of it was answered.

It was dark and as they alighted from the train; the gusting wind blew the rain in all directions. The wooden station building creaked, and the light from the gas lamp above the ticket office window spluttered. The rain suddenly started falling more heavily, and Edward bundled Jorgen into a cab. The boy noticed pungent smells in the air from the nearby chemical factories. The cab driver, who knew Edward, spoke in an accent he found difficult

The Lucy Effect

to follow. He heard the word *Cowley Lodge* mentioned. The cab passed several trams, their electric lamps shining brightly giving comfort to pedestrians, who were mainly workmen dodging puddles as they hurried to their homes or to the public house. It followed the tram track to the north of the town up a brew along North Road. Eventually the driver slowed down and turned left. Through the condensation and the rain on the windows, Jorgen could just make out a row of large houses in the gloom. This was St Helens, the town of strange smells and accents.

Cowley Lodge was a large property. It had suited Edward, a solicitor, when he and his wife moved in with their son in the late 1890s. It was one of several houses built for the professional classes in the Cowley Hill area of the rapidly developing industrial town. Because of its elevation, the air was cleaner compared to that of the industrial heart of the town sited at the lower levels of the Sankey Valley where the smoke and foul-smelling odours prevailed. From the windows on the north side of the house one could see miles and miles of arable farmland dotted with woods rising to gentle hills on the horizon. Edward knew Jorgen would not be able to see any of this until daylight; the night was pitch black, and the rain was lashing down in the high wind as they took leave of the cab. When they got into the house, Jorgen refused the supper Edward offered. Edward took him upstairs and opened a bedroom door. The room smelt musty. He told Jorgen to use the bathroom next door and to make sure he washed behind his ears before he went to bed. He promised to come up later to say prayers. Jorgen obeyed the request without question. There was no point in doing otherwise.

He spent little time in the bathroom. The bright electric lights and his tiredness brought on a headache. The bedroom was more inviting. There was no brightness about it. A single lamp was its only light source, and it cast comforting shadows. On the bed was a dusty nightshirt, which he put on quickly. It was a bit tight.

When Edward returned, they knelt together at the side of the bed to say prayers. The light went out, and Jorgen was on his own again, completely on his own for the first time in his life. There was a lump in his throat. His tears were torrential like the rain he could hear. He moaned almost silently so that the man who thought he was his grandfather wouldn't return. Eventually he calmed down, and the last thought he had was that, as the sun rose, he'd be away seeking his great aunt as Papa wanted him to. The thought comforted him.

In the first few seconds of his waking, as the sun crept into the room through a chink in the curtain and gently warmed his face, Jorgen hadn't a clue of his whereabouts. He'd never slept in a bedroom other than his own tiny one, and he stared at the shapes of the unfamiliar furniture and fittings. Outside, the sounds he was used to – ships, loud-mouthed people, street traffic, and tens of church bells tolling – were replaced with an eyrie quietness. Then the horror and numbness of the previous evening struck him. He yanked the cotton sheet instinctively over his head to blank the world out. He thought he would cry, but he didn't. He listened for sounds in the house, but there were none. He gingerly drew the sheet back and noticed that the new day's rays of sunlight that caressed and warmed his face also exposed fine dust particles that dulled its brilliance. His desire to escape had become a victim of his dulling grief. But there was a flicker deep down in his mind that surprised him – an interest in the new world he faced. It was tinged with guilt.

Jorgen arose from bed, dressed quickly, and explored the bedroom. He looked at the books. He'd never seen as many in one place. They were all for children, and some of the titles he recognized from school. There were boxes of toys in a wardrobe together with boys' clothes. The clothes were neatly grouped on hangers, but they were all too small for him. He realized they must have belonged to Edward's grandson. The room hadn't been used for months, if not years, so his assumption was that Nathan was no longer around. He heard voices of children outside and went over to the window. The bedroom was at the front of the house. When he looked out of the window, he noticed a garden and, across the road, a school. Boys about his age – eleven – were walking into the school through the main entrance. There was a quiet orderliness about how they conducted themselves. His former plan of just dashing out of the front door completely receded. At least living with a man who seemed to like him because he resembled Nathan gave him the opportunity to look for his great aunt. She couldn't live too far away.

Downstairs in the dining room the maid had set one place at the table. She had made the breakfast and gone as usual. Jorgen later learned that she would come back at five and prepare a hot meal and would make sure she wasn't around when Edward returned. This was how Edward wanted it, how he needed it. He'd retired after the tragic death of his daughter-in-law and Nathan, and when his son left home, he had hidden himself away from the life he'd once lived. Each day he would leave the house before lunch and travel by car or train to nearby towns. He'd visit restaurants, hotels, libraries, and art galleries. This was his new life, deliberately and obsessively constructed to push the old life to one side and to fill the void of time left. The acquaintances he'd made in these places he kept at arm's length. He was a mystery to them. He'd be the one asking the questions and would rudely avoid talking about anything of a personal nature, so they never ventured to ask. To them he was a retired gentlemen inclined to be generous and of substantial financial means. For Edward, that's all they needed to know.

Chapter 28

It was nine when Jorgen entered the room. Edward explained that he had finished writing a note for Mary the maid asking her to lay two places in future, as he had a guest staying. Edward stared at the boy and said nothing. Jorgen caught his heart beating rapidly. Had the old man realized? Was the charade he now wanted to continue no longer playable? The features on Edward's face, which the previous day had beamed with joy and gratitude, now indicated the opposite. It was the blue grey eyes that said the most. They were blank. Edward looked down at the note he'd written and suddenly, as a car engine starts up spluttering at first but gradually becoming stronger and stronger with the occasional missed beat and finally purrs into life, his expression changed to full joyful recognition.

'Aghh, Nathan,' he said. 'Get a plate and help yourself to breakfast. You look half starved.' As on the previous day, the man proceeded to shower Jorgen with questions. Jorgen was amazed at the sudden change, but remained silent. Edward didn't seem to mind, and Jorgen realized that he was happy just to talk and didn't need a response.

Jorgen observed this strange behaviour of Edward's again later in the afternoon. The weather had improved, and they'd spent the day on the promenade at Southport exploring the arcades and operating the penny machines. Finally, they had gone onto the beach. Jorgen realized that Edward was reliving times when all the family had come out for a day, years ago. He could tell this because Edward seemed to be imagining that other people were there. He talked to these spirit people and would occasionally bring Jorgen into the conversation. Jorgen was struck dumb, but Edward seemed to barely notice his silence. The old man was acting out a scene played over and over but with slight variations each time. Jorgen wondered what had happened to the man's family. He knew the man thought he was his grandson, Nathan. And there was Emily, the man's wife. When Edward first mentioned her name, Jorgen was shot through with cold shivers. He thought Edward was speaking to his dead mother – the mother who'd died when he was seven. There was a warmth and gentleness in the way he spoke to her, just as he remembered the way it had been between his parents. Strangely, this brought him comfort, a feeling of belonging to the family.

Jorgen managed to cope with this behaviour, but became embarrassed when people stared and giggled. To Edward these people didn't exist; he recognized only Nathan and the invisible family. On the way back home, they stopped off at a hotel in Scarisbrick. Jorgen realized that this was a place that Edward's family had visited a great many times. A friendly waiter, well known to Edward, came to take their order,

'Ah, sir, is this your grandson?'

Edward looked at him and then turned slowly to Jorgen and back to the waiter. The vacant look in his eyes had returned.

'The boy...?' Edward said, staring right through Jorgen as if he wasn't there. Jorgen looked down at the white tablecloth and noticed the almost invisible pattern of silver thread. In places it disappeared only to reappear further on when he traced it with his finger. There was silence. It continued. Jorgen anxiously tried to trace the thread that he'd lost sight of. He wondered what was going to happen. The waiter appeared to be uncomfortable over being so forward. Then Jorgen found the thread again.

'I'll get your dishes, sir,' the waiter said as he over stroked a well-trimmed ginger moustache and hurried away. When he returned, everything was as right as rain. There was a sparkle in Edward's eyes as he joked with his grandson. The waiter placed the dishes down and huddled the tray under his arm. He nervously joined in on the tail end of the laughter that was taking place between grandfather and grandson, all the while stroking his moustache.

'Is there anything else you require sir?'

Edward looked at the waiter briefly as if he was a complete stranger, but then there was blessed recognition.

'Oh, no. That'll be all.' The waiter seemed relieved. Likewise, Edward's inner voice declared that he shouldn't pay a visit to this hotel in the future. He would stick with new places. In the weeks that followed, it would be only these places that they would visit.

****

Jorgen was not looking forward to the afternoon trip the next day. He was convinced that Edward would start speaking to himself again and worried the old man might expect him to join in the conversation. Jorgen hoped to avoid this by moving away from Edward at the first sign of being roped into the scene that was being played out. As it turned out, the boy was spared the blushes. The strange behaviour of Edward didn't recur, and as the day went on, Jorgen relaxed. His shattered world dissolved off and on when he became interested in whatever Edward was showing him. In one of the museums, as he turned a corner, a skeleton of a prehistoric monster massed before him. It was so enormous it took his breath away. Minutes later, guilt invaded him as he remembered who he was and why he was there. It was difficult to get away from. In most of the main streets of the city there were large collections of anti-German posters and graffiti.

Chapter 29

On the second day after their return home from a trip, Jorgen explored the gardens at the back of the property. He thought a detailed knowledge of the area might be useful if he had to make a quick getaway. He'd never seen anything like the garden that he encountered. It was totally alien. Even Jorgen, in his youthful innocence, wondered what it all meant. Ahead of him were three areas of land surrounded by five-foot trellises. Each area was slightly more elevated than the previous one. There was no grass or flowers apart from unhealthy-looking plants in stone pots. The ground where the grass would be in an ordinary garden was covered in a mass of pea gravel with flat slabs of granite set into it. He realized they were paved steps meant to be followed, and they led from one level to the next. Jorgen chose to avoid these, preferring to scrunch along the bone-dry gravel as he made his way to the third level. There was a gate at the entrance to the top level – the strangest one he'd ever seen. It consisted of two six-foot upright posts, one at each side of the entrance, and two cross pieces at the top, the higher-placed cross piece longer than the lower. There was a different feel to this level. There was a backdrop of cherry trees and cloud-pruned trees that provided shade and encouraged moisture. Placed on the ground were large stone pots containing large acer plants, and a stone water feature that looked as if it had not been used for a long time. In contrast to the dryness and lack of life on the other levels, here on this level there was a hint of quickness and movement. The breeze in the trees created motion and rearrangement. The invading shrubs on the sides of the trellis were pushing through and making headway. They'd joined tufts of grass that had fought their way through the gravel.

A section of the trellis to Jorgen's left, the direction he knew would lead to the main road, had been pushed down by the weight of the wandering, exploring shrubs, and he scrambled over it. The undergrowth was dense, and he found it difficult to see where he was headed. He hadn't realized the garden was so big. But he navigated using the line of cherry trees that ran all the way along the back and sides of the property. Suddenly the shrubs ended. He was met by a well-kept lawn bordered by many standard rose bushes. He'd reached the side of the property that ran along the main road. Close to the wall stood a large hut with windows covered in thick dust, curtained with cobwebs. A large rusty padlock was fixed to the door. This building was run down like the dry garden. Tall thistles in bloom surrounded the hut like over-zealous sentries with their blue busbies swaying in the breeze guarding a precious place that no one was to enter. Jorgen went over to a window and peered in. At that moment, Edward started to bang on one of the French windows and ran into the garden to confront Jorgen. 'You must never, ever go near that hut!' he warned. 'It's dangerous. You could have an accident. D'you hear me, boy? Never, ever!' His face was the colour of beetroot. He wrung his hands together, turned his back on Jorgen, and remained there several minutes staring at the hut.

****

One night about a week later, Jorgen couldn't sleep. He kept thinking about the last hour he'd spent with his father, turning over and over in his mind the events as he remembered them. When he'd exhausted every aspect of this memory, his thoughts moved on to how he was going to find his great aunt. So far there hadn't been an opportunity to do anything. Edward was with him all the time. But this wasn't his main concern, as Edward at least offered him some security, which provided him time to think out any plans he might have. The stumbling block was that he had no idea where to start the search. All he knew was that she lived in an area called Windle. Irritated, he banged over on to his other side in an effort to ward off these thoughts that inevitably led nowhere. Eventually, he fell asleep. He had a dream. There was a house that he instinctively knew belonged to Frau Stocker, but he couldn't see it from the road he was on. It came into view only as he walked down a drive lined with blackened, dead trees. The day changed to night halfway down the drive, and the black, skeleton-like trees branches began to seek him out. He was so petrified, his only thought was to run away, but the bony branches prodded him and then carried him aloft towards the front door. The next moment he was sitting in a comfortable armchair like the one in Edward's lounge. Slowly, his surroundings became Edward's lounge. The door opened. An old lady walked in, but as she came nearer, she changed into his mother, and he suddenly woke up.

When Jorgen came down to breakfast the following morning, he was tense. Every muscle in his body seemed as tight as a rusty screw. It was the tension of conflict – the urgent need to resolve an issue without the means of carrying out the resolution. Edward was opening some letters with a silver letter knife at the table. That's when the notion grabbed Jorgen's attention. As Edward came to the last letter, he sighed and thrust the blade of the knife in a rough manner underneath the red wax seal, and the envelope tore apart. He swore. Jorgen had noticed that the old man couldn't seem to stand anything that was not as it should be. Edward tried to straighten out the envelope and its contents, and seemed more concerned about the condition of the paper than about the message in the letter. That's when Jorgen decided he must try to escape the stalemate he found himself in. He decided to visit the post office.

****

They'd arrived home at four, and it had taken Edward another fifteen minutes to settle down in his chair and fall asleep. Jorgen had no idea where the post office was located except that it was somewhere in the town centre. On one journey in the car they'd driven through the centre, so he knew how to get there. He estimated it would be a fifteen-minute journey on foot. Then he'd have to locate the shop. That would mean that he'd be away from the house for about an hour, which happened to be how long Edward's afternoons nap usually lasted, although Jorgen couldn't be certain. He'd rarely been in a post office before, but he knew the people who worked there dealt with letters, and they'd probably have lists of names and addresses. He intended not to speak to anyone, but to just have a look around.

Jorgen stole out of the house when he heard Edward snoring away and arrived at the centre in reasonable time. Locating the post office was another matter. He didn't want to ask the way. He was conscious that he still had a slight German accent, but the nasal English he spoke was a trademark of '*Liverpudlians*'. It would be a giveaway if anything went wrong. People would start wondering, and before he knew it, the place would be swarming with constables. But in the end that's what he had to do. Time wasn't on his side.

Out of breath, he was finally standing in front of the post office door. Perspiration trickled down his temples and his bright-red cheeks. People would notice; panic was just around the corner. He imagined Edward sitting in his chair. He imagined the newspaper falling off his lap and his eyes opening. Suppressing

The Lucy Effect

the vision, he thrust the door open. The bell rang too loudly and for too long.

People were in a queue. Everyone stopped talking to see who was making the racket. Jorgen quickly understood that there was a knack in not making the bell ring so wildly. He couldn't have made a better job of a conspicuous entry if he'd purposely set out to attract attention. Jorgen turned away quickly. He wanted no eye contact with the staring throng. He started looking at the items of stationery that were for sale and glanced briefly at the other customers who had lowered their voices and were talking about him. A small girl with blond curls smiled at him. He looked away. He clumsily knocked a small tower of rolls of string over, and one sailed towards the girl. She picked it up, let go of her mother's hand, and offered the string to Jorgen. The postmistress shouted out, 'Hey, what are you up to, laddie?' There was nothing for it. He had to run. He yanked the door open with some force, and with the sound of the wild bell ringing in his ears, he ran out of the shop. The woman with the child darted out of the shop and gave chase, but Jorgen was too fast. He could hear her daughter screaming. Jorgen didn't stop until he reached the house. He went around to the back garden and climbed over the wall. He noticed Edward still asleep on the chair. *Thank God*, he said to himself. *Thank God.'*

Chapter 30

On the Monday of Jorgen's fourth week at Edward's home, several events occurred that would have significant repercussions for the boy. In the morning, Mary, the maid, left later than usual. Edward had asked her to go on an errand. As she was walking down the path, she happened to turn round and look back at the house. At the same time, Jorgen happened to be looking through the window at the top of the stairs. When he saw Mary, he realized with horror that she was the woman who'd chased after him at the post office. What if she told Edward? At least she hadn't rushed back to the house. Perhaps she hadn't seen him after all.

It was at the end of the afternoon later that same day, when Jorgen and Edward returned from their trip out, that Jorgen accidentally discovered the rusting key to the padlock that secured the hut door. He'd been in the pantry looking for some cheese that Edward had asked him to bring out for supper. He'd stumbled in the darkness and knocked the key off its hook. Edward came in to see what all the noise was about and saw Jorgen picking the key up off the floor. He was angry and made Jorgen promise never to touch it again. So Jorgen put it back quickly on its cup hook next to the other, smaller, shinier keys in the pantry. But Jorgen had made the connection between the rusty key and the hut and began wondering what it all could mean.

Part of the answer came the following day before Jorgen was due to set out with Edward for lunch. Jorgen was gently opening the

The Lucy Effect

French window that led into the lounge where Edward was taking a nap.

'Hey, is there anyone there?' a young voice shouted from the road. 'Can you let me have my ball back please? It's gone into that hut!'

Jorgen stopped in his tracks. It seemed unreal, for it was the first voice, apart from Edward's, that had directed a reasonable question at him since he'd been in St. Helens. The boy repeated his question in a louder tone as if he meant business. Jorgen stepped outside, gently closed the door, and ran along the garden path to where he thought the noise was coming from. And then he glimpsed the boy through a hole in the privet hedge. He stopped. What should he do? If he responded, it could have consequences that he might later regret. It could give the whole game away. Then again, maybe this boy could help him.

'I'm coming!' Jorgen said in the best English voice he could muster. He moved into the line of vision of the curly-haired, blonde boy.

The boy was slightly taller than Jorgen and a few years older. He wore the uniform of the boys who attended the school on the opposite side of the road to Cowley Lodge.

'Oh, super!' the boy said. 'You're foreign, aren't you? I can tell by your accent. Is it Belgian or Russian? Wait till I tell the others! Super!'

'Stop, please!' Jorgen shouted in such an authoritative way that the boy immediately obeyed. His beaming face changed in an instance to one of considerable curiosity. His blue eyes shone brightly. The boy was begging for an explanation.

'Do you really want your ball back?' Jorgen asked, his voice taking on more of a foreign accent. 'If so, you mustn't tell a soul about me. To you I don't exist. That means to any of your friends and family I don't exist. Do you understand?' he added firmly.

Taking up the game, and without hesitating, the boy said, 'Yes! Super! I agree. I've never seen you. You're non-existent – invisible even. By the way, my name's Montgomery. What's yours?'

Jorgen nearly laughed out loud, but contained himself.

'Where do you think the ball is?'

'It went through one of the windows in that shed.' Montgomery was pointing to the hut, which was surrounded by weeds.

Jorgen hesitated. The picture of an angry, red-faced Edward floated through his mind. But he was desperate. He had a strong feeling that Montgomery might help him.

'Wait a minute,' he told his new acquaintance. Jorgen remembered the large, rusty key hanging in the pantry. He ran off and headed round the house to the kitchen. He was back in no time, but he couldn't get the key to budge in the lock. Perspiration trickled down his face, and tiny flakes of rust and dust stuck to his sweaty hands as he repeatedly tried to move the key.

'I can't budge the darn thing,' he said angrily, and he bashed the key against the iron of the padlock.

'D'you want a hand?' Montgomery asked meekly, a hint of surprise in his voice. 'I can shimmy over the wall.'

In no time, the boy was standing next to Jorgen. He took hold of the key, and mustering a great deal of force, he turned it in the lock. This time the padlock sprang open, and it fell to the ground. Before Jorgen had the opportunity to respond Montgomery said,

'You'd done most of the work. The dastardly thing was ready to open as soon as I touched the key.'

Instinctively looking back at the house for any signs of Edward, Jorgen slowly pushed the squeaking door open. Both boys could never have imagined what was waiting for them.

At first they couldn't see the rich decoration owing to the accumulated cobwebs and dust. But when they started removing some of the cobwebs with artists' brushes they'd found in a jar by the door, they couldn't believe their eyes. The room measured about twelve by ten feet. It had been decorated to a high standard. Thick, embossed lilac-coloured silk cloth with large floral patterns covered the walls. Gas lamps were fitted on two of the walls. There were easels and painting materials at one end of the building. The floor at that end had been laid with lino material. There was no sign of paint spillage. Several classical Japanese landscape paintings hung on the walls. Jorgen was suddenly covered with goose pimples. He had a strange feeling about the paintings. They had a link to the dryness of the gardens, but he couldn't work it out.

Jorgen felt Montgomery staring at him. He could tell that the boy instinctively knew that Jorgen had never been inside that building before and was amazed at what he was seeing.

'Do you know what these are?' Montgomery asked, and without pausing for a response, he continued. 'Japanese ink-washed art. I've seen such paintings before. They're all the rage in Paris.' He turned round to face Jorgen and added, 'You've not been in here before, have you?'

'No,' Jorgen said meekly.

'Why ever not?'

'I don't live here.'

'Where are you from then?' Montgomery said brightly.

Jorgen didn't respond and moved away.

At the other end of the hut there were two small, ornate, round brass tables with matching chairs. One of them was covered with gingham check tablecloth and laid with tarnished silver cutlery and soup and dinner plates for two people. Everything was covered in dust. Wine glasses had been placed next to the plates. An unopened bottle of wine and a corkscrew had been set next to a burnt-down candle in the middle of the table. On the other side of the candle was a small basket containing what looked like the putrefied remains of bread rolls. The other table was bare apart from a copy of *The Times* and an ashtray full of cigar stubs. Everything was laden down with thick cobwebs and dust.

Jorgen was the first to comment.

'What was this place used for apart from painting and eating? And why here? There are so many rooms in Edward's house that he could have used.'

'Who's Edward?'

'The man who owns the house.'

Montgomery, who'd walked over to the bare table, started to speak, but stopped abruptly. 'Take a look at this,' he said, pointing to the newspaper.

'What?'

'The date – Tuesday, seventeen September nineteen ten. This must have been the last time anybody was in here. The table's set for two people'

Jorgen interrupted,

'But where's the other food? The soup and the main course? Why just the bread and wine?'

'That'd be the hot food,' Montgomery said. 'Perhaps it was in the kitchen and they were going to get it when they were ready to eat. Something must have stopped them having the meal that night.' Montgomery slowed down the words in his last sentence as if deep in thought.

'How'd you worked out it was night-time?'

'Candles,' explained Montgomery.' You wouldn't have a meal in the middle of the day using candles, would you? And anyway they could have used the gas lamps.' He paused and looked around the room.

'The newspaper, though. They don't arrive here till late in the afternoon. I think the candles were there because they wanted to make it romantic.'

'Romantic – what's that?' asked Jorgen.

The Lucy Effect

'It's what adults like doing with each other – you know, kissing.'

Jorgen remembered his papa kissing his mother, but there were no candles around at the time. A lot of things that adults got up to mystified him, so he let it pass. He noticed that there was a space on the wall where a painting had been. It must have been the biggest in the hut. A similar-sized painting was in the main lounge; in fact, it was the only painting hanging in the house. It was a picture of Edward and a woman. He had his arm around her. Jorgen had guessed it was his wife. 'I think I know what this is all about,' Jorgen said, smiling. He felt he'd got one over on Montgomery. 'There's a painting missing here, and by its size I'm sure it's the one in the lounge above the fire place. I'm sure it's his wife, Emily'

Montgomery, who seemed now not to want to be outdone, butted in,

'This is their special place! I bet she died the day after the date on the newspaper or shortly afterwards.' He glanced at the wall clock that had stopped many years ago. Seeing the clock must have reminded him of the present time.

'Golly, look! I've got to get back to school. I'm sure dinner time is over. See you tomorrow if that's okay.'

As Montgomery ran out of the door, Jorgen called after him, 'Haven't you forgotten something?' But it was too late; he'd gone. Jorgen picked up the cricket ball and started shining it on his trousers. As he walked out of the hut, the ball sparkled in the sun. Its reflected redness had a warming affect, and the solid, hard feel gave him a sense of strength.

Chapter 31

Montgomery visited the 'Cafe Secrete' as he called it the following day at lunchtime. He told Jorgen the hut reminded him of a place in Paris he'd been to with his parents and sister before the war. It was the general décor, but especially the furniture, the gingham table cloth and the Japanese style of the paintings that illuminated the memory. Although his friends were curious about his absences at dinner time, he told Jorgen that they accepted the story he told him of visiting a relative who was in need of help. He made sure he wasn't seen going into the house across the road by slipping down the side street and using the gate at the back.

Jorgen handed the cricket ball over as Montgomery sat down. He was about to ask his new friend if he wanted some pop, but Montgomery started to wave his hands about. Jorgen had observed the previous day that this was a sure sign that words were going to spill out of the boy's mouth.

'You're not related to Edward are you?'

Jorgen shook his head. He was unsure whether he should tell Montgomery about his situation. There was a pause. Montgomery stared at him and waited in silence until Jorgen couldn't stand it any longer.

'Edward picked me up in Liverpool,' he said quietly.

'What d'you mean, "picked you up"?'

'He mistook me for his grandson and grabbed me.'

'And you went along with him of your own free will?'

'Yes. He said he was going to St Helens.'

'You're talking in riddles. What d'you mean?'

So Jorgen embarked on his harrowing story. He mentioned Edward's strangeness and said that most of the time the old man earnestly believed that Jorgen was Nathan, his grandson. Montgomery interrupted here and related stories he'd read in the newspapers about people living two lives – even people who had two spouses, neither of whom knew about the other. Jorgen didn't believe a word of these stories and put them down to skulduggery. He found it easy talking to Montgomery when the boy wasn't interrupting. There were hardly any traces of deliberate bossiness as had been the case with some older boys he had known. Montgomery wasn't averse to hiding his feelings; he'd blurt them out, but always politely. Trust was gradually building between the two.

Both of their personal needs in the friendship seemed to be satisfied. Montgomery seemed bowled over by the exotic nature of his new friend's plight and was certain he could help him. Jorgen needed someone to confide in and break the monotony of his current life of virtual imprisonment. But more importantly, he was sure he'd found a way of tracking down Frau Stocker. Montgomery's family were well to do and had many contacts in the town, and Montgomery swore that he would never let his parents know about their friendship. After Jorgen's recent experiences, he knew that nothing could be relied on, but he had no alternative. He had to trust Montgomery.

Montgomery was late leaving. It was mainly his own fault; he'd kept interrupting Jorgen's story. Some of his questions weren't relevant, but he seemed intrigued by Jorgen's life in Liverpool. Jorgen realized Montgomery couldn't help asking the questions. Jorgen had to virtually push him out in the end, and they couldn't stop laughing.

Jorgen's friend didn't turn up on the Wednesday, which worried him. But on Thursday when they met, Montgomery explained that he'd been on detention owing to his late return to school.

'So what excuse did you give?' Jorgen asked.

'I said I was helping a German avoid capture, of course.' His face remained straight, but he couldn't hold it for long when Jorgen's lower jaw dropped. After some horseplay between them, Jorgen continued his unfinished story, insisting that Montgomery shouldn't butt in for his own sake – and his school's. When Jorgen mentioned that his great aunt lived in Windle, Montgomery's face brightened, and he stopped his friend, who was in full flow. There had been no hand wave warning. He explained they were in luck. His parents knew the area very well, and there was a chance they could help. The boys spent their whole time together discussing how Montgomery could approach the matter with his parents without giving too much away. Towards the end of the visit, Jorgen became frustrated with Montgomery because the boy was continually dismissing his ideas. Montgomery seemed unaware of how his friend felt. Jorgen's anger approached boiling point as Montgomery announced that he could get a paper round in the area.

'Stop!'' Jorgen said in a voice that needed several decibels shaved off. But it had the desired effect.

Montgomery's face showed disbelief followed instantly by a fierce frown.

Jorgen continued, 'You mentioned weeks back that everyone in school was talking about the *Lucy* going down and Germans being rounded up. You could ask your mates if they know of any Germans in St Helens.' Jorgen had calmed down by the time he finished his suggestion. Montgomery thought about this and said,

'Not such a bad idea. I have a Commie teacher for history – bit of a pacifist. I could say that it was to do with an essay. My parents would fall for that line as well.'

Jorgen was pleased that his idea had gone down well.

'You could try that before any paper round.'

'No, I'll do that as well.'

Jorgen thought his friend had had the last word again. There was no malice in this, though. He was grateful for all the help Montgomery offered. Jorgen was excited. He felt the chances of meeting his great aunt had moved closer. What would her response be? His father had never talked about her; she wasn't part of the family history, unlike his aunties and uncles in Germany. He'd been too young to have picked up on any conversations his mama and papa might have had concerning Frau Stocker.

The boys parted. Jorgen could hear Montgomery whistling as he walked along the path to the back entrance, making sure he was out of sight of all who might take an unwelcome interest.

Edward woke up, startled. He could hear the chants of a strange bird in the garden that he couldn't recognize. But he'd seen it a few moments ago in a waking dream – a large bird, similar to a grouse, but with much brighter colourings. Reds, greens, and even a hint of orange figured in its plumage, and it had the palest of blue eyes. It had something in its beak. The eyes changed to the darkest shade of blue. He knew it had been doing something illicit. Emily might have been able to tell him the meaning of all this. She was that way inclined. These thoughts were curtailed when he heard the back gate shutting. He got up to investigate, but there was no one there except his grandson.

****

Montgomery was at the breakfast table the following morning. He'd been first down after he heard the gong. As well as preparing the breakfast, sounding the gong was one of the maid's tasks. He'd just helped himself to bacon, sausage, and eggs from the silver chafing dishes that kept the food piping hot when the maid gently placed the neatly folded local newspaper on the table. She smiled at Montgomery. He smiled back. He knew she loved the way he appreciated her cooking. Ravenous, he'd demolished half of the bacon when he realized that he'd forgotten the sauce. He went to fetch it and was amazed to see part of a headline on the newspaper: 'Aged German Lady...' He couldn't see the rest of the line because of the way the paper had been folded. The start of the second line began, 'At Home...' He was just about to open the paper when his father walked in, followed by his mother and older sister.

'Morning, Monty. Anything of interest in there?' his father said with a smile on his face. 'It seems to have dragged you away from your breakfast. That's a first!'

'Yes, the porky never leaves his trough,' Ann, his sister, said good-naturedly.

To complete comments from the trio, his mother added,

'Oh, leave the lad alone. He needs all the education he can get!'

'Morning, everybody. No, I just came for the...' He let his sentence taper off, and he returned to his place smartly with the sauce bottle. After dousing his food with the brown liquid, he resumed his well-developed habit of devouring food as fast as he could.

'By the way,' muttered his father, his mouth half full, 'you mentioned yesterday evening that you wanted to ask me something important.'

With his mouth emptied of food, Montgomery caught the last four words.

'Erm, no... I mean I might do. It all depends...'

Delightedly, Ann cried, 'Oh, subterfuge! Subterfuge, it goes on!'

Now normally Montgomery would have relished the attention and bantering. He'd be the one to start such play. His reply was a bit on the thin side, however.

The Lucy Effect

'Ha, ha – the joke's on you. Just wanted to see how you'd rise to the bait. And you did. Ha, ha, and you *did*!' He emphasized the second 'did' by stabbing his last piece of sausage. He excused himself, got up from the table, and rushed out, explaining that he had schoolwork to finish. In his bedroom, he wondered how he was going to get hold of his father's newspaper. His father always took the paper to work with him, and he either left it there or on the train. The solution came quickly and was simple – he'd buy a copy with his tuck money and charge his friend tuck to offset his loss. One way or the other, his lunch-time visit later in the day was looking as if it could be a very eventful one.

Chapter 32

Jorgen arrived at the Cafe Secret earlier than usual. He was excited. It wasn't a boiling-over sort of excitement – more a gentle simmer. He was expecting that Montgomery would have some news for him. He'd poured himself a glass of lemonade from the stock they'd accumulated in the shed and sat down. He was surprised to hear the gate bang. It was too early for Montgomery. But who could be using the gate? No one ever did. There was a noise of swiftly moving feet. The door of the shed flew open. Jorgen nearly knocked over the chair jumping up. He was so unnerved. It was a red-faced Montgomery who confronted him. He carried a newspaper and didn't look too pleased. Far from it – Jorgen had never seen his friend looking so down in the mouth.

'What's going on, Montgomery? You've scared the living daylights out of me.

Montgomery was out of breath. He was shaking his head.

'It's the worst possible news I'm afraid.' Jorgen observed the newspaper in Montgomery's hand. For one dreadful moment he thought that his father had died.

Between breaths Montgomery continued, 'Your great aunt is dead.'

'Are you sure?'

'It's in black and white – her full name, Heide Getrud Stocker, and an address in Windle.' He placed the newspaper on the tablecloth, and he made eye contact with Jorgen, who had glanced up at him briefly. Montgomery began to read, 'Mrs Stoker had been dead for about four weeks. A neighbour said that he was shocked at her death but had not been surprised that she hadn't been discovered for so long. Mr Osbourne said, "She lived the life of a hermit, never seeing anyone." Police stated that they could not find any papers in the house that indicated whether she had a family or not.' Jorgen looked up, but before Montgomery could say anything, they heard a noise outside one of the windows. It was Edward. He was looking straight at them. They managed to get out of the hut just as Edward rounded the corner.

Furious, Edward gave chase but tripped on a paving stone, fell, and banged his head on the closed gate. He fell, unconscious. The boys didn't wait for a confrontation with Edward. 'Wait for me in the woods in the park,' shouted Montgomery. 'It'll be very late, though.' Before Jorgen could reply, Montgomery was off making for the school. Jorgen kept running towards the park, which was about 600 yards away. He occasionally turned round looking for signs of Edward. In the park he stopped running. Some women – they looked like maids or nannies – were pushing prams. They'd been glancing at him. He smiled, and they continued gossiping. He walked around the perimeter of the park keeping to the wooded area out of sight. Finally he decided to plant himself in the middle of the densest area of woodland.

Jorgen sat there for an hour. All seemed lost. The hoped-for refuge with Frau Stocker that had been constantly on his mind since he'd deserted his papa had vanished in the cruellest of ways. He couldn't go back to Edward. What would be the point? He and Montgomery had desecrated the mausoleum that Edward had left in memory of his wife – or that's how it would look. Through the gap in the foliage he noticed a park bench. He made his way towards it. A nearby church clock struck four. The park was virtually empty. He heard the excited cries of children in the distance. He wished he could be one of them. They were playing without a concern in the world, and their mother would be taking them home shortly. They'd have tea and perhaps in the evening their father would be home from work early. He'd have a scrub up, and a dish of steaming hot meat and vegetables would be waiting for him on the table. Afterwards, when the children were ready for bed, he would read them stories. The mother would light the candles and take them upstairs. Jorgen wondered where he'd be sleeping that night. He heard the voices of older children from somewhere in the park. He dashed back to his hideout and crouched down. They were wearing green uniforms – the uniform Montgomery wore. Jorgen wondered if his friend was with them. But he didn't see him.

Four hours passed. The church bells seemed to be issuing a warning. Each time they rang, panic started in Jorgen's stomach and ended up as tight as a noose around his throat. There was no sign of Montgomery. That's when he started wondering whether his friend would show up at all. Montgomery was in enough trouble as it was. Why would he risk getting into more? Jorgen wished he had the photo of his parents. It always calmed him down. He had put the photo together with the sovereigns in an old cloth pouch that Edward had been throwing away. They were in his bedroom. If Montgomery was coming, he knew it would be very late. He decided to go back to the house when it got dark and retrieve the pouch. It was risky, but he was desperate and losing hope. The photograph meant so much to him. It represented the only connection he had with his past.

Jorgen was in one of the lounges. He was perspiring. There'd been a window open at the back of the house. The problem was that, if Edward was following his usual routine, he'd be in the next room studying his family Bible. After about an hour, at ten on the dot, he would retire to bed. It was ten to ten. Jorgen could hear wailing coming from the room, and then it stopped. In between sobs, Edward started talking to himself. Jorgen felt a tinge of pity. He opened the door to the hall quietly and started walking up the wood-panelled staircase. His heart was pounding. As the stairs

The Lucy Effect

wound round and he could no longer see the room Edward was in, he relaxed. He ran up the second flight into his bedroom and gently closed the door behind him.

At first he didn't recognize the room. It was 'his' bedroom. But the table and chairs had been turned over. A mirror had been smashed. The curtains were down, crumpled on the floor. The side of the bed had been lifted up and was resting on a small table. Fortunately the pouch and photograph hadn't been discovered. He'd placed it behind the bed partly covered up by a rug. Edward had wreaked his revenge on the boys' sacrilege. Jorgen wondered what exactly Edward now thought about his grandson. As these thoughts clamoured into his mind, he heard the telephone ring in the hall. After a few more rings, Edward finally answered it. Jorgen opened the door slightly to eavesdrop. Edward was talking to the police. There was mention of two 'evil vagabonds', one in a Cowley College uniform who had 'dirtied and despoiled the objects inside'. Then he caught the words, 'never seen them in my life before… yes the newspaper… no it wasn't mine.'

Edward placed the handset down and dialled a number. He burst into tears when the person answered. It was difficult to hear the conversation, as Edward was sobbing and blubbering for most of time. But the call went on and on. Jorgen heard the town bells chiming eleven o'clock. There was now a greater need for him not to miss Montgomery. Although the police didn't know who the Cowley boy was, they might be able to trace him. Jorgen had to warn him. The bells rang the quarter of the clock. There was no time to wait. He went into the large bedroom that Edward occupied at the rear of the house. As he was climbing out of the window, his foot knocked a vase off the windowsill. It smashed on the wooden floor. He managed to get a good hold of the drainpipe and climb down as quickly as he could. When he looked back, he saw the glowering face of Edward. He was shaking his fist and shouting at the top of his voice, 'Come back, you young scoundrel!'

Chapter 33

Jorgen sped off into the dark night clutching the pouch that contained the photograph. He didn't stop running until he reached the park and was out of sight of the road. There was not a soul around. The bells struck the quarter hour, but he didn't know which quarter. He was convinced that he'd missed Montgomery; that is, if he'd actually turned up. It had started to rain heavily, and the temperature had dropped. He was feeling miserable. The clocks struck midnight. It was like the drawing of a final curtain that was completely closed on the twelfth strike. The show had ended. Should he go to the police? Give himself up? No. He started to walk. He had not a clue as to where he was heading. He strolled out of the main park gates. After a minute or so, he heard the unmistakeable sound of horses' hooves on cobble. It could be danger. Edward would have called the police. He tried to hide behind a lamp post even though it was still lit. The horse and trap drew up beside him. Jorgen awaited his fate.

'Sorry I've taken so long. I'm not surprised you thought I'd given up on you.' It was Montgomery! 'Had to wait till all was quiet. Then when I was about to walk here, it started to pour down. So I went back for the pony and trap. Took me a quarter of an hour to hitch it up, and half that time to get down here. I circled the park once as best as I could, but there was no sign of you. I was on my way home, so you're lucky I caught up with you.'

Jorgen stepped into the trap.

The Lucy Effect

'Thanks. I must admit I was thinking you'd given up on me. Sorry, but how did you manage all this without someone hearing you?'

'Oh, the stables are a bit away from the house. Everybody had gone to bed by ten, even me.'

Jorgen had to smile. Montgomery was wearing a gabardine trench coat two sizes too large for him. But the hat was the most comical. It was an old concertinaed top hat! He handed Jorgen a similar coat. It was a perfect fit. He also handed him a bowler hat. Off the pair went at a gallop. At times Montgomery had to stop, because when they were soaked by torrential showers, he couldn't see to drive.

'Where are we going?' enquired Jorgen.

'My house. We have a dry cellar. I've organized blankets and some food.'

'Do your parents know?'

'What do you think?'

'Look, I've been thinking. You've done enough for me. You're in trouble as it is. I overheard Edward on the telephone talking to the police. He told them that one of us was wearing a Cowley College uniform.'

'Crumbs, you didn't go back to the house, did you?'

'Of course I did! I needed something. You wouldn't understand.' There was silence. Jorgen knew his friend didn't want to talk. Montgomery maintained a steady speed. The roads were deserted. The early morning hour, together with squally showers, meant that even the very few who might have ventured out were under cover somewhere, if they were sober. The others slept beneath soaking newspapers.

Jorgen suddenly shouted in an unconvincing manner,

'Look, stop! Let me out. You're just getting yourself into more trouble!'

Montgomery slowed down and allowed the pony to do the piloting. Turning to Jorgen he said,

'Not on your life. I'm not going to desert you – ever. Golly, we're true friends, patrons de la Cafe Secret!' He pronounced this in deep-throated French.

Jorgen, relieved, couldn't do anything but smile. The heavy shower had stopped. The pony knew where it was going and pulled off the main road onto a half-cobbled way full of pot holes. The trap bounced about, and Montgomery slowed it right down. They turned into a drive, and Montgomery announced,

'Here it is Stoneworthy Hall.

Jorgen saw before him, through the water-ridden darkness, the outline of a massive building. In his eyes it looked four times the size of Cowley Lodge. The pony turned down a narrow drive and then trotted through gates into a walled compound. Along two of the walls there were stables, and they headed for one in which a lamp shone.

'Jolly good girl, Bess', Montgomery whispered. 'The servants' quarters are nearby,' he said to Jorgen. 'We need to keep our voices down.' Steam rose from the pony as the boys unhitched her from the trap. When they were finished, Jorgen followed Montgomery down a paved path, which followed the contours of the building. They reached a back entrance. Here Montgomery fumbled round in the darkness and got hold of a spirit lamp and lit it. They entered the hall in the kitchen area. They passed storerooms and reached a large room. Brass pans that hung from a rack on the ceiling briefly sparkled as Montgomery's lantern passed by. Jorgen felt hungry as the aromas of recently cooked meat and herbs filled his nostrils. They entered a corridor, and after passing a number of doors on their left, they stopped at an alcove on the right-hand side. This led to a door. It was open. They went down stone steps. The cellar was huge and was divided into several rooms. Jorgen observed spiders' webs as the light caught huge, wide pillars of wood that stretched from the floor to the ceiling. These webs massed in the corners between the ceiling and the pillars. Jorgen tried to obliterate this sight from his mind. He had a deep fear of spiders. There was a lamp shining on the floor of the final room they entered. This room backed onto one of the outside walls. Jorgen became calmer when he realized there were no pillars in sight.

Montgomery had prepared a bed on the floor. There were blankets, sheets, and even pillows. Next to the bed was a chamber pot, and on the bed there was food wrapped up in greaseproof paper together with a bottle of lemonade. Montgomery bade him good night and said that he would try to see him early in the morning, although this might be difficult, as the cellar was off the main passage the servants used. Jorgen sat on the bed and opened the package of food. He heard the sound of a distant bell. But he was asleep before the clocks struck the first hour of the day. The lemonade was a sleeping companion, and the package of food fell on the floor. Mice were aroused by the smell of cheese.

Chapter 34

Jorgen woke up in diffused sunlight. It was entering through the cellar's frosted windows on the other side of the wall. For the first few seconds he was in a daze. The previous evening's escapade dawned on him when he spied the greaseproof package. Miraculously, the mice hadn't chewed through it. He tore open the wrappings and devoured the sandwiches. He had no idea of the time, and he didn't venture into any of the other rooms of the cellar, conscious of the multitude of spiders webs. He stood on a wooden box to get a view of the outside through the window grids, but the glass was not clear enough for him to see anything.

Sometimes he would catch the noises from directly above in the kitchen and the servants' quarters. On one occasion he scrambled close up to the box to avoid being seen when he heard the rattle of the cellar doorknob, but no one came down the stairs. The hours passed slowly. He would doze off now and again. Then he made a discovery. He'd taken the loose lid off the box to see what was inside. It was full of books and even some comics. He imagined it was his friend's doing. Montgomery had thought of everything. Jorgen smiled at the chamber pot, which he'd used and placed as far away as possible from the bed. But there was a limit to Montgomery's skill in solving problems. What could he and his friend do now? Only wait. But for what? Jorgen felt so lonely and vulnerable. He was at the mercy of factors he couldn't control. And all the time his friend was getting himself into a heap of trouble.

Then the darkness came. He knew it must be at least ten at night. He'd lit the lantern. It cast flickering shadows around the room and beyond. There were fewer noises from above. Most of the servants were in bed in preparation for their early-morning rising. He heard scratching sounds and imagined the worst. But he realized it was mice. He lay still and the little critters gingerly approached his makeshift bed, whiskers twitching searching for food. Suddenly they scattered as a key turned in the cellar door. Jorgen jumped up and just missed crushing a mouse crouched behind the box. To his relief, it was Montgomery. He was carrying a basin of water and towels. He set these down and picked up the chamber pot. Keeping it at arm's length and holding his head back, he clambered up the stairs. He returned with food and clean clothes in a cane basket.

'I'll leave your clothes in with mine for the maid. She won't notice; she's that way inclined. How are you, by the way? I trust the modern conveniences meet with your approval?'

'Not so bad, really, considering,' said Jorgen. 'But I'm not too keen on the other guests. Don't know about you, but I can't stand spiders!'

'Oh, sorry about that. Could bring in a couple of bats to see them off I suppose,' he said, smiling. Then he added, 'Would bats suit sir then?'

Jorgen was undressing at the time and threw his trousers at his friend. Montgomery ducked and caught them in the basket and then lay down on the bed. He looked very serious. Jorgen plopped himself on the floor and sat hugging his legs. His new trousers were far too short.

'What's up?' Jorgen asked in a subdued voice.

'Some trouble at school. The police have been in. They're interviewing everyone. Of course no one's admitting to being in the Cafe Secret, so we've all been on detention. Some of the lads know I've been going off at lunch times and have kind of been putting two and two together. They got me coming out of school. Threatened me that there'd be fisticuffs if I didn't do the honourable thing and admit tomorrow at school that I was the Cowley boy in Edward's shed.'

'Oh, no!' cried Jorgen. 'I knew this would happen! What did I tell you? What are you going to do? And don't say take a beating. It'll all come out in the end, so taking a beating won't help. You've got to own up. Tell the truth about the cricket ball and that you thought the other boy was Edward's grandson. You'd just become friends, but when Edward caught you, both you ran off and that's the last you've seen of him.'

'I already told Papa exactly that at dinner tonight.'

'What?' Jorgen said, completely stunned by the announcement.

'Had to,' admitted Montgomery. 'The headmaster said that the police would visit the home of every third-year pupil. I realized the game was up. And of course I'd come to the same conclusion you did – that the best way forward now would be to own up.'

Jorgen noticed that his friend was close to tears. His anger was smothered.

'What did your father say?'

'That he was very displeased with my behaviour, and he couldn't understand how I'd been allowed out at lunchtime. But it was my not owning up to the affair that bothered him most.'

'So what's going to happen now?

'He's going up to school with me on Monday. The police will be there. He's already let them know. Rest assured I'll not mention that you are here.'

'But how long can this go on for? We'll be discovered, and you'll be in deep trouble – not just because of all that's happened, but I'm the son of an enemy alien!'

'Look, must go. We'll see what happens on Monday.' Before Jorgen could say anything, Montgomery was climbing the steps and was gone.

Jorgen reached for the pouch and took out the photograph of his parents. He picked the beef sandwiches up without looking away from the photograph and greedily ate them. He thought his parents were telling him that there was nothing he could do. He had to accept what was happening and not be upset. That night he dreamed of giant spiders. They had spun a deep web around him. But there was still an opening left. He was racing to get out before he was entombed. Beyond the hole there was the familiar comforting sound of ships on the river. Would he ever hear them again?

Montgomery visited in the late afternoon on the Monday. The turning of the key had sent Jorgen into a panic. *It can't be Montgomery*, he thought. *It's far too early.* He'd been trying to work out a way of reducing the smells created by using the chamber pot. Nothing would make him venture beyond the room he was in to solve the problem. So he'd decided to turn the wooden box over the pot. Now he couldn't move the box in time to provide cover for himself, as the pot was under it. So he lay down and pulled the bedclothes over himself. The person who approached walked steadily towards him. Then the footsteps stopped. The fingers of the person's hand clutched the bedclothes and tried to yank them back. Jorgen tightly clasped the eiderdown with both hands.

'Jorgen, what on earth are you playing at? It's me, Montgomery!'

'You could have shouted out that it was you! It's still light. I thought you'd never come down at this time of day!' He looked at his friend.

'What's happened?' he asked, his voice rising in panic.

'I've been suspended from school for a week. When I go back it'll be the cane for me. But I'm not bothered.' He paused. A patch of sunlight caught the redness of Montgomery's hair. 'I told them the story that we agreed was the best one to tell. So they think that the last time I saw you was on that Friday. According to the police inspector present, whom Papa knows, Edward does not want to pursue the matter of us breaking into the shed. But he does want the boy who was impersonating his grandson to be apprehended.'

Montgomery could have mentioned more, but he didn't want to upset Jorgen. The inspector had had a quiet word with his papa after the meeting. He said that Edward had been very angry about the other boy who'd hoodwinked him into believing that he was his grandson – the grandson who had been killed in a train accident along with his mother and grandmother four years ago. Police questioning had revealed that the boy had broken into the house and wrecked a bedroom, and that Edward thought he had stolen some jewellery that had belonged to his wife, although he wasn't certain.

All this new information about Jorgen had left Montgomery in a quandary. He wondered just who was telling the truth. Edward was a respectable man – a solicitor, an acquaintance of his papa. Would such a person lie? No doubt it was the fact that Edward knew Montgomery's father that Edward had made it known he wanted all charges to be dropped against Montgomery. Edward had said it was the other boy who had cunningly led Montgomery on, just as he himself had been deceived. In the next breath he'd called Jorgen malicious and devious, and declared that he must be brought to justice.

Montgomery had remembered that Jorgen had told him about his mother and brother dying in a train crash five years ago. It was strange that Edward had mentioned the very same thing. Too much of a coincidence, but what did it all mean? Had Jorgen read a newspaper report about the accident and used the facts to gain his sympathy? One task he must carry out was to search Jorgen's belongings for the stolen jewellery. He couldn't believe what he was thinking. He found himself looking at the facial features of Jorgen. He saw honesty. Wouldn't he have just scarpered when the game was up? And how had he come to know about Frau Stocker?

Chapter 35

When Montgomery had gone, Jorgen took out the photograph of his parents immediately to calm himself down. They hadn't talked about what they were going to do, but Jorgen knew that Montgomery wouldn't let him down. But he didn't want to see his friend take any more risks on his behalf. So it was up to him to act. His gaze fixed on the wooden box, which he'd placed at the entrance to the adjacent room. He wondered whether it would be possible. There were no thoughts about what he would do after he completed the task. He lifted the box off the chamber pot and he carried it over to the wall beneath the window grid. He picked up the knife and fork that Montgomery had left with his food, hoisted himself onto the box, and began chipping away at the mortar that held the grid in place. It was going to take ages.

****

It was later the following evening when it all went wrong. Montgomery had brought some food in and left. They hadn't talked much. Once his friend had gone, Jorgen had started chipping away again at the mortar with the knife. When the key turned once again in the door, he panicked and fell off the box. The knife shot away out of his hand as he hit the concrete floor. By the time he'd picked himself up, Montgomery was in the room, and Jorgen was in full view. Montgomery was holding a folded newspaper. Eying the mortar on the floor and the knife he shouted,

'What on earth are you doing?' His eyes scanned the box, which was covered in debris, and he looked up and noticed the window grid surrounds and the missing mortar. He also noticed a money pouch lying next to the bed. Before he had a chance to say anything, the door of the cellar squeaked open. The game was over.

As Ann reached the halfway point on her descent down the cellar steps, she halted. Should she continue? She'd followed her brother from his bedroom on the landing. There had been something in his erratic movements – a certain nervousness – and besides that, he had been carrying a large basket that she'd never seen before. But as she stood there in the coldness and dark, a thought entered her head. Perhaps she shouldn't go any further. She was a sensitive fifteen-year-old and mature for her age. It might not be in either of their interests for her to surprise him. But it was too late. Montgomery had spotted her.

'What are you up to spying on me?' he shouted angrily. He seemed to be attempting to obscure something from her line of vision.

As she came closer, she knew he was hiding something. The lantern spluttered, and the light increased. Somebody was standing behind her brother.

'Who's that?' she asked, matching his anger.

'Oh, it's no good,' Jorgen said, moving into the light. 'Hello. I am Jorgen Roth, and your brother has been helping me.' Well-travelled Ann recognized the slight German accent right away. She instinctively covered her mouth with her hand as if she hadn't wanted these unimaginable words to be spoken.

'Dear God!' She gave Montgomery a piercing look. 'This is the boy the police are looking for, isn't it? The one you told them you hadn't seen since you ran away from that shed at Mr Aughton's! You've done something terribly wrong, Monty. How could you?' As she spoke, her thoughts chastised her for not turning back on the cellar steps. They kept telling her that all this wouldn't have happened. There was a chance it might have gone away. Now because she knew, the whole family would know. They would be shamed. This couldn't happen. She wouldn't permit it to happen.

Jorgen interrupted her thoughts.

'Please don't blame Montgomery,' he said. 'It's all my fault. I shouldn't have let him get involved—'

'Shush,' Ann interrupted in a determined voice. 'We must act right away. There's no point in going on about who's the villain in the piece.' She turned to her brother. 'You'll have to get him out of here right now.'

'But we can't abandon him just like that!' Montgomery said this in a half-hearted manner.

'We must for our family's sake!' she countered.

Jorgen nodded in approval.

'But we can't just chuck him out,' Montgomery said with more conviction.

'No, I didn't say that. I know somewhere not far away from here where he'll not be disturbed.'

'Hang on,' Jorgen cut in. 'Don't I have a say?'

'No, you haven't a choice,' Ann said firmly. 'Either hand yourself in or fend for yourself. We can't continue to be involved.' Ann was preferring that he wouldn't hand himself in. She actually hoped he'd be apprehended by the police on the run and there would be little chance of a comeback on the family. They'd be out of the picture.

'Look, I don't want to hand myself in to the police,' said Jorgen. 'They'll put me away. I have friends in Liverpool. They might help.' He was floundering. He did have friends in Liverpool, but he doubted they could help. Everyone lived too close together and knew everyone's business. But the idea of being put away made him think that returning to his neighbourhood was the better plan, if he could call it that. At least he'd be nearer the place where he'd last seen his papa. And for all he knew, he might find out what had happened to him.

At half past eleven Montgomery and Jorgen hitched the pony and trap up and set out. It was a warm pleasant night. The sky was clear. There were myriads of stars. It seemed too perfect in comparison to the mood the boys were in. The plan was to drop Jorgen off in a gazebo on an estate several miles away in Rainhill. Ann was friendly with the daughter of the family who owned the land. She knew they'd be able to gain access, and it was rarely used so Jorgen wouldn't be disturbed. He could remain there for as long as he liked, but he would have to fend for himself. There was a station nearby, and he could get a train to Liverpool. He had money, so that wouldn't be a problem. They nearly missed the turn off for the estate, but Montgomery caught sight of the gazebo, a large rounded building with stone walls. It was shaped like a lighthouse and had a dome at its top. This was Jorgen's destination. The boys hastily got out of the trap and shook each other's hand. Montgomery passed Jorgen a lantern and wished him luck. There were few words spoken. Jorgen had noticed a coldness in Montgomery. The pony and trap vanished into the darkness. He turned round and looked at the strange building caught in the grey light of a waning moon. Jorgen was on his own once again. The world seemed boundless, and he was the minutest of specks.

Jorgen hadn't slept all night. The folly was full of strange noises. Floorboards creaked even when not walked over. The slits in the folly's walls posed as windows. They followed the spiral staircase all the way to the top of the eighty-foot tower and a viewing platform. Creating a giant musical instrument, they encouraged the wind to speak with multi-pitched voices. But it was the out-of-this-world cries of unknown wild animals in the nearby copses that gnawed at his nerves. Jorgen had never

The Lucy Effect

experienced the country at close range, and as he went in and out of a half sleep, he imagined the creatures involved in ding dong verbal battles with the gazebo's voices. He heard scratching noises as if the maddened gangs of animals outside had had enough and were trying to get in.

He left the gazebo early. His only aim now was to reach Liverpool as soon as he could. It was dark, and the rain pelted down. He tried to keep under the trees for shelter. Underfoot, the ground was treacherous, and he slipped every so often on the sodden undergrowth. He discovered a path that gave him greater confidence, but hadn't realized that it led to a gulley. Suddenly he was pitched forward. He felt searing pain in his right foot as sharp iron teeth snapped tightly shut on it. He fell headlong into the mud and let out a yell as much as his dirt-filled mouth would allow. Tethered by the trap, he screamed and shouted until he was hoarse. Then he noticed a man with a gun.

Chapter 36

On the Monday of the following week, within ten minutes of entering Quirk's Orphanage for Boys in Catherine Street Liverpool, everyone bar the absentees on that morning knew that Jorgen was German. The news spread like a forest fire in a wild wind that blew in all directions. He'd been brought in by two police constables just before breakfast. That in itself caused more than the usual amount of attention a boy received when he first walked into the building. The headmaster had not been around, so the party had been dealt with by the deputy, Captain Swithins, who had behaved impeccably. He was a man who was always careful not to stand on a single worker ant in the company of even the most humble of entomologists. Once the paperwork had been completed and the constables had left, Swithins jumped out of his chair and stood inches away from the boy.

Jorgen stood awkwardly his right foot was still painful when he put his weight on it.

'Well, Hun boy, we've got you now!' Swithins said. 'Constables said that no words come out of that mouth since you were captured apart from whinging, hey. We'll have you talking like it comes out of the other end too quick for your liking, Hun boy!'

There was silence. Beads of perspiration trickled down Jorgen's temples and cheeks. Swithins took his time as he paced around the boy. He'd picked up a cane, and he tapped the end of it on the floor in time with his leather-on-lino footsteps. He looked at the boy closely and smiled. Again he stood facing Jorgen, a hand's length between them. He pressed the cane, at first without much pressure, on the injured foot. Jorgen let out a yelp.

'What's up, Hun boy? Explain yourself!' Jorgen remained silent. He dug his fingernails into the palms of his hands. He was shocked. How could it be happening? Swithins was a schoolmaster. The man's behaviour was beyond his comprehension.

'I didn't hear that, Hun boy,' Swithins said with a snarl. 'Speak up!' Swithins sank the cane further into Jorgen's foot. The searing pain was unbearable.

'Please stop,' he blared, his face contorted.

'Please stop what, Hun boy?'

Jorgen couldn't think what he had to say. He looked into Swithins' white, tense face. Piercing dark eyes looked down on him full of hatred. In a flash he knew what it was: 'Sir'.

That was Jorgen's painful baptism into the orphanage. Half an hour later he found himself in the attic, also known as the goal, on solitary confinement after a fight with three other boys, which had been orchestrated by Swithins.

Jorgen stared at the rusty grate in the cold fireplace. It contained only a thin layer of grey dust and clinker. There were three other aspects of the attic that claimed Jorgen's attention – the plain, dark-brown and bottle-green walls thick with dust; a dirty brown ceiling crisscrossed with lines where the plaster had fractured; and the one he spent most time with – only because it was next to the wooden bed where he lay – the slate rooftops and blackened chimneys that were just visible through the small windowpanes that were more grime than glass. This was his sixth day and night in the room without any human company. He had another to go. The clocks in the city chimed twelve. His stomach churned. His heart pounded. It was time. Heavy footsteps progressed up the wooden stairs, the man cursing at each step. The clunk of the tray as it was placed on the landing floor. The deliberate rattling of keys in the door lock. Then the hated form stood erect before Jorgen. His face was smooth skinned, the nose red like a cherry, his mouth small, his lips thin barely parted, his eyelids half closed like those of a haughty camel. All of this combined into a face that, when smiling, seemed pleasant enough and trustworthy to those people who were unaware of his darker side. To the boys he persecuted day and night, nothing could be further from the truth.

'You're not still 'ere are you, Hun boy?' Jorgen jumped to attention. 'Oh, I see you've left unwanted business for me.' The man glanced at the chamber pot. 'Why on earth did you do that? You know it doesn't pay.' He banged the tray containing the bread and water onto the wooden bed. Little water remained in the cup. The man lifted the thick cane off the tray. 'Bend!' he clipped. Jorgen automatically fell onto his knees and draped himself over the bed, his eyes screwed shut as he waited for the blows. There were always three thwacks aimed at his backside in rhythm with the syllables of 'un-wan-ted'. Jorgen held the tears back until the key was turned in the lock and he heard Swithins' heavy steps on the landing outside, then he pushed himself up onto the bed using his good foot and lay on his side; to lie otherwise would be too painful.

He'd lain on the bed for ten minutes before the keys in the lock turned again. A boy had been sent to collect the chamber pot and tray. Jorgen relaxed. It wasn't 'Bullhead', the boy who'd picked a fight with him on the first day and who continued to make his life a misery. Swithins had ordered this boy to collect and empty the chamber pot from the room. Each day the boy had punched Jorgen on a part of his body that was covered by clothes to avoid leaving tell tale marks. This new boy was black. But it wasn't the colour of his skin that seemed out of place to Jorgen; rather, it was the fact that he smiled at him as he collected the chamber pot and tray, and then he closed the door quietly. Didn't he know Jorgen was German?

The tall black boy returned the following morning just before lunch on the day of Jorgen's release.

'You have to come with me now please,' he said. 'My name is Vincent, and I know you're called Jorgen. I hope your injuries are not too painful. I will assist you down the stairs and will be very careful. We must go to the dining room for dinner.' Vincent was taller than Jorgen and a few years older. It was the way he spoke that intrigued Jorgen. He enunciated his words at a snails pace without any hint of an accent, and he showed Jorgen colossal respect. This respect was not just in the way he spoke, but was also in his body language, and especially his gentle smiling eyes and the way he helped Jorgen up and held him securely around his waist mindful of his injured foot. Other young blacks he'd met were rough and ready and spoke pigeon English.

The other boys were filing into the hall. Jorgen was amazed at how many of them there were. At the end of the hall was a raised dais on which the head, his deputy, the matron, and the teachers sat at a long table facing the boys. Below and in front of the dais stood another table at which older boys were serving hot food. Four rows of tables and benches that sat twenty boys per table were set at right angles to the dais. Vincent helped Jorgen to their places at the end of a table and went to get some food for both of them. On his return, he sat down and started eating. Jorgen was still standing, and with some difficulty began to eat the dinner that Vincent had placed in front of him. It was too painful for Jorgen to sit down.

Swithins hadn't noticed Jorgen at first, as he'd hurtled off the stage to give another boy a clip around the ears because he had been whispering, but when he was returning to his place, he observed Jorgen. He made for the end of the tables.

On the stage the matron whispered something to the head, and as Swithins reached Jorgen, the head shouted to him to desist. 'Have Vincent take the new boy to the sickroom,' he ordered.

Swithins returned to his seat sat down heavily and yanked his chair closer to the table. His face was red. Moments later, in a show of temper, he pushed his unfinished meal into the centre of the table and rose, knocking his chair backwards onto the floor before rushing out of the dining hall.

The sickroom smelt of a mixture of carbolic soap and iodine. Jorgen lay on his side on a bed that had the whitest of cotton sheets that he had ever seen. The room was warm even though the window was open. The sun, high in the sky, had vanquished the morning mist many hours ago. He felt drowsy, but his new friend's infectious laughter pulled him away from sleep every time it was ready to overcome him.

'I think we should steer well clear of Swithins,' said Vincent. 'He'll have it in for us for sure. You should have seen his face when the head told him to stop. He couldn't believe his ears! But it was the matron's doing. They don't get on those two – Swithins and Matron. She will be having a few words with him when she discovers the state you're in. The head wouldn't have done anything if she hadn't been there. Swithins seems to rule the roost along with the head. He's got some hold on the head.' Vincent spoke slowly and seemed to choose his words with care. There was a softness in his voice, which soothed Jorgen.

'How long have you been here?' asked Jorgen.

Vincent was looking out of the window. Jorgen followed his gaze. The smile vanished from Vincent's face when he spotted Swithins with Bullhead on the playground. The smile soon returned, however.

'Since the end of May. It was at the time of the riots. Our house was set alight and—'

Jorgen interrupted.

'But I thought it was only Germans they were after.'

'No, it spread to others whom some people consider "different". For many rioters it was just an excuse to rob and loot and get some excitement. But with us...' He paused, and Jorgen noticed tears welling in his eyes. 'It's because we're German.'

'You? German? But how can that be? You're from an empire country, aren't you?'

'Yes, but from the wrong empire – the German African Empire.' Vincent stifled his tears and put on a faint smile, but Jorgen could tell by the tautness in his face that he was upset.

'But what on earth are you doing in Liverpool?'

'My tribe sent me to get an English education.' Jorgen wondered why, as his English was better than his own. 'I came in July last year with my uncle from Kamerun,' explained Vincent. Then he broke down. His body shook as he sobbed, and he turned away from Jorgen.

There was a pause in the conversation as Vincent composed himself. Jorgen didn't know whether he should ask but he plunged in.

'What about your uncle?'

'My uncle. The last time I saw him was that night in May when it began, after the weekend the *Lusitania* went down. We got separated, and when I went back to the house early the next morning, it was still burning. There was nobody around. I went to the police station, but no one knew what had happened to him. They brought me here and said they'd make further enquiries, but I've heard nothing.'

There was a knock at the door. They were both startled. Nobody knocked to come into any room at Quirk's usually. It was the matron. Neither of the boys had met her, although Vincent had told Jorgen that he had seen her at school assembly the previous week when she'd been introduced to the staff and boys. She was in her forties and wore a dark-blue, knee-length uniform with a leather belt that pinched in her already-slim waist. A nurse's starched cap was perched on her head, secured with hairpins, and she wore black stockings and shoes, which were highly polished.

The clothes made her look stern, but her smile and kind eyes soon put pay to such ideas.

'I'm Matron,' she said kindly to the boys, 'and I don't think I've cast eyes on either of you. What are your names?'

When the boys had responded, she continued, 'Right. Roth, let's have a look at you then.' She checked a sheet of paper she held in her hand.

'I see you've been with us for only a week and have been in detention during that time for fighting.' While Jorgen explained to Matron what had happened, she checked his injuries. Her smile vanished and her bouncy, bright speech lowered an octave and became serious.

'We'll treat these weals on your bottom with iodine just in case they turn infectious. But I think there'll be a visit to the hospital to have someone look at that foot. No work for you, young man, school or otherwise. You've got to rest that injury. I'll have a bed made up for you in this room for the time being, and we'll see how you get on.' Her smiled returned, and as she was about to go out of the door, she said to Vincent, 'I'll get some hot water arranged, and he can have a bath here, but you'll need to assist him, Eteki.'

'Attacki! What sort of name is that?' Jorgen said, and like a safety valve blowing, bursts of hearty laughter released their tension.

Chapter 37

The following three weeks saw Jorgen settle into the routines of the home. The regular sequence of events during the day calmed him. The bell woke him at seven. Breakfast was at eight, dinner at twelve, tea at four, and bedtime was at eight. School and play occupied the other hours of the day. On two of the days, he'd gone to the hospital with Matron. It reminded him of a special day in the past. He remembered vividly the day his mother, weeks before she'd died, took him somewhere on their own and fussed over him a lot. It could have been any kind woman who sparked this memory; it happened to be Matron.

For Vincent, too, life at the home had improved. The constant bullying by Bullhead and his gang, which had gone on since his first day, suddenly halted. What surprised both boys most was how Swithins and Bullhead now deliberately kept out of their way.

The boys in the orphanage had already benefited from a changed regime that had been put into place after the new matron had been appointed. It was evident in the dining hall. Swithins was no longer pouncing on boys who talked at dinner and boxing ears. The prefect on the table would issue a verbal warning instead. Swithins still marked down these infringements in his small notebook, but as there was no immediate pleasure in punishing the boys, he seemed less interested in their behaviour, and the boys noticed that he would sometimes forget to note down a boy's name for a later ticking off.

These changed patterns in discipline caused difficulties for the head. Just before Swithins' appointment, there'd been a problem with the accounts, and the head had been to blame. He hadn't committed a criminal offence, but he knew it was a sacking affair. He'd appointed Swithins mainly because of his financial wizardry even though his references were poor. He had allowed him to take over the books, and within days the orphanage's financial problems were resolved. Swithins never let the head forget how much he owed him. The head had given him a free hand in the area that most interested him – discipline. He'd allowed his deputy to get on with it, although at times he felt uneasy about the more extreme of his actions.

That was until Matron came along. She held an important bargaining chip. She was a family friend of the orphanage's newest and most generous benefactor, who was also a trustee, and she held strong views on issues like discipline. So the head realized he couldn't ignore her. He also realized that the relationship between Swithins and Matron was extremely contentious. He had to keep them apart at all costs. The situation was a powder keg waiting to blow.

Swithins also couldn't ignore Matron, and this bothered him. He was aware that the head saw her as something of an independent modern-day lady with a penchant for trouble, but to Swithins she was a meddling suffragette, and he was desperate to be rid of her, but he knew he had to be careful.

****

Jorgen was allocated a bed in Vincent's dormitory with the under tens. They should by all rights have been in the older boys' room, but there hadn't been any beds. Vincent had mentioned to Jorgen that it was a good job, as Swithins was the master responsible for that dormitory, and Bullhead and his henchmen ruled the roost there. All dormitories were locked after lights out at 7.30. The master responsible for the under tens' dorm was known affectionately as 'Biddie' Jones. He slept in an adjacent bedroom on the same landing. He was a small, quiet, balding, and bespectacled Welshman. When he was in a good humour, he hummed Welsh hymns and occasionally called his boys by their first names when they were not in school. He allowed them to talk in the dormitory, but would never let it get out of hand.

In those weeks Jorgen and Vincent got to know each other well. It was inevitable. They had been thrown together because the boys, particularly the older ones, saw them as the enemy. The focussed hatred of the times that affected most institutions in the country ensured the boys were subject to sly digs and vicious name-calling to which most of the staff turned a blind eye. That didn't seem to be the case with Jones. Jorgen and Vincent sensed this atmosphere of support from Jones even though he kept his distance.

Jones wouldn't condone that sort of behaviour in his classroom or dormitory. He was averse to any display of favouritism being displayed to any child. Jones seemed to know that the boys supported each other and he left them to it. Often when he checked the dormitory at nine he could hear Jorgen and Vincent nattering away and shook his head to his invisible audience and walked away. Little did he realize that a plot was a-foot.

Jorgen was determined to find out about his father. He realized the only practical way forward was to visit the neighbourhood where he'd lived and ask questions. It would be impossible to do this during the day, for they were never allowed out of the orphanage unless supervised. Then Vincent had an idea, although he told Jorgen that he thought it posed too many risks; in fact, initially he hadn't wanted to mention it. His plan was that Jorgen should deliver a note late at night to his best friend asking for any details on the whereabouts of his father. He should ask the friend to send the message back in some way. Then it all started to fit together, as one idea begat another.

Kenny had been Jorgen's best friend before the troubles began. He happened to have a newspaper round and was likely to be the first one up in the morning and be the one to discover the note. The orphanage used a swimming baths that Kenny was familiar with. Kenny could screw up his return message underneath a loose stone that was part of a water fountain that both Kenny and he knew about. This could be done on the day Jorgen and Vincent would be at the baths with the other boys from the orphanage. The only other arrangement to make was the evening on which Jorgen was to venture out, and that was easy. It was to be after ten, under the cover of darkness the next Saturday. That way, if he'd been up half the night, he wouldn't have to face a full day's lessons the following day. Remembering his last excursion in St Helens, he murmured that at least a visit to a post office, especially one with a bell, wouldn't be on the agenda. Vincent interpreted this as a chant to ward off evil spirits. So, curiously to Jorgen, Vincent responded by nodding his head and repeating what Jorgen had said to himself.

Chapter 38

The big night came. Jones had turned off the lights and bade all the boys good night at 7.30. Jorgen and Vincent hadn't made any noise until they were sure everyone in the dormitory was sound asleep. They'd spent the time before the departure going over their plans and making sure every contingency was covered.

It was a cloudy evening, and darkness arrived early. Just before ten, Jorgen slipped out of the open window and climbed down the drainpipe. But he lost his footing halfway to the ground and fell heavily on his right foot. Jorgen didn't seem to move, and Vincent was about to climb down to help when he saw Jorgen pick himself up off the ground. He hobbled to the perimeter fence and just about managed to lift his body over. Vincent looked on anxiously. He knew he couldn't take Jorgen's place. He'd never be able to navigate the city, most of which was unknown to him. There was nothing he could do. He pushed the window further up and hung half of his body out straining to see whether his friend was still moving. He caught sight of him turning a corner, and then he was gone out of sight. The next three hours or so seemed like twelve. He'd never before been so anxious. When he was anxious, he usually paced around. This was impossible in the dormitory, so to compensate he got in and out of bed repeatedly. Every so often he walked to the window. His walk was as hushed and as purposeful as the one used when hunting and animals were near, and the snapping of a twig would put pay to bagging game.

At the window, his hunter's eyes tried to pierce the dark as he willed the figure of Jorgen to spring out.

Vincent was asleep when his friend returned. Stones struck the window. Some entered the dormitory, hitting the ceiling and bouncing onto the floor. A pebble hit his bed. He jumped up. Forgetting his earlier hunter's guiles, he rushed to the window. Jorgen was clutching at the drainpipe with one foot on the ground. His lips were moving, and he was making sounds. But they were inaudible; Vincent couldn't understand a word. Waving, Jorgen beckoned Vincent to climb down. As Vincent reached the ground, he noticed curtains move in the dormitory above. Jorgen whispered,

'I can't climb with this foot.'

Vincent thought it was too late to whisper now.

'Get on my back.' He crouched down with some difficultly in his tight-fitting nightshirt. 'I can bear your weight, but I'm not sure the drainpipe will hold. It seems a bit loose to me.' They were about one foot away from the window when there was a to-and-fro movement of the pipe. Suddenly the bracket above them detached from the wall, but Vincent had already grabbed the windowsill. Working together, the boys managed to pull themselves into the dormitory. Half the drainpipe fell to the ground, but the sound was muffled by the grassy lawn.

'Phew!' remarked Jorgen. 'That was close!' But before he could say anymore, a key was thrust with force into the lock, and the door burst open. Swithins bounded in, closely followed by Jones. The game was up.

Swithins said nothing, although his contorted face said it all. He darted to the half-open window and saw the broken and rusted drain pipe lying on the lawn.

'Right,' Swithins growled. 'Downstairs double quick to the office, and wait there.' He had his cane in his hand and whacked Vincent on the back as he approached the door. Jorgen, who had fallen to the floor, was struggling to get up, but he fell back down. Jones quickly intervened, obviously sensing Swithins' mood, and asked Vincent to help his friend. Swithins shot him a scathing look of anger. As Swithins walked out of the room, he shouted at Jones, at the same time turning to cast his eyes over the boys in the dormitory, who by now were fully awake and sitting up in bed.

'You're far too lax, far too lax. There'll have to be changes here!' Swithins warned.

The boys, who had been excited spectators at the scene, lay down almost in unison when they overheard these words. They knew it was dangerous to cross Swithins, especially in the state he was in.

The two boys waited outside of the head's office for four hours. Jorgen had spent the first two hours lying on a bench opposite the office in defiance of Swithins because of the pain in his foot. At six o'clock he'd had to give up the post. It was too dicey. The imagined wrath of Swithins was a hundredfold worse than any beatings he could inflict. Word had spread rapidly, and a string of boys came to see the spectacle of the absconders. Jorgen and Vincent were like the Christians paraded in the Roman coliseums before the ravenous lions leaped. The offenders stood there till breakfast was over. Jorgen was leaning on his friend keeping his injured foot off the floor when a door opened. To their relief, it was matron. The boys sprung apart as if the door had been a switch that had turned on a jolting current. She looked at them but passed by the expected smile absent.

The next time Jorgen saw her was through the banister rails when he was on all fours crawling up the wide oak panelled staircase with Swithens literally on his heels. His cane was aimed at Jorgen's feet, when they stopped moving he would take a swipe enough to smart but not to injure.

'One hundred and sixty eight hours in the clink for you me boy, not one less, that'll loosen your tongue all right'.

Swithins was smiling. Although the head had tried to intervene, a week in the goal had been the outcome of the meeting for Jorgen. Vincent, for his part, was denied treats for the same period of time. The head was in an impossible position, as Jorgen would not mention anything of the night's excursion. The questions fired at him were met with a stolid silence. Swithins had wanted to use the cane, but the head had intervened. As Swithins left the office dragging Jorgen by the ear, his boss reminded him that he wouldn't countenance the goings on of Jorgen's last incarceration. Swithins had scowled.

Matron, heckles raised, cried out, 'And what d'you think you're doing, Mr Swithins?' Swithins knew that the head would not intervene in the melee that followed. The last time he'd seen the head, the man had been in his office, sitting at his desk, head down, pretending to go through some papers. Swithins also knew that the head could hear every word that passed between himself and Matron.

'I beg your pardon. Who on earth do you think you are, woman?'

'As you well know, I'm the matron of this establishment, and you, sir, are its affirmed bully. How dare you propel this injured mite up the stairs in that manner!' It was at this point that Swithins jumped down two of the stairs together and placed himself a few feet away from Matron. He clutched her arms in vice-like grips and proceeded to shake her. He'd lost it. His face turned purple with rage as he looked her squarely in the eyes and mouthed obscenity after obscenity that included words such as *Hun* and *Jews* and *out of place* and *bombardment* and *blown to pieces*. The sounds echoed around the nearby rooms, and children ran to doors hoping for a glimpse of the action only to be shepherded back onto their pews. Teachers lingered at their classroom doors not wanting to miss a second of the astounding confrontation unfolding before their eyes. Matron was normally a person who could easily take

The Lucy Effect

control in a quiet manner and never showed panic, but now she screamed. Suddenly the head was in between them parrying blows delivered by Swithins. Some male staff members came to the aid of the head and gradually calmed Swithins down. They dragged him from the staircase to the head's office and slammed the door.

By this time, Matron, who was shaking in fear and anger, found herself sitting on the stairs attempting to restore her usual unshakeable composure. Jorgen had retreated backwards down the stairs on all fours, and he reached out his hand to comfort her. For a split second she succumbed to his offer and placed her hand on his. New born tears prickled in her eyes, but she aborted them as she realized she could not allow herself to be treated in such a way by an orphan. She stood up, having finally brought the trembling under control. Vincent had run over to Jorgen and was helping him up. Matron, now fully in control, led them both to the sickroom and quietly closed the door behind her.

Swithins was suspended for a week pending a meeting of the board. Matron curiously had not asked for his dismissal on the grounds of the assault. This had partly swayed the trustees not to go down this road, but it was the head who'd managed to carry the day. He'd argued that such an action wouldn't be in the interest of the orphanage, because it would bring the matter to the attention of the outside world, and the orphanage was likely to be at the mercy of the newspapers. Their patrons and creditors would be very displeased, and the future of the orphanage and its staff would be compromised. Of course the children's lives would be disrupted as well. The head was secretly relieved at the board's decision, as he wondered how Swithins would react if he was told he'd been sacked. He might spill the beans on the head's underhand activities in dealing with the orphanage's financial affairs.

Chapter 39

While Swithins was out on suspension, Jorgen and Vincent were moved to the senior dormitory, as two of the sixteen-year-olds had left for domestic work that week. The head hadn't wanted this, as he realized Swithins' dismissal wasn't going ahead, but what could he do in the circumstances? The beds that Jorgen and Vincent had occupied previously had already been taken by younger boys who'd been on the waiting list for weeks. Jones was looking after the dormitory; he was under the impression he was doing so until the head found a replacement for the Deputy Head. Swithins' sudden absence created problems for the school. Classes had to be rearranged and supervision duties changed, but this didn't affect the children. Quite the opposite; the oppressive atmosphere that Swithins instantly created as he walked into any room or corridor affected everyone within range. Now this oppression was gone, and there was a liberating lightness that wasn't just exclusive to the children.

When Swithins returned to the orphanage after a week's absence, he learned that Matron had objected to the board's decision to sack him. In fact, she was the reason he still had his job. He was amazed that she'd reacted in this way and couldn't fathom out the reason. At first he was a bit suspicious, but Matron seemed to be making a genuine effort to leave the past behind them. She smiled at him whenever they passed. In the dining hall, instead of appearing to be just about bearing Swithins sitting next to her, she engaged in conversation with him. Initially he

The Lucy Effect

responded with a polite yes or no, but little by little, he gave in. And there he was at the end of the first week chatting to her about Jorgen of all people. This deception wasn't easy to go along with, but he knew he had to do it for the sake of his job. The kernel of hatred still burned ferociously deep inside Swithens for all that Jorgen stood for, and all that he had done to him.

****

Jorgen and Vincent first heard of their tormentor's return when they were in the senior boys' line in the corridor on their way into the hall for morning assembly. In Chinese-whisper-style, the message of his reappearance spread down the line rapidly. Unlike Chinese whispers, the message hadn't changed in substance by the time it reached the last boy in the junior line. Staff members tried to hush the excited whispers, but they were unstoppable, and the staff members gave up in the end. At first Jorgen was hoping beyond hope that it was a trick – something cobbled together by pranksters for an easy laugh afterwards in the playground. But he knew by the way the staff didn't seem to have the will to snuff the news out that it was true. He glanced back at Vincent, who was six boys behind him in the line, to see his reaction. His white palms shot up, and his mouth moved in an exaggerated fashion framing silent oaths in his native tongue. Jorgen prayed, not with hands together, but with white-knuckled passion as his nails dug into his palms. But his prayer was not answered, as there on the stage was Swithens, thin lips tightly shut, eyes all over the place, and next to him a smiling matron. Just before all the boys had finished trooping in, Matron turned to Swithins, still smiling, and said something to him. He moved his head slightly in her direction. A brief smile flickered and was gone. Jorgen had seen it all now. Not only was his arch enemy back again, but he seemed to have Matron in tow. There was a knot in his stomach, his right foot twinged, and he shuffled from one foot to the other. He caught Vincent looking at him. Jorgen mouthed a silent 'in lavs' to him, and Vincent nodded.

The lavatory stood next to the main school building on the playground. It was a more recent addition to the main hall, as it had been purpose built when Quirk's Mansion was purchased by the charity. It meant that, when the boys were out of doors in the games field or playground, they had no need to re-enter the building, so the doors could be locked for security purposes. High, rusting fences surrounded the whole of the plot that had been Quirk's Mansion, replacing the hedgerows that had been present when the estate was created in the eighteenth century.

The lavatory was something of a safe house where boys sought refuge. The place stank to high heaven, so refuge was bought at a high price. The building contained rows of cubicles with barn doors that didn't reach either the floor or the ceiling. It was possible to hide if someone was looking under the door, but impossible if they gained the higher view. It was standing room only, as use of the toilet seat, if there was one there, was not recommended because of their unhygienic state, although for many boys such conditions were normal and they couldn't care less. The striking feature of the cubicles was the primitive artwork on the walls describing all sorts of bodily functions. Boys being boys, each was hell bent on producing the most shocking image. The Bullhead clan used four of the ten cubicles, and woe betide anyone who might enter and be caught.

It was playtime, and Jones was on yard duty. Half the school had gone off to the baths for a swimming competition. The day was scorching hot, and the aroma in the lavs was breathtakingly strong. All this meant that there were fewer boys around, and of these none would willingly seek out a hot, fly-ridden khazi. If Paul and Vincent were caught, they knew Jones would be lenient; in fact, in all probability, he'd leave them alone. It was an ideal opportunity for them to have a private chat. Now that they'd been moved to the senior's dormitory and were seven beds apart, chances of quiet talks were almost nil. When the coast was clear, Jorgen and Vincent darted into the toilets separately and carefully chose two adjacent cubicles that were for the commoners. Jorgen pinched his nose and tried to reduce his breathing because of the number of flies. In the end he gave up both, as they made speaking impossible. He spoke quickly and in short spurts, not letting Vincent respond, as he desperately needed to deflate the ballooning anxiety that was building up.

'Bloomin' heck – the pong! How come he's back? It's the worst thing. Did you see Matron? She was smiling and chatting with him! Who'd have believed it? He attacked her. You saw it. What's going on?' He had to pause; his mouth was thick with flies.

Vincent gave Jorgen's words some thought, and in a slow and calm way, as the flies didn't seem to bother him, said,

'What you see and believe sometimes are not the truth. You would know this if you played chess. To topple a king, you might sacrifice queen.' This was the future Prince Eteki speaking, but Jorgen couldn't understand this statement and dismissed it as mumbo jumbo.

'Chess – what's that?' His voice rose an octave. 'What are you saying, Vincent? That she's got a knife behind her back and is waiting to get him?' His shirt was sticking to his sweat-covered torso. He was irritated that Vincent seemed to be talking in riddles. Vincent didn't respond. Jorgen figured he was waiting for him to calm himself down. Jorgen's temper could be like a red rag to a hot, sweaty bull.

'I must get away,' Jorgen stated. 'They've got my sovereigns. I'll get hold of them, go down to St James Street, and get in touch with me friends. They might let me stay. If they don't, well there's that big hotel next to the railway station. I'll stay there.' There was silence, and Jorgen was suddenly overcome with vertigo for the first time in his life. When he looked at the door, he saw a shimmering, jewel-shaped object moving in his vision. He kicked the door open and ran outside and crouched down thinking he might vomit. In between gasping and retching, he took in deep gulps of air and soon felt calmer. The diamond had disappeared, only to be replaced by Vincent's face. As his friend bent over him, Jorgen gradually felt more himself.

'What happened in there?' asked Vincent.

'Just felt strange, and I was seeing things like glittering diamonds that floated in front of my eyes – but nothing was there. Then I was walking all over the place like when you come off the Walzer at the fair.'

'Probably the heat,' advised Vincent. 'But you should have grabbed out for that diamond! It might have come in useful on your travels!' he teased.

Jorgen did not respond. Instead he piped up angrily, 'Have got to do something right away now that Swithins is back. He's definitely going to be out for my blood.'

Vincent hesitated as if he was sorting out the right words.

'Look, wait till I find out if that friend of yours has left a note for you at the baths. If he has and wants to help, then maybe you could think about that. But it's risky. Absconders who don't return are expelled, and who knows what would happen to you then?'

Jorgen didn't respond, and Vincent seemed encouraged.

'You could go to Matron and tell her about your father and what you've been through since May. I've told you what happened to me. Matron's written to the Red Cross to see if there's any way they can help me return to my homeland. They might be able to find out where your father is.'

'But you don't understand,' said Jorgen as he turned towards Vincent. 'My papa told me that, as a German and a child without a family, I'd be imprisoned in the workhouse. That's why I haven't given anything away.' Jorgen's anger showed in his strained face.

'They know you're a German anyway, and what do you think this place is if not a sort of prison?' asked Vincent. 'We're locked in here and are ordered about. Why would they send you to the workhouse? Maybe they would if you did bad things. Running away might be bad to them.'

At that moment the bell rang, and they ran towards the boys who were lining up in front of Jones, who turned and unlocked the door to the school entrance.

'Promise you'll wait till Wednesday before you do anything,' Vincent whispered, and Jorgen nodded. He didn't hear Jones tell them off for talking. He was deep in thought about how to keep out of Swithins' way for the rest of the week.

Chapter 40

Swithins had maintained a low profile on his return, making sure he kept in line. He was on a probationary period for three months, so any harsh direct physical contact with Jorgen and Vincent he'd left to Bullhead's mob. There were beatings in the lavatories when Swithins was on yard duty, beatings that left no identifying marks and no witnesses. Even if there were witnesses, they wouldn't dare report these goings on. At night-time the mob gained access to the dormitory early and soaked their beds with water. On the first night, they thought it was a one-off welcoming gesture from Swithins. When it was repeated on the Tuesday night, they knew otherwise.

There was no point in Jorgen and Vincent complaining. The mob's nocturnal activities were carried out in silence. It was too dangerous for them to cause a rumpus, so any beatings, to the relief of Jorgen and Vincent, were out of the question. There were no witnesses to the bed wetting, as all the boys in the dormitory were terrified of Bullhead. Jorgen and Vincent had approached Matron, but without any evidence, she'd not been able to follow up on their complaints. As well, since the incident on the stairs, Matron's attitude to the boys seemed to have changed. She remained friendly, but the unconditional support had evaporated. They didn't know what was going on with her. When they'd asked about Swithins and why he was back, she'd just buttoned up.

****

The tall iron gates of the orphanage were unlocked and creaked and whined as they were opened. Vincent accompanied a partner, and in twos in crocodile fashion, all of the senior boys marched for over a mile to the public baths in Steble Street. To locals they were a familiar sight, and only a cursory glance was offered. From strangers there would be smiles and laughter and occasional applause as Swithins' brigade of senior boys marched in step as their master barked the orders. Vincent was at the end of the line. He'd been placed there deliberately. Swithins, who'd positioned himself behind the column, held a white baton and occasionally tapped Vincent on the neck and levelled derisory remarks at him. He'd allow the boys to laugh quietly and then ask Vincent why he wasn't laughing. Swithins felt his old self again. A fresh breeze was blowing up from the river, and the restrictions that had irritated him over the past few days in the home had been lifted, even though he realized it was only temporary.

The baths had been built in the 1870's and were showing their age. The changing rooms were in dire need of decoration. The paint on the window frames was flaking. There were patches of wall tiles missing, and the lower walls were showing signs of damp. The gas-light fittings on some of the walls were missing, and occasionally the gas was left on accidentally. The strong aromas of gas mixed with ammonia never bothered the boys. As soon as they entered the building and heard the wild shouts and screams of the other children, there was only one intention on their minds – to get into the water as quickly as possible. It was the third time Vincent had visited the baths. He was a strong swimmer and hadn't been beaten in any of the organized races. This was in spite of the handicaps that Swithins imposed on him when he was on duty. He justified it each time by saying that Vincent was nearly twice as tall as some of the other boys, which gave him an unfair advantage. There was some truth in this, so Vincent didn't mind. On that day Swithins seemed bent on ensuring that Vincent wouldn't come first in any of the events.

As the best swimmers prepared themselves for the off, Swithins approached Vincent and said loudly, his face beaming,

'Boy, you've been the biggest of cheats in the past in the way you've swum haven't you, Eteki?'

Vincent knew he had no other option.

'Yes, sir,' he replied quietly.

'Speak up, boy. Don't be shy. What did you say?'

Vincent shouted, 'Yes, sir!'

'Well then, to put matters right, I'll tell you when to start. If you lose the race, you'll have to come out and get changed immediately. Do you understand, boy?' As he uttered these last four words, he banged his baton in time against a nearby pillar.

The race that was to last four lengths was started. Swithins blew his whistle, and five boys dived in. Vincent stood waiting for a few seconds and stared at the boys in the water, and then he half turned to check what Swithins was up to. He found the man's eyes fixed on him. In turning, Vincent had glanced at the water fountain adjacent to the changing room door. That was his target. He thought Swithins wouldn't have a clue, but he'd accidentally given him the opportunity and the time to check the water fountain for the note. Vincent was determined not to win, and when Swithins blew the whistle for him to dive in when the other boys had completed two lengths, he knew he'd got nothing to worry about. He'd swim as fast as he could and would never catch the leader, and Swithins wouldn't fathom out the game he was playing.

After the race, as Vincent walked back to the changing rooms, he glanced round to see whether Swithins was checking on him. The man stood with his back to Vincent, whistle in hand. As Vincent neared the water fountain, he heard the whistle sound twice, which meant some of the boys had to get out of the pool. This was his chance. He bent down and turned the water on and

The Lucy Effect

began to drink. It tasted stale. He feverishly started searching underneath the bowl with one hand. At first there was nothing. He looked up in the direction of Swithins and saw him talking to one of the boys. Furtively, Vincent stooped down to examine the underside of the basin. It was there. Vincent, heart pounding, grabbed at it. At that moment there was a long blow on the whistle with a short blast at the end, which was a signal for all boys to stop what they were doing immediately. Vincent froze. Even his hand that clutched the note was motionless.

The words he feared the most in that split second moment of time echoed around the cold ceramic walls of the pool, and in Vincent's mind they went on forever:

'Eteki, stop what you're doing at once!'

Vincent, nearly as quick as it takes a frog's tongue to retrieve a fly without sound, bravely stuffed the note into his swimming costume and recited the briefest of charms for deliverance in one of his many tribal tongues. Swithins, who was at the other end of the pool charged along its edge knocking boys out of the way. Some unfortunate ones landed back in the pool. There was red burning hatred in Swithins' eyes. They were fixed on Vincent's squirming frame. Slightly out of breath, he stood a few feet away from Vincent, who unfortunately for Swithins, was about five inches taller than he. So rather than looking into his nostrils, he had to bend his head upwards when he spoke.

'Give me whatever you're hiding in your costume, black boy!'

'What's that, sir?'

Swithins looked at Vincent, incredulity in his expression. Vincent' enunciation had been very close to London English.

Strangely, Vincent's fear had gone. It had evaporated when Swithins had stood up to him. He hadn't realized how much taller he was than the master. He actually thought he could see the very same thought at the back of Swithins' fear-filled eyes! It could have been the chant he'd continued to recite silently. Whatever it was, he felt his strength and calmness merge together as one. It was as if he was one of the many stone columns that held the roof of the baths aloft – strong, cold, and unconcerned. Swithins caught sight of the note bulging in Vincent's costume. He reached in and grabbed it.

'Take that, you liar!' Swithins raised the white baton high in the air and was about to strike Vincent's left shoulder. But to Swithins' great surprise, as he swung it to connect with the target, the boy's muscular left arm parried the blow, and the baton shot out of his hand and bounced twice on the tiled ceramic floor before it scuttled into the pool. Never in his years of teaching at the orphanage had he been attacked by a boy. He was stunned into silence. He gazed at Vincent, who stood a few feet away and was staring him out. He didn't notice that Vincent's lips were moving minutely. He was still delivering the chant. The other male teacher in attendance, who'd taken some of the boys to the changing room, dashed to the pool area to see what all the commotion was about. Swithins said nothing. He pocketed the note without glancing at it and started walking out of the baths. His face was void of expression.

Vincent stopped the chant immediately. He was worried he'd overdone it, but he couldn't tell, as he'd never used it before.

The strange thing was that, all the way back to the orphanage, Swithins seemed to be in a world of his own. Even when his colleague tried to engage him in conversation, he remained silent. There was no drilling of the boys. Whereas usually silence reigned, the boys chatted in hushed voices to each other. Swithins didn't challenge them. They'd witnessed an unheard-of event – a boy striking a teacher.

By the time they reached the gates of Quirk's Orphanage, the story had changed and had Vincent as the first one to land a blow. That blow had not been a parry, but a determined strike at Swithins' chin that had sent him reeling over nearly ending up in the water.

Chapter 41

Later that afternoon, Jorgen and Vincent were in the lavatories. Swithins' 'henchboys' had been sniffing round all afternoon intent on collaring Vincent. They'd heard the rumours and couldn't believe them. Jorgen couldn't believe that Vincent was feeling sorry for their mutual enemy.

'You're feeling sorry for Swithins? He deserves all he gets and more!' Jorgen said the words without compunction. They rolled out well oiled by the memory of the beatings he'd suffered at Swithins' hands.

'I think I overdid it with the magic. It worked too well. Everything has been taken out of him except his breath.'

'You don't believe that stuff do you? It's mumbo jumbo!'

'I beg to disagree,' Vincent said politely to Jorgen. 'Gods are very powerful, and if you believe and make the victim believe, the magic truly works.' Vincent didn't sound as if he was really all that convinced, but he wasn't going to let go of the belief. Jorgen knew his friend still maintained a true and strong connection to his homeland.

'Never mind about that. Did you read the letter?'

'No. I'm sorry. But at least we know he answered.'

'But we don't know what he said, and Swithins has it, and I'm at his mercy.'

'Swithins is not well, as we know, and nothing's happened so far. If I were you, I'd throw myself at the mercy of Matron now that Swithins has got the note. Put your two pence and a ha'penny in before he does.'

'But she's on his side, and that makes it different from the way it was before. You know she's not the same with us.'

'Yes, but I think all the trouble has made her think she can't get too close to any boy and be so intimately involved. That's why she's changed. The way everything is easier for us here now since she started hasn't changed, has it? Look, she's on duty today. Go and see her.'

At that moment they heard boys' voices outside. One sounded like Bullhead. 'Come on, let's dash before they come in,' Vincent said. He led the way shouting tribal words at the top of his voice, followed closely by Jorgen. They took the boys outside by surprise and managed to break through their ranks as they hurried over to the safety of Jones. If any showdown was to break out, Vincent was determined that it should happen when they were ready for it and had some advantage.

Although he didn't understand all of Vincent's highbrow words, Jorgen got the sense of them. That was enough. After tea he made straight for Matron's door and sat outside her room. He was ready to move away rapidly if Swithins or one of the gang members appeared. His thoughts were on Swithins, and Vincent's notion that he wasn't well because of the magic inflicted on him. Suddenly, out of the blue, Matron's door opened, and Swithins emerged. His face was ashen. He didn't look at Jorgen; he merely dashed away. Matron had jumped up and was in pursuit when she noticed Jorgen standing at the door. She stopped. She was flushed, as if her heart was pounding. She hesitated for a moment before saying anything.

'What is it, Paul?'

Jorgen was surprised that she called him Paul, but there was no smile on her face. She looked stern. It put him off, and he got up and started to walk away.

'Wait,' she said. 'Come back. I know you need to talk about something important.' Jorgen turned and observed a faint smile, which grew wider chasing away some of the worry lines on her face. 'I've had a difficult day,' she explained. Jorgen wondered why an adult had spoken to him in that way. It was almost as if he'd become an equal, which made him feel uneasy. She walked back into the room, and he followed meekly.

Jorgen told her almost everything that had happened to him. He didn't admit to the break in at Edward Aughton's. At no stage did she interrupt him. It was only when he mentioned what had happened since he'd been at the orphanage and particularly about Swithins that she held her hand up. 'Can I trust you not to repeat what I think it's important for you to hear?' she asked. He replied yes, but he wasn't certain that he could.

'Why do you think Captain Swithins is like that?' Jorgen shook his head slowly. It was the first time he'd heard a member of staff refer to Swithins as Captain, although everyone knew he'd been a captain in the infantry.

'I must say first that I can't agree with the way he treats you and Vincent and the other boys in any way. That's why I've tried to change how you're all treated. But for your own sake, and the way you feel about what's happened to you here at the orphanage in the future, it's important you know some of the reasons for his behaviour. Do you understand what I'm trying to say?' Jorgen nodded, although he didn't understand the bit about feelings. But he was intrigued to know what exactly would be coming next. 'Captain Swithins was serving on the Western Front Have you heard about the Western Front?' To Jorgen it was all foreign, but he nodded. 'He'd been involved in several charges against enemy lines at the first Battle of Ypres, leading his men right up to the barbed wire only to have to retreat because of losses. On the last charge, his batman's head was blown off just as he went over the top. He was a very close friend of the captain's, and the captain went back to help and was so overcome with grief and horror that he ran away and kept on running. He was in hiding for days.

Fortunately, some of his battalion who knew what had happened came across him. They didn't want to turn him in, because they knew he would have been sent before a firing squad. So they looked after him, hiding him in a derelict farm.'

Matron was interrupted by a knock at the door. It was the head, and she walked out of the room and closed the door.

They stayed just outside the door. Jorgen could hear their voices. Although he couldn't make out everything they were saying, he did hear Swithins' name mentioned over and over again. During the conversation beyond the door, Jorgen was having his own inner conversation. He tried to understand what Matron was getting at – that Swithins was brave, but also a coward. It didn't make sense. What had that got to do with the beatings?

When Matron reappeared she looked even more flustered than before.

'Sorry, Jorgen. What was I saying?' A faraway look, maybe focussed on the mixed up feelings which haunted her about Swithens, invaded her eyes. Before Jorgen had a chance to answer, she continued, 'Oh, yes. Captain Swithins. His comrades dressed him up as an ordinary soldier and managed to spirit him into England secretly. But, of course, he couldn't go back to his hometown, and he had to change his name.' She paused. By this stage Matron had calmed down. Unknown to Jorgen – and indeed to Matron – she was using the narration of Swithins' story to reinforce her desperate need to look favourably on him and give him the benefit of the doubt.

She continued, 'He lived in the county of Middlesex in the south and moved up to Liverpool where he wasn't known. He was interested in the teaching of boys and bringing a bit of discipline into their lives as we all know too well.' Again she paused. 'Do you understand all I've mentioned?' Jorgen nodded his head. He was anxious to get to the end of the story smartly. He desperately wanted to mention the Red Cross as Vincent had advised him.

Inside his anger drum was expanding moment by moment; it was ready to burst.

'So he applied for the deputy's position here. He forged his character references, which included one from a head of a fictitious school in Oxford. He was well educated and so had no trouble obtaining the position at the orphanage.' Again she hesitated as she seemed to search for the right words. 'According to the head, he knew nothing of all this, and...' Again, she paused. 'It was only when Captain Swithins was reinstated to his position that this all came out. He revealed it all to me. It was very difficult for such a proud man to admit to desertion and cowardice, but he did. I wanted you to know all this, because it might help you to forgive him. You see he was taking it out...' Before she could finish the sentence, Jorgen flew out of the chair, opened the door, ran into the hallway, and slammed the door behind him. His over-inflated anger drum had finally burst!

In the hall, standing at the bottom of the staircase, was the head overseeing the line of boys as they marched up the stairs for their baths and bed. Jorgen joined Vincent, who refrained from asking questions. The thunder filling Jorgen's face said it all. It was evident to anyone who looked at him that the lighting of any touch paper would spell immediate disaster.

The head saw this, and also witnessed the opening and closing of the sickroom door again as Matron made a brief appearance and gave up any idea of pursuit for the second time that evening. He moved his head slowly from side to side and looked up with knowing eyes at the old chandelier hanging high up from a wooden beam in the ceiling. He obtained some crusts of comfort at the thought of the dramas that had been acted out within the light of its candles, but then had inevitably been forgotten over the decades.

Part IV
The Coming Together: 19th July 1915 to 13th August 1915

Chapter 42

At the central police station, Detective Constable Gilbert Pomfrey had just left a meeting to do with a murderer on the run. He'd been glad to escape the heavy pipe and cigarette smoke that had built up over the hour in the operations room. He was disappointed that he'd not been given a more important role in the case. But he was happy enough. The case happened to be of national importance. He had a fantasy about solving it; that is, more the end result of solving it. He could see himself frog marching the Hun after overpowering him. The image sent a wave of goose pimples stampeding over the length of his large frame. But it was going to be difficult. He'd drawn the short straw. He'd been placed on the night shift and was to tail one of the suspect's accomplices. She'd been up to her neck in it a few months back, but they didn't know whether she and the villain would make any contact. They were using her as the sprat to catch the mackerel, but it was a long shot.

Gilbert had just enough common sense to know that he'd been deliberately left out of any serious police work on the case. He was always given the dull legwork. There was a simple reason for this. Gilbert was incompetent. He'd been shifted from uniformed to plain clothes not because of any promotion, although this is how he broadcast the change, but because he could be more closely watched than when he was patrolling the streets of the city, sometimes causing mayhem. He would have been sacked early in his career, but he had connections in high places that meant he wouldn't be going anywhere until he got pensioned off.

Derek Mellor

It was eight o'clock in the evening. Gilbert and a colleague were outside the hospital in a car. His colleague was the most hated detective sergeant in the unit, and Gilbert knew it wasn't going to be a pleasant night. There would be no words passed between them unless it was official business. Detective Sergeant Mackintosh, known as Macka but not to his face, had told Gilbert that he'd be on his own for an hour or so every couple of hours starting at midnight, as he had to attend to some important business. This sounded a bit fishy to Gilbert. He wondered what the DS was up to. There was no way he'd be assigned other tasks, given that the current case was a high-priority one.

It was about ten o'clock when Macka got out of the car and went off in the direction of the city centre. He'd banged the car door shut in anger. Gilbert thought the banging was due to the door not closing properly. Another person witnessing the scene in the terraced house opposite moved a lace curtain panel.'

Hay, youse, what yer think ye're doin', all that din ye're makin'? Yer be wakin' the dead!'

The verbal instructions given to all officers when on surveillance duty were that no contact with the general public should be made unless the public's safety was at risk or specific information was required from the public that was pertinent to the case. Finally, no information should be made available to the public about aspects of the particular surveillance. So a woman shouting at them should have been ignored. But Gilbert felt he and the police department had been affronted; he was seething. *How dare she?* he thought as he pounded on her door. He heard keys being turned, and then the door opened wide. In front of Gilbert stood a woman of small height but with a round body and face. She was partly covered with a huge shawl that she'd wrapped herself in. Her chin sunk into her neck, and the hanging flesh wobbled like a turkey's wattle as she spoke.

'What d'yer think ye're doin' bangin' on me door and splinterin' it?' She held her arms akimbo presenting herself as an impenetrable castle. He observed her prickly strength and quickly pulled his warrant card out of a pocket and pushed it close to her nose. The woman's body became less tense, her arms dropped to her sides, and the previously narrowed lips expanded as a smile broke out.

'Well, yer should've said, constable. I'm as law abidin' as any. Come on in. 'Ave just this minute put kettle on the stove. Would yer like a cuppa?'

Gilbert was pleased with the complete climb down of the woman. He loved to see people's reactions when he pulled the card out.

'Yes I will,' he said haughtily, 'but bring it outside to the motor car.' He went outside and stood by the car and lit his pipe. It was a pleasant evening. Things weren't so bad. He'd have a nice cuppa, and the sarge would be away for another hour or so. He heard footsteps on the lino in the hall and the clink of crockery. He walked up the steps to the house and gently pushed the door open. A tray was thrust into his hands. That's when he heard the sounds of what he thought was a horse and cart stopping and starting These sounds were augmented by heavy footsteps, the closing of a car, door and a breathless sarge. He'd been found by the most hated man on the force with a tray in his hands on a doorstep.

Macka gave Pomfrey a rollicking and postponed his nocturnal activities, calling Pomfrey a buffon, and saying he didn't want to let him out of his sight. They spent a long, silent night together in the car. Macka's anger permeated the atmosphere for hours, demonstrated by clenched hands on the steering wheel, the low growl as he muttered under his breath, and occasionally the long drawn out sigh. At 7.50 in the morning, a young woman emerged from the hospital drive. Gilbert was dozing in the back. Macka got out of the car and opened the rear door. He cupped Gilbert's chin with his gloved hand and turned his face in the direction of the woman. He kept it in that position,

'You don't move from here. You've done enough already. The next shift will be here in ten minutes. Tell them what's happening. If you don't know what that is, it's that girl you're looking at now, and I want you in my office at ten sharp. If I'm not there, you wait!' Macka banged the door shut, crossed the road, and started tailing the girl.

For the next five minutes Gilbert sat as far back as he could in the seat and closed his eyes. This was the worst trouble he'd ever been in, and he was trying to work out his excuse. There was a knock on the car door, and there was his saviour peering through the misted glass.

'Nasty piece of work, that man,' said the woman. 'I saw him goin' after that girl. D'yer want that cuppa you didn't have?'

He was feeling benevolent towards her.

'You couldn't do us a favour, could you?'

Her eyes lit up.

'What d'yer mean?'

'Well, if anybody comes from the police, just deny that all this happened. You know, I didn't see you the whole night. There'll be something in it for you.' He winked and added, 'Yes, I'd love the tea.'

As Gilbert stepped out of the car to greet the old woman with the tray, a nurse slipped out through the hospital gates. She was wearing lipstick and a dark green coat. Gilbert hadn't noticed her.

When the relief car turned into Brownlow Street, its occupants caught sight of the girl and were vigorously attracted by her looks. They wondered what she was doing, all dolled up so early. The car stopped opposite the hospital just as the old lady was taking the tray indoors. Gilbert ran over to them hoping they hadn't seen anything.

'Can anyone drive the car back to the nick?' He pointed at the car. 'Macka's deserted me after that girl.'

****

Macka, in the meantime, had tailed the girl to the end of Skelhorne Street where she started to run. He knew she hadn't noticed him, and he was sure she was heading for Lime Street Station. Maybe she'd left it too late for a train. Then for a moment he lost her in the bustle of the crowd. He saw her dash into the station entrance. He ran wildly along the length of the station forecourt from platform to platform. It was the noise of laughter and merriment that alerted him. He observed her on platform three. She'd joined a group of what seemed to be four close friends. They were hugging and kissing each other in what Macka thought was a bit of a showy display. To make entirely sure it was O'Sullivan, he got her image out nestling in his warrant card. He moved closer to the group. She turned as she made her way to the carriage. Macka was only a few feet away. He got a whiff of perfume, but this was forgotten instantly as he looked at her face. She half smiled as if he was someone she might know. It wasn't Bridie O'Sullivan.

Chapter 43

Over on Platform One, Bridie and Paul boarded a train. After their clumsy meeting of the previous day, Paul was determined, right from the start, to put her at ease. He had some help from the train as the carriage jolted, when the engine was attached. As Bridie went to sit down, she stumbled, and Paul had to steady her. They both laughed, and this buffered away their tension. They had a compartment to themselves, which made it easier to talk. As the train pulled out of the station, smoke blew along the side of the carriage, and for a few seconds obscured the view. They didn't notice the four young people on the nearby platform waving ferociously at a girl as she pulled the window down, and a uniformed man, rifle slung over his shoulder, who kissed her. Paul and Bridie were too engrossed with each other. Whatever happened beyond the smoke was inconsequential. It was another world, far away – a world of ever-changing patterns of the comings and goings of people, of continual movement. Alone in the compartment, they enjoyed a special stillness and were unaffected by the noise and swaying of the moving carriage. Gentle words and looks, and the sweet first touches were the coming together of their longings. He placed his arm around her, and her head sank onto his shoulder.

The train wove its way out of the city and picked up speed. Periods of conversation alternated with moments of silence and tenderness between them. Paul did most of the talking. By the time he'd brought Bridie up to date with the essentials of what had happened to him since they'd last been together, they were

The Lucy Effect

approaching St Helens. He became pensive, and Bridie looked a bit perplexed.

Paul's last visit there with his family had been disastrous. Frau Stocker's husband had died several months before their visit. She'd not welcomed them. They'd sat in the best room where the underused lonely crockery on display in a cabinet sparkled calling out to be touched. There had been no hospitality – no cup of tea, no cakes that used to be offered when Paul's uncle was alive. But most hurtful, when she did speak, she spoke briefly, and only when they asked her something. The children had remained silent, almost in shock. It had been so different when their great uncle had been around. He obviously adored them and treated them as if they were the children he didn't have. That was why Paul had doubts when he'd told Jorgen to go to his great aunt's home. He wasn't sure of the reception he'd get. But a child in distress – her own kith and kin – surely that would have moved her.

'What's the matter, Paul?'

'I'm having second thoughts about you being here with me,' he told her. 'If we get caught, you'd be up before the magistrates before you could say "Jack Robinson".'

'But I've told you before, Paul, the chances of that happening are very poor. They're not looking for a couple. You said yourself that it was a good idea. Anyway, I'm not leaving you. So you can please yourself. Keep holding my hand, or I'll just latch myself on to you in such a way that people will wonder what's going on!'

With that she stopped speaking, although Paul kept on trying to persuade her to remain at the station. He was amazed at her stubbornness. Her beautiful green eyes sparkled, and she just nodded and smiled whenever he spoke. And Paul couldn't do anything other than give in.

In St Helens the couple hired a cab. It followed the tramway to the north of the town. The police had halted the traffic at the crossroads were the trams terminated, known locally as the

Green. Paul became anxious. He wondered whether they were on to him, but relaxed when he heard the strains of a military band. It led a parade of recruits for the Western Front, and the spectacle had attracted a large crowd that was being controlled by mounted police. Paul and Bridie spent several minutes at the Green and then travelled a short distance on the road to Ormskirk, eventually stopping at a property opposite Windle Grange Hall, an early Victorian property. Paul told the cabby to wait and helped Bridie down off the vehicle. Bridie eased Paul's increasing tenseness by squeezing his hand as they walked down a short, tree-lined drive. The house was whitewashed, but only parts of the whiteness showed, as the walls were mostly covered with thick ivy. Paul took hold of the weather-worn brass woodpecker doorknocker and banged it on the brass plate a few times before standing back. There was no answer, so he repeated the action. The door was opened by a man whose face indicated that he was not very happy about being disturbed by the uninvited.

'What's this? You're not tinkers are you? I'll call the constable.' It was obvious they were not tinkers; neither did they look like ordinary people. Particularly Paul, whose dark complexion and moustache looked very theatrical, and he was dressed in fine clothes.

'Oh, donna shut the door, sira, pleasa letame explain,' said Paul. The man looked even more confused and couldn't seem to find words to respond with, so Paul quickly continued, 'You see, I looka for my aunt. I thought she lived here. Her nama was Mrs Stocker.' Paul paused, and silence reigned. The man at the door seemed to be weighing up what his response should be to this unwanted intrusion. Paul took the initiative once more,

'I would hava written, but a visit was quicker. I hava not much time.' The man seemed to be about to interrupt, but Paul went on, 'Does Mrs Stocker liva here? Please, I needa to know.'

The Lucy Effect

The man said, 'No,' and made to shut the door, but just then Paul said to Bridie that it must be the other hall across the road. But finally the man spoke up.

'The old woman's dead. Died in April. I bought this house from the government. She was a Hun, did you know?' Then he banged the door closed as if to say good riddance to bad rubbish.

Paul and Bridie slowly walked along the drive in silence. Paul felt tears prickling in the corners of his eyes. He closed his eyes and desperately tried to stall the flow. There was a knot in his throat. It surprised him that he felt so upset. He quickened his pace, pulling Bridie along. The cabbie had the door open and helped them up.

'Let's get out of here smartly,' said Paul. 'To the railway station, cabbie.' Paul had jettisoned his Italian accent in the heat of emotion. He shut the window, fell into the open arms of Bridie, and sobbed uncontrollably. It wasn't the old woman's death particularly, it was all the other losses. Bridie did her best to smother the sounds. His breaking down would attract attention. Such emotion wasn't acceptable in polite society, especially for a gentleman. There was no doubt the cabby had been privy to all that had gone on, but fortunately the noises of the town increased as they neared the station and blocked out the outburst. Eventually Paul quietened down except for an occasional shudder like distant rumblings, the dying embers of a passing storm.

The carriage was half full at the start of the journey back to Liverpool. In whispers, they went over and over the implications of what had happened. Could the man at the property have lied? Frau Stocker could have been there; maybe Jorgen was there. But he'd seemed genuine enough. What's more, Paul couldn't imagine his great aunt contemplating having guests. Paul's trick of saying they were going to the other properties had worked. It was possible that his aunt had died; she must have been in her eighties. But if she'd died in April, and if Jorgen had gone to St Helens, and if he'd found the house, his aunt wouldn't have been there. She'd have been in the cemetery. Then, the house would have been unoccupied. There were so many unanswerable questions. They should have at least checked the cemetery, but Paul hadn't been in any fit state to pay a visit anywhere.

They alighted from the train at Rainhill, and Paul hailed a cab to take them back to the city. He wanted to avoid the police at Lime Street Station. They seemed to flock there later in the afternoons, like brooding starlings in a favourite spot. Bridie and Paul parted near the hospital, although neither wanted to. She'd arranged to meet her friend. Paul insisted she stick to the arrangement. The moment she was gone, Paul felt desperate. Although he'd enjoyed Bridie's company so much, it had been a wasted day. How was he ever going to find his son? Perhaps the time had come to hand himself in. Bridie wouldn't be implicated then. Why should he spoil her life? Maybe the authorities would help to find Jorgen. But why would they go along that particular road? He'd be a dead man with all the charges hanging over him. He'd never see Jorgen again.

It was at this point that his mind, out of the blue, suddenly conjured up an image of Paddy. Paul remembered his friend saying that, when you are stuck for knowing what to do and which way to go, you had to let your mind go 'seriously' blank, as Paddy had put it. You had to make a real effort; halfway houses weren't in the deal. When you got to this state, an idea would just pop up out of nowhere. Paul started the process, but all that happened was that in his mind he heard Paddy's voice talking gibberish. This sort of stuff might have worked for Paddy, but he was away with the fairies sometimes. Then it dawned on him.

Chapter 44

Two days later, in room 416 at the Adelphi, Paul was dozing. There was a knock at the door, and Paul jumped out of his chair. He hadn't requested room service, and he waited at the door. There was another knock, and the bellboy shouted, 'Telegram, sir.' It was from Paddy in response to the one he'd sent. It was not signed, and much of it Paul had to work out. Paddy was being careful. The decipherment took a few hours, but he eventually pieced the message together. The gist of it was that an Asiatic gentleman would contact him at the Adelphi in the next week or so, and for him not to worry about the problem. All would be resolved.

That afternoon, Paul had arranged to meet Bridie at the cafe near the Adelphi. When she didn't turn up, he started to worry. As he was about to leave, he found Bridie's friend waiting for him outside. She looked tense as she handed a note over, and then she left immediately. His face turned a shade paler when he read its contents. The note was rambling; it had obviously been hurried.

> Firstly, I'll say I've not told the police where you're staying. So you're safe for the time being. But I've told them everything else I know about you. How could you, Paul? They'd seen me on the train at Lime Street leaving for St Helens. I admitted that, but even though they shouted at me and told me about all the violent crimes you've committed, I kept silent. I didn't believe

> a word they were saying. It couldn't be true of my Paul. That was until they brought Lady Winnington in to the police station, and she told me what you'd done to her husband. We were both in tears. Goodbye.

The gnawing insecurity that had plagued Paul over the past few months returned with a vengeance. Although Bridie had said in her note that the police were unaware of his whereabouts, he didn't know whether he could trust her. He couldn't interfere with Paddy's arrangements of someone contacting him at the Adelphi. It would be too complicated, and so he had to remain there until the meeting had taken place.

He booked himself into a small hotel nearby. The windows in his room faced the Adelphi. If the police called in the night, he wouldn't be in room 416, but he'd know of their visit. That was if he kept alert during the night. As he had to be watchful of the police during the day as well, he spent his time drifting between a nearby cafe and the other hotel. Occasionally he would pop into the Adelphi to show his face so that the staff didn't come to any conclusions about what he was up to.

Paul didn't know how long he could keep the present regimen going. It had been a week and he hadn't been sleeping much. How could he with the chance of a police raid continually in the cards? His inactivity had plunged him into a depression that went hand in hand with the anxiety. At night he often found himself walking round in circles in the small bedroom he occupied. The floorboards would creak, and some people had started to complain. It was this that finally triggered Paul into deciding to telegram Paddy immediately. His friend needed to know the urgency of the situation. He had to hurry up the contact. It was also desperate that he choose another venue for the meeting;

meeting at the Adelphi was out of the question now. Otherwise everything would be lost.

Paul walked into the Adelphi and went over to the telegram office. A bellboy he knew approached him. A Chinese gentleman had called the previous evening and asked to meet Paul in the hotel foyer that day at ten. The hotel staff had tried to contact him, and had even entered his room when they failed to get an answer. It was 9.45, so Paul hurried to his room to rescue his belongings. He couldn't stay a moment longer at the hotel. When he returned to the foyer, he settled his bill at reception and had to endure the niceties of polite conversation at the same time he was continually looking out for the Chinese gentleman.

Chapter 45

Chung Hai affectionately known to his European friends as Hahyoo, hadn't any idea of his mission. He'd been asked to assist a good friend who was a fugitive on the run. He was uneasy about the task. It was his first visit to England. He had no idea what to expect. Hahyoo was an ex detective sergeant who'd served with the Hong Kong Marine Police, as had his father. In fact, his father had been one of the first Cantonese-speaking officers on the force in the 1870s, which boosted the prestige of his family in the community to no end. For Hahyoo it had been the ideal job, for not only did it uphold family tradition, but the pay for Chinese workers was the best in the crown colony. Those were the surface benefits. The deeper value was in the work itself. Each day he stepped into the office he'd have no inkling of what surprises were ready to take hold of him. Occasionally a case would come up that would stretch his mind in all sorts of directions, like a challenging chess game might. The application of his logic and the final creative spark that led to a checkmate in the case were like drugs. He could hardly wait for the next fix. Hahyoo knew he was damn good detective, but he didn't let it go to his head. Boasting was alien to him, a complete unknown commodity.

The fact was that he surpassed, as the gigantic Yangtze River makes the Re River appear as if it was a mere stream, other officers whether European or Indian, in solving cases that seemed intangible and impossible to unravel. So, automatically these flowed his way. Such was the trust bestowed on him following his meteoric rise in the ranks and the extent of his success. What's more, he mixed socially in a discreet way with European officers and civilians and was accepted by them. This he saw as essential to his work. Missing buried pieces of the jigsaw in a case could be uncovered from these sources. The hierarchy turned a blind eye to this fraternization; they could see the benefits, even though the behaviour was officially frowned on. So why should such a successful detective, who might have climbed further up the ladder, have arrived a day ago in the port of Liverpool, no longer an officer of the Hong Kong police but a business partner of a charmed Irishman?

Hahyoo had encountered Paddy on official business when the Irishman was on a visit to Hong Kong to clear up a business dispute with a rival shipping agency. His business was booming in the port, with the operation handling the largest volume of goods – especially silk from Canton – through the colony and the Chinese mainland. Hahyoo had been brought in to solve a case of fraud that had been resistant to the efforts of other officers mainly because of their lack of understanding of local customs and the language. During that time he'd had a lot of contact with Paddy, and they had become friends. Without telling anyone at first, even Hahyoo, Paddy had helped Hahyoo's family out over a financial issue, a problem they'd never shared with their son. Their landlord had been about to turf them out. Paddy somehow heard of this and ensured, through his contacts, that overnight the family became the landlords themselves. The family were unaware of the identity of their benefactor, and if they'd known, would never have accepted Paddy's offer. Hahyoo soon figured it out, but wisely never mentioned a word to anyone. His family would have been mortified.

This action of Paddy's cemented their friendship, and sometimes, rather than stay at the stuffy Metropole Hotel, Paddy would frequent his friend's small house in Ling Sing Street in Sheung Wan overlooking Victoria Harbour. Hahyoo's parents lived in an adjoining building. Typically, eager to learn and enjoy, Paddy threw himself into Chinese family life. He visited markets that he discovered along the unlikeliest of narrow roads and dusty alleyways. There he would haggle with traders, remembering his market stall in Dublin, universe upon universe away. With the younger males of the family, he'd shout the odds in heated mah-jong games while players satisfied their appetites with steaming fish and congee bought from food hawkers swinging along with their pots on shoulder poles. Paddy would buy trinkets for the family, and on one occasion even made them a gift of a songbird, which they of course named Paddy. The bird immediately learned to say 'Paddee' with a long *e* sound in the Chinese way, and that word could be heard for many years in the household. It was impossible for the family to forget him, not that they wanted to. This contact between the two friends unfortunately turned out to be Hahyoo's undoing, as he was reported to the authorities by a Hong Kong crime gang who harboured a massive grudge against him, as many of course did.

Because it was a legally formulated complaint, Hahyoo appeared before a panel of officers, and the issue of his over closeness to Paddy was brought out. He was severely reprimanded, relieved of his stripes, and placed with a uniformed branch of the Hong Kong police in a predominantly Chinese area in Wanchai. Hahyoo was lucky not to have been sacked, and it was only because of his excellent service record and his reputation that he was kept on the force. The Hong Kong police force had effectively lost their best officer, and Hahyoo had suffered his greatest fate.

Paddy was hounded by guilt. He felt he had been the culprit, and the worst of it was that, not only had Hahyoo fallen from grace, but his family had also. Their family honour had been dealt a severe blow, sending them to the gutter as vicious and jealous neighbours concocted far-flung tales of the abuse of Hahyoo's position in criminal activities and debauchery. So Paddy had no alternative but to offer Hahyoo a job as his superintendent of security in Hong Kong at six times his most recent weekly salary. Hahyoo couldn't refuse. This new position crushed all the gossip – a European firm offering such a prestigious job with respect measured in pounds. The family's honour was restored, if not elevated, and whenever Paddy visited the colony, he stayed with his Chinese family. If he didn't, Hahyoo's mother would read the riot act to him when he did call, with his namesake chirping occasionally in support!

Chapter 46

At precisely ten o'clock, Hahyoo entered the reception hall of the Adelphi Hotel. He was directed to the main lounge, but couldn't see the man called Paul. There was no one around with blonde hair. All the guests started gawping at him. It wasn't everyday that a Chinese person was seen at the Adelphi. Most people thought that he must be a person of importance, but he was not dressed in the manner of the high class; rather, he wore the bowler, white shirt, and starched collar of the lower class. His dark, ill-fitting suit – his hands were hardly visible – had seen many sunrises.

Suddenly, from behind, a man appeared who looked Indian. Hahyoo knew many Indians, as they served in the Hong Kong police. He was suspicious of the stranger's moustache. It was too perfect, obviously false. His dark hair was not the texture of an Indian's; it was too matte and again perfect. He was carrying a suitcase. Then it dawned on him: this must be Paul.

'Good morning,' Paul said stiffly. Hahyoo noticed taut lines on the man's face, and worried eyes. When he shook his hand, it was damp.

'Good morning,' Hahyoo clipped in three clearly separated syllables, the best English he could muster. He placed both his hands round Paul's in order to make him feel more relaxed, and he held them for a few seconds. Hahyoo thought he detected a bit of relaxation in Paul's manner, and a shadow of trust in his eyes.

'Look, if you don't mind, could we go somewhere else fairly sharpish?' Paul said anxiously as he rose from his chair picking his case up.

'Of course.' Hahyoo was surprised to see Paul heading for the reception hall and not the lift or stairs. Then it clicked. He was leaving. That was the reason for the suitcase. He followed him out of the building and across the busy road. Paul didn't seem bothered about the trams, and fearlessly wove in and out of the dust-clad vehicles that clanged their bells fiercely. He seemed intent on reaching a destination as quickly as possible. Hahyoo followed in a discreet fashion, carefully crossing the road. People stared at the well-dressed Chinese man with his short, Chaplinesque moustache, and hardly noticed the desperate actions of his acquaintance.

Finally, Hahyoo saw Paul enter a café. When they were finally both seated comfortably with a pot of tea, Paul explained all that had happened to him. At the end of nearly two hours and many cups of tea, he'd finished the tale. It had obviously been harrowing for him to go through some of the narrative, especially at the beginning. Hahyoo had been patient and hardly interrupted Paul apart from the times when he needed to clarify a detail. He would then scribble notes in pencil in a pocket notebook. But he tried to maintain eye contact even when he was scribbling. He was used to such a performance.

'Well it's quite a story, and very sad, very sad,' Hahyoo said at last. 'Paddy asked me help you. And he is here in Liverpool in few days. Is important that you know I work for your friend, and he is my friend also. I was a detective sergeant in Hong Kong, and that is where I live now and work for Paddy. Is my first time in Liverpool. Is to help you, but also Paddy wanted me to see what he does in Liverpool, so I arrive last week on one of Paddy's ships.'

Paul was intrigued that Paddy had ships and employed people in Hong Kong. But most of all that he'd shipped a detective to England to help him.

After finishing lunch, they walked to Paddy's office in Water Street; however, Paddy wasn't there. Hahyoo told Paul he'd found him a safe house, and if he didn't mind, he would take him there. The thought that it would be the house in Rodney Street crossed Paul's mind, but surely Hahyoo wouldn't be that stupid. Paul waited outside the office, as they'd agreed the fewer people who saw him the better. When Hahyoo returned, to Paul's surprise, he literally jumped into a parked car with impressive agility and beckoned him to follow.

'At the railway station there are many police. Car is safer,' said Hahyoo. And he added with a smile, 'Not to worry. I am good driver. If drive in Hong Kong, very necessary. Roads bad.'

'We're not going to Rodney Street then?' Paul was relieved as Hahyoo shook his head.

After driving for a few minutes, Hahyoo asked Paul to pick up a map from the seat in the back.

'You help me please. Map. Please read and tell me the way to go.'

Still bewildered by Hahyoo's antics, Paul took hold of the map and at first had difficulty focussing on its pencilled markings. Then, totally shocked, he realized where the pencil markings ended up. It was in an area he knew – Blundellsands – but that wasn't all. When they finally arrived and pulled into the drive, Paul recognized the hall right away. It suddenly dawned on him where Paddy got his ideas of hiding out in the least-expected of places.

Hahyoo parked the car near the entrance, and they walked into the house. It looked very different than it had on the rain-soaked day he'd left in a panic holding a gun into the side of Lady Winnington. It had seemed greyish and oppressive then, but now it was full of colour and life. He guessed this might have been because of the chronic state of panic he'd experienced at the time, but he did notice obvious changes. Several of the rooms looked lived in. Dustsheets had been removed, and flowers had been arranged artistically in large, royal-blue, enamelled vases decorated with golden dragons. The floral decoration, he thought, had to be the handicraft of a professional female artist. He couldn't have imagined it was the work of Hahyoo, even though he seemed to be a man of surprises.

In the kitchen, where the aromas were predominantly of exotic spices, whereas previously stale cabbage had reigned supreme, china crockery filled the shelves in much more abundance than would have been appropriate for a house that accommodated up to ten people. When Paul made a quick tour of the downstairs rooms, he noticed that the large dining room contained a long table and about sixteen chairs. They'd not been there last time.

It all came out when Hahyoo told him that Paddy had bought the house shortly after he'd read about the murder. He'd been looking for a house in that area away from the city centre for some time. He wanted to use it as a residence and a place to carry out his vital socialising. It was on one of his house-hunting trips when Paddy was returning from Liverpool to Dublin that he'd been arrested following the events of 7 May. The murder there had put buyers off, and so the price had been reduced, making the house an attractive proposition. Paul was about to say that he was the one being blamed for the murder when Hahyoo mentioned that everyone knew he wasn't responsible. It was as if he'd read his mind. This stopped Paul in his tracks.

Hahyoo responded to Paul's reaction.

'You know Paddy. Is very resourceful. Has many acquaintances, some more important than others, although he values them equally. This lord and lady, Paddy has friend who was close to them. Very unhappy couple. Those who are close to family also know the truth. The lady killed her husband. No doubt. But people believe lady. She is powerful. She has much money and many high-ranking contacts.' Hahyoo paused, obviously waiting for Paul to say something.

'I'm so pleased he believes that,' Paul finally said. 'It's the truth, as I told you before.' He paused. He was still trying to take it all in.

'Well, when he bought house he'd not had news you were a suspect,' explained Hahyoo. 'But did when he signed papers. Also knew you were not responsible. Thought would be difficult to clear your name at moment, better later. When you contacted him, he very happy. He said God made happen as made buying the house happen. Thinks like Buddhist – all things linked. It would be safest of houses to stay in until plan is worked out.

Paul interrupted him,

'Plan? What plan?'

'Oh, so sorry. A plan he has, but only if you agree.' Hahyoo looked at Paul with a modicum of compassion.

'I don't know plan. Paddy keep things close to heart till last moment. Maybe so can change it to keep face. Or maybe is thoughtful and wants us not to worry.' This made sense to Paul. It was the Paddy he knew.

'I must tell you what I do tomorrow. You told me last words you spoke to son were about travel to great aunt's in St Helens,' Hahyoo said, slowly flicking through the pages of his notebook.

Paul nodded but remarked,

'But she's not there, and neither is Jorgen.'

'Yes, but need to find out more, much more. Tomorrow go to St Helens by train to make enquiries. You will be sleeping when I go. It will be on first train. Will need address of great aunt. Please write in notebook.' He handed Paul the notebook, which was filled with page after page of beautiful Chinese logographic script. Paul didn't want to spoil it by adding his rigid style of writing English, but the very action of writing down the address made him feel that Jorgen was that little bit closer. Hahyoo had that effect on him – the overwhelming assurance that all would work out, in its own good time.

Chapter 47

As Hahyoo alighted from the empty carriage at St Helens Central Railway Station, he sensed many eyes on him. He was aware most people had never expected to see a Chinese man in a small town, and if they had, they would have expected a person like one they'd seen in a pictorial representation in a book, perhaps wearing traditional, loose cotton clothing and a 'pigtail'. They would not have expected a Chinese man wearing a dark suit and tie topped off with a bowler hat and carrying a bag with an umbrella perched on top. People would remember him for a long time. A bit of a handicap for a detective. As with many things, however, his uniqueness did have advantages. People are inquisitive, and as he'd found since his arrival in England, ready to talk to him, especially as he was always purposely smiling and therefore inviting conversation.

His first stop was the post office, the local repository of gossip. He knew from experience that it could be a gold mine for extracting the important piece of information to kick-start the beginnings of an investigation, and so it was. Within minutes of his presence, after he'd mentioned he was in the employ of a solicitor charged with looking for a foreign boy, the information started flowing. What's more, the prize was that he was told to come back later to meet Mary Shuttle, Edward Aughton's maid, who had the inside story. Next, he went straight to the newspaper office where he hoped to corroborate the information he'd gained at the post office. Later, he went to look at the records in the library for similar reasons.

In between his errands at the newspaper and library, he returned to the post office and took Mary Shuttle to a nearby hotel for tea and scones so they could talk privately. He suspected she would be in her absolute element to be in an encounter with an exotic stranger, which she probably could never have imagined happening in several lifetimes, and to place the crown on it, it would be the king and queen of a future gossip to boot. Along with this went the pleasure of relating the occasion repeatedly until her first performance and its content bore little resemblance to the latter ones. This, strangely, had been the result of the expectations of her audience, some of whom made it their business to seek further renditions. And, finally, the refreshments. To the dismay of Hahyoo, she insisted on pouring the tea, and before he could plunge a stopper into the cow's teat, she'd already milked both cups. Hahyoo was too polite to comment. He had to grin and bear it. Not only was it a counterfeit tea by the nature of its inferior grade, but the milk had ashened the brew and made it insipid. He attempted unsuccessfully to push thoughts of his delectable Keemun tea to the back of his mind as he sipped the wretched stuff. Still, Hahyoo was not disappointed. He'd gained all he needed and more. It was like the tea store that, in a heavenly season, protected by the goddess Guanyin, was bursting to the brim.

Hahyoo arrived back at Blundellsands late in the afternoon. He let himself in and found Paul in a lounge chair fast asleep. Next to him on a table were an empty glass that contained the remains of an alcoholic drink, and an ashtray full of cigarette stubs. Hahyoo smiled to himself and tried as hard as he could to quietly close the door on his way out so as not to disturb him. But Paul must have been asleep for some time; his sleep must have been light. The noise of the door had wakened him, and he called Hahyoo back onto the room.

'Sorry to disturb,' said Hahyoo. 'Sleep is precious. Makes mind healthy.' His words were spoken gently, slowly, and quietly, as if he was helping Paul to rise out of his slumber, an action that was as important as sleep itself. It had the effect of slowing Paul down, and he stretched his arms outward in a slow fashion, causing an expensive ornament on the table to wobble nearly out of control, but he managed to rescue it. But the pattern of rest was broken.

'Ha, you awake now. So sorry.'

'How did you get on?' asked Paul anxiously. 'Is there news of Jorgen?' Hahyoo observed a desperate tone in his voice. The man looked pale and was urging him to say the words he'd been waiting to hear for so long.

'Is evidence boy with foreign accent same age as Jorgen stay at two addresses in St Helens. Is reported as well and contented—'

'Where is he?'

'That I don't know.'

Paul started howling and muttered words in German that Hahyoo couldn't understand. This continued for a while, but Hahyoo didn't interrupt.

Finally, when Paul started to calm himself, Hahyoo handed him a newspaper and said, 'First thing you do is look at artist sketch of boy and tell me if it like Jorgen.' If Paul had looked at Hahyoo he would have noticed lines of tension in his usually pacific face.

Paul peered at the newspaper. His whipped-up storm of anguish vanished, and his whole demeanour changed. He suddenly jumped up and shouted out with exaltation.

'That's him! That's my son!' He laughed and slapped Hahyoo sharply on the back.

'That very, very good Paul. Am happy. Now we know for sure Jorgen was living in St Helens two months ago. I don't know where he is, but think is not far away. We know he is well, and tomorrow when visit St Helens again find out more. Look, tell you what happened.'

After going over in detail the day's events, but missing out bits that he thought either might cause unnecessary worry or he wasn't clear about, Hahyoo summed up all the information for Paul, occasionally referring to his notebook:

'This is what know from evidence. Jorgen stayed first with Edward Aughton. Is not known how came to be there. Edward is prosperous solicitor. Lives in large house on own. His life has been tragic. Wife died some years ago, and then daughter-in-law and grandson died in train accident in Liverpool.'

Paul asked when that was, saying that it was a bit of a coincidence.

'About five years ago,' said Hahyoo.

'My other son and my wife were killed in the same incident. Don't you think there could be something in that?'

'Yes, that is strange, but could be just fate for both. Sometimes these things happen. Until know more about the stitches in the cloth and how lie with each other, we leave it. Edward we know has mania, affects his mind. One witness, Mary the maid, said he lives in two worlds. The past and now. She hear him talk about grandson running away from house. Maybe thought Jorgen was his grandson when he was in past. But when in present Edward doesn't know him, and thinks he is not a good boy. We know Jorgen left Edward's when Edward found him with a boy called Montgomery in a garden building. That was the eighteenth of June reported in newspaper. Is last we hear of Jorgen, but I have idea that this boy Montgomery might know more. Only a hunch. If not, it has to be police, but this has many problems. That is what I do tomorrow. Try to see boy.

Chapter 48

The following morning Hahyoo called at the post office again to confirm the address of Montgomery's family. He took a hansom cab to Windle and asked the cabbie to wait on the opposite side of the road to the mansion for as long as it took. The cabbie shook his head, and Hahyoo suspected the man wasn't used to Chinese men, and that could make him uneasy. But when Hahyoo offered twice the fare at that moment and twice when he returned, the driver dropped his guard and almost snatched the coins offered.

As Hahyoo strode up the drive, he noticed the stables and the rear entrance to the building, and for a moment he wondered whether he should go that way. This had always been the case in his hometown when he called with official business to the homes of the wealthy. A Chinese man, whether a police officer or not, was always considered a servant. It was only the Europeans who were allowed the privilege of the front entrance. Hahyoo knew, however, that he had to be seen to be on their level. Wasn't he supposedly the employee of a law firm? He saw eyes peeping around the lace curtains as he stepped into the porch. As he was about to bring the doorknocker down with as little force as possible, the door creaked open slowly. There before him was a maid dressed in her black-and-whites. Behind her was another person, straining to see what sort of creature was at the door. A lady appeared from a room to the side. She was dressed in a long, purple, silk dress, which she swished anxiously about to avoid suitcases that filled a quarter of the hall. Perhaps she suspected they were dust ridden.

'I'll deal with this, Jennings', said the woman, and the maid scurried off along with her inquisitive colleague. Hahyoo knew that, according to normal practises, Jennings would have dealt with any caller who was not expected. She would have asked the caller to write to the lady of the house for an appointment. She wouldn't have given her employer's name, so any opportunist caller would rarely have graced the porch again. He understood that, in this case, Mrs Wilson must have seen Hahyoo approaching and must have been intrigued to know why a Chinese man wearing a bowler should be knocking at her door.

Luckily for Hahyoo, everyone was at home. Mrs Wilson told him the family would be off to Ireland the following day. He noticed train company travel labels attached to the larger pieces of luggage. The whole family were assembled in the best lounge, which pleased Hahyoo. It was the first time he'd been in a wealthy person's house in England, and he was struck by the brightness of the colours and richness of its furnishings. In Hong Kong in the houses of Europeans, furnishings and decoration were more austere and dull and of an older era. In the lounge he observed pale oaken floors that were covered in a large Chinese carpet that was royal blue with a lotus pattern in cream. Wicker chairs held in reserve stood on the oaken floor. Hahyoo joined the family, who were seated on two luxurious white-coloured leather Chesterfield sofas set around a large rectangular table. Montgomery sat on his own next to Hahyoo. Hahyoo couldn't take his eyes off the carpet, and was deep in thought about the meaning of the patterns in which the couches and table where placed. His memory, which had been the downfall of many a criminal, appeared to be switched off in that area of his mind where he imagined colour and shape flourished. These thoughts were suddenly halted by Mr Wilson's voice.

'So how can we assist you, Mr Hahyoo? I trust I've pronounced your name correctly.'

'Very correctly, sir.' Although he'd actually sounded the last syllable 'you' rather than 'yoo' as most English people did. Hahyoo was about to speak when Mr Wilson started up again.

'You mentioned to my wife something about an acquaintance of Montgomery's, a brief one might I add.'

Hahyoo observed that the word *brief* was spoken at a higher pitch than the rest of the man's words, and that simultaneously the speaker placed his first finger and thumb in an arch round his chin. Hahyoo took it as a challenging posture as much as one of curiosity.

'Yes, that is what I find out talking to citizens of St Helens and reading newspaper, a brief, as say, acquaintance.' He placed both hands on his lap and smiled, his lip lifting his meagre waxed moustache. He continued,

'I work for Collins Solicitors in Liverpool. I am agent.' Hahyoo disliked telling lies, but he knew there was some truth in it. These were Paddy's solicitors, and they knew about this escapade and would vouch for his lie, reluctantly, if there was any comeback. This was sealed by the salient and most important fact that Paddy was their main client. So he moved on.

'I look for German boy who is relative of lady who died in Windle here in May this year.' Hahyoo noticed that Montgomery's head sank, like a stone rushing for the dark anonymity of the bottom of a pond. He seemed to be looking at the patterns in the carpet. Hahyoo momentarily diverted his own thought to the pattern, and then the meaning came to him in a flash. 'We know Montgomery spent some time with this boy, a week I think.'

Mr Wilson folded his arms and interrupted.

'I think the time my son spent with this boy was only the lunchtimes, and then only for half an hour a day and not for the full seven days of the week. It was four days, if that, so in my reckoning that is no more than four hours – hardly any time.' Hahyoo nodded in an exaggerated fashion, and Montgomery's sister joined her bother and looked down at the carpet. The blue lotus carpet carried a secret Chinese message. It was 'truth.'

'Very true, very true,' Mr Wilson confirmed. There was a pause until Mrs Wilson asked whether Hahyoo would like some tea, but he declined remembering the tea he last drank in public.

Everyone relaxed, including Hahyoo, who turned to Montgomery and smiled.

'I have one question for Montgomery, because of course, I need to find boy.' He didn't want to mention Jorgen's name. He knew Mr Wilson wanted to keep right away from any personalisation of the matter. 'I ask very, very big favour of you, Mr Wilson.' The smile remained on his face as he turned towards Mr Wilson, checking for subtle movements in the man's facial muscles. They weren't forthcoming. 'I need to speak to your son on his own—'

Mr Wilson, voice raised, interrupted, 'No. I am very sorry. I cannot allow that. Even with the police, I was present, or a teacher accompanied Montgomery.'

'I understand, Mr Wilson. There was disappointment in Hahyoo's voice that he failed to hide.

'You can ask him in our presence,' said Mr Wilson. 'That will be all right.' His voice was softer, more conciliatory.

Turning to Montgomery, his smile still there but not as full, Hahyoo said,

'Do you know where boy went to when you were discovered at the solicitor's house? Did he say anything when he left you?'

Mr Wilson quickly responded. 'No, nothing at all,' he said. Montgomery turned his gaze to the carpet again and then to his father, unable to look at Hahyoo. 'Montgomery would answer in the same way wouldn't you?' continued the boy's father.

Montgomery nodded and looked at his sister, who just stared back at him.

Hahyoo had his answer but not the details.

Hahyoo sent the cabbie away and asked him to come back later to pick him up at the end of the lane. He didn't want the family to know he was still around. He walked a little way past the house and strode into a thicket. He cursed politely when he realized he'd torn his trousers at the front, and the tear was visible. Sitting on the stump of an oak tree, he prepared himself for a long wait. The two children knew more about where Jorgen had gone. It was obvious in the way they'd responded to the questions. He would wait until one of them came out of the house. It was his only chance. The luggage in the hall suggested they would be on their way to Ireland probably the next day.

Chapter 49

It was in the middle of the afternoon before Hahyoo heard activity in the courtyard – horses hooves on cobblestone. He jumped up quickly and managed to increase the length of the tear in his trousers in the process. When he'd confirmed that the rider was the daughter, he forced his way through the vegetation, his hand protecting the tear. He ran into the road, but the pony was off at a gallop in the opposite direction. Again a polite curse. Fortunately there was no one around, and he walked past the house in the direction of where the daughter was heading and concealed himself behind some bushes, careful not to make the tear any worse. He just hoped that she would ride back the way she'd gone.

There was little movement of pedestrians, animals, or vehicles. It was a hot afternoon, and he thought that the heat was keeping the majority of Windle's inhabitants indoors. In the distance, he heard the sound of a horse galloping. The horse came nearer all the time, and then it slowed down and turned off into a field and was gone. False alarm. The sweat was pouring off him. He had to keep his bowler on to protect his bald head. At least he was under a tree in partial shade. Suddenly he heard the sound of a horse in a gallop over soft ground. He assumed it was the previous rider returning. The sound suddenly stopped. He was a stone's throw away from the gate that led to the field. He checked to see the rider who was closing the gate, but he recognized the pony first and made his way onto the lane. The daughter was about to remount, so he ran as fast as he could, holding his bowler over the tear in his trousers. He shouted out for her to wait. She hadn't seen him and turned around. Out of breath Hahyoo reached her and said,

'Please, I must talk. I think you know something more about Jorgen.' There was no need now to tread carefully.

'Who do you think you are making such a suggestion to… I'll get my father!' She attempted to mount her horse, but he placed his hand that held the bowler onto the saddle. This exposed the tear in his trousers.

'Sir, what…' She pointed at his trousers, and he swiftly moved the bowler off the saddle down to the tear. 'How dreadful!'

'I apologize, miss. Very sorry. Accident in bushes. Please if allow me to speak. I keep bowler here.'

He wasn't certain how she would react, but he took the plunge at the same time, and momentarily an image of the carpet flashed through his mind.

'I know, miss, that you and your brother had contact with boy after he ran from house of solicitor.'

Victoria flushed and at first was speechless.

'How could you know such an occurrence happened?' This question confirmed Hahyoo's suspicion that she suspected he knew more than she hoped. He also saw that she realized, as she finished the last word, that she had virtually admitted the fact.

'I do,' he said. Then he paused to increase her anxiety. 'I have to tell father that this has happened. He does not know about it.' Again he paused.

'Please don't inform my father,' she pressed. 'He will be so annoyed.'

Hahyoo cut in. 'I need to know one fact, nothing else. Where he stay when you last saw him?'

'At first he seemed genuine, but Montgomery found out…'

Hahyoo held his hand up and shot her a sincere smile and spoke softly,

'Please, miss, all I want is where he last stay. Otherwise I tell father.' He knew Victoria had no options. She blurted out the address and mentioned the lighthouse gazebo in the grounds of the estate where they'd dropped him off.

Chapter 50

Hahyoo caught the train to Rainhill the following day. Paul had insisted he accompany him, but Hahyoo didn't think it was a good idea and used the familiar excuse of increased police presence at the railway stations. Paul was tense, tightly coiled like a new spring. Hahyoo knew that, if anybody crossed him, he was likely to explode. At the station, Hahyoo hired a motor cab. The driver didn't seem surprised; perhaps the word had got round. Hahyoo told him the address and requested the driver to park on the lane outside the entrance to the estate and wait for him. The driver seemed to have no qualms about this; perhaps he anticipated a large tip. Another reason for Hahyoo's suspicion that his reputation had preceded him.

Hahyoo scanned the treetops for a sign of the gazebo. It didn't take long to spot. He had a quick look round, but there was no evidence of anyone sleeping there or indeed having occupied it in any way in the recent past. He wondered if he should have trusted the girl. But he knew she was telling the truth. It was his craft to know. He retraced his steps back to the main tree-lined drive and started to walk uphill towards the hall. He caught glimpses of its red-bricked exterior through gaps in the trees, and then suddenly it came into full view as the drive turned sharply to the left. It was a magnificent Victorian building with huge bay windows that gave views of three lawns that gently dropped down, bounded by two stone walls complete with steps. Framing the lawns on three sides were copious rhododendron bushes that gave way to a background of thick woods. At the rear of the hall was a sparsely planted wood. The scene created an impression of a completely separate world.

This propelled Hahyoo into deep, peaceful musings about the hall's favourable feng shui positioning with its trees dissolving bad *qi*. He was suddenly jolted out of this thought oasis when a man approached brandishing a two-barrelled shotgun. He'd emerged from the rear of the property. The style of his clothes indicated that he was a servant, most probably a gardener or gamekeeper.

'What's your business?' the man said gruffly.

Hahyoo was happy that the gun was pointed at the ground.

'Very sorry, sir, to disturb.' At this point he raised his bowler. 'May I introduce myself? I am agent for Collins Solicitors of Liverpool. I come to find out about a boy who stayed here in the gazebo one night in June. He was eleven years old with blonde hair. Spoke with foreign accent. Perhaps you know of this?'

'Not a dicky bird, Chinaman, so be off with you!' He raised the gun.

Hahyoo didn't know why, but he thought the man knew something. It was the way his eyebrows moved.

'Please. I give you money.' He took out his wallet and revealed a five-pound note. He was taking a chance. The man could take the money and throw him off the property. There was no one else around.

The man seemed to be mulling this over. Hahyoo recognized that he was on the right track and pulled out another note. The gun dropped. Hahyoo knew he'd reeled him in.

'All right. But on one condition – that nothing comes out that will look bad on me. You must swear on this.'

'I swear that no one know about the matter, ever.'

'The lad got caught in one of me traps, so I took him in cart straight to hospital. That's where I left him. Last time I saw him he was going in ter hospital. I'm not supposed to be usin' the traps.'

'Please, which hospital?'

'Why, local one – Whiston.'

****

Hahyoo was waiting in a small corridor outside the administrator's office in Whiston Hospital. His only previous experience with the inside of a hospital was the contact he'd had visiting prisoners in the Tung Wah General Hospital in Hong Kong. There were few similarities. Whiston was huge in comparison and was comprised of a number of departments that Hahyoo had no idea about. Many of his countrymen were suspicious of these Western remedies, but he'd witnessed the value of them many times. In the office, clerks occasionally would look through the window to get a peek at the curious oriental man who sat patiently waiting to be seen. When the door opened and he was asked to enter, people stopped what they were working on and followed his every movement. He tipped his hat to them, and he smiled. They all smiled back. At one stage, as he entered the inner office, he thought they might applaud as he turned to face them for the last time, but the hospital administrator took hold of one of his arms and led him into the office politely.

The administrator had a file open on his desk. After they'd sat down he said,

'I understand that you're wanting to know where a boy, who was treated here during a week in June, was discharged to.' He stroked his thick moustache as he looked up at Hahyoo.

'That is correct,' Hahyoo replied.

'We can't just give out information to all and sundry, you know. First I must ask some questions.' He proceeded to ask Hahyoo who he represented and why he wanted the information. He also asked for the boy's name and for other personal details. Hahyoo was surprised that the hospital didn't have a record of Jorgen's name. The administrator said that the boy had withheld it, along with his address and other matters about his background. Hahyoo tried to fill in as much as he could. He gave Jorgen's address as his great aunt's, and said that she was deceased. In reality, this had some truth in it and it offered some explanation as to the boy's circumstances. The administrator seemed pleased enough with everything, so Hahyoo was expecting to be provided with the details of Jorgen's discharge location. The administrator closed the file, twirled his moustache, and stood up. Hahyoo dutifully followed.

The administrator held out his hand.

'Thank you for the information. We'll be in touch. Good day, Mr Hahyoo.'

Hahyoo turned to go and said,

'Please excuse, sir, what you mean "be in touch"?'

'As I said at the beginning, we cannot disclose information to all who ask. There must be an official reason. Your request will be decided upon by a subcommittee.'

'Sorry, sir, but you understand what I ask? Need information trace boy because of great aunt's estate. It in interest very much of boy.'

'Yes, yes. But there is a due process that we have to go through.'

'Can you say, sir, that it will meet with success?'

'Indeed I cannot,' said the administrator impatiently, and he led Hahyoo to the door.

Chapter 51

A week later a letter was delivered from the hospital administrator. It curtly said – in a few short lines – that, owing to the regulations, patients' personal information could not be given out. A magistrate's order would be required. Paul, in a fit of pique, ripped the letter up in an exaggerated fashion, and flung the bits into the air, all the while bawling expletives in German. Hahyoo entered the kitchen to see what the commotion was about and noticed the pieces of paper on the floor. Paul continued to blast his foul language out, but at a higher volume at Hahyoo's appearance.

Hahyoo picked up some of the pieces and shook his head slowly from side to side.

'Is very bad. Very bad. Do not waste anger you have. Use it to get address. Come we sit and talk.' He gently took hold of Paul's arm. Paul had quietened down somewhat, and let Hahyoo lead him into the lounge.

'When I go to hospital I see many things. I cannot help it,' Hahyoo explained. 'My mind work this way. It good for police work. I see how to get into places without being caught. I look at what is around – where furniture is and what it is. In my mind I have these pictures. They stay with me always. I wish I could get rid of some horrible ones. Not possible. But I glad I have this. Have to put up with bad. Like life, bad and good come and go. Is how is.' His voice was hushed, and his speech slow. It meant that Paul had to really listen to the words carefully. No longer were the hurting images he'd recently experienced so prominent.

There was silence for a moment, then Hahyoo continued.

'It possible to see address in file.' Now his words were not hushed or slow. They offered a challenge: 'We go to hospital at night. Me to find. You to guard. I know where files kept. What you think?'

'Do you have to ask? You're amazing!'

Hahyoo responded with a tittering laugh – a repeated 'he he' with the smallest of breaks in between the two words, over and over again. Paul couldn't help but laugh, which made Hahyoo's tittering increase in volume, which in turn encouraged further laughter in Paul. Paul knew that Hahyoo had taken his response as a resounding yes, and all that needed to be done was to burgle the administration office of Whiston Hospital that night.

****

They had to use the car; if the plan went wrong, it was their best hope of escape. The train would have made it easier to get to their destination, but Lime Street continued to be populated with police officers on the lookout for strange characters. Not so good for oriental and- Latin-looking men, especially travelling together. Neither of them knew how to get to the hospital directly, and there were no maps. The journey to Liverpool was straightforward; it took them forty minutes. They tried to navigate to Whiston by following the railway track out of the station, which they thought went straight there. They'd been travelling for an hour without spotting any signpost for Whiston. Hahyoo asked Paul to pull up and buy some matches at a shop they'd passed. They needed them for the night's task, and Paul could ask the way to the hospital. Paul walked back to the shop, and Hahyoo waited. On Paul's return, Hahyoo observed his face. It was as if an outsider had beaten the field and he'd won a packet.

The Lucy Effect

'You pleased with yourself. Is it something in your hand? It can't be matches. Must be newspaper,' Hahyoo said.

'Spot on, Hahyoo,' said Paul. 'I'm impressed. You ought to be a detective!' His smile widened as Hahyoo graciously accepted the irony. Paul thrust the newspaper onto Hahyoo's lap. An artist had drawn a likeness of Paul's Italian face, but had gone overboard on the moustache.

'The tash,' said Paul. 'It's as good as the man on the Bryant match box!' He shook the box right next to Hahyoo's ear. And as we're on the subject why couldn't we have brought flashlights instead of matches?

'Flashlight too noticeable inside room, matches better can control light'.

****

They had parked the car out of sight in a dirt track, un metalled lane. In the distance, the hospital loomed black, obscured by the brilliance of a setting sun. Paul and Hahyoo had passed the time by relating stories to each other. It was mainly Hahyoo who was the narrator. Paul couldn't get enough of his police tales, which included pirates and triad gangs with, of course, the exotic colony of Hong Kong as a backdrop.

'I think we go now. It dark enough.' Hahyoo had taken off his bowler and placed a black scarf around his neck tucked into his dark jacket. He'd persuaded Paul to wear dark clothes. 'You have matches?' Paul nodded. 'Please follow me. Keep close all time.' They crossed the road, which was empty of people and traffic. The only light came from a few gas lamps, which they avoided. There was no moon. They climbed over a wall several yards away from the entrance to the hospital, and Hahyoo quickly got his bearings. The administration building faced the entrance gates at the end of a short drive. Following Hahyoo's example, Paul hugged the side of the main ward building as they walked slowly down the drive. They were in luck. The hot evening had meant that windows had been left open even in the administration block. Hahyoo had told him that they had to be on the lookout for any watchmen who might be scavenging about. These were old men who remained on building sites all night keeping guard for a pittance, normally asleep for most of the night. He said he was used to them in Hong Kong, so he assumed they would be sleeping in their hut, or maybe not. It was a warm night.

Hahyoo climbed in through the open window first. Unfortunately, when he got inside, he tripped over a chair and went sprawling full length onto the floor. He knocked books and files off a desk as he tried to break his fall. Hearing the noise, Paul followed him in immediately, although the plan had been for him to remain outside. As Paul helped Hahyoo up, he heard Chinese words spoken quickly. He knew they weren't obscenities, but he thought he would check with Hahyoo later. The two lay on the floor for a few minutes to ensure they'd not been heard.

'Sorry for accident,' said Hahyoo when they realized all was quiet. 'Please go to window to look out. I check to see if door is secure.' The door was locked, so Hahyoo lit a match. Covering it with his hand on the window side, he walked carefully over to the cabinet that contained the files. The door wouldn't open. This didn't deter Hahyoo. He blew out the match, took a metal object out of his inside pocket, and started jiggling it in the lock. It was open in seconds. After lighting another match, he pulled out the drawer labelled 'Discharges'. The file for June 1915 was near the front, and he quickly found Jorgen's papers.

'Found it!' Laying the file on the desk and holding another match as close as he could, Hahyoo scanned each page carefully. Apart from the medical information, which indicated the boy had needed an outpatient appointment, the file detailed the circumstances of his admission. He'd been found by a member of staff walking away from the hospital, but they had persuaded him to stay for treatment. The report mentioned the boy's refusal to give any information apart from his name, which he had accidentally blurted out. They picked up that he must be of German origin because of his name and from the language that the night staff had observed when he was having nightmares on the ward. Upon discharge, the police had called to take him to an orphanage. It was impressed on the officers that the boy must attend for outpatients. At this point the light of the match died at the same time as Paul said,

'Let's go then. Don't just read the thing! We'll have plenty of time to do that.'

'Very sorry, but no,' said Hahyoo. 'It must seem that no one been here. Don't forget have good memory. I almost finished.' He lit another match.

'There's someone out there!' Paul warned in a harsh whisper. 'Put the match out!' From the light of a gas lamp on the other side of the drive he could see an old man with an oil lamp. He wore a flat cap even though it was a sweltering night, and braces held up his baggy trousers over a collarless shirt.

'It's the watchman!' said Paul.

'Please tell me when he go. I read one more paragraph.'

'He's turned the corner.'

After that it was straightforward for the pair. They drove to the railway station that they'd passed on the way to the hospital and followed the line. Once they came across signposts for Liverpool, the navigating became easier. Hahyoo remembered the way back to Crosby from Lime Street. On the way he related to Paul everything he'd read, apart from the address of the orphanage. Hahyoo thought that, in the excited state Paul was in, he might want to pay a late-night visit and attempt a rescue. That was completely a non-starter of an idea. Paul insisted that

Hahyoo tell him, but Hahyoo held fast saying they'd talk about it the following day. Hahyoo was relieved he hadn't taken the file. He was convinced that, if he had, there would have been no stopping Paul.

Chapter 52

It was about one in the morning when Paul and Hahyoo arrived at the house. Hahyoo immediately noticed it. There were two lights on, one upstairs and one on the ground floor. As he stopped the engine, Hahyoo said,

'Did you leave lights on in house?' He'd observed a large, shiny object in the drive near the window from which the light shone. His view was partially obscured by some bushes, so he jumped out of the car for a better look. It was a car – a car that Hahyoo had noticed the police in Liverpool used. His heart took off at an incredible rate until he heard himself saying, 'Calm... calm,' and started taking deep breaths. He thought it peculiar that there was only one car. He'd expect at least three if they were apprehending an armed man, as Paul was believed to be. It was also odd to see house lights on unless they'd been there some time after carrying out a search.

By this time Paul had got out of the car. Both men crept around the side of the house to the back entrance. No lights were on at the back. Hahyoo pointed to the kitchen door. It was locked. He pulled out some keys on a chain, and they were soon in the passage that led to the back kitchen. As they passed through the kitchen, Hahyoo knocked a small table over and cursed. He took out his old service revolver.

'Don't be alarmed,' he told Paul in a hushed voice. 'I have this to warn or defend, not to injure or kill.' They checked all the rooms downstairs, including the lounge where the lights were on. There were no signs to indicate the room had been searched.

There was nothing out of place. Hahyoo turned the light off, and they started to climb the stairs. Halting at the bedroom where light was shining from underneath the door, Hahyoo sensed that the room wasn't empty. Holding the gun in front of him, safety catch off, he signalled to Paul that he was going in. He turned the doorknob slowly until he knew the latch had disengaged, and with all his force, he flung the door open. The door collided with an object that gave way and fell to the floor. A man was on his back. There was blood on his forehead, but Hahyoo saw this only briefly, as he turned the light out. If the person had associates, they'd be down on them within seconds. Hahyoo and Paul lay behind the sofa after Hahyoo had felt his way in the darkness to close the door. They waited. Nothing happened. There were no sounds of movement or voices until from over by the door there were signs of life as the man started to get up. He was obviously dazed, as he stumbled. Hahyoo crept over to him on all fours. His eyes had become adjusted to the dark. He was behind the man who'd attempted to stand up again. Hahyoo jumped up and was right behind him.

'You stay still. Is better for you!' he said. He nudged the gun into the man's back.

'What sort of a welcome is that, Hahyoo?' These words were said in the broadest of Irish accents. Hahyoo couldn't believe his ears.

Paul and Paddy embraced each other for several minutes. Tears fell in between volumes of rapidly fired words, from Paddy in particular. Paddy had a rough outline of what had happened to Paul from his contacts in Liverpool and from reading the newspapers, but he knew that Paul knew only snippets of Paddy's life since that explosive early morning greeting on the beach at Blundellsands. He was soon to find out the details over a few whiskies. Paddy was revving himself up for one of his epic craics.

The Lucy Effect

Paul and Paddy sat on a sofa together in the best lounge. The chandelier and wall lights, all electric, lit up the scene as if it was a stage. Hahyoo, who'd diligently remained out of the limelight, sat in an upright chair at a distance from the sofa, which emphasized his respect but also his recognition that, at that moment, he was not a main player. Paul and Paddy needed the time to reflect and adjust, to fit as comfortably together as they had previously. This was assisted by the alcohol they drank. Hahyoo was drinking tea. A clear head to him was secondary only to the nourishment of good food and non-alcoholic drink.

Hahyoo had several Liverpool commercial directories to hand, which he'd laid out on a mahogany card table. The Quirk's Orphanage for Boys in Catherine Street, he found out, was a charitable trust whose main benefactor was the Church. It was for boys aged six to fourteen, sometimes sixteen if employment wasn't available. According to their main advert, which appeared in all the publications, they were successful at placing boys in the merchant navy. Their educational standards were second to none, and in the next sentence there was a bizarre boast that they had the lowest number of cases of illnesses in children in the Liverpool and environs. This was followed by a complementary statement that they had one of the best-equipped sickrooms with qualified staff. A telephone number was displayed with a request to contact the head or deputy in the first instance. Finally a list of the benefactors was displayed at the bottom of the advert in bold script. Hahyoo wondered who the advert was aimed at. Presumably not the illiterate parents or their children. He thought possibly the first benefactor on the list.

Meanwhile, on the sofa, centre stage, Paul and Paddy were well into their craic. Paul learnt that his friend had been close to death on a few occasions when he was on the trawler returning to Douglas, and again during the brief journey to the private hospital in Douglas. Somehow he'd held on. Loss of blood was the main problem. He was quickly transferred to Nobles Hospital in upper Douglas. His friends and business partners were concerned that his identity must not be revealed, as he was still a hunted man. They'd hurriedly fixed up papers that satisfied the hospitals that he was a resident of Douglas. He was given blood, which was a risky business, but he pulled through, and the bullet was removed. Fortunately, no vital organs were affected, and he was transferred back to the private hospital.

Paddy mended quickly and was up and about in no time. Within a couple of days, he'd contacted Hahyoo about Paul. Hahyoo was already on his way to Liverpool from Hong Kong, and on the advice of his solicitor Paddy had handed himself in to the police and was given bail. At the court hearing, the four-leafed clover was in the ascendancy for Paddy. He was found not guilty on the charge of murder, and a verdict of misadventure was pronounced by the court, much to the displeasure of the family of the victim and most of the public gallery. In the local press, a headline read 'Escapee Friend of German on Trial for Murder'. They had been after his blood, and there was a near riot outside the court. Paddy had immediately caught the ferry to Liverpool, and after attending to some work in the city, he'd motored to Blundellsands. There hadn't been any time to contact Paul and Hahyoo, and anyway, he liked surprising people. He told Paul that he was not so sure about people surprising him though, after the recent debacle.

Finally Hahyoo joined the other two on the sofa at the alcohol-powered insistence of Paddy. Hahyoo left some space between himself and the other two. After some catching up with his friend, Hahyoo manoeuvred the conversation round to the evening's events. Paddy plied Hahyoo with a range of superlatives over the burglary, and the latter's face offered a wise smile and he waved his hand dismissively. Hahyoo tried to quote the proverb about the proof of the pudding being in the tasting, but he got it mixed up.

Paddy ribbed him over this for several minutes with wild twistings of the meanings of not only the phrase, but its individual words. As they retired to their beds, all of them realized they had to test the reality of the facts that had been uncovered. That would mean tasting the pudding with the head at the orphanage.

Chapter 53

Hahyoo was first to rise and was impatient to start his day. He picked up the telephone's earpiece and turned the generator handle rapidly to connect with the operator. He was apprehensive. This was his first occasion using this type of telephone.

'Can you connect with Quirk's orphanage, please?'

'Would you mind repeating that, sir?'

'Sorry speaking. Please, you connect me Quirk's Orphanage.' Hahyoo's mixed-up words further confused the operator, who began to ask him to telephone later and speak to her superior, but suddenly, he felt the earpiece taken out of his hands.

'Excuse me friend here,' Paddy cooed into the mouthpiece. 'He doesn't appreciate the wonders of this incredible instrument like you and I, me love. What he was trying to say was, can you put us through to Quirk's Orphanage?' It took the girl a second or two to respond. Paddy suspected she was overcome, as women so often were, with the enchanting lilt of his accent along with his forwardness. And, after all, that had been his intention all along. In the meantime, he cast a warm smile in the direction of Hahyoo, who simply shook his head.

'One moment please.' There was no 'sir', but there was a definite lightness in her voice. 'You're through. Bye-bye,' she said with a hint of laughter. The phone spluttered and then a stern sounding male voice clipped,

'Quirk's Orphanage,' said a voice. 'Headmaster speaking.'

There was a pause, so Paddy responded,

'I work for Collins Solicitors in the city—'

The head interrupted, 'Your name?'

'Mr Kirwan.' He used Seamus's name; at least he was Irish. There was another pause. Paddy continued in a voice he hoped was the opposite to the one he used in his previous conversation with the girl, 'We are searching for a boy whom we understand is an inmate at your establishment.'

'Understand from whom?' was the curt response.

Paddy hesitated.

'Look, can I send my man in to see you?'

'When?'

'This afternoon.'

'No. I shan't be in.'

'Later this evening, then?'

'One moment.' He heard the rustling of paper. The head seemed to be checking his diary. 'Not in till Friday, at ten.' The man didn't wait for a reply; the telephone went dead.

'Right then, that's it,' Paddy said.

Hahyoo picked up Paddy's displeasure.

'So we go to tomorrow morning?'

'No, this afternoon. I have this strong feelin' we won't be gettin' any place wit' that man, and besides there's method in me mad thoughts. Wait and see.'

****

Hahyoo had drawn the short straw. Paul and Paddy had persuaded him that it would be so strange for whoever was on duty to be confronted with a charming and seemingly naive person like Hahyoo, they'd be putty in his hands. This wasn't the way he saw it. The others had much more to lose than he did. That was the real reason. But he wasn't bothered. He was aware that it was in his interest. Recent events in Paddy's life had reinforced this idea. 'No Paddy, no job' came into his mind as it had only a few weeks previously when Paddy had mentioned the task waiting for him in Liverpool.

As Hahyoo entered the gates of the orphanage, these thoughts were still on his mind. He calmed himself down by starting his breathing exercises as he walked up the steps and entered the reception area. He stood in the hall in between the office and the staircase. In the distance he could hear children's voices. They were outside playing. He retraced his steps back to the entrance porch and looked around for a bell push. He was about to press it when a female voice asked,

'Can I help you, sir?' Hahyoo noted it was said with warmth.

'Oh yes. Very sorry for disturbance.' He bowed as he said this, and Matron responded with a smile.

'I come from solicitors about a boy we try to trace.'

Matron held her hand up to stop him.

'Pardon me for stopping you, but you need to talk to someone else. The headmaster is not in, but his deputy is here. Would you like to talk to him?'

Hahyoo agreed, and she showed him into the office. 'Wait here. I'll get Deputy Head Master Swithins,' she said.

As Swithins walked in, Hahyoo sensed a man in torment. It was not so much the tautness in his face, and the folding and unfolding of his arms, but the terror he saw deep in the man's eyes. Swithins sat down behind the desk. Hahyoo sat down opposite him, realizing that he was not going to be asked.

'I come from solicitors,' he began. 'We look for boy Jorgen Roth. From our investigation we know he here or has been here.'

'That is confidential.' Hahyoo noticed that Swithins almost added the word *sir*, but must have thought better of it. Hahyoo cut in,

'We offer good money. One hundred pounds.'

'How much?' Swithins asked with incredulity.

'One hundred pounds cash.' Hahyoo emphasized the word *cash*. 'A pretty penny, yes?' Swithins nodded, his mouth half open.

'You have boy here tomorrow. Ten o'clock. I give you fifty pounds now and fifty pounds tomorrow when you hand boy over.' Hahyoo became aware of his rapid words and that he sounded as if he was dealing in commodities, so he consciously slowed down. 'And no one else to know. You say he ran away. You understand?'

Swithins nodded as he covered the page of a newspaper up with a large battered register ledger that was lying on the desk. Hahyoo noticed this and wondered what it meant. Was it a nervous response or something more sinister?

Paul and Paddy were waiting in the car.

'Didn't it go all right?' Paddy asked. Hahyoo knew that his unsmiling face must have given him away.

'Yes, too well.'

'What d'you mean?'

'We buy *Liverpool Courier*. He not surprised when I ask about boy. No response in his face. He very troubled man, though maybe that was reason. He cover newspaper, so I could not see.' The sentence was garbled and very unlike his normal logical and quaint English.

'Hold on,' Paddy said. 'What d'you mean about hidin' the newspaper?'

'He cover newspaper when I say not to tell anyone about deal, and say that boy ran away.'

They all knew that they had no alternative but to go through with the deal, and time wasn't in their favour.

'Ye're overdoin' yer t'inking. Yer brain'll fry if ye're not careful,' said Paddy. 'We've got no other option. Just have to take care.'

They bought that day's edition of the *Liverpool Courier*, and when they came to the advert it was obvious that Hahyoo's hunch was correct. The police were offering a reward for the capture of Paul or information leading to his arrest. But, again, Paddy counselled for action rather than delay. The other two were not happy. But hadn't the cat jumped out of the bag and screamed unearthly infant cries? Everyone would know what was going on. Paddy thought otherwise as he planned to tinker with the actions of the proverbial cat. The others wondered whether Paddy knew more than he was letting on.

Chapter 54

At half nine the following morning, Paddy, disguised and dressed as a chauffeur, parked the car in a side street opposite the playing fields at Quirk's Orphanage, making sure it was pointed in the right direction for a speedy getaway. Hahyoo was to bring Jorgen over the playing fields and head for the car, and Paul would assist his son over the fence. For the purposes of quick recognition, Paul had reverted to the face that Jorgen would know him by. If anything went drastically wrong, Hahyoo would fire a shot, and Paul and Paddy would make a dash for it and leave Hahyoo to his own devices.

Hahyoo was none too pleased about this decision. Not so much because of the likelihood of his capture in such circumstances, but rather because he didn't like the idea of discharging his pistol with children around. There were no protests. His only reaction was to engage his mind. He wanted to tap its positivity, so he uttered the mantra 'I will succeed. I will succeed' in his native tongue and kept repeating this until he thought it had permeated his subconscious and established itself within to be called upon if necessary.

Hahyoo rang the bell, and the door was opened by Swithins. Hahyoo observed a passing smile, and his heartbeat increased. His mood wasn't helped when he noticed Swithins was walking down the hall towards the office at a slow pace. He was time wasting.

When they'd sat down in the office Hahyoo asked,

'Where's Jorgen?'

'You're early. I'll go and fetch him.' Swithins was out of the office for five minutes. Hahyoo noticed that the newspaper was still on the desk underneath the register. To confirm his suspicions, he checked the page it was opened on. He'd been right. This deputy was greedy. It was nearly ten to ten. When Swithins returned there was no sign of Jorgen. Seeming to anticipate Hahyoo's response, he said,

'He'll be along shortly.'

Swithins sat down and started looking at some papers on the desk. Hahyoo remained silent for a few minutes and calmed down taking deep breaths. His mantra came to mind. When he'd finished this exercise, he took the pistol out of his inside pocket and pointed the barrel at Swithins head,

'Look, I don't like what I do, but I think you trick me.'

Swithins seemed paralysed by fear, and Hahyoo could tell the man's mind had momentarily receded to some faraway, and possibly frightening, place. He didn't seem able to speak. 'Where money I gave you?' Hahyoo demanded.

Swithins fumbled with the drawer and eventually took the bank notes out, which Hahyoo grabbed. 'Now,' Hahyoo said, pushing the nozzle of the gun against Swithins' forehead, 'pick up mouthpiece of telephone. Ask someone to bring Jorgen here quick. Very quick!'

His hands shaking, Swithins did as he had been told. After a few moments, there was a knock at the door. Hahyoo noticed the time: three minutes to ten. Hahyoo got up from his chair, backed away towards the door, and opened it, still holding the gun pointed at Swithins. By this time the deputy head had his head down on the desk. He was sobbing like an infant out of control.

Hahyoo turned briefly and saw Jorgen standing in the doorway, his mouth open in shock. He grabbed the boy as gently as he could and said,

'Don't be afraid. Paul – your father – come for you in car. It's on road. He say, tell Jorgen that he hope you not spent sovereigns he gave you when you separated, and he was pleased you went St

Helens. Now we must go quick. Police come.' With these words, Jorgen seemed to relax a bit. As they ran across the playground towards the playing fields, Jorgen slowed down. Hahyoo noticed that the boy was looking directly at a tall black boy, and the boy was looking back at Jorgen.

Vincent knew he must speak to his friend, who was approaching him rapidly. He couldn't believe his eyes – a Chinese man and Jorgen running towards the fence! Vincent didn't have to think about it. He joined Jorgen. Both boys began to laugh the laughter of care-free innocents escaping constriction.

Hahyoo had no choice in the matter. He could clearly hear the bells of what must be police vehicles. Jorgen increased his speed when he saw his father on the other side of the fence. He soon left the other two behind. There was no time for any sort of emotional reunion. No time for anything. Paddy was revving up the high-powered car. All the doors were opened, and Paddy half glanced at Vincent as he piled in along with Hahyoo and Jorgen.

They were unsure of police tactics. At least the city force had few cars, so their options were limited. Paddy sped away from the orphanage. The engine roared. Its rasping tones reverberated around Victorian structures and cobbled streets. Paddy prayed aloud and sometimes swore whenever he imagined danger. He was doing both now.

Paul's knowledge of the city's back streets enabled them to evade the police without too much effort. Once they were clear of the city boundary, they relaxed. Jorgen clung to his papa, and his father's arms cocooned him. He felt that he could never let him go. How many times in the past few months had he dreamt of what was happening at that moment? Suddenly this strong emotion of sanctuary ruptured. He didn't know why. He felt he was submerged in dirty, thick water, floating, unable to see with clarity. The events of the last half hour hit him – the unreality of it all. It was like the plot of a 'penny dreadful'! The terrifying was possible, all the time. No eventuality was impossible. A precious dream of a jewelled, sparkling, never-ending waterfall could suddenly turn into a nightmare of a dark, foul-smelling pond. The four months of separation and its horrific reality created a kernel of doubt within him, and his mood changed from elation to anger. How could his papa have put him through all that? It was his fault. He pushed Paul away angrily.

Vincent wanted to comfort his friend, but thought it might upset Paul, so he stared out of the window at the deep, lush greenness of the countryside. Its alien presence invaded him. He yearned for the sunburnt dryness of his native land, the stretching plains of huge un travelled distances, the fond sounds of insects, even the pesky ones. To Vincent his present experience was also unreal. A moment ago, he'd been a child in a school, and here he was in a car, treated almost like an adult. The certainty of the days ahead had gone. Every road they turned down northwards was one more road away from his uncle. Now, what would happen?

Paddy's thoughts, unsurprisingly, were quite different. His concern was the black lad. Why was he a passenger? He'd introduced himself right away. The boy seemed polite and well educated. Paddy showered him with questions. Hahyoo must have seen that Vincent was getting upset, as he intervened in a good-humoured way, saying that looking into the eyes in sincerity when talking was like an undoubted experience of heaven.

Paddy couldn't hear Hahyoo's gentle voice above the roar of the engine, but got the feeling tones of the message and shut up.

Paul's initial joy on the reunion was tempered with sadness. He couldn't quite understand the sudden change in Jorgen and put it down to over-excitement and, like Vincent, tried to seek solace from the view through the car window. Jorgen sobbed for the rest of the journey, but the engine smothered most of the sound to the gratitude of the car's occupants.

Chapter 55

Hahyoo was pouring boiling water on his favourite tea. He had taken great care of this precious commodity since leaving Hong Kong. He kept the Keemun in an old tea caddie decorated with golden dragons on a red background. It had belonged to his grandmother. The role of cook had been foisted on him his first day at Blundellsands. He didn't mind, as the most important part of a meal was the accompanying drink. No one else could brew Keemun tea as it should be brewed. In fact, no one else could brew tea apart from Paddy, whose tea was always Indian and came with milk even though Hahyoo would request none. It was an insult to the leaf. He took a tray with the drinks into the lounge where they were seated on the two sofas.

'You were a bit slow wit' the drinks there, Hoo. Ye're slippin!' Hahyoo ignored him but half smiled when he added, 'I might take to dockin' yer wages.' Sometimes Hahyoo didn't know which way to take Paddy's humour.

Paddy must have sensed these thoughts, as he said,

'Ye're noodle dish knocked me out good style! Where'd yer learn to cook?'

'Everyone cook at home. Everyone join in good atmosphere.' He was wanting to respond in a more comical tone, but he didn't have the thoughts, never mind the words. Instead, he became serious.

'Look, we must talk about what we do now.' He took a sip of his tea, which had an immediate calming effect. Most noticeably, his calf muscles, which were prone to tension, relaxed. 'Is very, very important.'

Paddy immediately gave him his full attention. Hahyoo knew that his friend would heed his next words. 'The police will look for Chinaman, and the newspaper will show drawings of me like they do. So from now I have to hide. Where can I hide? Can't stay here. Neighbours see me. They tell police. We need to hide car we drove from orphanage. Maybe somebody see.' He stopped and took another sip of his tea.

'All right,' Paddy said. 'I take yer point. I'll be on the blower later and make arrangements fer tomorrow.'

'But need to go now,' urged Hahyoo. 'Today is dangerous to stay – for us all.' His manner was more resolute than ever.

'What d'you think, Paul?' asked Paddy.

Paul seemed surprised that Paddy would be asking him. But Hahyoo noticed that Paddy was behaving strangely.

'Hahyoo talks sense,' said Paul. 'It's too risky to hang about.' He looked at the others as if to gauge their reactions to his response.

'Look I suppose it's a good time to tell yer what me plans are fer yers all,' Paddy cut in. 'You can tell me what yer t'ink.' He paused and looked around at the group. 'I've got yer a ship leaving Liverpool fer New York and the Americas tomorrow early—'

Paul sprung to his feet.

'Good God, Paddy, that well takes the last biscuit!' he shouted. 'I've had enough of you knocking us over like a cheap set of skittles on a whim, and all the time having us believe that we were shouting the odds! It's not the first time, and you know it.' His face reddened as the volume of his voice rose, but Hahyoo believed that the man would be able to control his temper. Like a watchman with a bull terrier, it would go no further than necessary.

'Bare faced, leading us on until the last minute, knowing exactly what was to happen!' continued Paul. 'You treat us like brainless lackeys!'

Hahyoo's embarrassment prompted him to look down at the table away from anyone's line of vision. He observed that on the table there was one biscuit remaining on a blue plate that had a gold rim. It was perfectly sitting in the centre of the blueness. He thought about spatial positioning and where people sat in relation to others and how they orientated their limbs. He believed it was to do with power and the way they ranked themselves in the pack. A notion carrying more weight and punch pierced his mind and made him smile. It was Paul's reference to the last biscuit.

Hahyoo had been suspicious of Paddy's behaviour the previous day. And now it all fitted into pace. He'd telegrammed Paddy about the whereabouts of Jorgen on the Tuesday, and Paddy had quickly arranged for the ships he had available in Liverpool to be on alert. So he'd known all along that the deadline was Friday the thirteenth of August even before he'd set foot onto the ferry in Douglas the previous day. No doubt if these plans had fallen through, Paddy would have worked out alternatives.

'You're as bad Hahyoo,' Paul continued, turning to Hahyoo. 'I thought I could trust you, the so-called honest Chinaman.' His eyes threw daggers at Hahyoo, who immediately raised his hand in self-defence.

'No, I knew—'

Before he could finish Paddy interrupted.

'Hahyoo knew not'ing of dis. Yer both know what I'm like. The least yer know, the better. Yer wouldn't be spillin' the beans, would yer, as there wouldn't be any beans to spill? The better for me, the ships, and all the other cogs, major and minor, who've had a hand in all this palaver. Look, in the end it's up to yers all what ye're going to do. I can't force you. I can only say dis. The sooner ye're clear out of Liverpool the better. The point is that it'd be difficult to switch a sailing to another port. The admiralty are closing down shipping routes fer passenger sailings and concentrating on freight and food imports. Because of the U-boat threat, it looks like the sailing tomorrow will be the last out of Liverpool carrying passengers. The way we got round it was by using a cargo ship with passenger accommodation. Although it could be done fer all of yers to go on a cargo ship to another destination as crew, there's far more admiralty checkin' in these vessels. The option would be fer yer to stay in hidin' in this country. But at some time, sooner or later, you'll need to be shipped out. When war's ragin' it's not goin' to be good fer any of us. And who knows when it'll all end?'

There was silence as the words sank in. Paul capitulated and walked over to Jorgen. He sat down and placed his hand on the boy's shoulder. Jorgen moved away, closer to Vincent. He'd avoided his papa since they returned.

'Look, Jorgen,' Paul said. 'New York. We've talked about going before as a family.'

At the word *family* Jorgen flew off the sofa, his face a mix of anger and tears. As he approached the door, he turned and shouted in German,

'I hate you. Leave my mama and brother here in the cemetery?' He slammed the door behind him. Paul rushed to the door, flung it open, and ran up the stairs after his son.

Hahyoo followed and managed to catch him up before Paul reached the bedroom that Jorgen was in. The boy had slammed the door shut and it sounded as if he was barricading it with heavy furniture. A reddish hue still clung to Paul's face. He was about to bang on the door, but Hahyoo pulled him to one side.

'He very angry, like you must be. Not good time to speak. He needs to get feelings out on own for now.'

'Why is he like this?' Paul said breathing heavily.

'He been through great deal. It pass through his mind time and again. Like badness from wound can fester in brain. That no good. Take time. You need patience of Buddha.'

'But what if he refuses to come with me to New York? I can't leave him here—' Tears shone in the corners of his eyes.

Hahyoo interrupted,

'You right. Can't stay here. Too dangerous. I see him when he calmer. I talk long with him, try persuade. Other problem is Vincent. He wants stay to find relative. It makes worse if he stay. It likely that Jorgen find harder to go as well.'

When Hahyoo and Paul returned to the lounge they found Paddy with a large glass of whisky in his hand. He was alone.

'How is he?' Paddy asked as Paul poured himself a whisky. Hahyoo sat down and started sipping his beloved tea.

'Barricaded himself in a bedroom,' Paul answered. 'We've left him. No point in making it worse. Where's Vincent?'

'Went after Jorgen. He seemed upset as well.'

Paul took a gulp of his drink and thumped the glass down on the table with great force, but then rearranged it more gently.

'That'll stir Jorgen up. We'll have to watch them. They could do a runner.'

Hahyoo interrupted.

'Very sorry, but that could be bad. Can't make prisoners. Think Paddy speak with Vincent. You have many contacts here who could find out about uncle. I can talk to Jorgen. Try make him understand.'

'I made no plans to ship another person out,' Paddy said. 'He won't have any papers. And the crew will be dead set against it. T'was touch and go whether they'd accept the invitation to our little shindig. We had to lean on them heavily. I could find out about his relatives as you say—'

Once again, Hahyoo cut in,

'Vincent would be arrested. He now one of us – criminal, apart from you, Paddy. Find himself, as you were, in a prison. Also it would be very good for you to help man who one day is to be chief of tribe. Good for business in Africa.'

There was silence. Paddy swirled the whisky around in the glass again and again. Hahyoo could almost see the words forming in Paddy's bright eyes.

'Well I suppose in fer a penny in fer a pound.' He tapped Hahyoo good-naturedly on his arm. Tea slopped onto the saucer Hahyoo was holding. He didn't respond. He'd got his way. To him it was the only solution, but he knew too well nothing was perfect.

Chapter 56

The adults agreed they would leave the house at 8.30 that night, head for the docks, and board the ship. Paddy arranged for them to be picked up by car. The one outside would be taken to the docks and loaded into one of the ship's holds. It would come in useful in their travels in the Americas. Additionally, the police wouldn't be able to trace the car. The ship's captain would have to be bribed for the extra cargo, and not just the car. There was Vincent as well. Paddy and Hahyoo were to try and bring the boys round to accepting what was going to happen and ensure that they were ready to be picked up on time.

Paul remained in the lounge, and the others went to pack their belongings. By chance, Hahyoo had to return to the kitchen. He'd forgotten his canister of tea. When he got to the hall he could hear the voice of Paul coming from the lounge. He thought it strange, as he knew Paul was alone. He tiptoed over to the door, and to his horror overheard Paul on the telephone speaking to a woman he addressed as Bridie. He was making arrangements to see her late that night at the pub opposite the Adelphi. It could ruin everything if it went wrong. Hahyoo tensed his muscles and grabbed the brass doorknob, but held back. To confront Paul at this time would be rash. It was obvious that Paul planned to leave the ship in King's Dock later for the rendezvous, and Hahyoo thought that discussing the matter on the ship offered more advantages. He didn't know the motivation behind Paul's desire to meet this Bridie. Hahyoo knew the man could be headstrong, and in his anger might leave right away now. That would be disastrous. No one else needed to know. Paddy was unpredictable when he was in a tight corner. Hahyoo would keep this close to his chest until they were on board ship where they'd have more control.

****

It took only one phone call to the emergency services carried out by an employee of Paddy's to obtain the information on Vincent's relatives, although the news was worse than he could have ever imagined. The charred remains of Vincent's uncle had been found in the wreckage of the burnt-out house. He broke the news to Vincent in as gentle a way as he could and spared him any of the morbid details. Paddy told him that the body had been buried in a pauper's grave in a city cemetery and it would be possible for the body to be exhumed and returned to their homeland. This was a bit of comforting blarney, but already there were seeds of a plan in Paddy's head to carry it out. Then his speech dried up, something that Paddy thought hadn't happened in ages... well, since the Isle of Man.

Vincent turned away. He dropped his head and sobbed. His body shook. To Paddy's amazement, however, the boy quickly controlled this wave of emotion. He lifted his head, straightened his whole body, and remained still. There was a gracefulness in this action, and to Paddy the boy seemed to have physically grown taller. After a minute or so when Paddy could just about catch some phrases that Vincent mumbled in his mother tongue, he turned, shook Paddy's hand, and said thank you. In some ways it was a relief for Vincent to know what had happened. He could now concentrate on moving on, and that meant a return to his village.

Hahyoo fared rather worse in his attempt to persuade Jorgen to change his mind. Each time he'd gone up to the bedroom, Jorgen had refused to open the door or speak. As Hahyoo returned to the lounge for the third time, Paul and Paddy were well on the way to finishing off the bottle of scotch on the table. They both gave him questioning looks as he sat down, and Hahyoo moved his head from side to side slowly in response.

'No sound from room,' he said.

'Did you check to see if the bedroom window was open, Hahyoo?' Paddy asked.

'Of course.'

Paul shuffled his feet and started twirling a strand of his now-natural-coloured, long, blonde hair between two fingers anxiously.

'Time's getting on,' he said. 'The car will be here in an hour. We've got to sort it out. Let me go and have a word. He needs to know how his behaviour is affecting us all – this shilly-shallying. We need to be stern, get him to face the facts.'

Paul got up, but Hahyoo also stood up and placed his hand on Paul's shoulder. 'No. It no good. Will not speak to you, am sure. Make worse. Leave it me one more time. I understand what you say.'

Half an hour later, Hahyoo stood outside Jorgen's room again. It would be difficult. What he was going to do was not in his nature, and it could easily backfire.

'Jorgen, your papa in mortal danger!' he shouted in as harsh a way as he could manage. 'You understand? His life is threatened. You want lose him? Only you might stop what wants to do. He does for you. Open this door. You can save him,' he finished angrily in a blaming tone. To his surprise the door opened slowly, but Jorgen wasn't behind it. He'd jumped onto the bed. He sat with his head bowed, grasping his knees so that his tear-stained face was mostly obscured. Hahyoo wasn't going to speak first. He observed the tension building up in Jorgen as the boy started to rock his body, the knuckles whitening as his hands gripped his knees.

Jorgen suddenly looked up. 'Why did Papa leave me? He shouldn't have left me,' he shouted, looking directly at Hahyoo. His eyes were red, and tears flowed down his cheeks. 'I told him not to make me go, but he just said, "Geh, geh, geh!"' For a moment Hahyoo felt he was Paul. 'Why? Why?' Jorgen rolled over on the bed and started to pummel the pillows with his hands, sobbing violently until this charge of anger exhausted itself. He then lay face down, whimpering.

Hahyoo walked to the bed and gently placed his hand on Jorgen's head.

'Your papa told you go because he loves you. He wanted you to be free.' Hahyoo's responses to Jorgen's questions were limited. He didn't know the whole story, so he had to prevaricate at times. 'You had chance on own. Not want you in orphanage. Not his fault didn't work out. If you'd stayed with father, you would definitely be in orphanage. Can't you see? Did it for you. It hard for him to do this. He did not know what would happen to you. In his mind you went to relative.' He paused. Jorgen seemed to be quietening down. His breathing was more natural. 'When he in prison, aim was to escape and find you. This was very dangerous for him. Your papa nearly shot and Paddy wounded. He has not had chance to explain everything. But I must tell you. Your father plan to see someone tonight because he upset what you said. He goes to see lady he know. Think that if he stay in England with you, better chance if he seem to have wife. So police won't know him. They look only for father and son. This is very dangerous. If he caught, will go to prison for long time – or worse may happen.' Hahyoo didn't want to elaborate. 'You must try to stop him. Let him know you only want be with him and safe in America. You can come back England when all is sorted. I know Paddy wants help your father and you. He risked life, got wounded for your father. You mustn't let them down. Better if tell him when get to ship and on own.'

Hahyoo wasn't sure that Jorgen had taken all this in. But there was no time. He heard a car pulling up outside.

'Come on, Jorgen. For your papa's sake, must go now.

Paddy opened the front door to find a chauffeur standing there. The parish church clock struck the half hour. The chauffeur hurried inside, shutting the door behind him, and followed Paddy into the lounge. The chauffeur started to undress down to his underwear,

'There's your kecks and jacket over there on the chest of drawers. You'll be pleased yer won't be wearin' mine,' Paddy said with a full beam of a smile. 'Yer know the plan. Take the other car to the ship, the *Prenton* in the Kings Dock and make sure it's loaded on board, in the hold mind. Oh, and don't forget yere uniform! ' The man, no longer a chauffeur was soon gone. There were no other pleasantries exchanged. Paddy, who still had his chauffeurs uniform on from the morning, added the peaked cap. He placed his arm around Hahyoo at the same time as he half covered his friend's face with his hand.

'Come on Hahyoo, ye're not feeling well. You've bin kiddin' us all along. Ye're really a hundred-yer-ol' sod.' At first Jorgen, standing near his father, appeared a bit confused, but then he seemed to realize what was going on as the others started laughing.

'Shhhow a bit of decorum fer an ol' gent,' Paddy shouted as he half carried Hahyoo to the car trying to make sure his face was covered and checking to see if any of the curtains in houses across the road were being moved, although he thought it pointless, particularly when the others followed carrying their cases. Paddy cursed and hurriedly snatched the cases from them muttering under his breath. Then he added, 'Aren't I a good enough chauffeur fer yous, yer bunch of idyets!' Jorgen and Vincent were laughing their heads off.

Chapter 57

Chief Inspector Louis Denning, an old timer brought in from Scotland Yard to get a swift result in the high-profile Roth case, sat at an unfamiliar desk. He looked up and out of the grime-covered bay window on the first floor of the central Liverpool police offices. A car with a thunderous engine was passing below the window, and smoke from its exhaust wafted in through the top open panes. He rose to his feet in haste, leaving his burning pipe on the desk, and looked onto the busy street scene below. He'd gauged that he first heard the car when it had turned into Dale Street from Castle Street several hundred yards way. It was travelling too fast. Drivers of vehicles pulled by horses and ponies were having difficulty keeping their animals calm. Some animals reared. A cart carrying a load of vegetables shed some of its load onto the road. The fabric roof was down on the car, and Inspector Denning could see its young driver turn his head from side to side enjoying the reactions of pedestrians. Some of them were obviously fearful; others were angry. And children looked on most amazed and excited at the sight. The speed of the vehicle made Denning think of the getaway car that had been used to lift the boy from the orphanage earlier in the day – the car nobody had seen although some witnesses had heard. it had been a high-powered car without a doubt similar to the one he'd just observed. He called someone into the office to ensure this latest driving infraction was being followed up.

Ever since his arrival and a quick appraisal of the facts in the Roth case, along with an assessment of the police personnel involved, he'd kicked himself for taking the job on. But he'd wanted to retire on the highest note possible. This case was of national importance. It had seemed a godsend, but now low, flat notes were depressing him, and their volume was increasing. The senior Liverpool officers concerned would never have been employed by the Yard. The way they'd tackled events so far was beyond belief. The day after his arrival, he put in a request for his right-hand man, Detective Sergeant David Kearney, to be despatched to Liverpool immediately. He had a talent for reviewing cases, a necessity if they were to get anywhere fast. Denning rang down to ask for a car to be made available. The train would be arriving at Lime Street in half an hour; he had arranged to meet Kearney there.

****

There was a silence. They'd exhausted all the gossip. Denning's facial expression had changed from the lightness of interest tinged with humour, to pensive furrows over his eyes, the latter firmly fixed on the clock in the office. Kearney was the first to break the feeling of unease,

'So they stuck you in probably the best office in the building 'cos of your chain smoking. That's a lark!'

'Think was more because of the way I stare at people, and you know what I mean.' Denning whipped his pipe back into his mouth and paused for thought. 'They had this meeting unbeknownst to me and then offered this place, because the chief constable is on leave, and it's quite private. I was in two minds whether to accept or not.' He paused again, but his pipe remained in his mouth. He puffed and mumbled, 'As you know, I like to be in the thick of it with the men. I can always pick up on things.' He took the pipe out of his mouth and knocked its contents into an ashtray. Out came his tobacco pouch, and he refilled the pipe. 'But then

I thought we'd need privacy. Didn't want to be overheard. They mightn't appreciate...' He didn't finish the sentence; his pipe needed attention.

Kearney got his head stuck in the Roth file, and when he'd had his fill he looked up and said, 'Right. Got it, what there is of it. Pretty thin on the ground, though. See what you mean about standards.' He flipped through the file as he spoke.

'Well, to be fair, some good work has been done – and then undone by other less-competent souls. It has weaknesses in its breadth. They should have widened the net a lot more from the beginning. This Lieber fellow – the one who escaped with Roth – they should have been onto him like a load of bricks. It's obvious that he's been involved all the way along the line. But he covers his tracks cleverly. That getaway car, for instance, must have cost a pretty penny. We know by the court notes from Douglas that Mr Lieber – known as Paddy – is a prominent, wealthy businessman, although we're not sure in which area of business. In fact, very little is known of him. He's the one with the cash and the contacts. But we don't have any concrete evidence to link him to the abduction. But nail him, and we could have our man in no time!' He took the pipe out of his mouth, twisted the stem off, and pushed a small, rolled-up piece of blotting paper into its orifice to clear out the gunge. 'Would you credit it? They were talking about using manpower to look for this Chinaman, but I'm sure he'll not be seen again. Don't worry. I've stopped this. But it shows their knee-jerk mentality. Another bothersome matter is that the police like to get their messages to the newspapers to show how they're doing, and the more bizarre the better. I didn't have a chance countering the Chinaman story, so it'll be out in all the papers tomorrow, you can bet your life on it. But it could do us a favour, take them off their guard.'

'D'you think so?' Kearney looked puzzled.

'No, of course not, I jest. It'd be like a preacher not knowing his scripture! They're far too clever. One of the tightest ships I've seen in my career. No, but there's always a weak spot, and if you keep ferreting, you never know—' Denning was interrupted by a knock at the door.

A uniformed officer popped his head in the door. 'They've found a dealer who sold a fast car last week in unusual circumstances,' he reported. 'Shall we follow it up, sir?'

'No,' said Denning. 'But get me a man to accompany Detective Sergeant Kearney to the garage to take a look.' The officer left, closing the door behind him.

Denning looked at his sergeant. 'You don't mind, Kearney? I know it's routine, but I can't trust this lot, and there might be something. But don't hang about. I want you back here for the wheat from the chaff sort-out meeting at five.

At four thirty in the afternoon, Denning received a phone call. It was from the local hospital. 'I've got a lady on the phone concerning Roth,' the caller said. There followed a pause. Denning could hear a flustered conversation in the background, and then an excited female voice came on the line. The woman sounded Irish and ran her sentences together nervously. 'Paul Roth has phoned me. You said I should telephone if he did.' Denning noticed that she was faltering. He wondered if she'd finish and hang up, and he was about to interrupt, but she continued. 'He wants to meet me. I didn't know what to do. He was so persuasive. I tried to get him to telephone again, but he said there wasn't time. He wouldn't tell me anymore.' She paused. He felt as if he could hear her thinking that she had to stop. She continued, 'He asked me to meet him in the Vine Pub next to the cafe we used to go to... this evening at ten. I agreed. I hope what I've done is all right, sir?' Denning thought there was little conviction in the last sentence. He even felt sorry for her.

'Couldn't be better, miss. You've done very well,' he told her. 'I'll send someone round straight away to pick you up so we can have a longer chat at the station, if that's convenient for you. By the way, my name is Inspector Denning.' He placed the receiver down. In his younger days he would be slapping the desk with both hands at this stage. Now he slowly took his pipe and his tobacco pouch from his jacket pocket and stuffed some of the fragrant tobacco tightly into the pipe's bowl. As he did this, he thought, *What a turnout someone's made a howler! We've got you now. No escape this time.* He jammed down the remaining pieces of the tobacco as hard as he could as if emphasizing the point. Then another jumble of thoughts from a deeper place bubbled up: *This is too easy. Are they playing a game? They couldn't be!*

Chapter 58

The steam ship *Prenton*, partly owned by Paddy, was berthed in King's Dock. The shipping company used this dock and nearby Wapping Dock, as they possessed a large number of bonded warehouses. Tax wasn't paid on imports until the goods were sold. This was handy for Paddy, as not only could he save money in the short term until items were sold, but he could hold non-perishables in the warehouses until prices rose and could pull in profit.

At 3,508 tonnes, the *Prenton* was one of the fastest ocean-going merchant steam ships. The *Prenton*'s main routes were to the United States, but on this occasion she was on an extended voyage that included South American ports. The *Prenton* boasted basic passenger accommodation that Paddy used when venturing out on trips that could be euphemistically described as 'quasi legal'. It had built up a notorious reputation in American waters, but they'd always managed to dupe the authorities and throw them off the scent. Since the beginning of the war, though, there'd been a couple of close calls as security tightened. On this night in King's Dock, viewed from the quayside, the *Prenton* stood in good stead with the look of a readiness to cope with anything that was thrown at her. The back light of a still, bright sky powered by the subtle deep orange glow of a sun not long ago set accentuated her statement of strength.

On boarding the *Prenton*, Paul, Jorgen, Vincent, Hahyoo, and Paddy were shown to their berths. There were normally two cabins set aside for passengers, but on this occasion the captain, who was livid about the circumstances, had to give up his quarters for Hahyoo. In animal terms, Hahyoo was a perfect model of the Siamese breed of cat, as he had a very deep and complete aversion to seawater. He had already announced that, once the ship was at sea, he would lock himself in the cabin and order that he would not be disturbed until the end of the voyage. The other travellers shared quarters, the adults in one cabin and the boys in the smaller cabin.

Within minutes of checking out the accommodation, Paul excused himself to Paddy saying he needed some air. The boys' cabin was next door to his own, and Paul was in luck – they were nowhere to be seen. There was no need to slip the letter under the door. If the letter had been intercepted, he couldn't have faced Jorgen, and his plan might have been foiled. He was ready to go. He would be talking to Bridie in the next half hour. The thought made his heart beat a little bit faster, pumping adrenalin round his body, alerting muscles and grey matter. At that moment, apart from exhilaration, bizarrely, his dominant feeling was one of romantic patriotism. He felt more German than ever. The child part of his personality took over. He fancied himself a secret agent stealing out into enemy-held territory to rescue his love and cement a newly made family together for the sake of Jorgen. He was desperate. Nothing would stop him!

After dropping off his belongings in the cabin, Jorgen searched for his papa. He wanted to make sure his father didn't leave the ship. He became desperate when he realized he wasn't anywhere to be found on the open decks. The only places he hadn't checked were the locked cargo holds. Of course it was impossible to check them, and it would be fruitless anyway. Jorgen dashed back to his father's cabin. It was empty. Where was Vincent? He'd know what to do. He returned to his own cabin. Vincent wasn't there. On the top bunk bed he noticed a letter. He stared at the words written in German. At first they didn't make sense. His mental defences wouldn't permit any encroachment of their meaning, meaning that brought back the memory of rushed departures, some more purposeful than others, but all without resolution. This was the frenzied mindset of Quirk's Orphanage. He read the note:

> 'Gone to visit a friend. If she says yes to the question I ask, then we can stay here in England. I understand why you want this. We don't have to go to New York. I will come back for you. Don't worry.
>
> All my love,
> Your Papa'

Chapter 59

Denning had ordered police to empty the Vine Pub in Lime Street of drinkers at nine. Detective Sergeant Kearney had wanted the public cleared off the surrounding streets as well because of armed police, but his chief had persuaded him that unusually empty streets would make Roth suspicious. This man would be on his guard, although there was a question mark here. All the other activities of the gang had been carried out in a professional manner. They'd covered their tracks like the abominable snowman, well within limits of evading capture. This new action of Roth's was insane; Denning was convinced that Roth's friends knew nothing of it.

Before Denning arrived at the scene of entrapment, he'd tried to obtain details on shipping and train departures that night and in the morning. All stations, docks, and roads, as much as they could be, were under surveillance, but the organization of manpower was causing a massive headache. Although Denning had requested extra manpower, he'd not had much luck, and time was in no way their friend. It was likely that Roth would be picked up, but the others could easily slip away. His thoughts stuck on this point as he walked out of the office. Someone called to him from along the corridor. It was the officer Denning was to have a word with before he left. The officer's face immediately gave away what was to come.

'Sorry, sir, we've not been able to find out conclusively whether there's any ship movement tonight or in the morning.'

'Bloody hell, man, why not?' Denning shouted in utter exasperation. The officer was one of his own men. He was standing there now before his superior, his head lowered, his hand tightly clasping the offending piece of paper. 'What about the harbour master?' Denning asked, though he needn't have bothered. He knew what was coming, so he cut off the mumbled response. 'Well, find him! You get out there with as many men as you can muster and root him out and let me know immediately if you get anything!'

Denning hurried out of the offices into the warm night. It was still light. The driver asked him where too. He replied, 'The Adelphi.' Looking out of the window at nothing in particular, he imagined himself on the night before they would leave Liverpool, having dinner at the hotel, celebrating the fact that Roth and the others were finally banged up. In his imagination, they'd finished all the courses and they were smoking cigars, he and his crew from London. Smoke was thick; so was the lewd humour. But he noticed he wasn't smiling.

Chapter 60

Jorgen dashed across to the loading side of the ship. He thought his papa could only have gone in the last couple of minutes. Incredibly, he spotted him. He was nearing the corner of the quayside that was diagonally opposite the *Prenton* by the warehouses. In the same split second, Jorgen spied cargo netting that had been tied to the top of the rail and thrown down the side of the ship. It was meant for sailors returning from late evening leave. It was the only connection with the dockside, as the vessel had been secured to sail on the early-morning tide. Holding onto the railing and springing up, he flipped himself round 180 degrees so he was facing the side of the ship, but he struggled to find his footing in the net. He slipped a few feet, but managed to stop the downward momentum. When he got close to the pathway on the dock, he swung himself outward and jumped to the ground. He lost his balance and, overcompensating, fell forward almost over the stone edge of the quay. Luckily he was able to grab a mooring post to break the momentum. He got up and ran. By the time Jorgen got to the corner of the dock where he'd first spotted his papa, Paul had reached the swing bridge. Jorgen had one advantage. He could outrun his papa.

Jorgen gained on Paul. There was no one on the quayside apart from a drunken sailor who was sleeping it off. When Jorgen arrived at the bridge he could see his Papa clearly in Cornhill. As Paul clattered along the street, the sound of his shoe falls reverberated in the tightly packed terraced streets. One dog barked, then another, as in colliding dominoes, and by the time

Jorgen passed the same spot, the neighbourhood was in uproar. A man sitting outside his front door threw a smoking clay pipe that struck Jorgen's shoulder as he passed. Hot ash flew everywhere. There was a dog at the man's side, but for some reason he kept him in check. Jorgen's father disappeared, turning right into Park Lane. Jorgen's stomach knotted. He increased his pace. There was just the church to get round. Paul boarded a tram at the stop by the pub, one block away from the church. Jorgen couldn't reach it in time. The tram accelerated rapidly beyond his reach. The tram, it's smoke-filled interior illuminated, clanged past with its high-pitched electrical whine. Normally this sound was a comfort to pedestrians at this time of the evening, but it was like an evil dragon to Jorgen. His papa was devoured by all the tobacco smoke. The situation charged Jorgen's half panic into a full-blown one. But then he was saved by a friendlier beast. It hadn't stopped, but it was travelling slowly – another tram. Jorgen jumped onto the rear platform, colliding with the conductor, and immediately ran to the front. He must keep his papa's tram in sight. The conductor yelled that he should sit down. There were no seats in the first two rows on the side opposite the driver from where he could get a good view. So he stood peering out of the window. The conductor again barked out an order for him to sit down. Reluctantly he went to one of the third-row seats, but kept bobbing up and down in order to keep a check on the tram in front. The conductor's face reddened; he seemed on the point of taking action. But rowdy passengers on the top deck needed to be sorted out first before it got any worse.

Fortunately for Jorgen, his papa's tram remained on the same track as his. Some passengers vacated the front seats as the tram wound its way round Queen Victoria's statute and into Lord Street. Jorgen pushed past the person sitting next to him who was reading and almost shoved the man's newspaper into his face. The man swore viciously. He'd that minute discovered a horse he'd placed a wager on at Haymarket was down the field. It was to be the last event there because of the war. Jorgen took no notice. He now had a perfect view of the tram in front. The conductor, by this time, seemed to have completely forgotten Jorgen. Jorgen could hear him. He was immersed in a heated exchange of words with the two drunks from the top level. The conductor soon had enough. He took both men by the scruffs of their necks and pushed them down the stairs. He pressed the bell to signal the driver to stop and ran down the stairs after them. As the tram slowed down, he kicked them off the platform and pressed the bell again for the tram to continue moving. It hadn't really even stopped. Yet another successful evacuation to add to all the others. The conductor's lips parted and he half smiled as he was applauded from up in the gods, and then moments later from the stalls of the tram.

The knot in Jorgen's stomach returned as he observed the tram ahead pulling away as it reached Elliot Street. The conductor was suddenly next to him. Then a knot in his throat joined the beast of a one in his stomach, and they both tightened.

'Fares,' said the conductor. There was no *please.* Jorgen didn't answer. He couldn't keep his eyes off the tram in front, but more importantly he had no money.

'Are you deaf, lad?' shouted the conductor. The passengers on the lower deck started to pay attention to the possibility of an encore from this showman of a conductor. There was no response from Jorgen, but he'd calmed down a notch or two as he noticed they were gaining on the tram in front as it slowed down to turn right into Lime Street. The adrenalin picked up. His attention was drawn to the platform side of the tram as it halted at a stop. Somebody got off. It wasn't papa. He couldn't see the man's face, but the clothes were wrong. As the tram started to move again he saw his papa. A light from a building illuminated his face.

'No one gets away with what you're playin' at, son!' bawled the conductor. He was about to grab Jorgen by the shoulders and throw him off the tram when Jorgen did the job for him. He ducked and rushed round the big man. The conductor's cap was knocked off. He fell into the arms of an old lady who was asleep. She shrieked. The conductor's cap wobbled at some speed along the aisle. It landed on the platform, and Jorgen jumped over it as he leapt from the tram. As he landed, he heard the passengers' replace adulation with laughter.

Jorgen tripped and fell as the tram turned into Lime Street. Fortunately there was no traffic around, and he managed to limp to the pavement. He only perceived pain in his ankle fleetingly, too concerned with tracking his papa. But he'd lost sight of him again. He must have turned off the street several hundred yards away before it intersected with a main road. Jorgen half ran, pain breaking into his consciousness as panic set in. There were no alleyways or even passages before the crossroads. His papa must have gone into a building. The only one he could see that seemed to have any life about it was the pub on the corner. The pub was well illuminated inside and out. Its polished red granite exterior and bow windows, caught in the glare of lamps, outshone the adjacent property, which stood neglected. The pub looked inviting, but there was something missing – the sound, of jollity, drunken voices, banged-out piano notes, and the general hubbub of a pub that was close to the bell for last orders. Even Jorgen, focussed as he was with the task at hand, noticed the oddness of it all.

Chapter 61

Bridie's memories of her visit to the police station and her conversation with Denning were all a blur. She couldn't remember a word she – or he – had spoken. She had refused a lift back to the hospital. In a daze, she walked out of the police station into the noise of an uncaring city. Across the road was a café. She sat at a table, felt dizzy, and closed her eyes. Someone asked if she was all right, but she didn't reply. Her eyes were fixed on the clock behind the serving counter. She watched the long hand moving. It seemed to move in an erratic manner as if it wasn't sure of its journey and final destination. In the end, a concerned waitress approached and asked if she'd like a cup of tea. She ran out of the café. Staring at broken paving stones, cigarette stubs, discarded clay pipes, and bits of paper picked up by the breeze, she became allied to this mindless detritus. The nagging thought started. Paul had telephoned. Hospital staff had watched, listened, and had been intensely expectant. Her heart surrendered. Why had she betrayed him – and not just once?

Bridie rounded the corner at the bottom of Brownlow Hill, and there in view was the Adelphi. A car door banged. It was him, Denning. Across the road was the Vine Pub. Was Paul there? Denning glanced back for a second. She turned cold, about to run. He hadn't seen her. She felt her legs continue to move forwards out of control. It all happened so quickly. A boy was grabbed and pulled into a passageway. Denning blew a whistle. There was a cacophony of barked orders. The boy and Denning disappeared. Then it dawned on her.

Bridie ran into Copperas Hill. There was a passageway around the back of the pub. It was known to both of them, and she was betting that Paul would use it. As she crossed the road, a man with a boy in his arms dashed out of the alleyway. Bridie called out. The pub's insides were bursting with noise now. She heard shouting and furniture crashing. She was nearly behind him. Breathless she shrieked his name. He didn't respond.

'Paul. I'm sorry...' Her voice sounded shattered. 'Please...' Then her voice was gone. As he turned the corner into Bolton Street, he glanced back. His face was tense. He was trying to form his words when the single shot rang out and scattered sleeping pigeons aloft. Bridie fell forwards onto her knees, holding up her hand. A farewell or a last desperate attempt for forgiveness – nobody would know. Paul kept on running. Tears prickled at the corner of his eyes. He shielded Jorgen. The next shot would be for him. *As long as Jorgen is safe*. There was an exchange of angry voices. It all happened in slow motion. A car pulled up. He didn't recognize the driver. A man was shouting in squeaky Cantonese. He was pulled in.

Hahyoo pushed Paul and Jorgen down onto the seat as a burst of shots hit the car. Paul caught one in his leg and rolled onto the floor in pain. Jorgen comforted him. Hahyoo ripped a piece of fabric from the hem of his shirt and applied it as a tourniquet. Paul's eyes screamed with bright yellow flashes, and he passed out. Hahyoo discharged his gun into the air. It halted the police's advance. The car sped away. A strange thought flitted across Hahyoo's mind. He hoped he hadn't injured a pigeon.

When Paul came round, he found himself in unfamiliar surroundings. He was in a car, but not the same one. He lay on a large leather seat in the back. Then pain struck him. One of his trouser legs had been torn, and a bandage had been applied.

'So you're back with us,' Paddy said with a cheerful lilt in his voice. 'It wus a close shave, that wus indeed.' Inside he was exploding with anger. Paul had put their lives on the line, but Paddy knew his friend must be going through hell. He held back. He would deal with the situation later.

Paul sat up.

'Where's Jorgen? He passed me in Lime Street. I realized the 'Vine' was full of coppers, and I was about to get away when I saw him. I picked him up. He was injured. I can't remember what happened after that.'

A smell of petrol breached Paul's nostrils as Jorgen opened the car door. Beyond the car he noticed a workshop and several cars, including the one he'd been in, parked up. Jorgen placed his arm round Paul who noticed he'd been crying.

'I'm sorry, Papa,' Jorgen said.

'Come on, son. You've got nothing to be sorry about. I'm the one who should be saying sorry. I've been a complete idiot. Nearly ruined everything.'

There was no mention of Bridie. Paddy and Hahyoo looked at each other. Their faces broadcast a mixture of pity and concern.

Chapter 62

Paddy was driving the special, large 1915 Mercedes 28 they'd picked up at his firm's garage behind the offices in Water Street. He was still wearing his grey chauffeur's uniform and looked anxiously into the rear of the car, as he drove towards the first police roadblock at the end of Water Street. His eyes scanned for signs of life of his friends. There weren't any. They were nowhere to be seen, but he knew they were there. He relaxed, smiled, and slowed down.

'What's your business, and where are you going?' snapped a sergeant. Paul would have immediately recognized the officer if he'd been sitting next to Paddy. It was the sergeant who had been at the root of all his trouble. But Paul and the others were concealed under a false floor in a cavernous compartment that was dimensionally similar to that of the car's cabin.

'I'm a chauffeur, and have to collect Lord Horwich from the Globe Hotel in Garston,' he said, his voice faltering. All this had been plucked out of the air, apart from the Globe Hotel, which he knew well. The sergeant looked at Paddy with contempt. He hated the Irish. All of them were upstarts. He saw no reason they should be employed by the gentry. There was a danger with all that Fenian nonsense. He pushed Paddy aside.

The sergeant had taken a personal interest in the hunt for Roth, and it showed. His wasn't a quick check of what, on the surface, seemed an empty car apart from the driver. He insisted that Paddy show him every inch of the panelling in the interior. It was as if he knew something.

But how could he? Paddy kept coughing, a shallow nervous cough. He was concerned that the officer would notice that the floor was too high compared with the other dimensions of the car. The fading light gave Paddy a slight advantage. The floor had been fitted expertly by a carpenter. The oil lamp carried by the sergeant was of no use in revealing joins that, even in perfect light, would have been difficult to spot.

When the sergeant got down on the floor, oil lamp in hand, and twisted and shuffled his body to manoeuvre it under the car, Paddy's heart started to run at a pace. The sergeant would be very close to the concealed passengers. If any of them made the slightest movement, they'd all be done for. Paddy started to whistle an Irish jig. Anything to distract the sergeant who'd stopped moving and lay silent. He whistled louder; he had no other option. There was a chance the sergeant might become suspicious. Paddy needn't have worried. The sergeant's red, smouldering face appeared out from under the car by Paddy's foot. He had picked up a large blob of oil on his nose. The rest of his body followed as he rolled over letting go of the lamp at the same time. Paddy had to jump out of the way. It was deliberate act by the frustrated sergeant. But it backfired. The oil lamp, its glass shattering, jammed under one of the wheels spilling oil, which caught on fire. This, slammed the brakes on Paddy's grease lightning formed muse that the sergeant had taken on the appearance of a rather Dark Father Christmas. Paddy uttered a cry.

'Me front tyre! It'll be gone! I'll have to move or there'll be murder to pay!' Without waiting for a response, he jumped into the car, released the handbrake, and pressed the starter button. The engine didn't explode into life, but the car started rolling forward.

'I've not finished with you yet!' shouted the sergeant. At that moment the engine fired. The tyre was ablaze. The sergeant was about to blow his whistle, but Paddy knew he had nothing on him, and he watched the sergeant lower the whistle as another vehicle pulled up. Petrol was a dastardly commodity if threatened by fire.

By the time the car reached Wapping Street, the flames from the tyre had been replaced by dark smoke. Paddy could hear coughing from the hidden passengers; he increased his speed. As he turned into the Wapping Dock, there was no sign of life in the dock offices, although he noticed light through the windows. The plan to doctor the staff's drinks must have gone smoothly – as smoothly as the best Scotch after several had been knocked back. He pulled round the building out of sight and released the others from the secret compartment.

On the quayside, the dockers in the pay of Paddy drained the car's fuel tank and disconnected the battery. Fortunately the fuel tank was on the opposite side to the smouldering tyre, which reduced the danger of an explosion. The dockers were taking no chances. They hurriedly attached the car to a crane with wire cables and chains and hoisted it up. It swung outwards as it was turned and positioned over the main deck, and then continued to sway. Its smouldering tyre, stoked up by the wind, showed signs of re igniting. They had no time to wait for it to settle, and down it went bouncing onto the deck where it struck a ventilator tube. Captain Johns, red faced, was having a fit. He'd refused to have the car on board, but had been unable to control events beyond his vessel, even though he'd bawled and bawled at Paddy and the others. Paddy's orders were set in stone. The captain now shouted orders to the crew to douse the tyre and the car with water. Paddy was standing next to him. The captain spun around quickly and deliberately collided with Paddy and then sped off. Paddy hardly took any notice. He was lamenting the damage to his precious car. It was only when he heard the ship's steam engines start up and the captain barking orders to cast off that he took notice. The *Prenton* turned slowly, manipulated by ropes from the quayside, and headed on a course through open dock gates and swing bridges that would take it into the Mersey Estuary. It was 12.50 in the morning.

Chapter 63

Denning, on his way back to headquarters, was out of his mind. How could what he considered a standard entrapment turn out in such a mess? A fatality caused by a man under his command. Any unnecessary death was inexcusable, but the death of a beautiful, young, innocent woman made it a hundredfold worse. He shouldn't have given the order not to cordon off the area. The girl should have been at least escorted back to her place of work, or even detained. He should have realized the true state of mind she was in. Then how did the pick-up car disappear so quickly, like a ghost through a solid wall? This gang knew what they were doing. He had been convinced that Roth had been a loose cannon going off on his own. The expertise was shown in the gang's ability to think on its feet – or tyres in this case – and come up trumps. Such a modus operandi he'd not witnessed before. The car pulled up at the police HQ, and as he angrily stormed through the doors and rushed down the corridor, he spotted Detective Sergeant Kearney.

'Kearney! Now! My office! Get the others. They should be back by now, the useless bunch.' He regretted the last few words. The men weren't to blame; it couldn't have panned out any other way.

The office was full of pipe smoke, and Denning noted the distinctive hiss of a faulty gas lamp that was in need of attention. It was eleven twenty. The men had collected outside the door, and he had kept them waiting, although not deliberately. He'd used the time to draw a pictogram of the choices they had left in the case.

He did this only if there was a huge possibility that those he hunted were about to escape the net. It was an obsessive act that verged on the murky outer territories of magic, with a dose of wishful thinking, as if the very action would herald success.

He'd drawn a solitary square at the top of the piece of paper. In it he'd written, 'Main aim: apprehend the offenders and others without any more fatalities.' The word *fatalities* was underlined. *What a joke*, he thought. From this square, solid lines ran to three circles, which he'd headed 'Docks', 'Railways', and 'Road'. In each circle he'd written a list of the actions needed to achieve success. The circles then fanned out in broken lines that ended in diamond shapes. In these he'd written factors that might cause problems. He'd drawn nine diamonds. This string of precious stones, synonymous with success, mocked him. He placed a cross on each circle and diamond apart from the ones under 'Docks'. He was about to change the diamonds to triangles when there was a heavy knock at the door, and he realized his foolishness. But he knew the way forward, if he could call it that.

'Come!' he shouted in as harsh a voice as he could muster. He waited for the men to sit down and for the shuffle of chairs to stop. Most of the Liverpool contingent of officers had their heads down. But one of them was intent on cleaning the nails of one hand with the other and then swapping over and repeating the process. Denning's gaze bore into the officer's eyes when he looked up briefly, like a rivet into steel plate, cold and angry. But the words that came out of his lips were quite the opposite.

'Look, men, I don't want to blame you in any way for what's happened. I take full responsibility for the death of that innocent girl. There'll be an enquiry, and I'm certain you'll all be exonerated. Right, gentlemen, let's get down to business.' His words sounded bright – even springy – a million miles away from how he felt. 'Let's clear up tasks outstanding.' The members of the Liverpool contingent looked bafflingly at each other. 'Right, Cummings, any news on the invisible harbour master?'

'None, sir. We're still chasing it up. His second man's in hospital according to his wife—'

Denning cut in,

'Bloody hell! Surely someone must know!' There was silence. Denning's thoughts were elsewhere. He couldn't get the Irish girl out of his mind. Her face, the soft innocence of her eyes. She'd trusted him completely. He knew it had been difficult for her to cooperate. He had sensed that she still had feelings for Roth. Denning had seen her waiting outside his office. She'd turned to leave, then obviously changed her mind about meeting him. But a clerk had got hold of her arm and led her in. If only the clerk hadn't. Her virtue and the idea she knew her place in the world restricted her from any action other than compliance. He remembered her sinking into a chair.

There was a knock at the door.

'Excuse me, sir,' a female clerk said nervously. 'Just had word. A couple of vans have arrived – reinforcements from Manchester.'

'Tell them, if they've got out of the vans, to go back in and await further orders.' He turned back to the men.

'Well, at least that's something. We'll leave them in reserve here, and if anything develops, get them to the spot right away.' Denning looked at Kearney as if he knew the detective sergeant was about to say something.

And he was right. Kearney spoke up. 'The docks are the only area where it's been difficult to achieve tight security. The main roads are blocked, and the stations are covered. Perhaps we should allocate a vanload of officers to the docks.' As Kearney finished speaking, there was another knock at the door.

'Excuse, sir.' It was the same clerk, this time with less anxiety in her voice. 'There are three charabancs full of constables and sergeants from Preston just come in, sir.'

'Tell them to do exactly what I said before,' Denning said.

Before he had time to start a new sentence, Kearney piped in. Denning thought, *Is this the new king come to take my crown?*

'Sir, I suggest we send a couple of the vans right away to the docks. Call off the search for the harbour master, and board and check out all the ships that are readying themselves to sail.'

Denning was thrown. That was the line he was planning to take. He was about to respond when a Liverpool officer blurted out,

'What about the *Courier*?'

'What courier? I hope your interruption is relevant,' Denning responded menacingly. He felt he was losing control.

'It's the local paper, sir. It'll have times of ships going out on the high tide.'

Denning jumped in, thoughts of Bridie far behind him. 'Why hasn't someone picked up on this before now?' He struck the side of his head with his pipe-free hand and looked around the room. 'Right, Cummings, get someone onto it immediately. It'll save us a heck of time if we know which bloody ships are departing and when.'

Denning glanced at the clock. It showed 12.30. His gut feeling was that the answer had to be at the docks. The railway stations had been covered, as well as the main roads out of Liverpool. The sea was the best option for the fugitives; it offered so many possibilities. They might never be seen again. He took a puff of his pipe, pursed his lips, and unconsciously exhaled a perfect ring of smoke. To Denning, the ring was a symbol of completeness. It egged him on, even though the sham diamonds still lurked in the far reaches of his mind

'I know its like placing all your eggs in one basket,' he said to the group at last, 'but I want all the manpower to be dispatched immediately to the docks area. We'll cover all the docks that are currently available for ocean-going ships.'

Cummings slipped back into the room and interrupted him.

'According to the *Courier*, sir, there is only one merchant ship that is scheduled to leave on the high tide at one in the morning – the *Prenton* at King's.

'That's our target!' bawled Denning. 'Get the Manchester and Preston lads over there now, smartish!' Half smiling, he was unaware that the smoke ring had vanished.

Chapter 64

Denning reached King's dock within fifteen minutes, closely followed by the officers in the charabancs. The clocks in the city were striking one. With Denning were Kearney and a local sergeant who had been on watch at the docks all night. He'd pointed out that the *Courier* had listed ships sailing on the high tide at one o'clock. But the *Prenton* might have already left its berth before one. If they were in luck, though, the ship could be one of the last ships in the queue both in and out of the dock. They'd closed all bridges half an hour ago as a precaution as soon as they'd got word of the likelihood of the docks being used for the gang's escape. This might have been done earlier, but they'd needed the permission of the harbour master. But Denning was now beyond care and had taken responsibility for the action, which he knew would cause havoc with shipping traffic. The shipping lines hadn't been notified.

There was no moonlight. The wind had brought clouds. It was pitch black on the quaysides apart from the round blotches of light surrounding the gas lamps. On the water, beams of light came and went. Officers were aware of the noise of engines and hooters; they could see the outlines of ships on the move. Carrying flashlights, they spilt onto the quayside and started checking the names on ships. It was a difficult task. Some nameplates were obscured; others were too far away for the flashlights to be effective. They shouted at sailors who had come out to see what all the fuss was about. But they all seemed to be confused about berth numbers

Denning and Kearney entered the dock offices. They'd been surprised that none of the dock's employees had come out to see what was going on. They quickly understood why when they encountered inebriated bodies. All were fast asleep with arms sprawled out on the tables or hanging by their sides. Bottles of whisky were everywhere. Kearney took a swig out of a half-empty one and spat the contents out immediately. There was a scowl on his face, 'That's doctored!' he shouted.

At that moment, the sergeant returned, his chest heaving, out of breath.

'They're having difficulty checking the names of ships still berthed, sir.'

'Get out there again, Sergeant, and spread the word. The *Prenton*'s definitely the one we're after.' He swung round to Kearney. 'Let's have a quick look at the paperwork here for a clue about where she's berthed.' After a couple of minutes, they found the name *Prenton* and the words *No 6 berth* in a book with a page headed 'Sailings... August 1915'.

They were out of the offices in a shot. Denning shouted out that the ship was in berth six. He kept repeating the words. They echoed in warehouse passages and entrances and skipped across the water to continue their pranks.

By chance, a solitary officer passing an empty berth picked out the number six on a slab. 'It's here, sir,' he shouted. 'Berth six is here, but its empty, or maybe I'm looking at the wrong berth!' They set out to check the two ships at each side of what they presumed was berth six. In the end, they had to board both, and it took several minutes before they were able to verify the fact, by talking to the drunken crew of one, that indeed half an hour ago the *Prenton* had sailed. It was obvious that the vessel was no longer within the confines of either dock. The hope was that the other bridges had been closed in time.

Denning returned to the police HQ in Dale Street. It was two in the morning. He telephoned the admiralty immediately and requested that the *Prenton* should be apprehended and fugitives should be arrested. The naval officer on the night duty watch asked for her approximate position and details of the arrest warrants. Of course Denning had no idea of her position. The officer promised to call back within half an hour.

An hour later, Denning was still waiting. During that time he'd been clearing out the desk of his personal belongings. He telephoned again. The officer apologized and said he'd been on the point of contacting Denning. Unfortunately they were unable to assist. All they could do was to alert all naval vessels in the vicinity to keep a look out for the *Prenton*. He added that the chances of locating her at this time were minimal, as the number of non-combat ships on post in the area had been reduced in May owing to U-boat activity.

Denning placed the receiver down gently and thought, *So that's it*. He was resigned to what would follow, and he left the police HQ without saying a word to anyone.

Chapter 65

Everybody, apart from Hahyoo and a Chinese member of the crew, were in the mess. They all had a drink in their hands, including the captain, who'd spoken few words to his unwelcome guests.

Paddy stood up and announced that a toast was in order. 'I just want to say a few words. At ten o'clock yesterday evening, I wouldn't have believed we'd all be here this very lunchtime waitin' for one of Hahyoo's culinary specials. It wus ever such a close-run t'ing.' He glanced over to Paul, who acknowledged the knowing look he gave him and raised his glass. 'I t'ink if we hadn't had the two cars to hand, especially the Mercedes with the hollow bottom as good as any of Hoodini's contraptions and got the car loaded on board in time with a blazin' tyre, it wouldn't have happened. Amazin'! 'Twasn't meant for movin' bodies, but it did us proud. So we've got two cars at our disposal for a grand time in the Americas. It's all t'anks to the crew and the lads.'

Paul interrupted.

'Who are the lads? How on earth did you manage to get them to the docks so quickly?'

'Funnily enough and don't ask me why,' he winked and nodded simultaneously, 'they were around in the dock offices drinking the good whisky as opposed to the tainted, on our behalf. That was a stroke of luck. We wouldn't have roused them if they'd been in the local.

'I'd like to t'ank the two boys. It's not been easy for either of them. So much to take in and get used to. But the way they handled themselves was just grand. And of course there's Hahyoo – always in the background, but at the front as well, one step ahead. What a team.' At this point, on cue, Hahyoo and Charlie from Canton came in from the galley with trays of steaming soup and dishes full of rice, meat, and fish complete with sauces. They sat down.

Paddy was still standing up with a glass in his hand.

'Oh, Paul, this one's for you. Seamus sends his best wishes, even though you did a bunk on him. He eventually realized what was goin' on, and it worked a treat. The police fell for it, as they do for a pretty, wide-eyed, innocent colleen in trouble'. A hush broke out around the table. He quickly recognized his insensitivity. He remained silent as the room did for several seconds.

'So finally, Paul I trink to you and all we've been through, partners in crime and havin' a laugh through thick and thin. Getting' Jorgie and yous back together. We did it, Paul, we did it. Here's to life, liberty, and the chasing of happiness. Now where have I heard those words running together before?' He raised his glass. Everyone stood up and drank each other's health.

As the applause died down and Paddy was lowering himself unsteadily into his chair, he observed the captain glowering at him. He immediately sprang up again,'Please be upstanding masters and gentleman once again,' he said to the assembled people. 'I'm so sorry to have missed out a very important toast. Apologies, Captain Johns.' The sincerity shone through Paddy's whisky-reddened eyes. 'I know it's been difficult fer yous, all this change an' messin about. I personally want to thank you, an' not just in words, but in deed, so am givin' you an extra bonus to compensate yous all.' A half smile tentatively rippled out on the captain's face as the red duster might gently flutter in the first breeze of the day. Everyone applauded and drank his health. Paddy slapped him on the back in a drink-laden, rough manner. The smile shot from the captain's face as if the flag had been whisked down suddenly and everything was as it had been before.

Chapter 66

A U-boat lurked at a shallow depth about a hundred miles off the southwest coast of Ireland. It was in need of some minor repairs, and it was on its last stretch of duty before returning to its base in Ostend. Kapitan Hellingen had just completed the log for the watch. He had been called to check an object that had been observed through the mist on a course that would shortly intersect with them by some tens of metres. It was a merchant ship. No matter what nationality, the Kaiserliche Marine – The Imperial German Navy – had ordered active service units to engage and destroy all such targets. To Hellingen it was almost begging to be devoured. The sea to the west, their alluring vast net waiting to catch this final morsel of their hunting spree to be savoured before thier departure home. He ordered the submarine to surface. The klaxons sounded for action stations, and the submarine rose gently as its ballast tanks were filled with air. The merchant ship had spotted them. It had changed course suddenly like a gazelle that had observed the fearsome yellow and black bands of a big cat even though it was some distance away. The panic-struck animal sensed that its adversary had no need of stealth. The attacker was suddenly upon its prey. The gun crew whipped the plug off the gun barrel, loaded the ammunition and attached the optic sights. The trigger hairs bore down on the shuddering heart of the vessel.

Hellingen was about to give the order to open fire after a last check with his binoculars. He was looking for a name and a clue about the ship's cargo, although it was likely to be empty and returning to the United States. He noted that it was unarmed, but couldn't find any sign of a name. As he scanned the decks, he could hardly believed his eyes. It was a car. Its waterproof coverings were flapping in the breeze. It wasn't just a car, though, it was *the* car. The most expensive Mercedes on the market. They were no longer available. The war had seen them off. Hellingen stood erect, transfixed like a statue for half a minute or so. The gun crew patiently awaited their captain's orders. He knew they would be wondering about his intentions; he wasn't a man known to shilly-shally.

Hellingen gave the order to fire a shot across the bow and signal the merchant ship to receive a boarding party. His second officer looked at him in disbelief, but Hellingen didn't care; he continued to contravene orders. It should have been a quick kill, but all Hellingen said was 'Spoils of war' in a vexed manner. The *Prenton* didn't respond. It was attempting to turn. Hellingen swore and ordered two rounds to be fired at the rear of the vessel. He was desperate. This target area was as far away as possible from where the car sat, its tarpaulin now wildly provoking him. The shells hit their target, and a plume of black smoke rose from the stern of the ship, concealing it briefly. Then, through the smoke, Hellingen observed flames. The ship had stopped and was drifting.

Hellingen and a party of armed crew approached the *Prenton* in a dinghy. The vessel had surrendered. A rope ladder was lowered, and Hellingen was the first up, pistol in hand. The fire was still blazing, and he ordered his men to assist putting it out.

Hellingen said to the *Prenton*'s captain, 'Do you carry munitions?' There was no response.

'Ammunition? Bombs?' he said in faltering English. Still no response.

Hellingen was becoming impatient. He strutted over to the captain, but at that moment Paul stepped forward and said in German,

'No. There are no shells, bombs, or smaller ammunition on board.'

Helligen was shocked. A German speaker?

'Are you German?'

'Yes, originally from Frankfurt am Rhiene,' Paul answered confidently. 'We need your help. Can you take us to Germany? You are our only option.'

Hellingen couldn't believe the words he was hearing. There was a pause. The only sounds were the sea, the voices of men tackling the fire, and the flapping tarpaulin that Hellingen had his eyes focussed on.

'My original plan was to set you adrift on lifeboats to be picked up by your navy,' said Hellingen. 'It might be dangerous for you to remain with us. But, actually, we could do with your assistance in getting this merchant ship back to our base.' As Hellingen said this he was making his way to the car.

****

The *Prenton*'s mess was full of German sailors, laughing and joking. They were overjoyed to have unexpectedly escaped from their herring can of a submarine. They knew from their last briefing with the captain that several of the crew would be sailing the *Prenton* back to base. It could be some of them. What a release. The presence of Jorgen and Vincent speaking their second language and making friends with young Germans only a few years older than themselves created a family atmosphere. The Germans treated them as younger brothers and passed around well-worn family photographs. They said little about the war. This was an occasion to savour. It shoved the war far away, completely out of view.

Hahyoo had confined himself to his cabin. Seasickness had struck. Their situation was in the lap of the gods. He'd moved the

The Lucy Effect

limited furniture around in the cabin to ensure the optimal feng shui combination. That was all he could do. He hated sailing. It coloured everything black for him. His logical mind would not operate as it usually did in normal circumstances. He was of little use. He'd told everyone he was retiring, as he was very tired. Hahyoo was aware that Paddy knew that the sickness was his Achilles heel, and he would be locked away out of the picture until he reached the steadiness of solid land. He'd want little food and even fewer visitors.

Hellingen was discussing with Paul how the men were getting on with the repairs. Only the steerage system had been affected, and its restoration was nearly complete. They would be underway in a few hours.

At the same time Paddy was trying to involve Johns in conversation. He responded to Paddy's chat in monosyllables. His face looked like the padlocked door of the Shylock Ale house in Dublin that faced the world with faded, black, flaking paint after the last call for orders. Johns' thoughts were sunk into the scene he had witnessed. Huns in his ship. He couldn't believe that Paddy had allowed it to happen. What could he do? Paddy's company owned the *Prenton* and him along with it. He'd been given a break by Paddy when he was down on his luck – very down. But this. This. Wasn't Paddy a traitor? He surely wasn't going to be one. He'd had it with Paddy. Non-cooperation was to be the order of the day, and maybe an even more drastic action.

Meanwhile, on the opposite side of the table, Hellingen's second in command was having thoughts that were not that dissimilar to Johns' about Paddy. What was Hellingen up to? Wasting time, endangering the boat and his men. He knew he'd been in touch with Ostend about the engagement and, more to the point, had been ordered not to waste time. He'd been ordered to return to base immediately. Hellingen, of course, had ignored the command. Hellingen's second in command knew it was the precious car. The captain was known for his reckless behaviour in and out of the boats. But he was seen as a hero, one of the most decorated in the Kaiserliche Marine. He could do no wrong. But surely this was unprecedented. What should he do? Take over? A mutiny? But the men would never follow him. The present adventure, he mused, would add that extra pinch of spice to one of their most successful missions.

****

Several hours later the *Prenton* was underway with the U-boat trailing behind, still on the surface. Hellingen was scanning the horizon for any telltale signs of smoke from British destroyers. But the light was fading. The moon and stars were not visible. There were dark clouds, and everything soon would take on an inky blackness and mix the sea and sky together seamlessly. Only the lights of the two ships were visible.

Paul had gone on deck with Jorgen to get some air. There was a freshening breeze. As they looked down, they could make out the white foamed galloping waves with the light from *Prenton*'s portholes. The effect was hypnotic. They stood in silence for a minute or so. Then Paul placed his arm round Jorgen and pulled him towards him. He told his son it went without saying he was overjoyed they'd found each other, and he apologized for what had happened to him. Not placing his mind in gear and with the best of intentions Jorgen blurted out that he was sorry about Bridie and her accident. Paul didn't respond. Jorgen glanced at him occasionally, as they remained standing there, staring at the ever-changing wave patterns until a sheet of lightening lit up the sky, bathing both vessels in a fleeting ghostly light. They could feel rain. There was a crack of thunder. The weather was changing for the worse.

The Lucy Effect

Hahyoo turned over in his dream to get away from the shot he'd fired at Swithins, not wanting to know the outcome of his rash action. He woke suddenly at the second blast as flashes of brightness invaded the cabin. The *Prenton* pitched. Hahyoo fell out of his berth and started to curse Paddy as politely as he could. Why had he got mixed up with him? If he hadn't, he'd be safely tucked up in his bed in Sheung Wan, Hong Kong, a poorly-paid but safe constable.

The storm was gathering in intensity, and only the *Prenton* remained on the sea's manic surface, for U21 had received an urgent signal. The storm they'd encountered was predicted to develop into hurricane proportions, so Hellingen had given the orders for the boat to be submerged for its own safety and the comfort of the crew. He was worried. His precious cargo on the *Prenton* would be exposed to the fierce storm. In a lightning strike of a throwaway thought, he'd half considered strapping himself to it for the protection of the car and not any other darker reason. The loss of the car could mean he'd pay a heavier price for his reckless actions. At least the car had offered a crumb of a consolation prize.

The others had different thoughts that kept the majority of them awake. It wasn't the loss of war loot that deeply worried Paddy. It was the ferocity of the storm made worse by Paul's equally ferocious snoring and complete unawareness of all the commotion. His only consolation, in glaring contrast to Hellingen's materialistic worries, was that the threat from British warships would be nil. They'd all be heading for safe harbour rather than hurtling around searching them out.

Jorgen and Vincent were up and about. They couldn't believe their luck – the overwhelming dare that the storm presented. Unknown to anyone, they managed to crawl on all fours along *Prenton*'s passageways, and up and down steps to reach the main deck. Who was to be the first one to reach Helligen's trophy? The special Mercedes, now bereft of its canvas shelter, clung to the main deck. The exhausted ropes and chains that secured it, strained and groaned as the deck heaved and danced with the waves.

A few nautical miles away the sea, wind and atmospheric pressure had been involved in a spiralling conflict. The wind refused to give up. It grew in strength aided by an alliance with a tropical cyclone. In the circumstances, it was a one-way battle. Even though the sea struggled heroically, it was made to climb and climb. Vincent was ahead of Jorgen crawling up the final set of steps to the main deck, having been flung back twice. Jorgen desperately tried to pass him as they reached the main deck. On the bridge, Hellingen's second in command saw Johns squirm as he peered through his binoculars. There was no reason to ask why. A gigantic wave was heading towards them. There wasn't even time to alert the crew.

A sequel to the novel is planned to be published next year.

Ten years on it's set in the St Petersburg of the 1920's. The tragic effects of the revolution are still being experienced mainly by the poorest who battle to make ends meet. The elite are forced to toe the party line for fear of incarceration or even worse. No one can feel safe.

Our friends find themselves in the thick of it. Struggling to establish business contacts they are faced with corrupt officials who have other more devious plans in mind for them. Will one of them find himself making the ultimate sacrifice?

Lightning Source UK Ltd.
Milton Keynes UK
UKOW02f0007030215

245538UK00001B/3/P